MUZUKURU

74-fzdp
11/22/94

MUZUKURU

A Guerilla's Story

Paul Hotz

RAVAN PRESS   JOHANNESBURG

Published by Ravan Press (Pty) Ltd
P O Box 31134, Braamfontein 2017
Johannesburg, South Africa

First published 1990

Cover illustration: Ramona Belcher
Cover design: Jeff Lok

Typeset in 10 on 12 pt Times Roman
Printed and bound by Sigma Press (Pty) Ltd, Pretoria

ISBN 0 86975 385 1

To those who fight for freedom

Author's Note

This book is based on interviews with people who fought in Zimbabwe's struggle for liberation. I have, on occasion, simplified the history in the interests of plot and narrative. My intentions were to write a novel, and it is as a novel that this book should be read and judged.

Deep pools become crossing points
— Shona proverb

Chapter 1

*P*ast Karoi the tar ends. The truck hits this pothole as it turns off onto the Binga road and slides all over the place. Everyone sobers up: ou Headlights packs away what's left of his brandy, ou Fudge puts down his guitar. This is it, you scheme to yourself, we're finally in the bush, things are serious now.

And you check the bush, check the bush as the truck trundles on through the TTLs, the Tribal Trust Lands, but there's nothing, nothing but a bunch of huts every kay or so, a boy with a flock of goats, a patch of mealies, a donkey standing in the shade of a thornbush. Yet, in your gut you can feel that the terrs must be out there somewhere.

You close your eyes and imagine a terr ambush — piling out the back of the truck with sten gun blazing, terrs falling left and right and General Walls himself pinning a silver cross to your chest, as your wife and your old man and your lightie look on applauding. . . .

You begin wondering about your lightie, your wife — what's she up to now? — and you look back at the grey plume of dust drifting behind you and up ahead where the road winds off into the hills and the heat haze, and the shivers start slithering up and down your spine. What've you got yourself into this time, how did you manage to land up here?

And hours later, when you're nodding off from boredom, the truck turns this corner and there, right in the middle of the bush, is this mammoth bloody fortress of yellow earth topped with barbed wire.

'What a place,' complains ou Soaps — he was our champion complainer, that bloke — 'A month of this is going to drive us up the wall and onto the ceiling.'

And though all of us loudly agree with him, there's no place that us ouens — ou Soaps included — would rather be. Hell — we're out in the bush for the first time, there's a chance of action — what more can you want?

Our convoy, a jeep and a truck, halts outside the gate and a dozen heads pop up along the wall. Our lootie shouts 'Black Boot', the password, the gate opens, and the convoy trundles through.

Ya, back in those days just hearing someone use a password seriously was a real thrill — it was the sort of thing you read about or saw in the movies.

But even so, as we drove on inside, I felt for a moment that maybe ou Soaps had a point: that place was bare, man, bare. About a dozen tents had been pitched at one end of the camp, and four- five trucks and half-a-dozen bulldozers were parked in rows at the other. And that, except for the shithouse and a single large thorntree, was that.

'Make yourself at home,' said this wit, one of the blokes we'd come to relieve. 'You're gonna get to know this place real well.'

We were led off to our tents, assigned our places and told to get ourselves organised. But me and my buddy, ou Headlights, we couldn't wait: first thing we sneaked off to check this lot out. While we were gawking at the bulldozers, we bumped into the wit — Roy I think his name was — who kindly volunteered to take us on a tour.

The bloke was as good as a guide book. He explained that bull-dozers had shovelled up the ring of earth around the camp, and showed us the peepholes that the guards looked through as they made their rounds. I stared out at the barbed wire, the 30-metre belt of bare earth, the 150-metre belt of clearing beyond it and the surrounding bush beyond that, and wondered what it would be like to be anchored there on a moonless night at three in the morning.

'One of the guards was blown to pieces about a year ago,' said Roy, as though he could read my mind. 'This terr, he crawled right up to the wall — through the barbed wire and alles — and dropped the goddam grenade in through the peephole. They had to scrape up the pieces with a spoon.'

Me and ou H were sort of quiet as Roy led us to the next item on his list of local attractions: the roadworks.

We climbed a koppie overlooking the site and rolled ourselves a reef. Off in the distance you could just make out the blue of Lake Kariba, and there below us miles and miles of dusty yellow road coiled off through the mopane scrub. Roy pointed out the lake and roads, just in case we had missed them, and began telling us all about the government's programme to build this mammoth road system in the area so's troops could be trucked in quickly if the terrs ever tried to invade again. Our job, it turned out, was to guard the roadmaking equipment.

And that, Roy informed us, was that. As we walked back to the base the guard on the gate, who was bullshitting with his buddies, waved us through with hardly a look. I was shocked. Hell, we were supposed to be out in the operational area.

'I thought security was pretty tight out here,' I said.

'Why? What's the problem?'

'The password. The guard didn't ask the password.'

Roy checked me out like I was so green I was leafing. 'There are 20 blokes in this camp,' he chuned me, 'he knows all of us pretty well by now — and who the hell ever heard of a goffel terr anyway?' He was right: none of us had. Hell, back in those days us ouens schemed the idea of a goffel terr — if we'd even bothered to think about a goffel terr — was as ridiculous as a bloke getting pregnant. I chune you if somebody had told me that one day I'd become a guerilla myself, I would've laughed.

That night the blokes we were relieving celebrated their departure. They'd shot two-three impala, and they'd stocked up with a couple crates of beer and a kilo of grade one stop.

What with all that fuel, it wasn't long before the party was hot and jumping. Me, I was going lekker there, a hunk of impala in one hand and a beer in the other, until I overheard Roy chatting to one of his buddies.

'Reckon we're getting out just in time,' he was saying.

'He's gotta hit the camp any day now,' the other blokes agreed.

Me, I look at ou Headlights, and he looks at me. What's all this about?

'What's the story here?' ou Headlights wants to know.

Well, this Roy, he shakes his head and scratches his gut and schemes well now, he isn't sure whether he really ought to tell us. Ou Headlights asks why he's keeping whitey's secrets for him, and Roy picks his teeth and sighs and then chunes us okay, okay now, don't tell anyone I told you but....

There's this hardcore terr in the area, this Comrade Bigfoot. 'No one has ever seen him,' Roy tells us, 'but eeh, man have we seen that houtie's tracks — he must wear size 15 boots — I'm not chuning you. He must be as big as a goddam elephant.'

'He's smart too, that Bigfoot,' his buddy chips in. 'Not even the best trackers in the Rhodesian army can follow him. One minute you're hot on his trail and the next — right out in the middle of nowhere — it just disappears.'

'On top of that,' chunes Roy, 'the bloke's really got it in for us. Some goffel spoilt his sister, and he's been after us ever since.'

'Ya, he hates goffels,' his buddy confirms, 'really hates us.'

'Eeeh, what he doesn't do when he gets his hands on one of us.'

'Better shoot yourself first.'

Ya, the pair of them, they told us quite a collection of stories about this Bigfoot. We heard how he had once strolled into this RDR camp dressed in a RAR uniform: five blokes were playing poker by the fire and the guard was busy rolling himself a reef. Bigfoot gooid a grenade into the fire — bwaaa — and took out all five one time. Then, before the guard could work out what'd happened, Bigfoot took a pistol and — bwa-bwa — hyperventilated the poor bugger's brains.

'I never read any of this,' I put in, wide-eyed. 'I never saw any of this in the papers.'

'Ya,' said Roy, very serious. 'You don't. That's one of the things you learn out here. There's an awful lot happening which the mense back in Burg aren't told about.' Another squad of cold shivers marched down my spine. What the hell were we getting into?

Ya, that night, I chune you, I spent half the time wishing that I was back in Burg, and the other half dreaming of winning a medal by wiping out Bigfoot and his buddies.

But, next morning, when the guard roster was pinned up and I saw that me and ou Headlights were on that night, I stopped thinking so much about medals. Hell, how could a bloke like me be expected to fight against Bigfoot? Why didn't the army do something about him — why were they allowing terrs like him to roam loose?

That evening I tried to get in a few hours' sleep before I went on shift, but it was no use. I lay awake and stared at the canvas. Over in the dump a hyena was nosing through the tin cans and laughing its lunatic hyena laugh, and off in the bush the owls were whoo-ooing as if a couple dozen people were due to die. I wished I was back in Burg, I wished I'd grafted at school and had made the right sort of friends, and had never gone on to reformatory or the army. If I was a teacher or a mechanic or something I wouldn't be stuck out here in the bush.

I was still wishing at 2 am when the guards coming off duty called me and ou H for our shift. Keeping close together the pair of us tiptoed to our post. In the darkness the walk to the bulwark seemed one hell of a lot longer than before.

Headlights put on a cup of tea. I started a circuit of the bulwark, sneaking along without a torch in case I gave my position away. It was so dark I could hardly see a foot in front of me. For all I knew they were already inside the camp, waiting quietly in the dark for me to trip over them. Outside the blasted hyena starts up again — jee-ah-ah-ah-ah-ha — and I look out through the first of the peepholes scanning that particular stretch of bloody Africa, telling myself that there's nothing out there in the dark, nothing worth worrying about, if the terrs hit the camp it'll be at sunrise when you're already off duty. And then — O Jisis — I check the things — terrs — a whole company of them — heading towards us.

'Attack!' I yell, shoving my sten through the peephole and opening up — pa-pa-pa-pa — 'Bigfoot.'

Then everyone's screaming 'terrs', 'terrs', 'attack' — and rushing to the walls with their stens. Someone goois a grenade — BWAAA — flares arc up into the night. The lootie — in skants — races round shouting instructions which no one can hear. Then, as the flares drift down and the firing dies away, each of us gradually realises that ya, out there in the patch of bush he's covering, there's nothing moving, nothing at all.

As the camp becomes quiet it strikes me that maybe I'd made one hell of a mistake.

'Hey — what's that?' Ou Headlights points to the light thrown by one of the last flares. 'There's something.' We all crowd around the peepholes, checking and checking, and as the flare falls ya, we can check that there is something out on the road, something is lying there. Me, I'm feeling relieved, I chune you.

'Looks like you've got something, Kiernan,' says the lootie. 'Good work.'

And as I'm wondering just what medal I'm likely to get the flares sink another couple feet and there, ya, we can all make out this great grey lump — this dead donkey.

Thereafter I was known as The Donkeykiller of Binga, or Donk for short. Ya, all that Bigfoot stuff turned out to be just a story and, as the lootie told us later, there'd been no terrs in the area for years. We were there to stop the locals stealing the road-making equipment.

The locals would rock up at the site with half their kraal in tow — old queens, snotty-nosed toddlers, doddery old madalas — the lot. They'd perch there gawking and gossiping as the bulldozers flattened trees and graders scraped the earth bare. Ya, we were the big entertainment out there in the bush — and the moment our backs were turned they'd grab anything they could lay their hands on. Picks and shovels you could understand, and wire and string too, but what the locals wanted with a dozen bulldozer voltmeters we never did work out.

Still, it wasn't our stuff they were scaling, so we got along fairly well with them. They sold us chickens and tomatoes when we were sick of our ratpacks, and some of the chicks would take a walk for a couple tins of bully beef or a few packs of smokes. (Me, I only went along once — I was smashed out of my skull at the time — cos I was shitscared of catching the clap. Or rather — let's be honest — I was shitscared of Naomi catching me with the clap.)

The locals also kept us supplied with stop. They were serious smokers, those okes, specialists in their mbanje. They were always discussing the crop — was it going to be as good as last year's, had there been enough rain?

The local connoisseurs kept telling us about this special pipe, a pipe so potent it could knock you flat on your back for an afternoon, and eeh, I chune you us ouens were eager to get a taste of this thing.

First chance we got, when the lootie buggered off to Binga one Sunday, ou Headlights — he could never sit still, that ouen, he was always looking for excitement — borrowed a truck, and talked me and ou Soaps and Fudge into coming along to investigate.

We found the kraal, no problem, and the madala who owned this phenomenon was only too pleased to take our 10 cents each and lead us down through the mealiefield to this small stream where he kept his apparatus: a tatty grass mat and a long red rubber tube which ran through the stream to a tin funnel that he'd propped up on a pile of stones.

In the shade of a nearby baobab tree, the morning's previous customers sprawled out with broad grass grins on their dials.

The madala waded across the stream to fill the funnel and light it. Once it was going, each of us sat on the mat and took a good long hit. The smoke was cooled by the water and, without realising it, you took this long deep breath. Me, I remember feeling sort of disappointed — was this all there was to it? — until I tried to stand, and tripped over my own two feet and nearly fell into the water.

Once we'd all had a hit we headed for the shade of the nearest tree. Ou Soaps began worrying about the lootie finding out about our expedition. Ya, he was a funny ouen that Soaps; when he wasn't complaining, he was worrying. Back in Civvy Street he was a security guard, and a preacher on Sundays. Not that it ever stopped him sinning along with the rest of us.

Then he went quiet, and we all just sat there and munched away on this pack of biscuits. I remember watching these tiny wasps diving and stinging this giant black shongololo as it tried to writhe away on its back.

'That lightie, he's going to murder that monkey,' says Soaps suddenly and, ya, I realise that for quite a while now I've been hearing this shrill eee-eee sound somewhere off in the distance.

I look up and there, maybe 20 yards upstream, this lightie's trying to lower a baby monkey, which he's got dangling on the end of a short grass rope, onto this wire car that Lightie No. Two is BRRRRMM-BRRRMing all ready for take-off.

'That lightie's going to murder that animal,' Soaps repeats. No one says a thing. That stop was really first-class. 'I don't like to see monkeys murdered,' he starts complaining. 'It's cruel. We should do something about it.'

'We don't need to get involved in any monkey business,' yawns ou Fudge, this large light fellow with skin exactly the colour of fudge made with condensed milk who liked to think of himself as a practical bloke. 'We got enough troubles.' Prophetic words.

Finally ou Headlights surfaces through the haze. 'These houties, they don't know how to treat animals,' he says. 'They shouldn't be allowed to have them.'

And with that, he pulls himself to his feet and strides over to rescue the ape.

'Gimme the goddam thing,' he yells and the lighties, they take one look at ou H heading towards them and drop the monkey, rope and all, and hare off into the bush.

The monkey doesn't stick around to say howzit either. With four feet of rope looping along behind it, the thing races for the nearest tree.

But the rope gets entangled in thorns and ou H swoops down and grabs the end and hoists the beast up into the air, and there it revolves shrieking and scrabbling.

The locals under the baobab tree are shouting at us. We can't quite make out what they're saying, but it doesn't sound too friendly.

'Maybe we should buy the animal,' suggests Soaps, a little nervous. 'We don't want trouble.'

'Screw them,' sneers Headlights, panting and indignant. 'They're just a bunch of goddam houties. And the way they treated this monkey — '

'We better get out of here then,' says Soaps, 'cos if we stay there are going to be problems.' And so off we went.

Back at camp, when the stop wore off, we found we had an unexpected problem: a baby monkey, its eyes hardly open, sitting in the bottom of an oil drum sucking its toes the way a baby sucks its thumb.

'Might as well graze it,' said Fudge, being practical again. 'The army doesn't allow you to keep pets anyway.'

'We're supposed to have saved the thing,' argued Soaps, all very upset. 'We can't eat it. Someone must want it' — he looked round at us ouens — 'they make first-class pets.'

But no one did, particularly. Headlights said it'd start fiddling with the spares for his bikes, and Soaps lived in a flat, and me, if I'd rocked up in Burg with that thing my wife would've thrown us both out. Hell, she wouldn't even let me get a dog.

While we were still trying to sort out what to do, the monkey solved the problem for us: he gnawed through the rope around his middle, jumped out of the oil drum and streaked to the top of the only tree in the camp.

And there he stayed for the next couple days. No one seemed to notice that he was up there, he was such a tiny grey-green thing, and most of the ouens were glad to be able to forget his existence. Me and Soaps, we gave him the odd banana and orange, and nailed a tin which we kept filled with water about half way up the trunk. The monkey ate the fruit but he raced off and hid himself in this old nest whenever we came near. Soaps christened him Chico, after an ape in a Tarzan movie.

Then Chico discovered barbed wire. One morning, about five bells, just before I came off guard, there was this shrill ee-eeing down by the trucks. I went over to check out the scene and there was the animal trapped in the rusty wire on top of the bulwark.

I found a ladder and, wrapping my hand in old rags, climbed up and freed the thing — which was maybe something of a mistake cos the monkey immediately latched onto me and declared me Mommy.

I wasn't charmed. What was I going to do with a baby monkey? I tried ignoring the thing in the hopes that it would look round for a more obliging mother — but no dice. He followed me everywhere and, whenever he wanted a more convenient place to sit, he'd run right up onto my shoulder — no matter whether I was shitting or shaving or what.

Come mealtimes, he'd perch at my feet, cock his head and watch me as I sampled the food, and the moment I'd swallowed a mouthful he'd be shouting for his share.

What with all this performing, it was only a matter of time before the lootie got to hear of this, so I figured I better try sort things out officially.

Now the lootie — Lootie Beauty we called him — was a bit weird; he'd rocked up at the camp with this fancy leather case crammed with suntan lotion, shaving cream, aftershave, deodorants, footpowders, Eau de Cologne and all kinds of muck.

There was a story that he'd once been a lootie in a honky unit — all our officers were honkies — but he'd made such a drastic balls-up that he'd been sent on to us.

Anyway, I asked to speak to him in private and spun him this long story about how we'd saved this poor little baby monkey from being tortured by the local lighties. Now we'd saved him, we weren't so keen just to abandon him. 'He can't fend for himself, sir,' I pleaded. 'He's too young. He'll be torn to pieces in minutes.'

Chico then stuck his head out of my shirt, hopped out onto my shoulder and tried his charm on the lootie. For once the ape behaved perfectly: the lootie stuck out his hand and Chico scampered up onto his shoulder and nestled up against his cheek.

'It's not everyone he likes, sir,' I put in, figuring what the hell, every little bit counts.

But, to tell the truth, I needn't have tried so hard. The lootie was an animal lover, a real rabid one, and all this talk of our dumb and helpless friends made him about as gooey as a chocolate in the sun.

'I don't think the intention of the army regulations is to slaughter innocent baby animals,' he said with feeling, and started telling me about the pair of cocker spaniels that he'd left behind.

Once he was all rubberstamped and legal, that ape took over. He pinched one of the lootie's bars of perfumed soap and grazed it and was so sick we figured he was finished. He fell into a pot of stew while he was investigating the kitchen, and nearly ended up as one of the ingredients. He borrowed a round from the armoury, and climbed up this tree and tried to eat it; he stole the only spanner small enough to close this valve that I'd opened to bleed brake fluid from one of the trucks; he ate my last pack of smokes on the day the camp ran out; he chewed up the laces of my boots just before an inspection; he shredded one of Naomi's letters before I had a chance to read it and he pissed on Headlights while the bloke was telling him to watch it or else.

Ya, ou H, I chune you he was flat. He wanted to put the ape up before the firing squad then and there, and I had to explain that all lighties go through difficult stages. 'My lightie,' I said, 'she spent years drawing on walls, but eventually she grew out of it. With any luck he'll grow out of it soon.'

'How long is it gonna last?' he wanted to know, 'and what are we going to do until then?'

But me, I had no more ideas. I'd tried them all and they didn't work.

'Hell, you and me — we've got to be smart enough to keep a baby monkey under control,' ou Headlights complained. 'What do their mothers do out in the bush?'

Well, if mother monkeys have effective methods of ape control, we never did discover what they were. Ou Chico, he did just what he liked, irrespective of all our yelling and screaming.

Midway through our stint at Binga, me, Fudge, Soaps and Headlights were informed that we were going on a three-day patrol with Lootie Beauty. It wasn't usual for the looties to go on such patrols, but apparently one of the main mannes figured it would do him good. The lootie, of course, wasn't too keen on the idea, and us ouens weren't exactly charmed either.

'With all that muck he smears on himself the terrs'll smell us 10 miles off,' ou Soaps complained.

'What I'm worried about,' reckons ou Headlights, 'is my arsehole. That bloke, he's a rabbit I'm chuning you.'

Actually, in spite of all the complaining, the patrol wasn't too bad. It made a change from standing round and looking at bulldozers. Ou Beauty agreed to let me bring Chico along after I'd given him this long spiel on how the animal would sicken and die if I wasn't around, and the ape kept us amused. Every couple kays we'd come to a kraal, and back in those days the mense were still pretty friendly. The lighties would come running to admire our gats, and there'd usually be a few squawks of surprise when someone spotted Chico.

Lootie Beauty would address the locals — with Fudge translating. He'd carry on for hours about the good government sending us miles out into the bush to protect them against the terrs.

'Do you know what a terrorist is?' I remember him asking one greybeard.

'Ya, baas,' the bloke tells him. 'The army has visited us here before.'

Just in case the whole story hasn't quite sunk in properly, Lootie Beauty gives him this long story about how the terrs want to steal the country and give it to Russia.

'Now what is a terrorist?' he asks again when he's finished. 'Tell me what these gandangas are.'

The madala, he's very pleased to be able to show that he's learnt his lesson, and informs us that these gandangas were devils who ate children, raped women and wanted to take away everyone's goats.

'Well, you've got the main idea,' reckons Lootie Beauty, very pleased. 'Now have you ever seen one of these gandangas? Has one ever been here?'

'No, baas.'

'D'you reckon he'd be able to recognise a terr after all that?' Fudge whispers, very dubious.

'If these gandangas come, you must tell us,' says the lootie. 'You will be given a big reward. Do you understand?'

'Ya, baas.'

The madala, he flashes this big smile and this old queen brings over a big pot of millet beer. The old bloke, he takes a swig and hands it on to Lootie Beauty who just stands there holding it not quite knowing what to do.

'It's just beer, sir,' ou Fudge whispers to him as the lootie stares suspiciously down at the whitish-grey foam. 'Nothing to worry about. You've got to swallow some or the locals will think you're rude.'

Well, the bloke he takes a deep breath, shuts his eyes and gulps down a mouthful as if it's medicine.

The lighties, they're sniggering at this performance until the madala checks them out with a naked eye there.

Then ou Fudge takes the beer pot from the lootie and downs about half of it at one go. 'Really lekker,' he chunes the bloke in Shona. 'First-class.' And suddenly there are smiles all round.

The pot is passed to me, but before I can even smell the stuff, Chico shoots down from my shoulder and bends over to take a sniff. I pour about a teaspoonful into my palm and let him investigate. He dips a finger in, samples it, decides ya, okay, and quickly laps the lot up. Then he licks his lips, somersaults up my arm, flips onto my head and slides down my neck where he lies like a fur collar. The lighties, I chune you, they really liked his performance.

But the lootie isn't impressed. 'Boys,' he says with a smile fixed to his dial, 'boys — it's time we started moving.'

'A little longer,' suggests ou Fudge, who's enjoying the show. 'We don't want the tribesmen to think we aren't polite, sir.'

'Enough is enough,' says the lootie with dignity. 'We are the

Rhodesian army, not a travelling circus. We must keep our distance or these people will forget that we are their superiors.'

Ya, that was the first and last time I ever heard a Rhodesian complain about the locals being too friendly.

Back at the base, this convoy heading down to the lake stops to pick up some equipment. Chico, being Chico, bounces over to check out the scene and, as the blokes are climbing off the trucks, he jumps aboard. In the back of one of them he finds this box of grenades which some idiot has left open. He lifts up a grenade, sniffs it and, probly scheming this thing is some new variety of hardshell fruit, somehow manages to drag the thing up the camp's solitary tree.

'That monkey, man — it's got a grenade,' someone yells, and all us ouens, we drop whatever we're doing and race over to check this lot out. Ou Chico, he sees the crowd gather and schemes he must be onto a good thing. He pulls himself up a branch or two higher for safety's sake. Whatever happens, he's not going to part with his booty without a fight.

'Kiernan,' the lootie shrieks. 'He's your monkey. Get a banana and call him down.' I tried to explain that the harder we tried to persuade Chico to part with his latest toy, the more he'd hang onto it.

But I could hardly make myself heard, what with all the suggestions flying around.

'Gooi a couple rocks.'

'Iron the thing out.'

'Chop the tree down.'

'Kiernan,' says the lootie, all very severe, 'go to the kitchen and get a banana.'

And while everyone's shouting, Chico begins to check out this find of his, trying to work out what all the excitement's about. He discovers that he can't bite through the shell, but the thing has a sort of stalk which is loose and jiggles. He sniffs at this lot — perhaps this is the way to open it up — bites it, and then gives the thing a pull.

'Watch out,' someone screams, 'the ape's found the pin.' Us ouens, we jump, I chune you, diving for cover behind trucks and bulldozers.

BWWWAAAAAA — and bits of monkey and shrapnel spatter against the trucks, and bits of shredded leaves spin down around us. Exit Chico.

There wasn't much damage, and luckily no one was hurt. One

truck had its windscreen shattered, there was a flat tyre or two, and a couple holes were punched through the canvas of our tents.

The two looties marched off to Beauty's tent to argue about who was to blame. Lootie Beauty wanted (so we heard) to know why the grenade had not been locked up as required by the regulations. The convoy's lootie wanted to know why we had ignored the regulation about pets in camp. After yelling at each other for half-an-hour, they began to understand that the other bloke's point of view might not look too bad in a courtmartial, and finally agreed that ya, it would be best for everyone if they just forgot the whole damn thing.

I shovelled all the scraps I could find into a cardboard box I'd scrounged from the kitchen. We buried him that afternoon, buried him smart, I chune you, slow marching to this spot outside the gate where me and Headlights dug the grave.

Soaps took the opportunity to get in some preaching practice, and told us all about Monkey Heaven where, he reckoned, Chico was already causing chaos, pulling the feathers out of angels' wings and fiddling with the harp strings. St Peter was already threatening to send him down to the Other Place.

I draped a small Rhodesian flag over the box, and Fudge sounded the Last Post, and we put what was left of Chico into the grave, rolling a large boulder over it to keep off the hyenas. Ya, it was quite a ceremony, that. Back in those days we were still playing soldiers, and everything, even death, was still a game to us.

Chapter 2

Ya, back in those days we didn't understand anything, we didn't question anything. We believed more or less what whitey wanted us to believe.

To explain it all properly I have to go back quite a ways, right back to the first years of Rhodesia's history, My father's father was Irish, his mother was Shona. The Irishman, Adrian Edward Kiernan, came from Cork and how exactly he landed up in Southern Rhodesia — as it was then — has been forgotten, probably for the good of the family name. He was the manager of a farm near Fort Victoria and there he took up with my grandmother, Elizabeth Gondodema, a 16-year-old farm labourer.

During his two years there she produced two children, my father, Patrick, and my aunt, Mary. Then Kiernan vanished — apparently he was fired for boozing. Whatever, he upped and disappeared leaving my grandmother holding the babies. She returned to her father's kraal but she didn't get along with her half-brothers, so she drifted to Salisbury where she found a job as a cleaner in a department store. When my father was about six, she took up with Desmond Gamba, a petrol pump attendant. My father and Gamba never saw eye to eye; my father couldn't forget his white father and Gamba couldn't forget his wife's white lover. There were battles, beatings. The day my father turned 15 he got himself a job in a clothing store and, when he received his first payslip, he went to board with a coloured family. He never went home again.

When World War II broke out my father enlisted. He served in Italy and North Africa and, to hear him talk about the desert war and the drive up the peninsula, you'd scheme he'd won the whole thing singlehanded. Actually he was just a glorified taximan — only white Rhodesians had been allowed to fight. Even so, he found that Civvy Street didn't suit him and a couple years after the war he re-enlisted, ending up as a clerk in stores.

Round about that time my grandmother died while presenting Gamba with their seventh child. My father didn't go to the funeral or, as far as I know, even visit her grave. Even now, he never mentions his half-brothers and -sisters. If it wasn't for Aunt Mary, who sees the one half-sister occasionally, I wouldn't have known the little I've put down here.

In 1952 my father married Doreen van Jaarsveldt, a tiny skinny woman so light that, as he was fond of pointing out, she could pass for Portuguese. In fact her people were from South Africa, and some of them were Moslems. She'd once lived in Jo'burg and she had a brother, Steve, who'd been locked up a couple times.

On July 7, 1952, I was born and my two sisters, Vera and Gladys — Kiernan family names both I'm told — followed just a year or two later. My mother grafted as a shop assistant, my father was promoted to sergeant. They bought this car, an old beat-up Austin Cambridge, and then a house in Arcadia.

My mother died of pneumonia when I was about 10. My father raised me and my two sisters and, I suppose, managed fairly well under the circumstances. Aunt Mary, who lived just down the road, did what she could to help out. She spent a span of time with the girls

— she called them 'the daughters I never had'.

Also my father got a 'girl', Agnes, to run the house. She was passionate about cleaning, that one; she was always dusting or wiping or scrubbing. Especially in my father's room: she often cleaned it when he was around, and they always locked the door whenever one of her cleaning sessions was in progress.

Agnes had been with us about a year when she suddenly up and produces this lightie several shades lighter than herself. My sisters oohed and aahed over the thing, and spent all day changing its nappies. My father, though, he was bothered by that baby and was always complaining about its howling, about how Agnes was neglecting her work. After a month of this she took the child off to the TTLs and left it in the care of her grandmother. Then a couple weeks later she left in tears. I never did find out why.

It was around that time that Smith declared his UDI. I remember the day well: me and my buddies had spent the day smoking stompies and roasting mealies. When I rock up at home round about five my father and his buddies were perched on the back verandah knocking back their beers and discussing the chances of a British invasion. Though they were all so solemn, so excited I didn't take any particular notice of what they were saying cos they'd been nattering on about this consti-watter and invasion and alles for months. I was about to sneak inside when my father called me over in his this-is-good-for-you voice: 'This is history, Eddie, come and listen.' Well, history was all dates and English Kings to me, but there was something so strange about my father and his friends that afternoon that I hung in the doorway undecided while he switched the radio on for the news. Smith was speaking; his voice was dry and flat but you found yourself caught up in the roll of his words:

'In the lives of nations there comes a moment when a stand has to be made on principle, whatever the consequences. . . . We may be a small country, but we are a determined people. . . . We have struck a blow for the preservation of Justice, Civilisation and Christianity, and in the spirit of this belief we have this day assumed our sovereign independence. . . .'

Then the buddies started up. 'What else could he do?'. 'The Brits drove him to it'. 'Look at the Congo, what happened there when the whites pulled out'. 'The coons here man, they're the happiest in

Africa'.

I'd heard it all before, so I sneaked on inside. Ya, back in those days I just wasn't interested in politics — notwithstanding the disappearance of all decent chocolate from the cafes and all the 'I hate Harold' and 'Harold is a pawpaw' bumper stickers.

The big thing in my life was hanging around with my buddies Turps and Lugs and Toofy, Aunt Mary's youngest, who'd been christened Adrian in honour of the Irishman and rechristened Toofy in memory of his front teeth.

We washed cars, carried packages — anything for a few cents — and smoked stompies when no one was looking. We called ourselves the Warriors and we schemed we were now hardcore ouens, real main mannes.

Ou Headlights was the boss. We call him Headlights cos he was so dark he shone as bright by day as headlights did at night. He wasn't yellow-brown like most of us goffels, or brown like most houties, he was black, as black as black paint. But he insisted he was a coloured. 'Look at my hair,' he kept telling us, 'it's straight. When did you ever see a houtie with hair straight like that? And my nose, it's pointy. Houties have flat noses.' It was the Indian blood which made him so dark, he said, not forgetting to add that Indians weren't the same as Africans. 'Those Indians, they ride elephants and build temples and stuff,' he told us. 'They're civilised.'

At school he was always battling some bloke who'd called him a houtie or'd asked him how much he'd paid to be registered coloured. One time he was flogged six for pouring ink all over the books of this bloke who was too big for him to fight.

Ya, ou Headlights, he was always in trouble. He'd started school a year ahead of me but, cos he never did any work and was always bunking, he'd been kept down a year, and we ended up in the same class.

Now don't get me wrong. He wasn't dumb. He could fix bicycles — 'Peddlers' we called him — as simple as two and two. By the time he was 12, 13 he was already pulling in a couple bucks every week with his repairs. He was also an expert in other things as well: in the vacant lot behind the cafe he taught me and Toofy and the rest of us how to roll a first-class reef and how to build a bottleneck that burned easily and evenly all the way down to the gerrick.

Some days we would skip school and he would lead us in an expedition to town or to one of the white suburbs. We roamed up and down streets of huge white houses set in acres of lawn, keeping an eye out for anything we could — to use Headlights' word — 'borrow'. One time he borrowed a peddler which someone had left to rust on his front lawn. He slapped a coat of paint on it and sold it for 20 bucks. Us ouens, we were impressed.

We raided the white areas quite often after that. Me, I mostly kept watch and daydreamt of meeting up with this golden-haired, fairskinned lass — very much the usual sort of thing. I did actually meet such a creature once. While I was perched on a rock across from this cafe keeping an eye out for stray cops while Headlights and the others were brightening the life of the shopkeeper. This chickie — she must've been 11, 12 — was a beaut, man, a real beaut, with a skin so light it was almost transparent. She wore this thin white cotton frock, and there was this red ribbon in her hair. She looked as if she'd stepped right off the lid of a biscuit tin.

This chickie, she looks round, and then floats over to me. It was just how one of my favourite daydreams began. 'Can I help?' I chune her, standing up into a dream world.

She looks me up and down and I sense eeh, she doesn't exactly find me satisfactory. 'What's the time?' she demands.

I didn't have a watch. I could've killed for a watch just then. 'Haven't got,' I had to admit.

'Poor little piccaninny,' she scoffs. 'No money to buy a watch hay?' And with that, she saunters off.

It was only then it struck me that she didn't have a watch either.

As I'm trying to work out what I should've said, the others were chased out of the shop by the swearing shopkeeper, and we all disappeared off into the nearest patch of bush to rook a quick reef and share out the loot.

As we chewed away on this bargain liquorice I told the others about this dream creature, this goldenhead. They weren't exactly sympathetic.

'Called you a piccaninny, did she?' says ou Headlights, those huge black eyes of his widening to headlight size. 'You should've told her — you're no bloody houtie — you should've spat in her face.' Ya, ou Headlights, he wouldn't take shit from anyone.

But me, I'm sorry to say that I wouldn't have followed his instructions. For weeks afterwards I dreamt of Goldenhead asking me for the time, and I'd pull out this large gold fobwatch just like one I'd seen in the window of a city jewellers. It flicked open at the press of a button, and told you not only the hours, minutes and seconds, but also the date and the month and the year. It was waterproof, it had 27 jewels, and its hands glowed in the dark. If you pressed the button twice it became a stopwatch. With that, I figured, I'd be able to give Goldenhead the time in a thunderstorm at midnight. I concocted dozens of fantasies about her desperately trying to find out the time exactly — immediately. Of course I'd just happen to rock up at the 59th second of the 59th minute of the 11th hour and I'd whip out the watch — with fairytale results.

My other favourite daydream was that doctors had discovered a magic formula which could turn us goffels white — not pinky-yellow, like most whites, but real white — white like icing sugar, white like paper.

Hell, you couldn't forget that whitey was tough, tough enough to rule the world. You couldn't forget that whitey was the one who'd rocketed into space, who'd painted the maps red, green and blue with empires, who'd invented cars and radios, aeroplanes and television and guns. At the flicks all the heroes were white. And we were half-white — maybe even more than half-white — ourselves.

But, of course, there was that other half. Being of Shona stock ourselves, we felt that we'd at least descended from the most civilised tribe in the country. Shonas, my father was fond of saying, were quiet, peaceable sorts, farmers, not real savages like the Ndebele who'd ripped through the country just before the whites arrived. Those with Ndebele ancestors naturally had other ideas: as far as they were concerned the Ndebele were warlike and noble, and the Shonas were gutless peasants, hardly better than slaves.

But, no matter whether your ancestors were Ndebele or Shona, you couldn't forget the fact that they were black. At school they taught us only European history. There wasn't such a thing as African history — a teacher once explained to us that nobody could remember what had happened before the whites came and started writing everything down.

Besides, back in those days we believed that all the blacks had ever done was fight and breed and, when it came to a fight, whitey had always beaten them anyway, except when they'd massacred defenceless women and children, or had overwhelmed some small band of hopelessly outnumbered heroes who'd stood steadfast to the last, firing until their rounds ran out. Hell, as my father used to say, no one was even sure that you could civilise blacks.

Ya, looking back, it's no wonder I was so keen to impress Goldenhead. I couldn't get her out of my head for months. With my share of the proceeds I bought this watch, guaranteed gold, from one of the local heavies. It looked pretty good, and it worked most of the time too. I kept it hidden from my father and only wore it when we went out on our expeditions. But I had no luck: I never saw the girl again.

With peddlers we had better luck: ou H got pretty good at borrowing them and, over the years, he must've picked up three or four dozen Raleighs and Peugeots as well as one or two Japanese models that had somehow, in spite of sanctions, made their way into the country.

The bloke hid his bargains in this old fowl-run in his parents' backyard for a month or two, and then fixed them up, swapped round a few parts, and painted them matt black. The garden boy bought the finished products, and wheeled them off to the townships where he flogged them for a mammoth profit.

Ou Headlights did pretty well too. What with his reputation as a repairman, his business began taking up so much time that he stopped bothering with school.

The headmaster wasn't going to complain and his father, who was dossing when he wasn't grafting, had no idea what ou H was up to. His old queen, this stiff-necked old cow who schemed she was something special cos she'd once been married to an Englishman, didn't care what he got up to as long as he occasionally slipped her a couple bucks for booze. Ya, she wouldn't lower herself to take a stroll down to the pub and get pissed with the locals, and knocked back the stuff at home behind closed doors instead.

Then ou Headlights sold all his peddlers and blew all his bread on this fourth-hand 50cc motorbike. He spent days fiddling with the thing, taking it apart and putting it back together again. He wasn't interested in going out shopping for bargains, he stopped doing repairs. His old queen muttered about the waste, the waste, all that good money gone to waste, and most of the Warriors got bored with this new story of his and wandered off to other battlegrounds. But me, I stuck around and, once he'd figured out the basics of bikes, we started hunting out bargains together. Our first target was a delivery scooter. We cleared about a 100 bucks, and it looked like ou Headlights was all set to make a success of his new business too.

Then, one fine day when his bike was in bits and pieces lying spread out on sheets of newspaper in the garage, his old queen sent him down to the shop for a bottle. As he's hobbling along there this cop on a bike pulls some old jalopy off to the side of the road, parks and goes off to write his ticket. Now ou Headlights, he checks out the cop's bike — purely a professional interest, you understand — and sees eeh, what's this? the cop has left the keys in the ignition.

Ou H, he just couldn't resist. He hops on the thing and — vroom-vroom — off he roars.

It wasn't like stealing, he tried to explain to the court: when you see a ten-dollar bill lying on the pavement you aren't going to walk past and leave it there crying for an owner. No, you are going to pick it up. Finders keepers, losers weepers.

The magistrate was not impressed; he sentenced Headlights and me — the cops found out all about the scooter as well — to two years reform school.

It was bad but not awful, I suppose. I did my best to get along. I played left-back for second team soccer, and learnt the basics of a trade — confectionery — as well as some carpentry and motor mechanics. For the rest I kept out of trouble, made sure I did just what everyone else did — one of those small, skinny lighties you see on the fringes of every school photograph.

When the pair of us were released we went straight to the army to do our national service. Though it was still voluntary in those days, us two didn't really have much choice. My father and ou Headlights' dad had this idea that a stint in the army would make men of us, and they managed to persuade the head of the reformatory to force us to sign up.

Me, I didn't need persuading anyway, I was dead keen to go. I'd been reading stacks of war books — Douglas Bader, escapes from German prisons, *The Battle of Monte Cassino*, the naval war, the desert war, *The Battle of Britain*, that kind of thing — and just then my one ambition was to fight for freedom and democracy and alles.

It looked like I'd get a chance too. Just a few years before, in '67 and '68, Zipra forces had invaded Rhodesia. The security forces wiped them out in no time and the survivors gapped it back to Zambia where they were said to be planning another try. Next time they crossed I wanted to be right there on the banks of the Zambezi waiting for them.

But I ended up a driver. That was all that coloured national servicemen did back in those days. We were given the minimum of military training — running, combat exercises, basic tactics — and we were taken to the shooting range a few times. That was it. For the rest they taught us driving and some elementary mechanics.

Still, there were consolations. Me and ou Headlights ended up in the same platoon, and the graze was okay. We were allowed to smoke and drink, and once in a while we were given a weekend pass. Besides, you could feel you were doing something — even if it was only driving a truck — for Democracy and the rest.

In spite of the fact that the papers were fond of repeating that Rhodesia's blacks were the happiest in Africa, we were called up to do our first additional camp about two years after we'd finished our national service. Though I complained loud and long about the call-up, I was actually quite pleased to go. What with the joys of marriage, fatherhood and a regular job — I was married with a lightie by then, and chief confectioner at Katz's bakery — I reckoned I could do with some time off.

Come call-up day us ouens were all lined up on the parade ground at Inkomo barracks, and this major informed us that we couldn't just be drivers any longer. In future, he said, us coloureds were going to have to play a man's full role, in future we were going to have to fight.

The whole bunch of us gave a cheer you could hear all the way to Burg. At long last we were getting a chance to prove ourselves!

When the major finally restored order he explained we had been transferred from our transport battalion to the RDR, the Rhodesian Defence Regiment. We would now be guarding strategic targets.

As our previous training had been a little too basic even for guard duty, we were sent on another training course.

It was on our second call-up, just three or four months later, that we were sent off to our base near Binga, where the strategic targets turned out to be road-building equipment.

Chapter 3

I t was disappointing but we did have quite a jol out there in the bush and back in Burg, when we were given a letter informing us that in 56 days' time we would be guests of the government again, I didn't know whether to swear or cheer. I picked up my bag and spear — I'd bought it off this madala for five bucks — and joined the mob straggling towards the camp gates.

Outside this crowd of friends and relatives waited. I shoved through the crowd. There wa-a-ay over in the back I checked Naomi holding Ruthie's hand and standing on tiptoes as she looked for me. I waved as I pushed towards her and eeh, I chune you when she finally spotted me and waved back there was a lump the size of a pumpkin at the back of my throat.

My old man, he was there as well, waiting to give the hero a lift home. Eeh, but I wished I had a few decent warries to entertain them with. 'I did pick up this spear,' I chuned them as I played peek-a-boo with Ruthie as we drove off. 'I took it off this bloke who looked suspicious.' It was a spectacular spear all right, bound with copper wire and beads, and with a big sharp head that looked as if it meant serious business. I never did dare tell them I'd actually bought the thing. Hell, it was the only souvenir I had.

Now my father, who'd fought in World War II and had worked in the Rhodesian army stores for years, was very keen on his military souvenirs. He had quite a collection of model tanks and aeroplanes which Italian prisoners of war had made out of scrap metal, as well as a few caps and badges and empty AK mags which troopies had given him.

So when we get home first thing he really checks that spear out, weighing it in his hand and running a finger down its blade. 'I wouldn't like to be on the receiving end of this,' he reckons. 'This thing is serious. You should hang it in the lounge.'

Well, Naomi schemes it's a first-class idea and heads off to the kitchen, pulls out the box of general junk and scratches around until she comes up with a picture hanger and some fishing line. Together we hung the thing up above the mantelpiece, above the family photographs.

We had quite a collection: in the centre there's a shot of me and Naomi, just married, in the doorway of the local Anglican Church; beside it was one of those large, old stiff studio portraits of my mom and dad and us three kids taken just after Gladys was born. My father looks impossibly young and trim, and as respectable as a preacher; my mother is just as I remember her. There was a shot of Uncle Ronald, Aunt Mary and ou Adrian outside their new house in Zambia; Ruthie naked on the lounge carpet when she was three months old; the Manchester Wolves the year we won the league; ou Numbers very smart in his military uniform; Naomi's aunts and uncles on the beach at Beira; Naomi laughing with a crowd of cousins; Naomi, about 16, in a fancy dress at a dance — it must've been taken just before we started going out.

Ya, I was only 19 and she was only 17 when we married. We'd known each other for years — hell, we'd practically grown up next door to each other. Her brother, ou Numbers, had been a serious member of the Warriors. Though he hadn't been much good at arithmetic at school he could sure as hell confuse any shopkeeper when it came to change. In those days Naomi was this skraal, dark-skinned lightie with long wiry pigtails who came shouting for him to go home. I can still remember her, hands on hips, in this pink dress she always wore, all puffed up as she informed us: 'Ma says....' After I was locked up, I didn't see her again for a couple of years. Then, one Friday night while I was doing my national service, I rock up at this scene at some connection's place, down a beer and ask this bird to boogie. As we're hopping around there it strikes me that she's sort of familiar. I check — double check — 'Naomi? Numbers' Naomi?'

'Yea,' she smiles. 'I was wondering how long it would take you to click.'

Well, she wasn't exactly a skraal lightie any longer: she was taller than me, maybe an inch or so, and darker — the colour of strong tea with a touch of milk — and these fine fat tits bulged in her blouse. Her hair was thick and black and hung down to her shoulders, and she had a smile that could've charmed a camel. Me, I was knocked right out. We boogied and talked, boogied and dopped, and late that night we took a walk and, behind the hall of the local Baptist Church, I spoilt her.

After that we saw each other whenever we could. A couple months later, just before I've finished my national service, she comes crying to me that she's pregnant, what are we going to do? Me, I'm scheming maybe we should think carefully about this little lot, there's no need to rush into anything. One of my buddies knows this bloke who knows a bloke who.... We're still thinking when Naomi's old queen somehow smells out what's happening and, next time I'm round she sends Naomi down to the cafe for smokes, sits me down and wants to know what's all this she's been hearing about me and Naomi?

'Me and Naomi, we get on,' I chune her, cautious-cautious. From what I'd heard, that old queen had a tongue like a panga and I didn't want to get her going.

'More than that,' she tells me, 'from what I hear, quite a lot more than that!'

Me, I stared down at the carpet. This wasn't the sort of thing you'd talk about with some bag old enough to be your mother. She didn't have any qualms though. She came right to the point. 'I hear you are a confectioner,' she said like it's right down there with street sweeper. 'Do you make enough to support my daughter?'

At that stage I didn't. I'd only been out of the army for a month, and I was still finishing my apprenticeship. But there was no help for it: Naomi's old queen wanted us married, and so married we were. We couldn't afford a place of our own, so we had to stay with her. She was a bossy old bitch, always trying to run everything for us, but as we didn't have any coin there wasn't much we could do about it. Then old Adams was fired for drunkenness and the owner of the bakery, Katz, made me his chief confectioner, and just about doubled my wages. Me and Naomi, we had a talk: we decided to put off having another lightie for a while, she found graft as a shop assistant and, with the additional income, we were just able to afford the payments on a house. Naomi's old queen lent us the money for the deposit — she was probly pleased to see the last of us — and we bought this cabin just down the drag from her. I began thinking about a car.

Once the spear had been hung and straightened, we had tea and this chocolate cake Naomi had baked specially for the occasion. I tried to scrape together some suitable warries, but I couldn't exactly tell my father how I'd come to be christened Donk, or exactly what we'd been up to when ou Headlights had rescued Chico. Actually, I needn't have worried: what with all the talk of war and gats, my father started parading all his own favourite warries, and he told us about Italy and North Africa all over again. 'You'll love being in the army,' he kept telling me. 'It's the best job a man can have.' Me, back in those days I schemed maybe he had a point.

When my father had run through his stories, I admired Ruthie's new doll and Naomi filled me in on all the local news: Vyvyan, her cousin, was about to be divorced cos his wife had found out that he'd been messing around when he was away on call-up; that bastard Robson was still leading Gladys up the garden path — now he'd taken some woman off to Victoria Falls for the weekend, but she still couldn't see through him. Vera was expecting, she was three months along, and so was Flo across the way, and Delia had just had another. Pickles had lost his job cos his boss closed the factory down and took the chicken run to South Africa, and Shireen had had to go out and get a job. . . .

Dad went off to his buddies at the bar, we played with the lightie till it was time for her afternoon nap, and then put her to bed and went to bed ourselves. That night for supper we had chicken curry that Naomi made — she was an expert in curries — and afterwards we went to the movies. Sitting there cuddled up next to her eeh, I chune you I was glad to be back home.

Next morning, Saturday, Naomi dropped Ruthie off at her mother's and went off to her second-hand furniture shop. Me, I sat around for a while, paged through one or two westerns, but eeh, I was too restless to read. I just couldn't stay still; I had to do something. Not even a pot of tea cooled me down. I tried to weed a flowerbed out back and discovered I was causing heavy casualties among the petunias. There was just no way I could manage gardening. I threw the spade down and headed over to ou Headlights to see how he was settling in.

I found the bloke in the garage, glaring at the engine of this 1950s Harley, which was spread out all across the floor, as if he's going to grab a hammer and start smashing it any minute.

'It's a bugger being back,' he reckons, wiping his hands against his overalls. His old queen is after him for coin, his dad wants to buy a new car and is asking for the garage back. 'We should've fucking stayed out in the bush — maybe we should just join the goddam army full-time.'

'We're goffels,' I remind him. 'The only full-time goffels are drivers and clerks — like my dad.'

Well, we reckon we're in need of consolation so we stroll down to the shab where we down a couple beers. And, as we're dopping there, we reckon, hey, you know, why not get hold of the rest of the ouens and get together for one big booze-up before we're back at the grind. Me, I'd finished off quite a few beers by then and I'm feeling quite charitable so I volunteer our cabin for the occasion.

Anyway, Headlights staggers off to organise everything and I lurch on home. Naomi's already there, waiting with the lunch, and eeh, I chune you, she isn't happy to hear about this little lot. 'You've been off with those blokes for months,' she yells, 'and you're not even back a day and you're jolling again.' And then she starts accusing me: I don't love her, I've been chasing after someone out in the bush, I'm just not interested in her anymore, her ma always said I was no good.

'Hell, keep your tits tied on,' I chune her. 'It's just my buddies coming round for a couple beers.'

But she was beyond little things like facts by then. 'If you're trying to get rid of me, why don't you throw me into the street? Nothing is worse than being ignored. . . .'

'Look, why don't you try listening to what I've got to say,' I put in, starting to raise my voice myself.

'But it's true,' she wails. 'You'd rather be with them.'

And, when she was carrying on like that, it was most definitely true.

Well, I can't admit that to her so I retreat into the garden and hole up there, drinking and sulking, until the ouens rock up, armed with a bomb of brandy and a couple beers.

We take up our positions in the lounge. Ou Fudge rolls a reef and ou Headlights checks out the spear on the mantelpiece and informs us he wants a bottle pickled terrs' ears on his. Then Ruthie waddles in, muddy and smiley, and I let her have a sip of beer cos she's been such a good girl all day. Next thing Naomi swoops in, snatches the lightie up and carries her off, kicking and screaming.

'Come and have a beer with us,' I call to her, but she's not interested in peace moves just then. When she's finished with the lightie, she stamps over to the kitchen and bangs all the dirty pots and pans into the sink. It's difficult to have a good time with that kind of racket in the background. 'Bloody bitch,' I'm muttering.

'Women,' sighs ou Soaps, who has been concentrating on the brandy. 'They're Adam's curse, that's what it is. Every time I do a marriage and there's some bride promising to love, honour and obey, I want to shout out she's a liar, a liar in the house of God. . . .'

We decided to head down to the shab. Me, I chune you, I was so flat I didn't want to lay an eye on that chick again. All that night I'm knocking the dop back and every once in a while me and Headlights and the others sneak off round the corner for a quick skyf. Somewhere along the line we land up at this scene — Fudge's brother's place, I think it was — and me, I try chatting up this cherrie but after hours of dancing and gallons of beer, she makes a duck.

I'm not quite sure what happened after that. Next thing I remember the sky is starting to lighten round the edges as I'm crawling up the path to the front door, puking into the pansies every couple of feet. I drag myself onto the verandah, bang at the door and Naomi opens up and she's screeching like a police siren. Me, I just pull myself inside and pass out.

The next morning, when I finally came round, even before I'd had a chance to swallow my coffee and aspirin, she began yelling at me all over again. I told her to shut up; my head was hurting. She did — and refused to speak to me for the next three days. But at least she was quiet. The whole of Sunday I spent sleeping off my hangover. Monday, it was back to the grind.

Three am alarm, 4 am bus, 4.30 at Katz's Confectioners. The graft itself wasn't too bad and Katz was generally okay. The shop was small and we made everything ourselves, which meant that us ouens had to be able to handle everything from sausage rolls to cream cakes and chocolate eclairs. It also means us ouens didn't just have to produce the goods, we had to produce top quality goods, the best around, cos the shop was quite a lot more expensive than the mammoth places near us.

My favourite graft was making wedding cakes, not cos I'm particularly pro marriage or anything, but cos I liked it.

To begin with we'd ask the customer what exactly they had in mind, and if they didn't like sultanas I'd leave out the sultanas; if they had a passion for candied pineapple I'd go heavy on the pineapple. Then I'd stir in the other ingredients, the sugar and the flour, the eggs and the spices, the lemon and the brandy and alles. Next you divide it up between the different pans. Sometimes it would be only two pans and sometimes there'd be a whole span. Once I had a chick who wanted a seven-tiered job, and eeh, I can chune you, that item was one grand piece of confectionery. I called it my masterpiece. Ou Katz, he just laughed, called me his marzipan Michelangelo and reminded me that the mense were going to graze the thing, not put it in a museum.

Well, after I'd baked the cakes — usually that was on a Monday — I'd let them cool nicely and trim them, brush on some apricot jam and cover them in marzipan. On Wednesday or Thursday I'd spoon on the icing and slide my baker's card across till the surface of each was as smooth as a still pond. Friday I'd do the sides of the cakes, and then on Saturday morning I'd add a bit of water to a little of the extra frosting and give them all a second coat. Then I'd set them aside and let them harden till, say, the next Tuesday or Wednesday.

When I came back to them it was to decorate and eeh, that was the lekker part, the part I liked best. I'd draw a plan on a piece of grease proof paper, the same size as the cake. Then I'd lay that item on the cake, prick my design through with a pin, get out my pipes — my star pipe and my shell pipe, my writing pipe and my petal pipe — and go to work making a rosette here, a tulip there, a 'Hilda loves Horace' in the corner and a fancy bow round the sides. Next I'd mould some almond paste into a pair of lekker wedding bells or maybe a dove and then, last of all I'd get out the little plastic bride and groom for the top. When I think of it now, you know, it seems odd to have been putting those honky figures on cakes that were meant lots of times for goffel, houtie or Indian chicks. But, eh, back in those days I didn't think of things like that.

Once I was back making wedding cakes it was as if I hadn't been away at all. From 4.30 in the morning to about 1.30 in the afternoon I grafted. Usually I'd make it back home by about 2, 2.30. After a shower, I'd have lunch, read the paper and then doss for an hour or two. Round about five, when Naomi got home, I'd wake up and maybe fiddle around in the garden for a while, or go to soccer practice or head down to the hotel or the shab for a few beers. At seven sharp Naomi served supper, and afterwards we usually watched TV until we went off to bed at about nine. On Saturday afternoons I played left back for Manchester Wolves and in the evening we'd go off jolling. On Sundays we slept and read the paper and in the afternoons we'd visit friends or relatives or watch soccer. Ya, it didn't take long for things to settle back into normal. Except, that is, for Adrian.

Just a week or two after I was back at graft, Adrian was making headlines. According to the papers he was a terr and he was in town. His was one of the first terr units to hit Burg, and back in those days none of us had ever heard of goffel terrs either. I chune you the whole place went frantic. There were cops on every street corner, bomb-drills in the schools, house-to-house searches in the coloured areas and every five minutes the radio was asking 'All those with information about the whereabouts of the following men to....' Ya, ou Adrian, he had the city running scared.

The cops visited us, they visited all the relatives. They searched our houses while the neighbours watched through their curtains. 'I'll turn the bastard in the moment I spot him,' I told this cop who questioned me. 'Me, I'm a Rhodesian, I'm completely against all this communism bullshit.' But I was so angry about the whole business the bloke must've schemed I might just be acting cos they kept watch on the house until he was caught.

Ya, two days later they discovered him and his buddy holed up with this mad old aunty in a house just round the corner from us.

About 80 police and troops surrounded the place and snipers were positioned on neighbours' roofs.

'We realised what was up and we tried to sneak away,' ou Adrian told me years later. 'We were down there in the garden, in this mealie patch, and we tried to crawl to the hedge. But, when we got there, all's we could see was this long line of boots. Our way out was literally blocked by boots. Three times this officer with a megaphone called on us to surrender or be shot. The last time he called, he gave us three minutes to decide.'

'Me and the other bloke, Comrade Terror, we had to make a difficult decision, a decision filled with mixed feelings. Our lives were in our hands. A shootout with the cops would've meant suicide. But at the camp, the commissars had talked as if surrender was the same as selling out. I wouldn't have minded if I'd died in battle because then I would have died like anyone else trying to free the country — but our situation was utterly hopeless. Even if I'd tried to lob a grenade or something, they would've shot us to pieces without it ever having left my hand.'

So Adrian and his comrade surrendered. The news came over the radio as I was lifting a pan of cinnamon buns from the oven.

'You know this terrorist they're talking about?' I remember Katz asking me. Me, I just about dropped the pan on my feet. For a moment there I was scheming someone had put the word in his ear.

'No ways,' I chune him, putting the pan down on the table. 'Why would I know someone like that.'

Which was — I'm not trying to defend myself — true in a backhanded way. At that point in my life I honestly couldn't figure out why Adrian had turned terr. And, when I got back home that afternoon, my old man was sitting there in the lounge telling Naomi he also couldn't understand why Adrian had done it. It just didn't make sense to us.

I emptied this bag of bargain buns into this plate on the coffee table. 'This goddam idiot must be insane,' I put in. 'A coloured terr — it just doesn't add up.'

'He's a fool, a complete fool,' my father says, uncoiling the cinnamon bun and dipping a chunk into his tea. 'All right, things aren't perfect here, but they're beginning to change.'

'I'd just like to see the goddam bastard hung —'

'He's your cousin,' Naomi points out.

'He's a terr. Here I am slaving my guts out to make a decent living and Katz goes and asks me if I know the bloke! What happens if he finds out?' Ya, back in those days I would never have believed that one day I'd be a terr myself.

Chapter 4

So you get the idea. That's the kind of people we were. You can understand then why the whole family found this business about Adrian being a terr a mystery, a big embarrassment. We all tried to keep the connection quiet, but everyone knew of course, and as you walked down the street the hair on the back of your neck prickled cos you knew damn well that all the people you were greeting would start on about the terr's family the moment you were out of earshot. I took to stating my position loudly to whoever would listen and every chance I got I wore my army clobber to prove just which side I was on.

I was wearing my army clobber when we went to this fancy nightclub the weekend before my third call-up. Me and Naomi, we boogied through a couple of numbers and then ordered a beer each.

We were getting all lovey dovey there when this honky in an RLI uniform, this blonde youngster with a bad case of pimples, wobbled over to our table. 'Howzit,' he said dropping himself into a chair.

I asked him if he wanted a drink. He did. By the look of him he'd had quite a few already. I ordered another round. I might as well admit it: I was pleased — proud — to have a honky, a troopie, sit with us at our table.

Naomi offered him a smoke, I asked him what unit he was in, and just as he starts to answer another two troopies, both of them drunk, swagger up to our table. 'Hay — Eric — nice goosey —' one of them announces at the top of his voice. He takes hold of Naomi's chair to steady himself '— big tits.'

'What unit you blokes in?' I repeat, ignoring the comment. I'm really sweating there, you check, really sweating. You never know with drunks. I figure if I can just get through to them, show them that we're all in this together.... 'I'm an RDR man myself. On Monday it's back to the bush.'

'Why don't you just bugger off now then?' the troopie says, checking me out with a wooden eye. And then he leans over the table and grabs at Naomi's breast.

'No,' — she slaps his hand back — 'no.'

I jump up. 'We'd better get going now — we must get back to the lightie.' I didn't want a scene; I couldn't have taken on all three of them, and in the old Rhodesia, if you had a run-in with whitey, you somehow always ended up in the wrong.

'Hey, hey hey,' shouts Eric, grabbing Naomi's hand, 'stay with me — let's go have some fun —'

She giggles and hesitates, or seems to hesitate, before she pulls herself free. Even now I'm still not exactly sure what she did even though I must've played and replayed that scene a thousand times in my mind.

'Not this one,' I yell, trying, you know, to sound firm.

I caught hold of Naomi's hand and practically dragged her to the door. As we went out the club onto the landing, I heard those footsteps behind us. 'Just walk natural,' I whisper to her, 'just....' But before we're even at the bottom of the stairs, the three army boys were up onto us, kicking, punching, swearing. Suddenly I'm doubled up on the pavement, the taste of blood in my mouth and some bloke swinging his boot into my gut. The door of the club opens again, there's a blast of music, and a shout, and the three blokes jump and run. It's then that I spot Naomi huddled up against the stairs, holding her head and moaning.

'Goddam honkies — they're bloody barbarians,' ou Headlights says after I'd told the ouens about it all as we were heading to this base at a tea plantation near Inyanga.

'Ag, you can't blame the honkies,' reckons Fudge — picking up the other end of the stick as usual. 'Bastards like that come in all colours.'

'Bullshit,' says Headlights, indignant. 'Ever heard of a goffel breaking a honky chick's — or any other chick's — jaw like that?

Fudge had to admit he hadn't. 'But it could happen — no problem,' he insists.

'No man, it couldn't,' ou Headlights informs him. 'This shows just what the problem is: the honkies, they've got no respect for us. They scheme we're just like houties.'

'Wish I'd been there,' reckons Sticks, this new bloke, a dark stocky fellow who was a storeman at a warehouse. 'I'd've taught them to watch themselves round goffels....'

'They probly would've broken your jaw too,' puts in Fudge.

But this Sticks lets us know he's done some boxing, quite a lot in fact, and he'd like to see which three drunken honkies could stand up to him.

'And when the cops rock up,' asks Soaps, 'what sort of trouble....'

'How long you going to stick around waiting?' Headlights snorts.

We were still arguing when we reached the tea estate early in the afternoon. The truck turns off onto this dirt road twisting off through dense forest high up into the hills, changes down to two as we ease down this steep slope through a small stream. The side of the road was thick with ferns and up on the hills these tiny waterfalls trailed off into spray as they tumbled hundreds of feet down the hillsides. Every couple kays we pass a kraal, and hordes of near-naked children rushed to the road, waving and begging for cents and sweets. Another turnoff and the track was banked with bougainvillaea and rusty barbed wire, and up in the hills you could see women at work, small brightly coloured dots moving in a ragged line through the rows of tea.

'Thank God you've come,' the ouens in the camp chune us as we debus. 'We were beginning to scheme we'd been left out here to die.'

'So it's hot-hot out here then?' I sneer, remembering all those Bigfoot stories. 'You want to get out of here before you're wiped out, do you?'

'No such luck,' they tell us. 'This place is as cold as frozen fish. The only goddam enemy out here is boredom.'

A year before, we were told, the terrs had visited the estate from Mozambique which was just a couple kays across the gomos. They politicised the workers until one of the bossboys reported them to the manager who called in the army. The terrs then disappeared along with the bossboy and had, by all accounts, kept their distance ever since.

We were holed up in this old overseer's cabin, a rundown place with a rusty iron roof, about 50 yards from a compound housing maybe 500 mense. As far as army accommodation went, the place was a luxury hotel: for starters we were sleeping under a roof, not just a tent; there was also running water, hot and cold, and screens to keep out the bugs as well as an inside toilet and shower. Even better, the lootie had his own quarters, a small cottage just down the drag. Just the camp's administration office was in the cabin with us. Ya, accommodation-wise we would've been in paradise if it hadn't been for Lootie Beauty.

It was ou Headlights who discovered the lootie's latest. While we're organising rooms and alles, he tiptoes in, rolling his eyes and motions us to follow. We sneak past the administration office, where the Beauty is chewing his pen and contemplating the wads of paperwork the previous lootie left him, on down the corridor to the shithouse. There, tacked to the door, with a pair of drawing pins in each corner, is a large notice in red ink. 'OC Only'.

'This wasn't here before,' hisses ou Sticks. 'I christened the bowl myself.'

'This is our goddam toilet,' ou H says. 'The lootie's already got one in the cottage — and hell, that's only 10 yards down the drag. What does he need two for?'

'Cos he's a big arsehole,' Fudge cracks.

'This is discrimination,' complains Soaps. 'Does whitey scheme he's too good even to mix his shit and piss with ours?'

'We should be grateful whitey wasn't so careful with his sperm,' reckons Fudge, 'otherwise we wouldn't be here at all.'

'The bastard,' says Headlights, 'we'll get him.'

We spent the best part of the next morning searching for suitable snakes, but the only one we were able to find was this bright green thing, about six inches long, which none of us could identify.

Back at camp we sat around watching the thing, its purple tongue flickering in and out, in and out as it nosed around the bottle, while we argued about what to do next. Soaps reckoned ya, this thing was a mamba for sure. 'Mambas are the bright green ones,' this instant expert informed us. 'I saw in a book once. If it bites the lootie he'll die and they'll hang us all for murder.'

But Headlights was not convinced. 'It's too quiet to be a mamba,' he told us. 'It's just a bush snake. It's harmless.'

Sticks, who'd once spent a couple months at teacher training college and was supposed to know about everything, had to admit that he wasn't sure. 'It's probly semi-poisonous,' he chuned us, trying to sound like he knew what he was talking about.

After an hour of arguing we decided ya, what the hell, ou Headlights had to be right. So next morning at about five bells one very cold stiff snake was emptied through the window of the OC toilet.

All's quiet until the lootie rocks up just after breakfast. As he's ambling down the passage what does he check but the snake sliding out from under the door of the toilet into the passage. That bloke, I chune you, he lets out a shriek like Russian tanks are invading from Mozambique. He shrieks so loud that us ouens, we don't even think about snakes and booby traps as we grab our gats and dive for our defensive positions.

It took quite a while to sort out all the confusion, and by the time Lootie Beauty had more or less restored order, the snake had slithered down this hole in the skirting boards.

We never did see the thing again but for the rest of our stay us ouens all wore our boots while moving around at night.

Still, the snake had kept us entertained and we were grateful. There wasn't much else on the go. Once in a while the lootie would call for volunteers and send off a patrol, and ou Soaps, our medic, was kept busy patching up people from the compound. For the rest all's we had to amuse us was a pile of tattered paperbacks, a radio and booze. Every Monday we put our coin together and bought ourselves a couple crates of beer. We made a law that everyone had to down at least one beer before breakfast, and there was always a competition to see who could knock back the most by lunchtime. Sometimes we'd play smashed soccer: every member of each team had to put away three-four beers and smoke a skyf.

One afternoon while I'm brooding there among the beer bottles, this old greybeard from the compound sidled up to me and asked to see the medic. I took him off to Soaps and the bloke starts off on this long sad story about his sick grandmother who lives in this kraal waaay off in the bush, can we come and see her? Ou Soaps reckons well, can't you bring her in, and next thing the bloke's whispering there's a terr holed up in one of the huts.

'Hey, hey,' says ou Soaps rather shocked. 'You sure he's a terr?'

After all, we'd been told that there weren't any in the area. Yes, the bloke insists, there's a terr. He's been shot in the foot, and his comrades have left him there until they can take him to Mozambique.

We call in Lootie Beauty and all the rest of the ouens, and the greybeard explains where the terr is hidden: the kraal, how to get there, even the hut. Then he asks for his reward — about 500 bucks a terr in those days — but no one was bothering with his problems just then. The lootie is wringing his hands and asking what, what are we going to do, and us ouens are telling him let's go, go-go-go-get him. Hell, it was our first chance of a fight and we didn't want to let it slip through our fingers.

But the lootie he decides no, no, he can't do it to us. We're not trained fighters, he's going to call in the fire force. He radios HQ and requests choppers, bombers, fire force. The main mannes aren't impressed. 'We get dozens of reports like this every day,' one of them informs him, 'and most of them are bullshit. Go take a look yourselves — and call us if you run into trouble.'

The lootie wasn't too charmed, but orders are orders. Leaving the madala in camp in the care of a solitary guard, the rest of us piled into our two trucks and off we trundled into the bush. Me, I managed to get myself onto the lead truck: after being nicknamed Donk I wanted a chance to prove to the ouens exactly what I was made of.

After half-an-hour driving along cattle tracks, the kraal comes into view. The children spot us at once — 'Mabhunu', 'soldiers', they're shouting and they all, even the toddlers of four, five years old, drop whatever they're doing and bolt off into the bush, goats and chickens just behind. Me, I'm scheming what's all this about? Though I'd stopped at lots of kraals, visited dozens of villages, I'd never seen anything like it. The locals had always been friendly, offering us beer and graze, and the lighties had always hung around us, admiring our gats, on the lookout for cents and cigarette butts. But that afternoon, for the first time, they ran.

The truck slams on anchors at the outskirts of the kraal, the sarge yells 'debus' and we all pile out, rifles at the ready, and surround the place, taking up positions in the mealie fields. 'If anyone moves, they will die,' the sarge yells three times in Shona, and then again in English to make sure everyone understands. 'Stay where you are and you will be safe.' The second truck stops, the ouens debus, split up and start searching the huts, checking each one just as we'd been taught: the one bloke standing by the door, gat cocked and ready to blast the place to kingdom come, orders the mense out, one at a time, hands over their heads, the other searching them as they emerge. Ya, even now, thinking back, I'm surprised at how well our unit performed that afternoon, how well we searched the people and marched them to the trucks and made them all lie down. Ya, we performed that search as if all of us — the locals included — had been doing it forever.

Two or three mense and a goat crawl out of the fifth hut, but somehow, ou Headlights, he isn't satisfied. 'Move out,' he shouts, kicking at the wall, 'or we'll burn the place down.' There's this rustle of something, and everyone — the villagers lying on the ground, us blokes surrounding the kraal — we're all staring at Headlights and the door of the hut. 'This is it,' I'm scheming. 'This is where the terrs open up.' The hairs at the back of my neck are standing on end, every second I'm expecting the rattle of rounds from the bush beyond us.

Instead there's a grunt, a hand appears in the doorway. Headlights, quick as a snake, grabs the wrist, jerks him out into the sunlight. There's a cry from the women, but we look at them with our guns and they go quiet. The bloke, his foot wrapped up in a dirty whitish cloth, sits blinking at the light and at the gats. Even from my position, 50 yards away, I can smell his sweetish stinky odour.

'Your situpa? Where's your situpa?' Headlights demands. The bloke starts mumbling something about having lost it.

'Bullshit. And your foot? What happened to your foot?'

'I fell baas, fell on a stone and cut it.'

'Lies,' says Headlights glaring at him. 'If that was the story you would've gone to the hospital. You wouldn't have stayed here to rot.'

The bloke, he takes another look at ou Headlights and his gat and out it all spills: ya, ya, he was with Zanla, he was a cadre but only because he'd been kidnapped — they'd threatened to kill him if he didn't co-operate. He actually wanted to give himself up, he'd been planning on it.

'I thought this area was supposed to be quiet,' I said as we boarded the truck with our prisoner.

'Hell, I hope there are at least a couple of other terrs around,' says ou Headlights jumping up beside me. 'This is more fun than smashed soccer.'

We took the terr to the nearest cop shop, about 40 kays to the south. The road was pretty bad, muddy and slippery, and it began to rain really hard just as we arrived. By the time we told our story and handed the terr over, it was dark and, according to the cops, the road was dangerous at night, too dangerous to take a chance, and so we had to stay over.

The army put us up in this old bungalow in a camp for white RDR troops, 'Salusa Scouts', middle-aged men who'd been called up to do guard duty. When those blokes heard about our capture, they invited the six of us into their mess and bought us drinks and cross-questioned us about the goings-on. Eeeh, I chune you we downed the booze that night. Those whiteys, they hadn't seen any kind of action at all, and they were so keen to hear about it that they kept the stuff flowing. Ou Headlights, he downs a couple double brandies quick-quick and tells the bar about searching those huts; how you feel the hairs of the back of your neck prickle and you know — just know — there's something hidden inside somewhere. Ou Sticks, he describes how Headlights grabbed the terr's wrist and yanked him out. More double brandies. By then just about every honky in the place is crowded around listening to us. Headlights, he starts to expand: he sounds like a pro as he tells the bar just how useless the houties are out in the bush, how they always throw themselves down behind cover and can't see what they're shooting at, how they always fire too high anyway. 'Just keep your nerve and go for it,' he chunes these blokes. 'You're as safe as if you're hiding behind a rock.'

He'd obviously been listening to troopies in the bars.

Then ou Soaps pipes up and starts spouting religion and Rhodesia all mixed up together, telling us what a blessed God-given country we've got the luck to live in.

Well, everyone begins to yawn, and the whiteys begin drifting back to their own tables.

'Listen to that goddam goffel,' says this honky who plonks himself down at a seat at this table just behind me. 'Isss all bullshit — awww bloody bullshit.'

'Bullshit,' Honky No. Two agrees. 'To-tal bull.'

'Bullshit,' states No. One again. 'Now me — I'm not fighting for that democracy and civilisation bullshit. I'm fighting to keep this place decent for the white man —.'

'Fighting,' chimes in No. Two, taking another swig of beer.

'And for, you know, my farm and my wife and my children. For what's mine.'

Well, bullshit to you too, I remember scheming as I staggered back to my bunk. What's going on here? What's this war really all about?

Next morning I was the only one of us blokes who made breakfast. As I sat there, head in hands, staring down at the skin forming on my porridge, one of the honky sergeants, this Perkins, came over and asked if he could follow us back to our base as he was taking a stick out to a farm nearby, and didn't know the road.

Well, it's quite fine by us, of course, and round about eight we got moving. I was at the wheel — all the other blokes were too babbelas — and as I drove along I remember scheming that the road was very quiet. No lighties ran out waving as we passed the kraals, no one was standing at any of the bus stops.

As I'm wondering if the locals weren't holding some kind of festival or a church service or something, there's this sharp corner up ahead, I change down, brake and — KKKKKKKKKKK — firing off in the bush to the right.

Me, I don't stick around to say good morning, I chune you, I jam that gear lever into second, shove my foot down flat on the accelerator, and the truck about stands on its arse as it climbs the hill. A side window shatters, I duck — PPPPPGGGGGGGWWAAAAA HHHHHhhhhhhh —

Then I'm lifting my head from the steering wheel and there's blood in my eyes. 'O fuck,' I say and try to wipe it off with my hands. The truck's smashed into a bank. Off to the right the AKs open up again and the rounds are drumming against its body. There's still blood in my eyes. It strikes me that maybe I should move and I grope round for the handle of the passenger door, open it a crack and half-slither, half-fall out.

The firing stops. 'They've probly pulled out — never stand and fight.' It's Sticks's voice. A blurry shape was in front of me.

'Sticks,' I said like I'm at the bottom of a mine, 'Sticks?'

'O — jisis — Donk — what hit you?'

I put my hand to my forehead, touched wetness. 'Dunno,' I said. It was much later that I realised I must've smashed my head on the steering wheel when the truck hit the bank.

'Hold still.' He wrapped one of the bandages from the first aid kit round my head, splashed my face with water from his bottle.

I blink and there, maybe 50 yards up the road, a truck lies on its side, these black figures crouching all around it. Terrs? Devils? On the roadside black trees shook leafless branches, and for a moment there I thought we were all dead and in hell. 'My God — what's that?'

Sticks spins, gat at the ready. He snorts when he sees where I'm pointing. 'Jisis — your brain must've been shaken loose, man. Those honkies — remember? They hit a mine.'

Soaps wavers in front of me, a quarter-jack of brandy in his hand. 'Mistake,' he apologises, 'grabbed it as I debussed. Instead of my gat. My mistake. My . . . .'

'Shut up,' roars Sticks. 'Shut the fuck up.' I shut my eyes and anchor there, anchor there, swaying. 'You know where the others are — Fudge, Headlights?'

'Back of the truck,' says Soaps. 'At least . . . .'

'You guys all right?' Sticks shouts. No answer.

Taking his knife he saws through the rope tying the flap of canvas to the cab, pushes it back and peers inside.

Fudge is there under a bench holding his head.

'You all right?'

'The terrs,' he babbles, 'I thought the terrs . . . .'

'Headlights?'

'He debussed. He . . . .' I was swaying and swaying.

We went round to the other side of the truck, and there we found him, lying stretched out in the grass. From the way he was lying there, head and arms at these weird angles, I could see he was dead.

'He said he was going out to get them,' Fudge says as he climbs out. 'He said he wanted the ears for his mantelpiece. He said . . . .' I had to sit down.

Sergeant Perkins comes up with three men. Their eyes are red, their faces, hands black and smeary. 'There's three hurt,' he tells us. 'But nothing serious.'

Sticks reported our losses: one dead, one wounded.

'We've radioed for a casavac,' Perkins says. 'We're going into the kraal to find the bastards. Coming?'

We didn't need a second invitation.

The kraal was just 100 metres on down the road. By the time we rock up the doors of all the huts are shut and even the dogs have slunk off. We spread out, surround the place. Perkins shouts for the people to come out, hands up, or else. In their twos and threes they emerge, their faces turned from us, lighties in their parents' arms, or clinging to their legs. There must have been at least 80 mense all lined up in this big bare patch of earth in the centre of the kraal. They stand there, silent, as Perkins watches them with his gat and the others hunt through the huts, searching for arms and propaganda and stragglers. Me, I just stood there, waving the flies away from my forehead.

There's this screech, shrill and shivery, as Sticks finds someone, a youngster of maybe 15, 16, hiding under a bed. He drags the kid from the hut and, twisting his arm behind his back so's he's just about doubled over, marches him across to Perkins.

'Why were you hiding?' Perkins demands.

'I was worried, baas,' the kid gasps.

'What? What've you done to be worried about?'

'. . . soldiers . . .' he manages to get out as Sticks yanks at his arm again.

'What've you done to the soldiers? What have you done?'

'Nothing baas. Nothing. I tell you true.'

'Bullshit.' Perkins belts the bloke across the face. Blood dribbles from his lip, from his nose. 'You're a terr' — clap — 'you planted the mine . . . .'

'Baas — no — ' The kid cringes, tries to shield his face with his hands as Perkins cracks him again — kwa — kwa — kwa.

'Don't lie to me — or I'll kill you.'

'Baas — please baas — I'm not lying.' Kwa — kwa — kwa.

'He knows nothing,' this old bloke standing in the line volunteers. 'He came back from the town today.'

Perkins beckons the old bloke to him. 'Who asked you to speak?' he demands. 'Who?' Kwa — kwa — kwa. The bloke grunts and crumples to the ground holding his head. Perkins kicks him in the gut.

'I don't know these gandangas,' the old bloke cries out as he twists to avoid Perkins's boot. 'None of us know....'

'Bullshit,' says Perkins landing a kick on the bloke's mouth. 'If you don't tell me — you'll die.'

'B...' the bloke begins and spits out a mouthful of teeth and blood. 'B....'

Perkins, he takes his gat, places the barrel on the bloke's forehead, fires — paa. The body jerks and twitches and there across the dirt the blood and brains have splashed out like this huge pink fan. Half-a-dozen lighties start to howl.

Perkins turns to the young bloke again and asks him all very polite what he knows about the attack.

'Nothing, baas, noth....'

Perkins puts his gat to the bloke's head, fires.

When the body is still, Perkins beckons over the bloke next in line. The bloke — he looked like a labourer, about 40 I'd guess — he just pisses himself. He's standing there and the pee is running down his leg. Perkins takes aim with that gat of his. That bloke, he starts talking and talking fast.

Chapter 5

I was flown to hospital where I was stitched up, X-rayed and given a shot to make me sleep. Next morning, still woozy, I was trucked back to the camp. I felt as if there was this giant child trapped in me; it was hysterical and beginning to howl and thrash its arms and legs about and there was nothing, absolutely nothing, I could do to control it. All that day I was perched there on the verandah, the blokes coming up to me saying, you know, how terrible it was about Headlights, what a great bloke he'd been and alles, and all the time the baby was howling louder and louder, kicking harder and harder. I remember ou Headlights sprawled out in the grass, the odd angles of his arms and legs, the piss trickling down the leg of the one bloke in the kraal, the youngster crumbling up and the other bloke's brains and bits of skull spread out like a pink fan across the dirt.

The baby squalled; I downed a couple beers in the hopes of shutting it up. Headlights dead: it seemed impossible. One terr accidentally fires straight, and ou Headlights is standing there asking for it. Hell, what with the way all the rounds were flying so wildly that morning, if he'd debussed say a second later or just a couple yards further down the drag, if I'd kept my head, if I'd kept the truck on the road, even a second or two longer, maybe the rounds would've only wounded him, maybe they wouldn't have hit him at all, maybe he'd now be a hero with his jar of ears on the mantelpiece. All cos of just a few seconds. If I'd thought more quickly, done my damn job properly, none of this would've happened in the first place. The baby was screaming by then, and throwing its arms and legs about wildly like a tortoise stuck on its back.

Headlights dead. Not seeing him again, not getting caught up in his latest crazy plan — jisis, I chune you it seemed impossible. It couldn't be. And he was so young: so was that lightie Perkins shot. It's one thing knowing in your mind and another to know in your gut that you will die too — and how easy it is — one slip, one second, one round and you're gone. That's it. Finish and klaar. End of story.

I rooked a skyf. That didn't help. Neither did a quarter-jack of brandy. Then eeh, I was bawling and smashing the furniture and pounding on the walls. My cut burst open and there was blood all over and the other blokes came running and grabbed hold of me. Soaps gave me a shot of tranquilliser, and next day I was told to take off the last week of camp and I was sent home. Shaken up by the explosion, the doctor said. Not too serious.

Back home I tried to explain all this lot to my father. He didn't quite get it. 'War isn't a Sunday school picnic,' he breaks in when I start describing the shootings at the kraal. 'But the terrs are doing far worse. Just come up to Cranborne some time — the place is chock-a-block with Afs who want to join up. Ask them why, and they'll tell you, "the gandangas just raped my sister", or "they cut my father's tongue out", or "they killed all my cows".'

And then he launched into his favourite warrie, one that he'd told me about a dozen time already. The terrs come into this kraal. They've never been there before and no one knows why they've come. They tell the first woman they come across to lie down, and then all 10 of them rape her. And then they catch her husband and tie him up and force the wife to cut off her husband's lips and fry them and eat them. Then they tell her to dig a hole. When she is finished, they ask her "is that how far you can dig?" and when she says yes, her hands are blistering, they shoot her husband in the back of the head and kick his body in. Then they tell her to make a big fire, and when she's finished, they tie her up with wire and throw her into it.

'And,' he finished up, 'they killed your friends. They're barbarians, those terrs.'

As the week wore on things got difficult. I didn't feel like going out and talking with my buddies; I didn't feel like staying at home. There was this burning in my gut, this restlessness, like when you've dropped speed: you want to do something, but you can't settle to do anything, and you keep walking up and down, up and down. I smoked a quantity of skywe to settle myself, and knocked back the brandy too.

I took a day off work for the funeral. About an hour before we were due to be picked up, Naomi took Ruthie off to her old queen's cabin, giving me strict instructions not to touch a drop while she was gone. By the time she got back I'd downed half a bottle. The lady, she had hysterics.

'I'm not going to let you disgrace the family,' she informed me as I staggered to the door. 'I've got to live with these people too.'

With a little stiffening, I figured, I'll be able to sort out this lot. I head over to the booze cupboard to pour myself a shot and the bottle has gone. Eeh, I chune you I could've killed for another drink then.

'Naomi,' I yell, 'Naomi. Where's my bottle?'

'You're drinking too much,' she shouts. 'Far too much. You're going to stop — from now — this minute.'

Me, I start pulling out the drawers, throwing open the cupboards, rummaging through the clothes. Naomi follows me, screams at me to stop, and the baby inside me starts screaming too. Finally I find the bottle tucked way back in the broom cupboard along with the ant killer and rat poison. A cause for celebration! I pour myself this triple tot — one as a stiffener, one for the baby, one to celebrate — and gulp it down. I grope for the bottle again and eeh, it's gone. Naomi had sneaked up and grabbed it and emptied it into the toilet.

The brat's shouting louder and louder. It's all too much for me, the whole damn scene. I stumble out of the house down to the shab and booze there in peace until I pass out.

On April 25 of that year, 1974, there was a coup in Portugal, and overnight the situation in Rhodesia changed. For years the Portuguese had been battling to hold onto their African colonies, and every year the fight cost them more: more men, more money. Even so, the liberation armies kept advancing: every year the guerillas in Mozambique, Angola, and Guinea Bissau liberated more territory, inched closer to the cities. The colonies were costing more than they earned. The main mannes in the Portuguese army saw that the wars were bankrupting the country, grabbed power and pulled out of Africa.

Up until then — and afterwards as well — most Rhodesians reckoned the terr threat was safely under control. They had pretty good reasons: Zipra's three invasions in the late sixties had all been smashed, and since then only small groups of guerillas had been able to infiltrate. Some Zanla guerillas had crossed from Mozambique but it wasn't an easy route: they had to foot it all the way from their bases in Zambia, risking attacks by the Portuguese and Rhodesians — as well as dysentery and malaria — en route. Those who did manage to cross were always short of supplies which had to be carried in by porter. Zipra and Zanla units had also crossed from Zambia, but the Zambezi and Lake Kariba were serious obstacles, and only a handful of mense lived in those areas anyway. A few Zipra units had also crossed from Botswana, but the government there wasn't too keen to help cos of the risk of retaliation.

But after Frelimo had liberated Mozambique, the president, Samora Machel, gave Zanla bases up and down the length of the border, all 1 100 kilometres of it. The border areas were ideal for guerillas as the country was broken and bushy and undeveloped; there were few roads; hardly any cops or government officials and a great many people who had no reason to like the authorities.

Ya, to those who thought carefully about these things, after the Mozambique coup Rhodesia began to look vulnerable, very vulnerable indeed.

Katz at the bakery was one of those who was worried. When I finally returned to graft there was bad news waiting for me: Katz had decided to sell up and return to England.

He called me into his office, this grubby little glass cubicle by the back door, and there under the nudie calendars and holiday and maintenance schedules he told me Rhodesia was going down the drain.

'The whites can't win this war now,' he said. 'The British and the Americans and the Russians won't let them. And when the blacks take over here it's going to be like the Congo all over again — you mark my words. There's no point in waiting round, things can only get worse....'

Me, I couldn't speak. Well, I'd been grafting there for almost five years: it was the only job I'd ever had. I closed my eyes and I could see one hell of a lot of hassle up ahead.

'... couldn't sell this place,' Katz was saying. 'Everyone is thinking about getting out ... closing down ... don't worry so much, Eddie, I'll find you a place. You're a good, reliable worker....'

He did ask around but he was only able to find graft for two of the 10 of us. The rest — me included — were given two months' salary and a reference. And that was it. I visited all the city bakeries and confectioners and just confirmed that there were no vacancies. The Situations Vacant column in the paper didn't help much either. I applied for graft as a truck driver, bus driver, pest exterminator, cook, caterer, carpenter, storeman, salesman, security guard and clerk. And so on. I had no luck though, none at all.

Every morning, after I'd answered all the likely ads in the paper, I'd head down to the shab for a couple of beers. But after I'd been looking for about a month, after I'd been turned down by a couple dozen companies, it just didn't seem worth the bother. I went straight to the shab in the mornings instead. Ya, in just over a month, Katz's coin was gone. We were living off Naomi's salary.

Luckily she'd managed to wangle herself fulltime graft as a manageress at the second-hand furniture shop. Her salary was okay; we could manage on it, just. But, of course, she wouldn't give me money for booze. It was her money, she kept telling me, she worked damn hard for it, and she didn't see why I should be allowed to blow it. Every morning she'd give me enough for bus fare, the paper and a cup of tea. Not a cent more, not a cent less.

'I never counted out the coin like this when I was grafting,' I complained. 'Hell, what I had we shared.'

But she wasn't sympathetic. 'You'll just drink it,' she told me. 'I work too damn hard for you just to piss it away.'

Still, every day I had enough to buy two shots of kachase and a stick of stop. And, if I hung around long enough, some drunk was sure to come along and fill my glass.

One morning while I'm waiting for a drink ou Sticks rocked up. He bought me a beer and we got talking. Us ouens we were both in the same boat, and it was sinking fast: the warehouse where he'd worked had closed down and he hadn't been able to find graft either.

'Typical of whitey,' I reckon. 'First he plants us in the country and then when things get warm, he jumps out and leaves us to fry.'

'There's always the army,' says ou Sticks. 'You can always catch a graft in the army.'

But the army didn't have any attraction for me just then. 'Let the goddam houties and honkies fight it out,' I chune him. 'I just want to keep out of the mess.'

'Hell, I schemed after they got your buddy you'd want revenge,' says Sticks, sort of puzzled. 'That's what I'd feel.'

And me, I remembered all these novels I'd read about the Rhodesian war, all of them about these blokes whose wives and children had been cruelly murdered by the barbaric terrs and how these blokes had then dropped everything else to go hunting for their revenge.

And it struck me, you know, that maybe he was right: it was the terrs, the terrs were to blame for this whole mess. If it wasn't for them I'd still have my graft, Headlights would still be alive. I wouldn't have to put up with Naomi counting out the cents and all her questions about the interviews I had lined up, and I wouldn't have to listen to any more of her lectures about how I mustn't lose heart. 'What the hell,' I chune ou Sticks, 'you've got a point. Let's go join up now.'

Chapter 6

'*W*e're always glad to have another coloured,' the white officer at Cranborne told us when we went to enlist. 'With the natural aggression you guys have, you make first-class soldiers.' I grinned; in those days I was still dumb enough to be flattered. Besides, we'd both just been paid out 400 bucks as a sweetener. Us ouens, we went straight to the nearest bottle store and bought ourselves a bomb of brandy each to celebrate. It was only much later that we read the small print and found out we earned only about half the salary of white troopies, and that we weren't paid during our one-month leave every year.

Me and Sticks downed a couple good sluks of that brandy before I hit out back to the cabin to tell Naomi the good news. But eeh, I chune you, that woman just about blew a dozen valves. 'You've done

WHAT?' she yells and slams the lid down on the curry and marches into the lounge where I'm pouring myself this mammoth dop.

'Joined the army,' I yell back. 'I told you.'

'Well go right back to them and tell them you've changed your mind,' she says.

'Listen,' I chune her, 'those terrs wiped out my buddy. I want my revenge. And anyway, it's a job.'

'You can get your revenge on one of your call-ups,' she informs me. 'And you can find some other job.'

'I've been looking for months — you know that.'

'Keep on trying, for chrissakes. Tell these army people you've changed your mind. . . .'

'I can't. I've signed. And anyway we need the coin.'

'You mean you need it to booze with.'

Naomi begins to blub. Me, I down my dop. 'I might as well be a widow you spend so little time here,' she sobs, throwing herself on the sofa. 'Even when you're home you're hardly here from one day to the next. Go — go on — get out — go to your army. It won't make one bit of difference. . . .' She starts howling even harder and I stop listening. She was fond of all that all-alone spiel, so fond of it that I probly knew it as well as she did. Me, I pour myself a quick shot and she ups and runs down the road so's she can weep all over her old queen's shoulder.

I swallowed the shot, poured myself another and drifted out to the back steps. It was twilight and the bats were swooping low among the oranges and bananas. I figured I could count my blessings: at least the bitch wasn't weeping all over me. But eeh, when she came back from her mother's she'd have just had a two-hour lecture on what a lousy husband I was and she'd be ready for battle. 'Fuck it,' I said out loud, and took a sluk straight from the bottle. I'd had more than enough of her nya-nya-nya for one day.

My whole life was being gnawed away by these nagging, whining women. I downed another dop and brooded about what a bitch Naomi was, what a botch I'd made of my life. Headlights was right: I should never have married her. She was impossible to satisfy: one minute she's complaining cos I can't find graft and when I sign up for the only graft going, she's carrying on like I'm all set to elope with a 12-year-old. Me, I was looking forward to the bush just then I chune you, anything to get away from her.

I was through with these women, I decided. I was sick to death of the whole goddam scene. Down at the shab us ouens drank and laughed and joked and had a good time. Why hang around the house waiting for the next round? I'd had enough. After another couple of shots for the road, I took off down to the shab and, for the next week, until the time came for me to turn myself in at Inkomo barracks, I drifted from bar to bar and shab to shab, dopping and stopping and dopping and stopping. I remember blowing the last of my coin in one of those moments of sodden clarity which come to you when you've been hitting the booze for a while. It was like I was standing outside myself looking down: there were streaks of dry puke on my clothes, stubble prickled my cheeks and chin, my breath stank of stale booze. My hands shook. I was a worm, a human worm, as Naomi would've said. One by one I emptied my pockets: my wallet with a card from Katz's Confectioners and a snap of Naomi holding Ruthie about a month after she had been born, a job application I'd never posted, the army letter stating I was signed on, three one-cent pieces, and one 10-cent piece. Not enough for a drink.

Me, I started chuning this bloke next to me, showed him the snapshot of Naomi and the lightie and told him how they'd both been wiped out in this car accident. I got so carried away by my story that I started to sniffle. It worked. The bloke bought me a quarter-jack of brandy, told me everything would come right and disappeared out the back when he thought I wasn't looking. Ya, during the next few days I got quite practised at bringing that snapshot out, and I chune you I didn't give a shit.

Come army day though, I pitched up at the barracks on time and more or less sober. Me, I was in a mess; my whole life was a booze-soaked, puked-up mess and I was sick of it. It was time to get organised, time for a change. I was in the army for a year — quite fine — and while I was there I would revenge my buddy. I'd also put an end to the dopping and the stopping, save every cent I could and write to Naomi and tell her how sorry I was about alles, that I was finished with my nonsense for once and for all and when my stint was over I'd find myself some decent graft in Civvy Street. All's I wanted was for everything to be back in place again.

While we were doing that refresher course I was really dedicated: if we were ordered to do 20 pressups, I did 40; if we went on a run, I kept going long after the rest of the ouens had pretended to collapse; if we were told to learn something, I learnt it off by heart. Inbetween times I kept to myself. I hardly ever spoke to the rest of the ouens; I wanted to be quiet for a while. In my spare moments you'd find me cleaning my kit or my gat. Ya, I used to really enjoy taking that gat apart, shining all the pieces one by one and then laying them all out in rows in front of me. Hell, I took that thing apart and put it back together so many times, I reckon I could've done it blindfold. Working on it relaxed me: each part had one and only one place, and all of them could fit together in just one way. There were no questions about it, no arguments about which piece went where. Just so long as you followed instructions, you were sure to get it right.

Then one afternoon, after inspection, the sergeant informed our platoon that only two troopies — me and this Bond character — were truly putting their heart and soul into the army. And, when he's finished telling everyone how good we were, he gave the pair of us the day off and marched the rest of the ouens over to the obstacle course.

Me, I scratched my head. I wasn't exactly happy with the situation. The ouens were going to blame us for their trip to the obstacle course, and a long hot afternoon with nothing particular to do loomed up ahead. If I'd had my choice I would've been out there with the rest of them, but if I'd volunteered they'd all scheme I was really trying to slime my way up the sergeant's arse. Out came my boots and my gat and I began giving them another clean. What was I going to do about the ouens? While I didn't particularly want friends, there was no point in collecting enemies. In future I'd make sure it looked as if I was doing just what the others did.

As I'm reassembling my gat this Bond fellow strolled over and offered me a smoke. He was one of those goffels who looks white from a distance — freckles on his dial, a touch of ginger in his hair — but when you were up close you could check how big and dark those freckles really were, and how that hair of his was coarse and crinkly in a way that no whitey's ever was.

First thing he told me he's called Bond after 007 in the movies, and he'd almost made it into the Selous Scouts. 'Ya,' he chuned me as he puffed out this mammoth wobbly smoke ring which collapses almost immediately. 'I know this war. I know it like the back of my hand.'

I nodded, and I guess he must've schemed I was suitably impressed cos he started on about his stint in the Scouts. 'There the arseholes we're with now would've had all their shit kicked out of them,' he told me. 'They say if they want to fuck around it's their business — but it's not. What's going to happen when we're out in the bush and we've got to rely on them?'

'Um?'

'In the Selous Scouts they just wouldn't have put up with it.' I picked up the firing pin of my gat and began polishing it carefully while Bond went on with his spiel. 'Man, all these obstacle courses and runs are nothing: there they'd make us run 30, 40 — even 50 kays.'

'Um.'

'One time they give you a matchstick — one matchstick — a water bottle and a roll of toilet paper, and they tell you to climb a tree and make a cup of tea for your instructor.'

Finally I took his bait. 'Ag, that's impossible,' I said with disgust.

But there was no stopping Bond. He rubs his hands together with the enthusiasm of a missionary breaking the news of Jesus's walking on the water. 'It's like this; say you're up a mopane tree, right? Now that tree has one hell of a hard core in the middle — okay? So it's not going to burn too fast. All that you do is to cut out a little hollow for your fire, and the chippings and the toilet paper they're your fuel. Then careful-careful you light your match and soon your instructor is sipping away. . . .' He wanted to impress me, he wanted to be friends, but eeh, I chune you, there was no ways I'd be buddies with that bloke: right from the start I could smell the trouble on him.

The main mannes were impressed by Bond, so much so that when our platoon was posted to the Honde Valley in the north-east, they made him corporal. Us ouens weren't so keen on the idea. He was always sucking up to the big shots and the ouens took to calling him 'the plastic whitey' behind his back or 'Plastic' for short. Then he was always trying to force us to be just like him: neat and tidy, always straining to do the right thing. He would've liked the floors of our barracks to shine like a mirror, our uniforms to be washed and ironed every day.

We were transporting equipment and supplies to camps near the border, driving over dirt roads and through 'terr-infested' territory. As you bumped along there was always this tightness in the pit of your gut; you couldn't forget that at any moment you could hit a mine, that just two weeks back a driver had been blown up only a couple of kays down the drag. At night eeh, you couldn't switch off, couldn't sleep, and after a couple days you start taking two-three-four dops of brandy just to quieten yourself down. Then, in the morning, you'd wake up with this ache in your head and this feeling — all's you could remember of your dreams — that something bad was about to happen. You begin taking a quick nip of brandy in the mornings to soothe the babbelas so's you're wide awake as you drive along, alert to scuff marks and patches of suspicious smoothness, any sign that something lay buried there, waiting.

Before long I was knocking back half a bottle a day. So much for my good resolutions.

I didn't keep my other resolutions either. I finally did write to Naomi about how sorry I was and alles, and about a week later she wrote back saying that while she was glad that I was sobering up at last and finally facing up to my responsibilities as a husband and father, she wasn't sure, she wasn't at all sure in fact, about us and our future together. She'd just have to see how she felt the next time we were together again. Then she got into the gossip: my father was now taking out this divorcee, Mavis Willoughby, did I know her? Ruthie'd had German measles but she was over them now; the doctor said her jaw had finally cleared up properly. 'But I still don't like going out on my own,' she wrote. 'I get a knot in my stomach and I start to worry. I told Vyvyan, and he says he will take me with him. It's very nice of him. Thank him when you see him....'

Me, I couldn't take any more. I folded up the letter, shoved it back in its envelope, and swallowed a slug of brandy. Ou Sticks, who was stretched out in the chair beside me, asked what the lady had to say for herself. And then it all comes out: I told him about Vyvyan who'd been divorced by his wife cos he couldn't keep his hands off the tarts. 'And now, the bastard is suddenly being so very sweet and kind to Naomi.'

'Ag, you've got nothing to worry about,' he tells me. 'It's the ones they don't tell you about you have to watch out for. She's just trying to make you jealous.'

But eeh, I couldn't forget about the letter so easily. I anchored on the verandah of the mess for the rest of the afternoon, downing the beers and smoking stop and trying to figure out what was what. I had these suspicions I couldn't talk about, not even with Sticks. Remembering Naomi's behaviour that night in the club (did she hesitate? she must have), remembering that Vyvyan was tall and light and handsome, I reckoned I just about had proof. Proof or suspicion okay, but what was I going to do about it? Ignore it? Never. Write a letter to Naomi forbidding her to see Vyvyan again? She'd just laugh. Scale a truck, head back to Burg, catch them at it, walk right in while they're rolling about in bed? I closed my eyes and saw myself ironing them out: Naomi pulling the sheet up over those big tits of hers and shouting 'No, no', and the two shots — paa — paa. After that the army could do what it wanted to me: DB for life or the gallows — I couldn't care. Or, better, I'd cross over to the terrs, and come back and hit this lousy goddam army which'd shipped me out into the bush even though there was fuck-all to do here. . . .

Me, I downed another couple of beers and a quarter-jack of cane and began slinging bottles at the mess's wall. I'd managed to smash about a dozen of them — and some other junk as well — before the ouens grabbed me and cooled me off in the shower.

Now Bond of course wasn't charmed by this lot. Next morning he calls me to one side and tells me though he's my buddy and all, as corporal he has to report my performance to the lootie. 'It's for your own good,' he says, 'you've been drinking far too much recently.'

There was silence as he waited for me to answer. If I'd given him a long sob story about Naomi, if I'd told him how hard I was trying to control my drinking and had begged — asked even — for one more chance, he would've been glad to oblige. But that morning I was just too sick, too slow, to care.

'Why'd you do it?' Bond asks encouragingly. 'Maybe we should talk this over. Maybe I can help?'

But I just wouldn't take the bait. 'When it's there I drink it,' I tell him.

Bond had no choice. Assuring me it wasn't personal, he marched me down to the lootie's office. Now the lootie, this Britz character, had just been transferred to the RDR and posted to the camp, and no one knew anything about him. It was only later that we heard the stories about him pissing on the colonel's roses in full view of the colonel's wife and daughter, and painting the major green at a regimental dinner.

But even when you walked into his office you could see this one wasn't your usual lootie. The place was a mess; beer bottles weighted down grimy sheaves of paper, the three ashtrays in the room were full, the picture of the topless cherrie was skew. The lootie himself sat at his desk, rumpled and unshaven, his head in his hands. 'What you want?' he growls after we come to attention.

Bond looks at him, soldier to soldier, and launches on the long list of my sins, and the lootie's head sinks deeper and deeper into his hands.

It's only when Bond finishes that the lootie finally lifts his head and glares at us through bloodshot, half-open eyes. 'Okay corporal,' he snaps, 'let's get this straight once and for all: we're fighting a fucking war, not holding a goddam beauty contest. As long as my men are ready to fight, as long as their guns are clean and in working order, I don't give an ounce of pig shit for all the other rules and regulations. So don't you come crawling up my arse with all this nonsense.'

Bond went green, the colour of mouldy cheese. I didn't know human beings could be that colour. 'Yes sir, sorry sir,' he was gobbling. He'd been straining so hard to do his best and he'd blown it, completely blown it. He turned and ran out the office, and disappeared for the rest of the day. Eeh, even I couldn't help feeling sorry for him — he was always trying too hard, that bloke, and you could see that sooner or later he'd tear himself apart.

Britz's popularity rocketed, and it rose even higher cos every evening, after he'd had a couple beers, he began drifting over to our mess and lecturing us about how he couldn't stand these officers in the regular army who were more concerned about the straightness of your trouser creases than the straightness of your shooting. 'Those blokes are a worse enemy than the terrs,' he'd inform us, beer in one hand, smoke in the other. 'They'll be the ones who defeat Rhodesia — you mark my words.' Then he'd rant on about how he'd been a soldier all his life, how he'd fought against communism as it had inched down Africa. He'd seen action in Mozambique, Biafra, the Congo where, to hear him tell it, he had been one of Mad Mike Hoare's best buddies.

'I've seen it happen time and again,' he told us. 'The blokes up at the top just don't realise that war isn't for gentlemen. Especially not here in Africa. Hell man, if this lot knew what they were doing they wouldn't leave me — an experienced bushfighter — to piffle away my time with a transport unit. I know what's got to be done — I could show them.' By this time the smoke is only a column of ash in his fingers and all us ouens have collected round to listen. 'Look — you've got to face it — the only way to deal with these wogs is to wipe out — obliterate — a couple dozen villages. Get them so damn scared that they shit everything but yes-baas out of their systems. You've got to fight terror with terror.'

To prove his point, Britz'd launch into one of his favourite stories. The one about the monkeys he must've told us at least 20 times.

'At a time when we were having trouble getting information out of the wogs, we captured a cageful of monkeys,' he'd begin. 'Our commanding officer thought they might come in handy so we kept them in a cage in the centre of our camp and starved them and tormented them with red hot metal bars and sharpened stakes and snakes and suchlike until they went crazy, bouncing against the bars and screaming the moment anyone came near. When they'd gone completely bananas we took all the prisoners out of their cells, lined them up in front of the cage, picked out a wog from the back, tied him up and threw him in. The monkeys screeched and clung to the top of the cage and hung there until one of them fell and landed on the prisoner and discovered that he was helpless. Then the monkeys, the whole tribe of them, jumped down and tore the bloke to pieces.

'We didn't have any trouble getting the others to talk after that.'

'Now that,' he'd say, taking a swig of beer, 'that is what I call a real war. This isn't much of a scrap here in Rhodesia — everyone is so goddam concerned with uniforms and strategies and shit. You know what I'm going to do one day? Resign from this useless army and join one of those private militias and go out into the bush and start doing this job properly....' Ya, ou Britz, he was a hardcore character that one.

High on Britz's hate list of fancy strategies was winning the hearts and minds of the people. In practice it meant only that every day the spare drivers went out on patrol. The idea, as this major who explained it to us said, was to show the villagers that we were on their side. 'They're just a quiet, shy people, and it will take a while before they will trust us,' he informs us as we sat in sweaty rows on our parade ground one long, hot afternoon. 'Understandably — because some of our policies in the past were hardly ideal. But we must make them forget all that; we must show them we are their friends, prepared to help.' Now as far as Britz was concerned, patrolling the area made good military sense but all this talk about winning the locals over to our side was one big heap of bullshit. 'I know these kaffirs,' he was fond of telling us. 'All this rubbish about helping them just makes them think you're gutless. They believe you only give presents to those who are stronger than you; as far as they're concerned all this aid and assistance shit is just an admission of weakness. The more you beat them, the more you take from them, the more they respect you.'

The main mannes, of course, were too soft, too liberal to admit the truth of this, his story went; they just couldn't face up to the fact that kaffirs didn't think like us.

And, flattered at being included in the 'we', the whole bunch of us nodded enthusiastically. Most of us — me included — probably believed him too.

Still, orders are orders, and out on patrol, all of us — Britz included — did more or less what we were told. I remember the first time we went on our circuit, following a muddy trail through a grove of wild fig trees down along this ferny, misty valley to a village of about 20 huts. We called the mense, lined them up and, with the rest of us covering, Bond and Soaps searched the huts. Nothing.

'We are here to protect you from the terrorists,' Britz announced, in English, and then gave the locals the whole spiel: if there was anything that they needed in the way of medicines, if there was an emergency and they had to get to town in a hurry, they'd better come to us. The locals scratched their heads. English wasn't their strong point. Bond, trying to impress, volunteered that he could speak a little Shona. You could see he was already imagining his 'invaluable help' being mentioned in reports.

Britz didn't seem too charmed. 'So make yourself useful then,' he snaps, flashing Bond this filthy look. 'And don't waste time either.' So Bond translates this whole story, and the headman then thanks everyone concerned for this most kind offer.

Then Britz had Bond ask if there were any terrs in the area.

The headman eeh, he didn't need a translator to understand that one. He just about tripped over himself he was so quick to tell us he knew nothing, nothing about them at all. 'Not in my kraal — never,'

he kept saying in English, shaking his head so hard I figured it was
going to come loose.

Nonetheless Britz, through Bond, reminded the gent and all the
other villagers of the penalties they'd suffer if they did not report
terrs: headmen could be locked up, huts burnt, cattle confiscated.

The headman wiped at the sweat on his forehead. 'Yes, my baas,'
he was saying, 'we report them first time we see them.'

Britz, of course, wasn't entirely convinced. 'We'll be watching
you,' he warned them. 'And don't think you can bullshit us.'

All the rest of that day we trapped from kraal to kraal, calling the
people together and searching the huts. They listened in silence to our
requests for information, our announcements of rewards and offers
of assistance. Not one person admitted knowing anything about the
terrs or their movements and not one person offered us anything to
eat or drink.

'You'd think we were lepers or something,' I scheme when we're
back in our camp. 'I wonder why the locals don't like us.' Ya, back in
those days I really didn't have much idea at all.

'Give them time,' — ou Clouds, this large light fellow who's always
stirring, mimicks the major — 'they are a quiet shy people, and our
policies have not been perfect.'

'When they get to know us better, things'll improve,' says Bond,
dead serious, 'but I don't know if it'll make much difference anyway.'
We'd been told different things by different honkies, so he must've
had a hell of a hard time working out exactly what to believe.

Next morning 'WaKe uP wazUkURu tHis Is NoT yoUr wAR' was
scrawled in large white letters on a boulder maybe 30 yards beyond
the perimeter of the camp.

The first we knew about it was when Britz started yelling. 'All those
on guard last night come here on the double,' he shouted, and me and
all the other offenders dropped our soap and combs and razors and
raced across the camp to this rise just beyond the officer's latrine
where Britz stood bellowing like a bull that's just discovered his cows
have been stolen.

'Now what,' he demanded, facing us, half-a-dozen shivering half-
dressed troopies all rigidly at attention, 'now what is the meaning of
this?' and pointed at the offending message.

'In Shona, sir,' puts in ou Clouds — playing kaffir as usual — 'it means nephew, sir. It's what the blacks call us coloureds, sir....'

'Johnson — you cretinous crossbreed — I didn't ask for a language lesson,' the lootie yells, turning bright red. 'Let me put it to you simply so that even scum like you can understand: I want to know how your black uncles managed to sneak right up to the camp and paint their message right under your goddam eyes.'

Ou Clouds, he contemplates that question, his forehead all screwed up like he's trying really hard, while the rest of us, we keep our eyes fixed on the ground as if an answer's due to tunnel out any moment.

'Well — what happened?' the lootie demands impatiently.

'Slippers, sir,' says Clouds suddenly.

'Slippers?' says the lootie, like he can't believe what he's hearing.

'Sir, in this flick I saw, the spies....'

Us ouens, we're battling not to laugh there as the lootie goes redder and redder.

'Johnson!' he yells, 'Johnson — shut that idiotic trap of yours before I shut it for you. Now let's have some sense on the subject. Jackson?'

Bond braces up, stretches himself even straighter. There's no sign of any laughter on his face and he's staring straight ahead just like the regulations require. 'It couldn't have happened while I was on guard, sir,' he says. 'Completely impossible.'

Britz nods. 'Kiernan?'

Me, I hadn't noticed a thing. 'I'm sure I would've heard if there was anything,' I tell him. And, of course, the other three blokes who'd been on guard that night all are willing to swear that they hadn't heard anything unusual either.

The cross-questioning over, the lieutenant sums up: 'The fact remains that even though every one of you say you were wide awake and watching, terrs managed to sneak almost up to the camp's perimeter. Now come on, you blokes — what's the problem? Are you really such a useless bunch of soldiers? Or do you really believe, like the terrs say, that this isn't your war?'

As Bond marched over to the cliff to clean this lot up, I couldn't help wondering about how I felt.

Well, being coloured in Rhodesia back in late '74, I didn't have an answer all loaded and ready to fire. O, if the lootie had asked me direct, I would've told him I was ready, willing and able to fight and die for Smith and Democracy, Rhodesia and Freedom, and I pretty much believed it myself. Still, the lootie was on target with those suspicions of his: most of us blokes weren't sure how we felt, weren't sure at all, and there were quite a few of us who had our own ideas, ideas of the kind we couldn't comfortably talk about with whitey.

'Those terrs have a point,' reckons ou Clouds as we're scrubbing away there. 'This war is between the houties and honkies. Why should we be involved?' He goois his brush into a bucket, dries his hands on his uniform, digs a skyf out of his pocket and lights up.

'Jisis,' says Bond, checking ou Clouds out as if the bloke has finally fried the last of his brain cells. 'That's bullshit, man. We're fighting the communists. The decent blacks are all on our side. . . .'

'Well,' says Clouds very sarcastic, 'that's whitey's story. Why is it that the locals won't have anything to do with us?' Next thing the pair of them are yelling at each other like a bunch of tomcats.

What with all the arguing it took us maybe an hour to scrub that cliff clean, and Britz he was flat, I chune you. When we rocked up back at the camp his fists were clenched so tight his knuckles were white. 'You useless kaffir bastards,' he screams at us. 'What in hell's name is going on? Do you think you're at a goddam Sunday school picnic or something? First you're all fast asleep while the terrs fiddle around outside the walls — and then, when I send you to clean the mess up, you loaf around chatting and smoking. You're a bunch of incompetent, drunken, half-breed, unprofessional dagga-smoking. . . .' And so forth.

He screamed at us until he was hoarse and then he started us running. Round and round the camp we ran while he stood in the middle and shook his fist at us. Ou Clouds, he decides he's had enough of this nonsense so he pretends to collapse and lies there in the dust like he's half dead. But Britz, he had no sympathy for us that day, no sympathy at all: he sends the rest of us running off to collect buckets of water and, when we come splashing back with them, he tells us to piss in them. Once we've all emptied our bladders, he orders us blokes to slop the stuff over ou Clouds. Eeh, Clouds, he didn't need a second helping, I chune you. He jumps up spitting and cursing, and runs, runs with the rest of us as we round the camp 15 times, 20 times, 25 times. And, though all of us had blisters by then, though our feet were bleeding and our muscles were aching, though every step hurt like hell, not one of us dared to stop and not one of us passed out.

That was the end of our beautiful relationship with Britz. As far as he was concerned, we'd proved ourselves to be on the same level as the houties and all his drunken visits to our mess, all his liquor lectures on the war and Africa came to an end. He became a real bastard, the sort of bastard Bond had been hoping for, the kind of bloke who'd cancel a weekend pass cos he had the babbelas and you didn't have a button. It was misery to be anywhere near him.

So, one Sunday morning, when there's a call for volunteers to guard this SAS camp while they're off on a mission, the whole camp steps forward. Anything to get away from Britz. Britz selected our stick. Anything, I suppose, to get us out of his sight. Within half-an-hour the six of us were bumping along to the border in the back of an old Bedford.

As we're winding off among the hills there, Bond, who is driving (that way the rest of us are rid of him) changes down to second, Clouds takes a hit of his reef and passes it on to me. I reach for it and — KKKKKKKKKKKK. The truck lurches, slips as Bond jams his foot flat and me and the others we're suddenly flopping round on the floor. The firing peters out — we must be through the killing zone — Bond slams on anchors. 'Let's get them,' he yells, jumping out of the cabin of the truck.

About 200 metres below us a unit of 10, 12 terrs were disappearing off into the bush. Bond opens up and the terrs scatter, diving behind rocks and bushes.

'They're too far,' shouts Clouds, 'let's get out of here.'

But Bond, next thing he's charging down that slope like a rhino. Sticks plunges after him and me, before I've managed to organise my ideas, I'm hurtling after them too.

One of the terrs shouts a warning and two of them open up — KKKKK — me, I throw myself down, and by the time I'm on my feet again, the others are a good 200 metres up ahead, doubling over and zigzagging through the bush of this koppie.

As I'm straggling along after them I check this one bloke trying to sneak away up this steep stretch of slope. He spots me just as I spot him, and while I'm standing there staring he unslings his gat — I fling myself down — he fires — KKKKK — and me, I scuttle for cover like a cockroach when the light's turned on.

That terr can't have had too much training or else I would've been finished, I chune you. I'm right out in the open wriggling through the grass — and his rounds whizz past miles over my head. I duck behind this rock, fire off two shots — paa-pa — which smack into the slope a couple yards to his right and the bloke he catches such a spook that he drops his gat and turns and runs.

Me, I stand up like I'm taking aim at a target at a shooting range, catch him in my sights, lose him as he lurches forward, catch him again and follow the instructions: 'grip your rifle firmly... don't allow it to jerk upwards... squeeze the trigger smoothly...' like there's this tape recorder in my head and the gat jumps and the bloke throws his arms back, crumbles and collapses sideways and rolls, back down the slope towards me and all the time I'm just standing there, mouth open, a shooting range target myself, watching the body as it comes to rest against the foot of this tree trunk and just lies there, slumped like a drunk.

Over to the right there's shooting, more shooting, and Bond's jubilant whoop, 'I've got one! I've got one!'

Me, I climbed up towards the bloke I'd killed. His chest was wedged in between the tree trunk and a rock. He was wearing the clothes that all the locals wore, baggy black trousers and a worn khaki shirt, which, from where I stood about a 100 yards off, looked as if it was covered with bright red patches.

'... really got him...' I heard Bond exulting.

Two terrs dead. We were heroes. When we radioed camp, Britz forgave us our sins, he even forgave Bond. We celebrated that night, I chune you, and there in the SAS mess we drank until we dropped.

'You and me — we're buddies,' Bond chuned me in between beers. 'Right from the beginning — right?'

He gripped my shoulder so hard it felt as if he was trying to crush it, and stared into my face. 'Okay,' I said, stepping back. 'Okay.' It was all too much for me. I went outside for a skyf and then sneaked off round the back.

The moon was as thin and white as an old man's hair, and the guard trudged silently around the perimeter of the earthworks. Somewhere out in the bush a jackal yowled. I felt something was about to happen, something bad, I didn't know why, and it was like I wanted to scratch at my face, feel my fingernails digging deep into my flesh and the blood beginning to run hot down my cheeks. Too much booze I figured. I shook myself, and went back into the mess and downed another beer, and then another. It was going to be a long night.

Chapter 7

C ome Saturday our entire stick was given a four-day pass. Me, I caught a glide to Burg, headed into the nearest bar to have a dop or two. I needed reinforcement before I took on Naomi, I chune you. After that last letter of hers I'd tried to write to her about a dozen times, but I'd never managed to get any further than 'Dear Naomi' without getting caught up in the bickering all over again. Finally, I'd given up and sent her this postcard saying I might come home for a couple of days some time. She never answered so I figured she wasn't going to throw me out.

Me, I perched there in the bar for hours trying to work out what to do. Should I hang around until, say twelve that night and then go round to the cabin and take a peek through the bedroom window? Should I just stroll round and check out the scene? After all, what with the neighbours and their gossip, Naomi would never allow any bloke to hang around late at night. Three o'clock, I figured if there was any funny business on the go that'd be the time. The lightie would probably be playing up at Naomi's old queen: no one would think twice about her cousin dropping round for tea.

When I finally pitched up, sucking a handful of peppermints in the hope that it would take the edge off my booze-breath, and saw the windows of the lounge open and the breeze ruffling the net curtains, the sunbirds at the honeysuckle round the side, the lizards basking on my crazy paving path, my gut gave a lurch and it was as if I was coming back from Katz's on an average afternoon, and nothing, not the war, not Headlights' death nor the closing of the bakery, had ever happened. Me, I leant on the gatepost to catch up with myself, and then sneaked off round the side so's I could stand on the drain and check out the bedroom. As I rounded the house, I spotted Naomi in the back picking chillies.

'Eddie?' she looks up in surprise. 'I didn't expect you home.'

'I didn't expect to be here,' I chune her, 'we've just been given this free weekend.'

Well, we both know what it's all about of course, and we both know that the other knows, and eeh, for a moment there I couldn't say a thing. 'Well — howz about a cup of tea?' I ask her finally, 'I'm dry.'

First chance I got, I pulled her into the bedroom, sat her down and asked her about Vyvyan: why had she been seeing him while I was up on the border risking my life for her and the country?

'Cool down,' she tells me, 'cool down. Don't believe all the bullshit you hear. There's nothing going on between us. We're both lonely. I don't have to live in the fridge just cos you've decided to spend your life playing soldier.'

'I'm glad to hear it,' I say. 'But what exactly have you been up to then?' Well, she humms and haas, mutters something about movies and a dance, and I go to the kitchen and rip down this calendar and start going through all the days I'd been gone, one at a time, and try to get her to tell me where she'd been, who she'd been with. She says of course she would very much like to help me — but she doesn't remember, she can't remember, it was a long time ago.

'Not so long,' I reckon. 'Only about two months. I've been around you enough to know you can remember two months back.'

But she starts to cry and asks me if I trust her.

'I'll trust you when you stop your stories,' I chune her. 'I know damn well that you remember.'

But she just lies there and the tears are dripping down her face and I grip her arm and chune her, 'Hey, you, don't you bullshit me anymore, I'm through with all that. I'm sick of bullshit, there's going to be no more bullshit in my life anymore. If you don't tell me where you were I'm going to twist your fucking arm until you do.'

'Are you threatening me?' she cries.

'Damn right I am,' I told her. 'We're going to get to the bottom of this for once and for all. I just goddamn want to know where you were on the fourteenth of May.'

She just howls louder. 'Okay, then, I'll give you something to howl for,' I tell her, and start twisting.

Up she jumps, tries to pull away. 'You hurt me,' she yelps. 'You goddam pig, you hurt me.'

'Ya, fucking right I did,' I agree, 'and I'm going to hurt you one hell of a lot more unless you tell me what's what.'

'You bastard.' She pulls away again, and I let her go, and she grabs Ruthie and screams out the front door down the drag to her mother's place.

And me, I chune you, I was shaking-shaking. The booze cupboard, it was still in the same place, and inside was this half-empty bomb of brandy. Ya, Naomi was always telling me how she could never stand the stuff. Another question. Still, brandy is brandy, and I poured myself a couple stiff shots just to steady my nerves, smoked this skyf I'd been saving for bedtime, and then perched on the floor there, in the lounge, and began to cry. I hadn't cried since I was a lightie, but I couldn't stop myself: I must've cried for about 10 minutes.

I had a couple more brandies to steady myself. Come hell or hot water I was determined to finish interrogating her that night. But she didn't come, didn't come. Six o'clock — Ruthie's bedtime — and still no sign. Seven o'clock — supper time. Nothing. I helped myself from the pot of curry on the stove. Well, if she's splitting, that's quite fine with me, I'm scheming to myself there. I'd be better off without the bitch. All these years we've been married she's given me nothing but grief. I'd be relieved to see the end of her — hell, I'd be free to chase all the young chickies again, free to dop as much as I wanted. Another couple brandies.

Come midnight though, I'm beginning to get worried. Maybe she's been in an accident, maybe she's run off with that bag of penguin shit, that Vyvyan. I remember the softness on the inside of her thighs, the kink in her spine just above her arse. More brandy. I just want her back all over again.

At 1 am that night she came back with Ruthie asleep in her arms, shushing me, when I opened the door, so's I didn't wake the lightie. Well, by then I was so relieved to see her that I'd forgotten all about fighting anyway. 'Sweetie,' I kept telling her as I kissed her ears, 'my sweetheart.' We put the lightie to bed, and then went to bed ourselves, and when we were finished I began cross-questioning her again, but she was asleep, or pretending to be asleep.

Ya, all the rest of the time I was in Burg we never did get round to discussing those questions and, while maybe it was unfair, I never forgot that she hadn't answered them and, at the back of my mind, I was sure she was up to something.

Back at Inkomo barracks at the end of our break, we found out that our unit had been redeployed. We were off to the Wankie area where we'd be supplying camps along the Zambian and Botswana borders.

'Eeh man, you should've checked what we put back these couple days,' ou Sticks was boasting as we perched there in the shade waiting for a truck. 'Brandy, cane, a bottle whisky from this cousin of mine down south — my liver isn't going to recover for a month.'

'It's not my liver I'm worried about,' schemes ou Clouds. 'My cock's the problem — I hope I've still got enough left to piss with.'

'If only we'd had a few more days,' ou Soaps starts, 'then we could've really relaxed.' Soaps, who'd signed up only a month or two back, had just been transferred to our unit, but that didn't stop him complaining about the lack of leave.

'Guess what I did,' Bond breaks in.

'Caught three kinds of clap when you pomped your mother.'

'Jisis, you blokes,' he says in a huff. 'Filth. No wonder whitey can't stand us....'

'Ag, let's hear his story,' says Sticks. 'So what'd you do man?'

'Bounty hunting — I went bounty hunting.'

'Is it, hey?'

'Me and my buddies. We were lucky, we all had leave at the same time.'

'Get anything?'

'Three,' says Bond proudly. 'That's four now, four notches in the barrel. We hit a unit of them as they crossed. Man, I'm telling you it was money for jam.'

'You're bullshitting us,' Clouds reckons. 'You spent your leave hunting terrs?'

'For sure man,' says Bond. 'In this goddam unit we just drive. It was lekker to see some action for a change.'

Us ouens, we schemed he was mad.

Now a couple days after we arrived at the camp, us ouens were sent out on the meat run: we picked up the meat rations for about half-a-dozen camps one morning and set off on our delivery route. Cos two trucks had been revved up in the last couple days, the rest of our stick came along for the ride.

The first stop was, naturally enough, our camp. We were sick of ratpacks and canned food; we wanted our meat ration into the kitchen and onto the stove so's there'd be curry or stew waiting when we returned.

Us ouens drag our supply into the kitchen, sit down for a quick cup of coffee. The cooks cut open the box to see what we've been given this week, and the smell hits us like a bucket of sewerage.

'Jisis,' reckons ou Bones, our company's cook, grabbing hold of his nose. 'This stuff stinks like a hyena's fart.' Putting on a pair of gloves he lifts this hunk of cow out of the box. It was green — I'm not chuning you — bright green.

'What's this?' asks ou Clouds, 'what've the mighty honkies done now? Crossed a cow with a cabbage?'

'We can't eat this,' pronounces Bones. 'This is rotten.'

'Hey,' reckons Sticks, 'considering some of the muck you serve us I was scheming you couldn't tell.'

'When I was in the Selous Scouts...' Bond begins.

It was then that I discovered a note, unsigned, pinned to the meat. 'Boil it with a little salt,' it read, 'it will taste fine.'

Okay, okay, as Corporal Bond tells us, this is the bush, we aren't home in Burg. We haven't got all day. So off we rattle with the rest of our load. At our next stop, this honky transit camp, we drop off five boxes of the stuff. While we're catching a quick cuppa there in the back we watch the cooks open the boxes: they're full of good, red meat, all five of them. 'It's the luck of the draw,' Bond tells us as we head back to our truck. At our next stop, this SAS camp near the border, it's the same story: their meat is 100 percent too. Ya, of all the five camps we supplied that day, ours — the only goffel camp — was the only one with green meat.

Back at our camp we showed the meat to Britz and asked him if he would return it. Britz, he burped. He was in a foul mood that day and he'd been drinking: the army had probly turned down another of his applications to be transferred to a fighting unit. 'If the army says it's all right,' he informed us, 'then it's all right. You bastards — you're too soft — that's your problem. In the Congo we ate meat with maggots crawling out of it... the stuff won't kill you.' Then he staggered back to his tent.

'Well, well,' said ou Bones, very dubious, 'I wonder how they cooked it with maggots and all? maybe boil it up first — with a lot of salt — and then curry it. Ya, a strong, sweet curry....'

But not even all the salt and sugar and chillies that ou Bones lavished on the meat could make it edible, and none of us could manage to down more than a mouthful. Next morning this whole carton of curry and the rest of the cow was carried out to the dump and buried.

That night the hyenas rocked up in their hundreds; to them curried green meat must've been a fancy high-class gourmet delicacy. They whooped and howled and snarled and celebrated all that night as they dug up what was left of the cow and devoured it. The smell we didn't get rid of so easily; it hung on in the kitchen for days in spite of extensive scrubbing, and every cup of tea we drank for weeks afterwards had this faint taste of decaying cow.

'You know what we should've done?' reckons ou Clouds one night as we're perching round grazing yet another of Bones's corned beef specials. 'We shouldn't have even bothered to argue, we shouldn't even have bothered to talk to Britz. If we'd just switched the labels with one of the other boxes, who would have ever been the wiser?'

'The whites would've kicked up such a fuss, they would've been given fresh meat anyway,' ou Sticks reckons. 'It's only us goffels who have to stomach it ...'

Only Bond tries to argue. 'It's just our bad luck,' he tells us. 'It's not race....' But no one listened to him. Us ouens felt that if there was shit around, whitey would make damn sure we would be the ones to fall into it.

Just after the green meat business, we took a convoy carrying supplies up to this new camp way up north on the banks of the Zambezi.

It was miles out in the bush, and there hadn't been much in the way of road for about the last 50 kays. The sun was setting and hell, we didn't know what was out there in all those miles of bloody Africa.

We put foot, put foot, slipping and sliding all over the place, and finally, when we showed up round about seven at night, the trucks and everything in them, all the drivers and escorts and cartons and boxes, were covered in mud.

Well, this sergeant in charge of stores gets out his torch, takes a look in the back and gives a sniff. 'I don't know why you damn drivers can't be more careful,' he tells us. 'Everything you bring here is always in such an appalling mess.'

Not even Bond likes this lot much. 'The road is bad,' he defends. 'You're lucky we're here at all.'

But that sergeant, he's not interested in our story. 'If you were professional drivers,' he informs us, pronouncing 'professional' as though he'd underlined it with a red pen, 'this wouldn't have happened.' And off he prances into the kitchen to call a couple blokes to help us unload.

And, I chune you, once we'd unloaded those blasted trucks and wiped those goddam packages down and stacked them in the kitchen, the sergeant he doesn't give us a beer or anything, not even so much as a cup of tea. Instead, he gets out his lists and counts all the boxes. 'I hope you lot haven't fiddled any labels,' he says as if he's making a joke, but you can see that behind it all the bastard is really dead serious.   Ou Bond, he's getting quite pissed off with that bloke too. 'We don't do that sort of thing,' he informs the sergeant, and then asks if we can perhaps have some supper, we've hardly eaten all day.

But that sergeant, he isn't so easily satisfied. He counts the boxes twice more and, when he finally has to admit that they are all present and correct, every last one of them, he chunes us okay, fine, but tomorrow morning before you go we'll take a quick peek to make sure that the stuff on the labels is actually in the box.

'Okay, okay,' says Bond. 'Where's our supper?'

Finally, the sergeant orders one of the cooks to 'throw something together for our friends' and, for all our trouble, we end up sitting outside (too dirty to eat inside, he informs us) on the stoep grazing half a can of cold bully beef and half a can of cold beans each. 'If I'd known this is what we were coming to,' ou Clouds says, 'I would've made damn sure that we got stuck in the mud and helped ourselves to the supplies.'

'If we were white...' starts Sticks.

'Ag, this sergeant's just a rabbit,' argues Bond, 'don't take it so seriously.'

'We could've at least complained to our officer,' says Soaps.

'If we had an officer who bothered about his troops,' Bond says. 'They....'

'We wouldn't have taken this shit,' ou Soaps says, 'if we were white....'

All this is too much for Bond. 'You blokes, you've got colour on the brain,' he chunes us and jumps up and strolls over to the honkies, about a dozen of them, standing at the other end of the stoep discussing cricket. We watched as Bond took out his smokes, offered them round, tried to make conversation. The honkies took his smokes, chatted to him for a while, then got back onto their cricket and ignored all Bond's efforts to chip in. Bond hung around on the edge of the group for a while longer, dragging on his smoke and puffing out those mammoth wavery smoke rings of his, but the honkies seemed to have forgotten he was there. The group was slowly closing in on itself, leaving him stranded on the edges. Eventually he gave up, and quietly dropped his smoke, ground it out with his boot, and disappeared off into the darkness. I remembered that Burg nightclub, me trying to be all buddy-buddy to the honky troopie who was only interested in chatting up Naomi. I closed my eyes; just remembering I'd been like that made me sick to my gut.

Next morning the sergeant insisted on going through the boxes with us before we left. We had our breakfast on the stoep — once we'd showered he decided our uniforms were too dirty for his kitchen — and watched as his helpers checked through the contents of all the boxes. Now in one they found three dozen winter sheets instead of two dozen mosquito nets. The sergeant, he really gave us a performance there: why were we bringing winter sheets out to the camp in the middle of summer? 'Don't you bastards know it's so hot out here you can fry an egg on a rock?' he chuned us. 'Don't you ever use your brains?' He tapped his skull significantly. 'Didn't one of you bother to give 10 seconds' thought to why you were bringing winter sheets out here?'

Bond pointed out, very polite, that we'd just transported the ruddy boxes, that we hadn't packed them or looked inside, that we'd had absolutely no idea we were bringing winter sheets to this particular corner of the devil's own country. . . .

'That's just what I said,' yelled the sergeant triumphantly. 'You didn't know what you were bringing. So why didn't you make it your bloody business to find out?'

And before Bond could explain all over again that we were a transport unit, only a transport unit, the sergeant asked what we were going to do about the shortage of mosquito nets. 'Malaria is a big problem out here,' he told us, 'the locals are dying like flies. How do you expect my men to lie there being bitten all night just because of your incompetence?'

By then even Bond has realised that this was one whitey we weren't ever going to get through to without an axe. He just gave up and promised the sergeant yes, yes, immediately we got back, first thing, he would take the sheets to the quartermaster, point out the problem, insist — yes, he would absolutely insist — that something would have to be done right away. 'Tell them to send a truck — or better yet — a helicopter,' the sergeant told us as we climbed back into our trucks. Just as we were revving the engines up another thought struck him. 'I'm going to send a letter — you'd better not sell those sheets on the way.'

'The bloke's mad,' reckons ou Clouds when we stop maybe 10 kays down the road to make ourselves a decent cup of tea. 'Crazy, insane, a real shithead.'

'After all that,' says ou Sticks, 'we should scale these sheets, sell them for what we can get. . . .'

'He'll write,' puts in ou Soaps, 'he'll complain to. . . .'

'Probly to Ian Smith and God on high,' snorts ou Clouds.

'Even if he writes what can they do?' argues Sticks. 'The sheets don't appear on the invoices?'

'It'd be stealing,' says Bond reluctant. 'We can't steal from the army.'

'Don't think of it as stealing,' I put in. 'Just remember how much more whitey gets paid — we're just doing what we can about the difference.'

But Bond wasn't convinced. 'Stealing is stealing,' he argued. 'We can't do that kind of thing if we want whitey. . . .'

'Why are you looking after whitey's things for him?' asks Clouds.

But Bond wouldn't be convinced. 'Stealing is out,' he declares. 'I'll report anyone I catch.'

Not that we listened to him, but all his sermonising didn't make him any more popular with us ouens.

When we came back from the trip we saw in the papers that Adrian had been sentenced to life imprisonment, and my father had written to say the story was that he'd escaped the death penalty only cos the government didn't want to offend the coloured community.

'I scheme it's a little late to worry about that now,' reckons ou Clouds, taking a hit of his skyf as we perch outside the mess waiting for our graze.

'They should've just hung the bastard,' says Bond, suddenly unzipping his lip. 'He should've been hung as a warning to all these goddam goffels round here who scheme they're so fucking smart.'

'But he's Donk's cousin,' Soaps objects. Me, I say nothing. Hell, everyone knew that this terr was my cousin and I wished they'd just quietly forget about it.

'I don't give a piece of curried dog shit whose cousin he is,' Bond chunes us, 'he's a terr and he should be hung.'

'Always whitey's arselicker,' sneers Clouds. 'D'you scheme they're going to give you a medal or make you a sergeant for this?'

'For fuck's sake man, I just want our people to have a little dignity.'

'Dignity? With blokes like you for whitey to laugh at?'

'You laugh at me for trying — but you guys — all's you ever do is sit round on your arses smoking stop like houties.'

Clouds starts imitating Bond with Britz. 'Sir — sir —' cringing — 'can I lick your arse, sir? Will you make me sergeant, sir?'

Bond takes a swing at Clouds but the bloke ducks, and next thing all the rest of us ouens are up and holding them apart.

Bond got drunk that night, sick, crawling, motherless drunk. Just after supper we found him lying in the dirt beside the shithouse cursing and spitting about 'goddam goffels' and 'goddam terrs'.

Well, Soaps went for water, Clouds to collect some coffee and me and Sticks, we tried to lift him. We weren't just being nice: our stick was on guard that night and if Britz found out ou Bond was pissed, we'd all six of us land in the shit.

But Bond, he won't have anything to do with the pair of us and he kicks and flails about when we come close. 'Terrs,' he's yelling, 'terrs.' Well, within seconds the whole camp is there standing around looking for these terrs, and, while everyone's trying to calm the bloke, up rolls the lootie who also smells as if he's been spending his evening emptying bottles.

Us ouens, we all back off, and Britz, he walks up to Bond and peers down at him. 'Jackson,' he asks, 'what are you doing on the ground?'

'Bond stares up, tries to focus. 'Fuckin' terrs,' he mumbles, 'fuckin' terrs.'

'Jackson,' says Britz, 'have you been fucking terrs then? I didn't know you were one of those.'

Which all us ouens in the peanut gallery found hilarious.

Britz sniggers himself and settles back against the wall. Bond is going to be the evening's entertainment. 'No, sir,' Bond manages to splutter, 'no, sir....'

'So it wasn't terrs then?' Britz says. 'Maybe it was pink elephants? Or big black spiders? What kind of man are you?'

More guffawing from the peanut gallery.

Bond, he manages to drag himself up onto his knees. 'Sir,' he says, 'that one' — pointing to me — 'is a terr's cousin; that one' — Clouds — 'is a terr arsehole; that one' — Soaps — 'is a terr lover. Waste of a brown skin.'

'But our terr's cousin is also a terr killer,' says Britz shaking his head. 'Have you by any chance been drinking?' More laughter.

And the whole scene probly would've petered out in a couple of minutes but, just then, this radio in one of the barracks announces: '...nine o'clock now ... music hour ...' and Bond tries to pull himself to his feet. '... gotta go ... gotta go,' he's babbling to himself, 'gotta guard.'

'Is he on guard now?' Britz demands, forgetting all about his jokes. Bond moans, there's a long pause.

'Yes sir, sorry sir, he is, sir.' I put in.

Britz glares at me. 'What've you got to be sorry for?'

Bond meanwhile hauls himself to his feet and promptly collapses back onto the floor.

Britz turns back to him. 'Drunk on duty, Jackson,' he says. 'That's a serious offence.'

'... apologise sir, I apologise.'

'I'm not impressed, Jackson. Stand up.'

Bond gropes about, can't quite make it. Britz grabs an arm and hauls him upright. 'Now, Jackson,' Britz tells him, 'you know damn well that I don't fuck around with all that brass button bullshit' — Bond nods dumbly — 'but I do insist that my men are first-class soldiers. And there's one thing a soldier absolutely never does — and that is drink while he is on duty.'

Bond, he just stands there, eyes closed, while Britz rants. 'I thought you were responsible, I recommended you for sergeant. But all that you're fit for is shovelling shit.' And with that he rips Bond's stripes off his uniform and throws them on the ground. 'Craik' — Sticks comes to attention — 'you take over Jackson's duties — as from now.'

By next morning Bond had disappeared. Now we'd been detailed to fetch this truckload of desks from this school to hell and gone out in the bush and we had to leave at first light. Us ouens, we combed the camp — no sign of him or his gat. We're all standing round trying to figure out what to do when ou Bones rocked up and chuned us ya, this morning the guards found a hole cut through the fence and a trail leading off into the koppies behind us.

Well, it was out of our hands, what with the hole in the fence and all, so Sticks went to Britz to tell him the story, Britz he had the bab-belas bad that morning and eeh, I chune you, he was in one hell of a temper.

'Come down,' Britz bellows at the bush. 'Jackson — come down immediately. If you're not here in five minutes you'll be cleaning the shithouse with your tongue.' No answer.

'Go and fetch the bastard then,' Britz yells at us, and as we're looking at each other trying to figure out what to do, there's this shot, this single shot echoing up amongst the caves at the top of the koppie. Somehow we all knew that it hadn't been fired at us.

We scrambled to the top of the koppie and there we found him: he was lying in this cave, splashed with blood and still half-alive. He'd rested the barrel of his gat up under his chin but he must've snapped his head back as he fired cos the bullet had missed his brain but where his nose had been there was this gaping red crater. A couple blokes turned to one side and were sick. I took off my shirt and someone crumpled it up and stuck it over the hole. Clouds ran for a stretcher, the pronto ran to radio the choppers. Half-an-hour later Bond was off on his way to hospital.

Chapter 8

*A*fter the shooting no one talked about Bond. Me, I had these nightmares and I'd wake up at two or three every morning sweating and shaking and shitscared of sleep.

Along with the bad dreams I had diarrhoea, the diarrhoea I always get when I'm nervous and boozing. Out on our supply runs I was always having to ask the driver to pull over so's I could do my business. Ya, my guts got to be quite a joke among the ouens and whenever we rocked up late somewhere, my guts would be paraded as an excuse. 'It's this character, sir — this Donk's guts,' the story ran, 'sir — he left a trail of shit between here and the last village, sir. Twenty times we must have stopped. . . .' Anyway, late one sweaty afternoon as we're bumping along the road to Wherever, I bang on the cab of the truck yet again and ou Clouds pulls over, and I debus and wander off into the bushes to do my thing. Except eeh, the bushes are about a 100 metres from the road, far too far, and I'm all set to squat there in the grass when this carload of honky chicks whizzes past shrieking and waving. That's too much for me; I turn and trudge off into the bushes. That car, I chune you, it changed my life.

Behind this wall of bushes I squat down, leaking and farting and — aaah — out it bursts. I'm just reaching into my pocket for my toilet roll when there's rustling in the bushes around me. I freeze — maybe it's a kudu or something — and then there in the thorns in front of me is the barrel of an AK.

I had no chance. My trousers were down round my ankles. My gat was lying on the ground beside me. 'Stand up and keep quiet,' someone whispered in English. Well, you don't argue with a gat. I stood up and stuck my arms into the air too.

He stepped out of the bushes. He was dressed in civilian clobber, dirty jeans and a rumpled shirt, and his AK was cocked and pointing right at my guts. Me, I just stood there. First thing he grabbed up my gat, slung it over his shoulder, then he unclipped the grenades from my webbing and stuffed them into his pockets.

'Pull up your trousers,' he ordered. 'We aren't waiting around for your friends.' I buckled up. With his gat he pointed to a thicket off about a 100 metres down the slope. 'Down there. You first.'

Just as we reach the thicket the bloke whistles like a guinea-fowl — 'oooeee oooeee' — and grabs me by the shoulder and drags me in. Me, I just about pass out; there in front of me about a dozen blokes are fingering their gats as they check me out.

'What's this. . .?'

'Who's he. . .?'

'A Rhodesian soldier,' the bloke cries out in a whisper. 'Comrades, I've captured a Rhodesian soldier.'

'What are we going to do with him?'

'Take him back — he'll give us lots of information.' The bloke turns to me: 'One wrong move and you've had it.'

I don't think I could've moved if I'd tried.

At a word from their commander, the terrs jump up, pull on their webbing. They fall into a single file, pull me in between two blokes with AKs, and then we're off, jogging north towards the Zambezi.

That's when the shots come, one — two — three. The ouens, they're scheming I'm lost. But I'd never been fucking lost — why'd they suddenly decide I was lost now? The terrs put foot. Me, I try to sort out my chances. When I don't show, the ouens would call in the choppers and the terrs'd scatter and I'd have a chance — if they didn't wipe me out first.

As we ran on and on I listened to the sky, waiting, praying for those choppers, trying to reach into the ouens' heads with telepathy, trying to tell my buddies what was happening. There couldn't have been more than an hour of light left at the utmost. And, if the choppers didn't find me before dark, well they needn't bother looking cos by morning I'd be so deep into the bush that they would never find me again.

Another couple shots — one, two — fainter now. The sky was darkening. Eeh, I remembered all the stories I'd heard about blokes who were captured, how they'd been interrogated, their fingernails torn off, their flesh burnt with cigarettes, and I silently cursed those ouens back at the truck. All's they were good for was sitting around smoking their stop and downing their dop. Ou Bond was right, they were useless. How long would it take them to wake up to what had happened?

As we pounded along I thought of ducking out of file, of gapping it into the bush. But hell, any attempt to escape would've just been a bad joke. As it was I had to battle just to keep up. The only thing that kept me putting one foot in front of the other was terror — I figured that if those blokes schemed I slowed them down too much, they'd wipe me out and not even think twice about it.

Hell, what would they take me all the way to Zambia for? I knew no big secrets. A captured enemy soldier to be exhibited to foreign newsmen? Why would they bother?

Me, I'd made such a mess of things. What would happen to Naomi and the lightie? How would they manage without me? I began to sniffle at the thought. But actually, when I began to think about it, I realised they'd be fine: even without any pension Naomi was earning enough to hold things together, and anyway she was pretty enough — and tough enough — to get some bloke to marry her, the lightie notwithstanding. Ya, next time round she'd make damn sure that she did better than an unemployed confectioner.

The sun slid behind a koppie and suddenly it was dark. We ran on and on until we came to this cluster of boulders at the foot of a gomo. Number two in the file gives his guinea-fowl whistle and everyone stops.

'Rush,' he announces and everyone leans themselves panting against the rocks. They're all checking me out like I'm the new monkey in the zoo.

'Guess what this one was up to when I caught him?' Head down I rest against this rock and wait for it all to be over.

'He was taking a shit' — a great roar of laughter — 'No joke. He was there straining away, his trousers round his ankles. I crept up on him. . . .' The bloke begins acting it out and eeh, I chune you, those blokes are just about pissing themselves they're laughing so much.

The performance over, he removes my rucksack and scratches through it until he comes up with this pack of smokes. He hands out a smoke to everyone, not forgetting me, and lights them all up with my lighter.

'So what do you call yourself?' he asks in English as he takes the first drag.

'Kiernan. Eddie Kiernan.'

'Well, Mr Kiernan,' the bloke says, 'I want to worship your gods. No, no — I'm not joking: you are a lucky man, a very lucky man. We are taking recruits,' — he motioned to the blokes who didn't have gats — 'back to Zambia. If I'd met you in the bush at any other time, I wouldn't have been able to give you the chance to introduce yourself. . . .' More cackles from the peanut gallery.

Me, I just stare at the ground.

'So where were you and your friends headed?' this other bloke asks. If you don't tell the terrs what they want to know, they cut your throat, no questions, ou Headlights had told us.

'There's a base down near Kazangula,' I tell him, trying to keep my voice steady, 'we were delivering supplies.'

Then and there I decide I'm going to be as co-operative as possible. Hell, I had nothing to thank the army for. 'It's a Special Air Services base. They'll hit Zambia tomorrow and some of our blokes will be guarding it while they're gone.'

It's about the only confidential information I have to offer, and the terrs aren't particularly interested. They don't have a radio to warn anyone in Zambia, and besides all I know is too vague to be of much use anyway.

'How long you been fighting for the dog Smith?' the commander asks.

'Hey — just cos I'm in the army doesn't mean I support Smith,' I
chune him. 'One of my cousins, he's a terr. . . .'

The comrades all smile, bright as knives. Terr, it strikes me, isn't
the right word for this company. 'Maybe you know him,' I begin to
gabble. 'Adrian Fredericks, the bloke they just caught in Salisbury.' I
didn't know about bush names then: ou Toofy was actually known as
Comrade Revolution — Rev for short — and he belonged to a
different party. They were still smiling. 'I've thought of switching
sides myself,' I babble on. 'Communism, all that — it's fine by me.
Hell, my grandma was a ho — an African. I mean — I can sympathise
with you guys.'

The comrades, they're perching there with their smokes, checking
me out with a naked eye, but I can't stop myself.

'Us coloureds aren't volunteers,' I gabble on, 'we're conscripts. If I
don't go when I'm called up I'll be jailed. And who will feed my wife
and children then? I've got seven of them.' Me, I couldn't stop myself.

When the smokes were finished, the comrades stood up and
stretched themselves, pulled on their gear and we started out again.
We kept moving right through the night, not running any longer, but
trapping, trapping. No one spoke, and we went on and on until it
seemed like we'd been trapping along forever.

At first light they finally stopped to doss. My legs felt as if there
were burning wires inside them. I couldn't have run away if I'd tried.
But those terrs weren't taking any chances: they tied my hands and
feet and hid me under a bush.

Ya, all the way to Zambia, they made damn sure I had no chance to
escape and, once we'd been rowed across the Zambezi by these
fishermen, I was handcuffed and taken to a camp near Lusaka. I
remember being thrown — no exaggeration — into a cell, but I'm not
too clear about what happened after that. I remember the lines in the
wood of this one bloke's desk, the smell of the shitbucket after it'd
been in the cell three-four days, the light that always seemed to be in
my eyes during the interrogations.

They wanted to know everything about me: where I'd grown up,
where I'd grafted; they cross-questioned me about the army, its
officers, the morale, the location of units, the feelings of goffels
generally, my father, Adrian — alles.

At first I gave them these stories, tried to prove that I hadn't
supported Smith and asked if I could join the terrs. But they don't let

you sleep much while you're being interrogated, and when you have to repeat the same story maybe 10, 12 times well, you can't remember what you've told them and what you haven't. Ya, by the time those blokes had finished with me, I reckon they must've known more about me than I did.

But there was one thing they never did find out about: my plan. I'd worked out that my only chance of escape — and probably survival — was to join them and sneak off when I was sent back to Rhodesia as a terr.

Chapter 9

*O*ne fine morning I was led off to the warders' bathroom instead of the interrogation room and told to clean myself up and shave. Afterwards they issued me with a clean pair of overalls, and gave me a big breakfast of sadza and sour milk.

Something was up. For the next few hours I perched there in my cell weighing up my chances: they'd just fed me but then they'd caught me out in dozens of stories; they knew I'd fought for Smith. Adrian didn't count, we hadn't seen each other for years. No ways would they recruit me. It'd be prison or the firing squad.

That afternoon, wedged between two warders, I was driven to the FC camp and led into this main manne's office. He sits me down and offers me a smoke.

'You are no more Edward Adrian Kiernan,' he informs me. 'You

are Muzukuru. That is your revolutionary — your bush name....'
They were accepting me as a terr — I'd be able to cross back to
Rhodesia and escape.

'I'm glad to see that you are so happy to join us,' the bloke says as I
break into this big grin. 'Your bush name is necessary to protect your
relatives....'

I stopped listening as he went on to tell me I wouldn't last 30
seconds if I tried to betray the struggle. 'Muzukuru,' I silently
repeated to myself. It's a Shona word for cousin, the word for the
sister's son. 'Muzukuru'. Well then, I was labelled from Day One. But
hell, it was better than 'Donk', and the main thing was that I was alive
and still in the game.

Military training isn't fun anywhere, I scheme, and the Tanzanian
camp was definitely no exception. We were put through the usual sort
of grind: an inspection at 5.00 in the morning, exercises at ten past,
and then a run. Round about 7.00 we'd be back for breakfast and the
rest of the morning we spent in class studying subjects like guerilla
warfare, conventional warfare, medicine, topography, armed and
unarmed combat and, of course, politics. At noon we broke for lunch
and during the afternoons there'd be more exercises, more classes and
by 5.30, when we finished for the day, all's we wanted to do was sleep.

After a month alone in a cell, being crammed in this bungalow with
about 20 trainees felt like being canned in a tinful of sardines.
Worse, those blokes they had every reason to be suspicious of me: I
was a goffel, the only goffel in the place, I'd been in the security force,
and I hadn't changed sides by choice. I stayed quiet, tried to blend
into the background; I never argued with anyone; I was always
nodding, smiling, volunteering — to shine the instructors' boots, to
scrub the shithouse. Not that my strategies helped much.

Right from the start this one instructor, this Comrade Banda, was
anti me. During the first inspection, while the whole platoon was
standing there at attention, he stopped at my bunk and started going
through my stuff item by item. He was out to get me. He didn't even
try to pretend. I'd had plenty practice at inspections over the years,
and I'd made damn sure I'd fixed up everything just right. Comrade
Banda, he couldn't believe it: he went through every last item a
second time — but still nothing. He was about to walk off to check the
next bloke out when suddenly he swung round and rumpled up my

clobber. 'Why isn't this clean?' he shouted. 'Exercise Number Nine —
ready position.'

I squatted down like a frog.

'Come on — jump.'

I jumped and he counted, and when he reached 50, he stopped and
asked me why I was demoralised. 'Don't you wish you were back with
Smith?' he says, checking me out with a naked eye.

'I'm not demoralised, Comrade.'

'You are. I can see these things.'

Me, I just hung my head. The bloke was using me to make some
kind of point, and there was nothing for me to do but string along.

Pushups were next, and he kept me at it, jabbing the barrel of his
AK into my back whenever I slacked. 'Come on, come on,' he kept
shouting. 'Do you want us to have to waste a bullet on you?' Finally
my arms hurt so much that I couldn't lift myself anymore, and I just
lay there, snivelling and aching.

'How can you be demoralised?' he demands. 'Didn't you hear our
Radio Zapu last night? Didn't you hear that our Zipra killed 200
whites last week?'

'No, Comrade Instructor.'

'Now Zapu Radio tells us only four of our gallant freedom fighters
were killed in all that fighting.'

'Yes, Comrade Instructor.' What else do you say when someone
tells you something like that? When Smith fiddled the casualty and
immigration figures you only had to multiply by five or 10 to find out
the truth. But those instructors, sometimes they got so carried away
that you had to divide by 50 or 100. Hell, if 200 whites were killed in
Rhodesia in a week, Smith would've surrendered or settled in a
month.

'And the Zanla cadres did some damage too.' To be fair the
commissars always did allow Zanla a couple kills, but never more
than a tenth of Zipra's score. 'They killed 15 — 15 of Smith's men —
and 10 of their gallant fighters died.'

'Yes, Comrade Instructor.' I tried to sound enthusiastic but my
performance didn't convince him.

'So who suffered the most then?'

'The whites, Comrade Instructor.'

'Why are you looking so sad then?' he demanded. 'Are you
mourning Smith's men?'

'No, no, Comrade,' I protested, 'I'm just surprised the fighters are so strong.'

'So you don't think it's true then? Do you think Radio Zapu tells lies?'

'No, Comrade Instructor. I think it's all true. Smith's propaganda. . . .' But he didn't give me a chance to get my line in.

'Smith's propaganda has rotted your brain.'

'No, Comrade Instructor.'

'We should just finish you now.' And eeh, I chune you that bloke checked me out like he wanted to cut my throat then and there. 'I can't understand why the big fish want us to waste our time on you — a coloured who fought for Smith! Why didn't they finish you themselves?'

After that little scene there was no chance that anyone would ever forget I'd been in the security force. The cadres avoided me, even my teachers wouldn't speak to me, and whenever Smith or the security force came up I could feel all their eyes burning on me, hot with hate. They called me Smith's son, sellout, traitor and imperialist hyena, and ignored me when I tried to explain myself.

Ya, those blokes, they did everything they could to get at me: at mealtimes I'd land up with less on my plate than everyone else, and if I left any item of kit lying around it disappeared. Hell, every time I had to go to the firing range with those guys I got the shivers. It wouldn't have taken much for one of them to 'accidentally' discharge his gat and blow me away.

But I chune you it was the assault course which really scared the shit out of me. The course itself wasn't much different from the Rhodesian ones: no targets of black men with guns jumped out at you but there was still enough in the way of barbed wire and general obstacles to make you feel quite at home.

It was the instructors who were scary. They had this habit of firing just behind you, the idea being, so they said, to familiarise you with the sounds of battle. They let it be known that there had been accidents on the course, blokes who thought they could be slack and who'd slacked themselves into a couple rounds. Of course instructors always tell you that kind of thing — in the security force it was just the same — but with that Banda blasting away behind me I was terrified, and I shot through the course like a rat racing to its hole.

Ya, that Banda he hated my guts. Even when the other cadres were to blame he'd land me in the shit. One night after supper, I remember, Comrade Instructor Banda strolled over to the edge of the parade ground where the cadres were perched with their buddies on these old tree trunks. He went from group to group and found all the Ndebeles on one side, all the Shonas on the other.

'Mix up, mix up,' he ordered them, and began cross-questioning each bloke about how well he knew the other language. Most of the blokes didn't know it too well, and Banda gave them a good swearing out. 'We are all Zimbabweans, all Zapu,' he yelled at us. 'We must be able to speak to each other.' Then he paired off the cadres Ndebele/Shona, Ndebele/Shona and ordered them to teach each other.

Then he spotted me. I was perching on this log alone cos none of the other cadres would tolerate me anywhere near them. 'So — we have one of Smith's sons here too?' he shouted. 'And I suppose you can only understand English?'

I said I could speak some Shona, which was true, but by then I was in such a state that I could hardly speak English, and the Shona just wouldn't come. All the cadres began laughing and jeering and Comrade Banda ordered me to do a 100 frog jumps for lying to him. When I'd finished he assigned two cadres, one Shona and one Ndebele, to teach me, instructing them to report me right away if I tried any Smith talk on them.

Ya, it seemed to me that my position at the camp was hopeless. One fine morning Comrade Instructor Banda would wake up with the babbelas and the belief that I was sabotaging the struggle. He'd finish me himself on the assault course, or call in Security and one dark night I'd disappear. The cadres would all scheme good riddance, and that would be that.

I had to escape. As I watched the comrades I weighed up my chances: getting out of the camp itself wouldn't be much of a problem, the guards spent most of their time sleeping. But hell, how could you manage out in the middle of Tanzania with no maps, no money and all of Zambia and the Zambezi to cross? Besides, as the camp commander had told us when we arrived, the penalty for desertion was death.

There was no way out — I was caught like a rat in a trap. I even tried to pray, even though I'd never had much of a handle on that sort of thing. And out there in the camp, when you looked out over those plains rolling off forever into the horizon, it was hard to believe that even if God existed, he'd be much bothered with me, stuck out there in the middle of the bush with a few hundred strays, while all of Africa's swarming millions teemed around us.

It all seemed hopeless, but even so I did what I could. I learnt the freedom songs, the slogans, and I said only what I thought they wanted to hear. I'd never taken much interest in politics before, and suddenly I discovered there were quite a few groups, and you had to know the correct attitude towards all of them.

I was a member of Zapu, and Zipra, its military wing. Zapu was the oldest of the parties — it had been around under one label or another since the fifties. Comrade Nkomo had led the party from the beginning, and when the commissars spoke of him they never forgot to call him 'the father of the struggle'. He had been locked up in one of Smith's detention camps for the past 10 years but, even so, what he said was law.

Two of the other groupings were breakaways from Zapu, and the commissars called them both 'insignificant splinters'. But even they had to admit that Zanla, the military wing of Zanu, which had broken away in '63 mainly cos its leaders didn't have much respect for Nkomo, had infiltrated far more troops into the country than Zipra. In fact — though this wasn't the sort of thing you could openly say — at that stage Zanla was more or less fighting the war on its own.

Instead, the commissars were always reminding us that, cos of the connection with Russia, Zipra was the best-armed and trained of all the liberation armies. Even if there were more Zanla cadres around, everyone knew one of us was worth 10 of them. You had the proof every time the commissars recited their casualty figures.

Frolizi, the other 'insignificant splinter', was an army without a party. According to the commissars, its members had been thrown out in 1971 for trying to introduce 'tribal differences' into Zipra. Frolizi then postured as the unity party in the hopes of getting cash from the Frontline states, but fortunately no one was stupid enough to help, and it was now battling to survive.

The fourth grouping, the ANC, was a party without an army. It was still legal in Rhodesia. The party had been formed to fight a new constitution that Smith had tried to sell to the world back in 1971.

The constitution sounded like a small improvement, but when you studied the thing you could see it was actually designed to keep the whites on top for a long, long time. Even so Britain agreed okay, if you can sell your constitution to the blacks we'll rubberstamp it, and sent the Pearce Commission over to gauge black feelings. The people were disorganised and all their parties banned. Bishop Muzorewa saw that the commission might just report in favour of Smith so he started his ANC to fight the constitution. The people flocked to join, and wherever the Pearce Commission sat the ANC made their feelings known. The British were forced to reject Smith's plan and, for a while, the ANC became very popular. But the commissars felt this popularity was just a temporary thing. 'When there is beer, a man doesn't drink water,' they told us, 'when the people can support us they will forget this ANC.'

I also made damn sure I learnt the Zapu version of what was happening in the struggle, and I repeated it every chance I got. We were taught that the struggle was still in its first, its defensive stage, when the objective was to wear down the enemy. Security forces as a whole, you check, are trained to fight a conventional war; they move openly in platoons, companies and battalions, and when they meet their enemy they hit him. Guerillas, on the other hand, move only in sections and keep well out of sight. You never fight the enemy head-on; instead you watch him, watch him, get to know all his movements, and then you choose your time and place and ambush him. Once you've hit him you disappear before he knows what's happening, and you stay disappeared until he's forgotten all about you. Then you hit him again.

By hitting here, there, everywhere, you stretch the enemy, forcing him to break up his companies and battalions, forcing him to send a stick here, a stick there, forcing him to guard every bridge, every farmhouse, every installation in the country. And, as you stretch him, he has to call up more and more men for longer and longer periods, straining the country's economy and the people's morale.

Equilibrium is the second stage. By then the sides are more or less equal, and the guerillas are beginning to operate in bigger groups, not just sections but platoons and even companies as well. You discover the weak point of the enemy, summon your troops together and attack. You are no longer running from the enemy; you are looking for him as much as he is looking for you. Your objective is to push the enemy back, right out of the TTLs, out of your remote farming areas, so that you can take over and build your base camps and administration there.

Next is the third and final stage, the conventional assault on the cities. Listening to the instructors' stories of the Liberation Army's final offensive against South Vietnam — sellouts slaughtered in the streets, mortars dropping on the suburbs — I tried to imagine the last battle for Burg, the gunfights along Rhodes Avenue, refugees jamming the city centre.

No, man — this is nonsense, I reckoned. The Rhodesian army with its jets and choppers and tanks being defeated by such a ragtag bunch of bandits? Never. Not until Nkomo paints the moon red and nails a hammer and sickle up there as well. These commissars have got to be cracked.

But the news from the struggle wasn't reassuring. One evening early in December we're sitting in our tent cleaning our kit when some bloke sticks his head round the corner and yells that Nkomo has just been released. Those cadres, they just about went mad, leaping up and jumping round shouting 'Bayete! Bayete!' Me, I figured I better jump around and yell Bayete too.

'Forward with Nkomo, forward with the struggle.'
'Smith must be going to surrender.'
'Freedom from the oppressors!'
'We'll drink Salisbury dry!'
'The people united can never be defeated.'
'We'll all get cars.'
'... home soon ....'
'Back to Zimbabwe.'

Me, I just couldn't believe it. I thought it was all some big misunderstanding.

We heard the full story a couple days later: the Rhodesians had released Nkomo and three or four other guerilla leaders, blokes who'd been locked up for 10 years or more, to discuss peace proposals with the presidents of the Frontline states.

When I heard that, I realised eeh, you couldn't just dismiss the guerillas' strategy as the ravings of a couple of cracked commissars: if Smith was talking to his 'communist terrorists' he had to be seriously worried about losing the war. And, when you thought about it, you had to admit ya, the commissars were right. You could see the strategy beginning to work: already the economy was starting to grind down, already the Rhodesians were being called up for longer and longer camps. Jisis — Rhodesia in the hands of the terrs? It was just too awful to think about. I figured that I might as well grab a gat and shoot everyone in sight and keep shooting until they gunned me down. It was all hopeless anyway.

Then, on December 8, 1974, the commissars announced that, to strengthen the struggle, Zanu, Zapu and Frolizi would all now join with Muzorewa's ANC.

The commissars pointed out that Nkomo himself supported the move, and explained that it would frighten Smith into settling. They also quietly let us know that the party wouldn't get a cent from any of the states supporting the struggle unless we stuck with the unity. 'And anyway this Muzorewa animal is only a temporary leader,' they told us. 'The people will be electing a new chairman soon, and Comrade Nkomo will win. We will coup Zanu, Frolizi and the ANC....'

Even so, there were quite a number of cadres muttering that Zapu didn't need any kind of unity and could deal with Smith very well all on its own.

Just two-three days later Smith announced a ceasefire. I felt as if the sky was falling, I chune you: Smith folding so easily — I just couldn't understand it. Why surrender to the terrorists? Why not go down with guns blazing? They would wreck the country anyway.

Still, I couldn't help thinking that if there was a settlement, I'd be home in just a few weeks — if Comrade Instructor Banda didn't shoot me before then. Home — man, I chune you that for a while I couldn't think about anything else. When I closed my eyes I'd see Naomi there in the kitchen making curry, Ruthie perched beside her pulling the head off her favourite doll. As Christmas came closer I found myself going through the things I'd normally be doing: every year I'd hose down the pine tree in the barrel on the back stoep and roll it into the lounge where me and Naomi and Ruthie would decorate it with streamers and tinsel and coloured lights. Ya, that tree seemed to be a signal for the start of the family Christmas season: the moment it was in place the cooking and squabbling began. There was always a big fight about when and where to hold the dinner — but it's my turn this year; no, no three years ago, you. . . . However, come the day, all the fuss and fizzle would've been forgotten and us blokes would retire to the back verandah and get pissed while the women clubbed together in the kitchen and complimented each other's cooking.

Man, I watched that camp radio like a dog whose owner is just finishing up a leg of mutton. Every time someone switched it on I'd sneak over and hang around in the hopes of hearing that the settlement had just been signed and we could all go home.

Instead we heard that the guerillas were insisting on majority rule as a precondition for talks, and Smith wouldn't agree. Ya, suddenly Smith didn't seem so sure about settlement at all.

Me, I chune you, I about cried. By then I'd completely stopped caring whether the country was Rhodesia or Zimbabwe, whether blacks or whites ran the place. I just wanted to be back at Katz's making sure that the first batch of bread was done by 5.15 sharp.

The only bloke who would speak to me, this Comrade Kwame, a tall bony 17-year-old from Harare, wouldn't have won any popularity contests either. The cadres didn't like him cos he was always whining about the filth and the dirt and the conditions in the camp generally. The place was pretty primitive — we were miles out in the bush — and the party certainly didn't have money for luxuries. Comrade Kwame wanted us to have more water to wash with — which would've been quite fine if we'd had a tap, but there at the training camp we had to carry every drop of water up from the river ourselves. More water would've meant more work, and when the instructors seemed to be taking his idea seriously eeh, the cadres wanted to murder the poor bloke.

Then there was the time he complained about the dirt in the bungalows. As a reward the instructors gave him the job of cleaning the camp toilets — I was his assistant — and the comrades called him 'Stinker', and began teasing him about his smell. Whenever he joined a queue or came into a bungalow, someone always held his nose and cried 'What's this thing now — a hyena's fart?' and Comrade Instructor Banda was fond of telling him that he stank so bad he could cross back into the country disguised as a skunk.

The comrades often played jokes on him. Once they stuck a boxful of shit next to his kit, and then wanted to know what all the stink was about. Even the instructors got in on the act. Now Stinker, he hated toi-toi — he would do just about everything to duck it. He was always at the medics, chuning them his back was paining, there was something wrong with his big toe. The instructors weren't impressed and, one time, after he'd limped his way out of the daily run, they decided to take us all tracking instead. The trail led down to the river where this herd of five, six elephants grazed during the day. We're moving along through the reeds when 'quaaa quaaaaa', and suddenly we check this thing, mammoth ears flapping, trunk curled, crashing through the reeds towards us. We didn't stick around to ask questions; we turned and put foot, I chune you, we put foot, ou Stinker, lame leg and all, way out in front of the rest. 'What's this lame leg business?' the instructors were asking him back at the camp. 'Are you trying to make fools of us or what?' And, after that, no matter what his excuse, every morning he had to run with the rest of the recruits.

Once while we were cleaning the shithouse, he told me the story of his life: he'd been looking for a way to study when he'd been tricked into joining up. Apparently he'd always wanted an education and had always done reasonably well at school. But, come Form I, he only passed in the second division, a reasonable pass but not good enough to win him a place in Form II at a black high school. His mother, a teacher, found him graft at this laundry and at night he studied by correspondence. Then, one day he heard a secondary school education could be organised for him in Botswana, and with the help of one of his uncles, he'd crossed.

And now he was missing his home: the sadza in the camp was too hard, like concrete, not soft like his mother used to make; we had to live in filth and he was missing his clean bed; everything was so dirty. Me, I caught quite a spook when he told me all this, I chune you. They just weren't the kind of things you said out loud in a training camp. 'I can't stand this place,' he told me. 'I want to run away back to Rhodesia.' Now me eeh, I couldn't figure out why the bloke was telling me this kind of stuff. It would've taken torture to get me to talk about escape. Did he scheme I was hoping to gap it as well? Then it hit me: this Stinker had to be Security. The instructors and the commissars must've sent him to feel me out.

In the middle of his story we were called to class. I followed along blindly and perched there shaking and trying to concentrate on the instructor's spiel. It was just the kind of thing those bastards would do. And I'd listened to him, sat there and listened and said nothing while he'd admitted that he was a traitor. Hell, that in itself would be enough to persuade Security that I was a sellout, a Smith sympathiser. There was only one solution: I'd have to prove to Security that I wasn't a threat — I'd have to report him.

So that night I sneak over to the Security bungalow and tell the bloke there that Stinker's talking of gapping it. The bloke nods, writes it all down. I'm a good comrade, he tells me, the kind of comrade the struggle needs. He gives me a packet of smokes and tells me if I hear anything else. I mustn't hesitate. . . .

I was sweating when I left. Stinker was the one cadre who'd been half-way friendly to me. What if he was now sent away by Security? What if he was just very young, a bit of a fool? I took one of the smokes, lit it, threw the others into the bush and went and hid myself in the shithouse.

For the next few days I waited for something to happen. But nothing did, and nobody acted any differently to him. He bumbled along as usual, and whenever we were cleaning the toilet he'd bring up his plan. I figured I had to have been right: he was Security.

Then everyone was talking settlement again, and I forgot about Stinker's problems. According to this one BBC commentator the South Africans were now twisting Smith's ear and dragging him to the talks. They'd even pulled their police home to show how serious they were. Meanwhile, the Zambians were making sure that the guerillas were in a mood to negotiate.

Ya, for a while there it looked as if a settlement was certain. When our training course finished in April, there was a passing-out parade and this big fish, who'd swum up all the way from HQ in Lusaka for the occasion, seemed to be preparing us for a negotiated settlement. 'We must ask ourselves what is our aim in the struggle,' he says, fixing us with a watery stare. 'We want power — power so that we can rebuild settler Rhodesia into our own Zimbabwe.' Loud cheers. 'In fact how we get the power is not the problem — just so long as it comes to our hands.' More cheers. 'If Smith says he will give us the power in three or five years, we will say — fine — just so long as he gives it to us. To free our country by the gun would take at least as long, and many comrades would die. How would your mother and father feel when the party tells them you are dead after Smith has asked to surrender?'

Ya, for five minutes there the Future was this sweet young cherrie wearing nothing but rose-coloured specs.

Not for long though. The big fish finned off to his waiting car, and the camp's Security commander strolled through the ranks, stopping at every platoon and reading out all the names of those cadres they'd decided were politically unreliable. Whenever he read a name out, two instructors jumped the bloke, blindfolded him, and led him off to a waiting truck.

As I watched the commander marching down the ranks towards me, I just about melted away, I chune you. I'd been one of Smith's men, I was a coloured, the only one in the place, and my instructors didn't like me.

The commander stopped beside us, looked at his list, checked us out. 'Comrade Kwame.' Stinker was right behind me. I didn't dare look round at him; I stood stiff, staring straight ahead. Two instructors grabbed him and led him off. The commander moved on, and the cadres around me quietly let out their breath. I closed my eyes, squashing back a scream. The commander halted by the next platoon and called out another name.

I never told anyone what happened there with Comrade Stinker. Hell, for all I know maybe it wasn't even my visit to Security which led to the bloke's arrest — maybe he talked to other comrades, maybe they pulled him in for something else altogether. No one ever told us, and I couldn't exactly ask. All right, my squealing like that couldn't have helped the bloke any, but what did he expect? Hell, spilling his story out like that he couldn't expect me just to listen like some padre. I was scared for my life. I wasn't just going to sit there and let them slit my throat like a sheep. Under those circumstances just about anybody would've done the same. Your first thing is — survive.

Chapter 10

*O*nce we'd finished our training we were bussed to the Zambian border where half-a-dozen army trucks were waiting. We were driven south for most of the day and then, late in the afternoon, the trucks turned off onto this dirt road which twisted off through rough, mountainous territory. For two hours the truck rattled along eastwards, and the only mense we saw were some lighties herding goats.

Just before sunset, out in the middle of nowhere, the trucks turned down this track which wound down the hillside into the valley. We're almost at the bottom when we round this corner and check this long green line of Zambian troops waiting for us. The trucks stopped, we debussed, yawning and stretching. 'Form up! form up!' the sergeants shouted, and slowly we all shuffled into place. Then the search began: every last one of us was forced to strip, and all the baggage was taken to one side where the Zambians picked through it piece by piece. I overheard one of the drivers asking what all the bother was about, and this sergeant told him no arms were allowed in the camp. I remember vaguely wondering what was going on. After all, the place was supposed to be a military base.

Only when the Zambians were satisfied that rone of us were carrying weapons did they march us down to the camp. We jumped this small stream, the Entrance stream, trapped through a stand of elephant grass, turned a corner and ya, there, tucked away between the foothills of the escarpment was the camp: this huge patch of bare reddish earth, the parade ground-cum-soccer fields, bounded by rows and rows of olive-green army tents to the east and west. To the north were a couple sheds and bungalows, old farm buildings which now housed the HQ, logistics, the clinic and the kitchen, and just beyond them was the Kitchen River, this clear cold stream where the camp took its water. This we later called the Zapu River.

Ya, there were so many rivers in the area that the camp was practically an island. The Kitchen River flowed into the Rat River, the southern boundary of the camp. It was a wide, warm river banked with beds of reeds which were crawling with rats, and when the food truck arrived late, or when we were sick and tired of sadza and beans, we'd trap a couple and grill them. Later the Rat River became the Zanu River.

As we marched into the camp we saw eeh, there were hundreds of mense around: guys on crutches perching together on a tree trunk at the edge of the parade ground, a bloke without an arm, and squads — there were squads everywhere — squads taking a quick smoke break in the shade, squads drilling, squads shouting slogans as they ran, squads of women even. Ya, in spite of all the talk of ceasefire and alles, you could see there was a war on.

We marched along the road to logistics, past the clinic and past the women's section where these chicks in khaki fatigues sat in circles outside their tents. A couple cadres shouted and waved and the chicks looked up and stared us out, but not one of them moved or said a word. We couldn't figure out what their story was.

But the Zambians at logistics, they were very welcoming, all 'comrade, comrade, comrade, comrade'. We were each issued a mug, a bowl, a spoon, a blanket and a groundsheet and every fourth bloke was handed a tent. Once we'd all been organised we were marched to the men's section and allocated sites near the Kitchen River.

That night one of the Zapu — ex-Zapu actually — commissars gave all us new blokes a lecture. The camp, he explained, held about 2000 cadres: about 900 from Zapu, 800 from Zanu, with the rest either Frolizi or fresh-from-homes. There were also about 200 refugees at the camp, most of them Zanu.

'This camp,' the commissar explained, 'is a unity camp. Cadres from all the parties have been brought here so that we can all be mixed into a single fighting force. You cadres have been recruited by Zapu — Nkomo is your leader — but remember that all of us, Zapu, Zanu and Frolizi, we are all now ANC. There is no more Zapu, no more Zanu, no more parties — only the ANC. We are now one party and one people.'

He called out one of the cadres and chalked 'ANC' in large white letters on his back. 'Long live the unity of the struggling masses of Zimbabwe!' he shouted.

We repeated the slogan.

'Come on — I can't hear you!'

The group roared it out again and again until you could hear our shouts echoing off among the hills.

The commissar raised his hand for quiet. 'With this unity we will scare Smith into surrender, and if there is no unity after victory, the imperialists can exploit the parties and make a civil war — that's what's happening in Angola now.'

'Long live the unity of the struggling masses of Zimbabwe!' we roared again.

'Our leader, Nkomo, the father of the struggle has put his name to this unity agreement,' he told us, 'and he doesn't want any of you causing problems — understand? Here at the Unity Camp you'll be lectured by commissars from all the different parties — not just Zapu. You'll hear a lot of rubbish' — laughter from us cadres — 'but you can sleep through it — just so long as you don't fight. Watch out for fighting — especially the Zanu cadres. They're trying to tell the world we're out to destroy the unity, and they're picking fights every chance they get. So whatever you do — don't give them any chance to make more of their lying propaganda. Don't get into fights with them because they will always run crying that you started first. Remember these are the orders from Father Nkomo.'

Another cheer. 'Forward with Nkomo, forward with the struggle. Long live the unity of the struggling masses. . . .'

Next day at breakfast I'm perching off to one side, as usual, when along comes this character with wires plaited into his hair so's it sticks out like the quills of a mangy porcupine.

'Forward with the struggle,' he greets me.

'Forward with the struggle,' I agree. That at least was a normal enough opening. Maybe we could become buddies.

'Are you for the unity?' he asks.

'Yes,' I say. Judging from what the commissar had told us, it was always the right answer.

The bloke nods, pulls a pair of little clay animals, the kind that children make, from his pocket. 'What's this?' I ask him.

'Unity,' he tells me triumphantly. 'The ox and the ass. And thou shalt not harness them together. God told me to spread the word.' The bloke he gives me a wink, pats his other pocket and through the material I can check the shape of a book, his bible. 'I've read it right through and that's what it says.' And with that he ducks off into the crowd.

Hell, this place is pretty weird, I'm scheming.

After breakfast there was toi-toi and then political discussion until lunch. The rest of the day was our own. Some cadres kept themselves fit with toi-toi: others played soccer or carved themselves kieries or hunted hares or birds, and one or two paged through the volumes of Marxist literature in the camp library. That first day I just drifted around, checking out the scene, and while I'm watching this soccer game, wondering about my chances of getting to play, there's this tap on my shoulder. My gut went cold, I chune you. I turned, expecting a dozen Security asking for an interview — but instead there's this goffel, this coffee-coloured pointy-faced fellow with no front teeth who introduces himself as Noah. 'Hell, it's lekker to check a little light out here in darkest Africa,' he says. And that, I chune you, is exactly how I felt too.

'Hell,' I said, 'you're the first bloke — except for that character with wires in his hair — to even speak to me.'

'That's ou Comrade Sputnik — those wires are his antennae for messages from the Lord — and I chune you he's no crazier than most of the ouens here. This place man, it should be called the Unity Nuthouse.'

We got to speaking about how we'd landed up in the struggle, of course, and I babbled out all my history: for about half-an-hour I jabbered away there, and eeh, I just couldn't stop myself. 'But don't get me wrong,' I ended up with this queasy feeling that maybe I'd said too much, maybe I was pulling a Stinker on him. 'I'm for the struggle. I understand all about oppression and imperialism and colonialism and racism and alles. I want to be a freedom fighter, and even if I hadn't been captured. . . .'

I sneaked this quick look at Noah to see how he was taking this lot, but eeh, the bloke, he wasn't even listening. We were walking past the women's tents and a couple of those large and silent ladies were standing around in one of their mysterious circles. Noah whistled, they ignored him. He whistled again. They just stood there, solid as tree trunks.

Noah was annoyed. 'You — you think you're pretty — hey?' he yells out, tossing a rock in their general direction. 'You think you're beauties just cos you've got big backsides? Well, you're kak, you're just a couple cows — I'd rather stick it up a dog any day. . . .'

'Hey, hey,' I'm telling him, 'cool down. We'll get into shit.' I'm shivering in my boots, I chune you. Two goffels daring to offend the flower of African womanhood — I could already hear the commissars.

'Ag, calm down man,' he chunes me. 'There's nothing to get excited about.'

'I've been locked up once and that's quite enough for me. . . .'

'I've been locked up three times and I don't give a shit.'

And that was his attitude. Back in Rhodesia he'd been locked up two-three times for minor things — smuggling a couple emeralds, selling stop, stealing a car — but nevertheless he'd still had to go to the army.

'Those fucking honkies,' he told me, 'they were giving me one hell of a hard time. I played kaffir, played kaffir until I just couldn't take it and after I told this whitey officer just what a useless arsehole he was, he tried to punch me out and I smacked him one with this bottle. . . .'

Noah crossed into Zambia hiding on a goods train and joined Frolizi cos he'd had to disappear fast after some incident involving a Lusaka barmaid.

'There was just one problem,' he chuned me. 'I wasn't long with Frolizi before I found out their houtie commanders are as full of shit as those honky officers!' And to crown everything, he tells me this long story about a houtie commander who'd murdered one of the goffel comrades and managed to duck punishment. 'If that goffel had been black,' he finished, 'Frolizi would've executed the commander, no question!'

Me, I was flabbergasted by all this talk. The bloke wasn't just laying his head on the block — he was sharpening the axe too. What was his case? Why was a bloke who'd been around for so long spilling all of this to some character he'd just met? Did he scheme he could trust me cos we were both goffels? I started thinking about Security and remembered Stinker and stopped.

Noah raved right on. 'Ya — these goddam houties don't treat us any better than the honkies. They call us "Smith's sons" and "sons of whores", and they're always trying to show you who is boss....'

Me, I grimaced, stared straight ahead hoping that no one had overheard us.

Noah, he gave me one look — 'For chrissakes don't tell me you believe all that phoney shit they feed you?' — and burst out laughing.

He was right, of course, he was right. I didn't believe a word of it. But however right Noah was, I most certainly wasn't going to admit it. I set my dial on stiff and kept my eyes front.

Ou Noah, he just laughed. 'Look — I'm not going to sell you out — we're goffels.'

I nodded quick and stiff — he was right but I just couldn't take it — and turned and lumbered off to the other end of the camp.

All that night I lay there in the tent, three ex-Zipra cadres all snoring around me, trying to figure out how to handle this lot. Finally I decided ya, he's a goffel, but dumb and dangerous. Whatever happens keep your distance.

And the more I found out about Noah, the more dangerous he seemed. Next morning at breakfast I got talking to this ex-Frolizi cadre who reckoned Noah had quite a number of nuts and bolts loose. 'That one,' the bloke told me, 'has a gift for finding trouble.' From day one when he'd argued with the commander about how many pairs of socks he needed, he'd been sinking deeper into the shit.

He'd been heard to mutter that at least the Rhodesians knew how to do things properly; he'd been caught listening to a Rhodesian radio station — the music was better, he said — and he'd been caught stealing sugar from the stores. His commander had had him tied to a tree for three days, but not even that worked. Afterwards he still caused as much kak as ever.

Well, once I knew the story, I dodged Noah whenever I could. He kept after me, slipping in next to me just after I'd sat down to eat, that kind of thing. He could see how I felt, but it didn't seem to bother him. Me, I was so worried I wanted to run every time he plonked himself down beside me. All the other comrades could check us, they would think I was his friend, they would think I was like him.

One morning, I remember the comrades were all gathering on the parade ground to hear this ex-Zanu cadre talk to us about the unity. I was perching there by myself, fiddling with a piece of wood, when Noah dumped down beside me again. It was just too much, he'd be heckling and jeering; I couldn't imagine lasting out the whole hour with him performing beside me. 'O hell — gotta go,' I told him. 'There's this bloke, this comrade I've got to speak to.' I jumped up, waved at the thickest part of the crowd, but Noah grabbed me by the arm. 'Your buddy can wait,' he said. 'I've got a couple things to talk over with you, Mr Goffel.' If I'd run and he'd grabbed me, it would've been like a lover's quarrel or something. I sat down and stared straight ahead.

A couple commanders were trying to shush the crowd. The speech would begin any minute. 'This unity business, it's real bullshit,' Noah says at the top of his voice. 'Stinking shit, with maggots crawling round in it.'

'Quiet, hey,' I whisper to him desperately, 'someone's going to hear.'

'Hell, comrade, you're green, man,' he chunes me like I'm sitting on the other side of the parade ground. 'No one takes this unity seriously. The whole thing's the concoction of the Frontline states and the OAU. No one would've bothered with it if they hadn't threatened to withdraw their aid. Like — just use your eyes: you'll see all the Zapu comrades together, Zanu together. And there're groups within them; it's all tribal, regional. . . .'

'Some people are for unity,' I said in case someone was listening.

'Man, they're just chuning you what their leaders tell them to say in public.'

Remembering that little talk the ex-Zapu commissar gave us when we first arrived, I figured maybe Noah had a point. Still, it wasn't the kind of point you made in the middle of a unity meeting.

Then this comrade, a huge bloke, very black and with shoulders like a boxer, strode up to the lectern and the crowd went quiet. There was just something about him; he was one of those blokes who seem to make the earth shake a little when they walk.

'Now that bloke,' Noah boomed out so loud I cringed and ducked down, 'that bloke is the exception. He's serious about this unity nonsense, so serious he's even pissed off his party's commissars.' Noah shook his head. 'Well, I s'pose it takes all types to fill the zoo.'

'Have you ever heard of London?' the commissar began slowly. 'How many of you have heard of London?' Maybe 20, 25 people out of the 100 gathered there raised their hands.

'Ignorant bloody peasants,' muttered Noah.

'Ssssh,' I whispered, my eyes fixed on the commissar, 'we're going to get into shit.'

The commissar pointed to one of the cadres. 'At school the teacher showed us pictures,' he said. 'It's a wealthy place, a big town.'

The commissar nodded. 'London is in England, the country Rhodes came from.' A sharp intake of breath at this. They all knew who *he* was. 'London is very big, very wealthy. Next to it Salisbury looks like a chicken hok. Now do you know where the English found the money to build their London?'

No one was answering this one so the commissar went on. 'From Africa, from Ghana, Tanzania, Zimbabwe. From all the countries of Africa. The English stole gold, ivory, cattle — and people — here in Africa and with that money they built London.

'That's what the colonialists are: thieves. They steal from the masses. They are ticks fattening themselves on the blood of the people. And anyone — black, white or purple — who steals from the people is a colonialist. Anyone who accepts our struggle is for us. In the struggle we are not racist, not tribalist....'

Noah, though, wasn't impressed. 'This idiot, he even wants to open up his unity to whitey,' he chuned. 'Why should we have to sit through this crap?'

'Sssh,' I began.

The commissar, he checked us talking there, stared us out with a naked eye as he went on. '... the unity is for everyone who....'

Me, I zipped my lip and stared straight ahead.

'All Africa has a single spirit,' he was telling the cadres now. 'All that separates us are the artificial boundaries of the colonialists — they are the ones who invented these countries, this Rhodesia of theirs, this Zambia. They are the ones who exaggerated this tribalism, put it in everyone's mind. In Zimbabwe it's Smith who tells us how different the Ndebele are from the Shona, it's Smith who keeps reminding us of all these old wars — if we all joined together and fought him as hard as we've fought each other there would be no more colonialism in our country by now.'

'Jee-sus,' reckoned Noah, jabbing me in the ribs. 'Listen to this bullshit. Tribalism Smith's invention! Hell, the Matabele and the Shonas have been at it ever since the Boers chased the Matabele out of South Africa. How are we meant to swallow this...?'

'Shut up,' I hissed trying to inch away, but right next to me there's this fellow with thighs as thick as logs.

What with all this racket the commissar stopped his talk, and glared straight at us. I dropped my eyes, but he kept on staring; he stared so long that everyone in the audience began turning and twisting in their seats to check what's happening. Me, I went cold: here I was suddenly on exhibition as a disruptive element, an enemy of the unity — goddam Noah — after me being so careful.

'What would happen if we won our struggle today?' the commissar resumed. 'Would the three liberation armies destroy each other so that the colonialists could come back and pick up the pieces? Are we going to destroy ourselves...?'

About half-an-hour later he finally finishes, and us ouens stand and stretch and begin slouching off towards the kitchen. 'That one, he's nuts,' says Noah rolling his eyes. 'These unity people must get in touch with reality....' Me, I chune you I'm hardly listening. I just want to belt the bastard. Since the day I'd been captured, I'd watched every damn step I'd made, I'd done everything possible to keep out of trouble and here's some loud-mouthed idiot sounding off to me in the middle of a goddam political education class like I'm his accomplice or something.

'I've gotta go,' I tell Noah and turn and step smack into the commissar.

'Watch it,' the bloke says, and eeh, he's towering over me like this angry black mountain.

'Pardon me, Comrade Commissar,' I blurt out. 'I wasn't. . . .'

The bloke he stares down at me like I'm this weevil in his sadza and it seems like forever before he finally opens his mouth. 'You,' he says. 'You. I've about had it with you two sons of Smith,' he says. 'You disrupt another lecture of mine and I'll crack your skulls like pumpkins.'

But eeh, man this was all too much for me. All these months I'd been careful, I'd held myself in check and made damn sure I didn't step out of line and now, cos of Noah's nonsense, this commissar is glaring at me as if I'm Smith himself.

'I wasn't talking,' I gabble like a scared schoolboy. 'It wasn't me. And Smith's not my father. Just because I'm lighter than you doesn't make me Smith's son — you said yourself.' Me, I'm so shocked by the defiance escaping from my mouth that I begin to shake. Any moment, I'm scheming, the bloke's going to belt me one, call Security and belt me one. But the commissar, he just stood there, his fists hanging indecisive.

'I apologise, comrade,' he says eventually, clearing his throat. 'You are right. I was not listening to my own lesson.' He sticks out one gigantic fist. 'Comrade Biani.'

Ya, that was Biani for you. Most blokes would've clapped you, but he actually listened to what you had to say.

'So then, how you feel about the unity?' he asked, as I began to register what'd happened and tried to stop myself from shaking.

'Hopeless,' said Noah. 'It's a fairytale, man — there's no way it's gonna work.' He went on about the situation in the camp, the incompetence of the leaders — on and on — but Comrade Biani listened quietly, patiently, though he must've heard all of Noah's points a 100 times before. When Noah had finished, the commissar turned to me.

'And what you think, Muzukuru?'

'Huh?'

'How you feel about all this? You agree with your friend here or what?'

I just looked at the guy. He sounded honestly interested. I didn't know what to say. It suddenly hit me that during my time in Security, in training, I'd turned myself into a chameleon. Everything I'd been doing and saying those past months had been to camouflage myself.

I'd listened to the commissars, to the cadres, to Stinker, to Noah, nodded to everybody, but kept myself under cover; I didn't have the faintest idea what I thought about anything.

'Well, I haven't been here very long,' I said, cautious.

'You smoke mbanje — dagga — comrade?'

'Hell — sure.' A skyf would've been really lekker. I turned to look round for Noah to see how he felt about this lot, but he'd disappeared.

Me and Biani trapped north along the foot of the escarpment for about a mile and then scrambled up a kloof until we came to the top of this koppie thick with wild oranges. We perched there on this rock in the shade and skyfed it up. Biani wanted to know how come I joined the struggle, and so I told him the tale of my capture. Eeh, the bloke he laughed so much he just about choked. Me, I didn't think it was that funny but still, I was glad to have him laugh — he couldn't be too anti-me then.

'But you won't go spreading it around?' I asked. I didn't want to be turned into Donk all over again.

'No — no — it's okay, man,' he spluttered, trying to get himself under control. 'So what's happened since then?'

I told him the rest of my story, assuring him I'd been anti-Smith from way back and leaving out any mention of Comrade Stinker and my escape plans. I told him how shit-scared I'd been out there on the assault course with Comrade Instructor Banda behind me and all the cadres making cracks about Smith, how everyone treated me like dirt cos they schemed I was a spy. And, when I was finished, he rolled another skyf and told me something of his own story, not all at once as I've put it down here, but bit by bit during all the years we fought together.

He was a Shona, a Manyika from round about Umtali, and had been with the struggle just over two years. His old man was a bossboy on a white man's farm and back when he was a lightie, he'd played together with the farmer's kids.

When he started school, he admired all those white youngsters, always so smart in their jackets and nice trousers. He wanted to look like them, but had only the one school uniform, which had been his brother's and it had patches all over. It wasn't till he was 11 that he was given his first pair of shoes, a pair which had become too small for one of the farmer's kids. 'I can still remember that day,' Biani told me, 'you don't know how happy I was to get those shoes. There were only two other kids in the primary school who had a pair of shoes, so from that day I was one of the big fish.'

He was an altar boy in the Anglican Church and in Sunday school had been taught that you would be what God has decided. At the time, he thought it natural, part of God's plan, that the whites should have the cars, the clothes, the cattle, the bicycles. But in standard five when he went to his first political rally, his thinking changed.

'We heard what our leaders were saying,' he told me, 'and we heard what was there, silent in our hearts. "A hungry man is an angry man," one of the speakers told us, and that phrase stuck with me. Oh, I'd never actually gone hungry you know, but I saw myself always walking with hunger: hunger for meat, for a new pair of shoes, for a bicycle, for a uniform without patches.'

In 1963, while he was visiting his uncle in Umtali, Zanu split from Zapu. 'The leadership of the new party, Mugabe and Sithole, criticised Nkomo for not being strong enough against the settlers; but tribalism was also there. There was rioting, the Zhii riots. Party supporters fought in every township in the country, and there were murders and rapes and burnings. Zapu held Bulawayo and Salisbury, but Zanu took the eastern part of the country.

'The sky over the townships was red,' he said. 'Our people were destroying themselves while the enemy — the Rhodesians — watched. It was then that I understood that for the struggle to succeed, there must be unity.'

When he was 14 he won a scholarship to high school and there he became friendly with a group of pupils who talked politics. One of the teachers explained to them how Moffat, the missionary, had come into the country with a bible and how Rhodes, the capitalist, had followed behind with his gun. The pupils talked about this and Biani wasn't the only one who decided to leave the Church. 'The Christians tell you not to kill, not to steal, but those Christians stole our country and murdered many of our people. In Church they tell you not to be envious, but when those Christians saw what a rich, beautiful country Zimbabwe was, they wanted it and took it for themselves.'

The pupils also discussed the education system. The African high schools wrote a very stiff exam, the Cambridge entrance exam, under very difficult conditions; the white schools wrote the same exam, but the government made sure they had everything, spending 13 times as much on every white pupil as on every black. 'We became awake to this,' said Biani, 'and we started complaining — about the books, about the classrooms, about the staff, the syllabus, everything.'

During his fourth year at the school, the pupils staged a food strike. They had been given boiled spinach — spinach boiled till it was just a tasteless green muck — served up with nothing to flavour it, and they complained that they couldn't eat the stuff. The headmaster, a short, pink South African with an RAF moustache, nicknamed 'Balloon' (because of all the hot air) told them to thank the Lord for what they had received, but next morning after assembly the whole school sat down on the grass and refused to move.

Balloon shook a fistful of twisted school knives and forks at them: 'This is what savages you people are! We try to help you and you still always complain . . . . Don't appreciate . . . no gratitude!' He finished by announcing that they'd be fed nothing but boiled beans and bread for a week. Next day the pupils struck again, and that afternoon Biani and five or six other ringleaders were expelled.

He went to Salisbury to look for graft, but couldn't find anything. That was back in 1971 when Smith was trying to talk Britain into recognising Rhodesia's independence. Smith came up with a new constitution which Britain agreed to rubberstamp and finance — provided he could sell it to the blacks. Now that constitution was a trap baited with British money for schools and hospitals; it was designed to entrench white power for another 150 years. Most of the leaders who could have warned the people were either locked up or else had fled the country, and for a while it looked as if Smith might just be able to persuade the British that the people supported their plan. Then the British announced that they were sending out the Pearce Commission to gauge popular opinion, and Bishop Abel Muzorewa began rallying the people. Biani started going to political meetings. He got talking to the mense there and before long he was helping mobilise the masses. 'Smith never expected us to win that fight,' Biani said. 'He expected us to say "Yes, baas, this is good. Thank you, baas." He expected us to be grateful to him for allowing the British to give us schools and hospitals. But we showed him, we showed him that we didn't want these scraps, we wanted what was ours — our country, our freedom.'

The Pearce Commission found that the blacks completely rejected Smith's new constitution.

Soon afterwards one of Biani's uncles found him a clerical position at the Rhodesia Timber Company. He got only five dollars a week, but in the beginning he felt he'd been very lucky to get anything. As time went on though, he became dissatisfied. 'Whenever I'd go to shows or fairs, I'd see people enjoying themselves, buying icecreams and beers, going on rides and the rest. I wanted to do these things too, but I always had so little with me.'

After about a year, he went to his boss and asked if there was any way he could improve on his salary or position. The boss wasn't encouraging, and Biani began to feel restless. 'I looked at myself locked in that job for the rest of my life, and I wasn't happy. I compared myself to the boys in the bush — they were our heroes and I wanted to be like them, I wanted to do something with my life, have something to show. One night my two cousins said they were thinking of leaving the country to join the struggle. I asked them if they were serious, and that night we made our plan.'

Next day Biani went to his boss, killed off a long-dead grandmother and chuned he wanted to go home for the funeral. The boss agreed and gave him a week off. He footed it over to Sound Enterprises and asked if he could put a deposit on a jacket. Sound Enterprises phoned his boss; the boss told them he was a good, reliable boy, and so Biani was allowed to put four dollars down and walk out with a 36 dollar jacket.

At his next stop he let a salesman talk him into putting down a deposit on a three-quarter bed with blankets, sheets, pillowcases, the works. The shop delivered the bed to his place that afternoon and he paid a bloke from his area who ran an unofficial taxi service, to strap the thing to the roof of his car and deliver it to his parents.

Finally he bought a bag, a good bag. 'It cost me nearly 50 dollars — or it should've — but I wanted to look right when I arrived at the struggle. Aah, but I was stupid,' he laughed. 'You know, I even believed I was going to make money out of the struggle. I thought I was going to be paid. The pay, it was all my own invention; I knew nothing about being a freedom fighter before I left and very little about the struggle. But I was young and when you're young, you're adventurous. Even if I'd known, I would've gone anyway.'

One cousin backed out, but Biani and his other cousin caught a bus to Umtali and then footed it to Mozambique where Frelimo found them and handed them over to Zanu. His first year was spent carrying ammunition from the Chifombo base through areas that Frelimo had liberated all the way to bases on the Mozambique/Rhodesia border. It was 15 days in the going and about eight coming back.

'It wasn't what I expected. In those days we had nothing, nothing but volunteers. Zanu couldn't train and feed us, or even give us all arms and ammunition. Sometimes we were walking with naked buttocks. There were very few guns and on the way back to Chifombo only one of the porters would be armed. If you were sick on the way back, you were going to die because we always left all our medicines with the fighters. My cousin died of malaria after six months; many were dying.' Biani was taken to Tanzania for six months' training as a fighter. 'By then I'd become a man. I knew what it was to kill and to die. I knew that the struggle mattered, not each one of us fighters. But, from the stories we were hearing about the leaders getting fat in Lusaka, we wondered whether they had begun to forget these things.

'Just after I came to Chifombo again, there was an election for the Dare and the Karangas, the southerners, took control from the Manyikas, the easterners. The new council promoted its own people, and blokes who'd hardly fought at all, fresh-from-homes, became commanders. Us cadres complained about this and the lack of supplies and the lack of guns, but no one seemed to listen.

'Not long after our unit left for the front one of the field commanders, Comrade Nhari, decided that this was all nonsense, the cadres in the front must have a say in the struggle. Him and his men attacked Chifombo, which surrendered without a fight. Next they raided the Zanu HQ in Lusaka and captured a couple of generals. There was some shooting, and some were sent to the front to see how the fighters had to live. Then they raided Zanu's Lusaka offices again, but this time Nhari and his men were not so lucky. The Zambian police ambushed them and captured them all.

'Tongogara, commander-in-chief of Zanla, then stormed Chifombo with 100 fighters who had just finished their training. About 50 cadres died in the fight, and afterwards Nhari and several of his supporters were tried and executed.

'Mataure, one of the three Manyikas still on the Dare, was among those shot; another, Mukuno, was suspended. Chitepo, the chairman, was the only Manyika left.

'Now I was in the country politicising the masses while all this was happening. We'd all heard rumours that Nhari was sending the big fish to us, but that was all.

'Then we were in an ambush and lost three men and had to pull back. We reached Chifombo not long after Tongogara. The camp was a wreck, comrades were dying. We couldn't believe what had happened: our own people were destroying themselves.

'Next we were told that Chitepo, our leader, had been assassinated. Us cadres were told his murder had been a Smith/Kaunda plot — Smith because he was trying to weaken the struggle, Kaunda because he wanted a settlement with Smith and Chitepo had refused to sell out. There were plenty other stories around too: some cadres were arguing Chitepo was killed by Smith's men alone, others saw South Africa in the background; a few remembered he had enemies in Zanu. According to one cadre, Tongogara was behind the murder; he said Tongogara believed this Nhari rebellion was a Manyika plot and he thought Chitepo had planned it.'

Biani discussed the stories with a couple of his comrades. Next thing there was this special parade and he was called out.

'Where did you hear these filthy lies about Comrade Tongogara?' this commissar was asking. 'Tell us for the good of the party.'

'I don't spy on my comrades,' Biani told him. 'We were talking, not plotting a coup.'

The commissar repeated his question, and when Biani gave him the same answer, clapped him one across the face. When Biani still wouldn't talk, he was shoved to the ground and kicked and beaten.

A big fish walking past stopped to watch just as the commissar landed a salvo of kicks in Biani's gut.

'Hey — hey — stop,' the big fish cries out. 'Weren't you one of the pupils expelled for leading the food strike at school?'

It was one of Biani's old teachers. They had often talked politics together.

'There must be some mistake,' said the teacher. 'This one can't be a reactionary. I know him. Someone must have confused him.' He turned to Biani. 'Tell us who confused you.'

Biani wasn't saying.

The main ou shook his head and turned away. 'He's badly confused,' he told the commissar, 'but he just needs to be warned.

Warn him, and I'll speak to him afterwards.'

Biani was taken off to the side of the camp and ordered to dig a grave. When it was finished, they made him spit in it. 'This is just to show you what will happen next time,' they said. 'Fill it up.' When he was finished they tied him to a tree and gave him 90 lashes.

He staggered over to his tent and collapsed. All that afternoon he just lay there, not moving, not saying anything. When one of his comrades came to him and said he must go to the medical people for treatment, he refused. 'I told him I was all right,' Biani said. 'I told him treatment was not necessary, and though he did not believe me, he left.

'I lay there paining-paining until late that night when a nurse — her name was Rudiya — sneaked into my tent and told me to get my back fixed. I refused, I told her it was not necessary.'

'The big fish won't like this,' she whispered. 'They think you are fighting them. There have been many bodies here.'

So Biani changed his mind. Rudiya helped him over to the sick quarters where she washed and dressed his back and put him to bed. He lay there for a week while outside the trials and parades and beatings went on.

Altogether about 150 cadres died.

'After that,' he told me, 'I was not happy in Zanu. Even when my old teacher had me promoted to deputy commander I wasn't happy. Zanu was falling apart. The cadres were fighting with the leaders, the leaders were fighting amongst themselves; we were capturing, flogging, killing each other and Smith was just sitting back laughing. I don't know what's what about Chitepo's death, but I still have the scars from the flogging. The axe forgets, never the tree.

'So, when the Zambian troops came with their guns and took away most of the big fish to question them about Chitepo's death and told us cadres that we were no more Zanu, but ANC, I wasn't sorry — I know, I know, like your friend Noah says, that there is not yet a proper unity here in the camp, but we must try to build one. It's our best hope.'

When we climbed down from his hideout he took me to his 'Unity Mountain', this rise near the Kitchen River where the unity mense had this encampment of eight or nine tents. He introduced me to the blokes, and we all went off to supper together, about 30 of them all arguing and squabbling about this rumour that the leaders were going to scrap the talks and send us all to the front. They didn't seem to mind being seen with me — they hardly seemed to notice me in fact — but question time came round soon enough. I told them about my past, and all very friendly and curious they cross-questioned me about my years fighting for Smith. Not one of them gave a sign that they schemed I was a spy.

Back at Unity Mountain we rooked a couple reefs, and three-four of the cadres began arguing about the new Zimbabwe. Me, I was fascinated: those blokes couldn't even agree what they were fighting for, but no one seemed to mind at all.

'This is a revolution of the workers and peasants,' argued Comrade Shungu, this short dark Manyika from the Mount Darwin area. Ya, he was one of the camp greybeards, one of the few old soldiers: he first crossed with the Zipra expeditionary forces way back in '67 and '68.

'Ag, forget all of his fancy stories,' threw in Comrade Hendrix, this skinny Zezuru with a big afro. 'It's simple: the mabhunu stole our country and we want it back.' Hendrix had been a buddy of Biani's since high school. They'd both helped organise the food strike but Hendrix had managed to duck expulsion, and went on to finish his A levels. He'd studied at the University of Rhodesia until the cops found out about his work for Zipra and he had to flee the country.

Comrade Shungu didn't like Hendrix's line at all. 'This settler nonsense is just an accident of history,' he told us, and went on to explain that once the struggle was victorious, we'd better replace the capitalist system with the dictatorship of the proletariat or we would just be replacing white exploiters with black ones.

'And end up broke like Tanzania?' Hendrix scoffed. 'We need industrialism, technology. We must learn these things, beat the West at its own game.'

'Why all this West nonsense?' this Comrade Lovemore broke in. 'When we've chased these mabhunu out why invite others right back in again? Why not make our own thing?' Ya, once Lovemore, a Kalanga primary school teacher who'd fought with Zanla, got started on his African socialism, it was difficult for anyone else to get a word in. Usually he was a really gentle sort of bloke, always willing to help, sharing whatever he had, but when he started on African socialism he overheated fast.

'Technology is not just for Europe,' cuts in Hendrix.

'Marxism neither,' adds Shungu.

'Why bother about trying to go back to the ways of our ancestors?' Hendrix asked. 'We've forgotten what they are, and even if we knew we probably wouldn't want. . . .'

Lovemore, he was so flat he couldn't keep quiet any longer. 'Africa is so sick with this white syphilis that maybe it can never recover,' he broke in, sputtering about Ubuntu, African Humanism, Western Individualism, and how the whites had only been able to invade Africa cos the tribesmen had never before come across people who snatched and grabbed and cheated like they did.

'Why can't we take the best of both?' asked Biani in his voice of reason. 'Why not the best of Africa, the best of Europe?'

'Maybe we will learn the worst,' suggests Comrade Bazooka, this Ndau with a hook nose like an Arab's. He'd been an electrician's assistant in the days before he'd become a Zanu commander. 'We are half learning from the whites,' he argued, 'we are learning to despise Africa and to smoke cigarettes — but not how to make his cars and radios. We are half-and-halfs now, like Muzukuru here — bastards. We are like toads: half for land, half for water, and not belonging to either.'

'This is nonsense,' Shungu told him. 'This stuff, it's just all the normal worries of the transition from feudalism to capitalism.'

'Look what Nyerere achieved,' started Lovemore again. 'And he only went half-way. Real African socialism. . .' and so on and on and on.

Ya, those blokes could talk, I chune you, they could talk until your ears were tired, but I always listened hard in the hope of convincing anyone who might be keeping an eye on me that I was serious about the struggle.

Comrade Shungu, at any rate, was so impressed that he volunteered to teach me African history and, to prove that my heart was in the right place, I gratefully accepted. I don't know whether all this was actually noticed but I did learn quite a lot of history.

'They have hidden our history because they want us to think we are rubbish — they want us to believe only they can rule.' That was his line. He spoke about the black Pharaohs of Egypt — I'd never thought of them as Africans before — and the kingdom of Kush; Carthage and Hannibal's invasions of Italy; Prester John and

Ethiopia; the West African kingdoms like Benin and Ashanti; the port cities of East Africa, Mombasa, Dar-es-Salaam and Sofala; and in Zimbabwe the Shona kingdom of Monomatapa and the Rowzi, who built the great stone city at Zimbabwe and the stone citadels up and down the country.

He told us of the wars with the Portuguese imperialists, the invasions of the first of the Madzwitis, Zwangendaba and his impis, Zulus fleeing their leader Chaka, and how they'd slashed their way through Mashonaland, destroying everything in their path. Then came the second wave of Madzwitis, the Ndebele under Mzilikazi. Running from the Boers and Zulus they crossed the Limpopo from South Africa, and seized southern Mashonaland, making its people their slaves. They raided the Shona tribes to the north and east, stealing the women and cattle, killing the men and burning the fields and huts.

After the Ndebele came the whites — and a long lecture about imperialism. Gold had been discovered in the Transvaal, you check, and the imperialists of Europe were burning with gold fever. There were stories of even larger gold reefs in Matabeleland and Mashonaland, and hundreds of schemers trekked to Matabeleland, and tried to persuade their king, Lobengula, to allow them to look for gold in his land. Among those who sent his men was the arch-imperialist, Rhodes. Though he already owned the diamond mines in Kimberley and the gold-fields of the Transvaal, though he was already prime minister of the Cape Colony, he wanted the mines of Zimbabwe also.

His men persuaded Lobengula to sign a treaty, the Rudd concession, but the whiteys who drew it up wrote one thing and told the king another. Lobengula found out about it, and tore up the treaty, but that didn't stop Rhodes: he sent his Pioneer column in to grab Mashonaland. His men divided the country up into farms, and stole all the cattle they could find. A few tools were taken from them so they massacred a village 'to teach the kaffirs a lesson'. They prospected for gold but didn't find much.

So the whiteys, these protectors of the people, began complaining about marauding Ndebele bands harassing the peace-loving Shona, and marched into Matabeleland to punish the plunderers. Two Ndebele regiments were wiped out in one battle, and Lobengula fled into the interior where he died.

The settlers called the country Rhodesia after their leader, and divided up the loot. They confiscated cattle for their herds, and claimed all the best land for their farms, recruiting the former owners as their labourers. The surplus people were chased off into the 'reserves' — areas with poor soil or tsetse fly that the whites couldn't use. Then came drought and rinderpest and famine, and many people died.

By 1896 the people had had enough. The Ndebele rose against the settlers, and the prophetess Nehanda, speaking with the voice of the spirit Chaminuka, called on the Shona to rise too. Many did and more than 300 settlers — one in every 10 — were wiped out in the fighting. For a while it looked as if these first freedom fighters would liberate the country. Then Rhodes went out, unarmed, and spoke to the leaders of the Ndebele and persuaded them to surrender. The Shona fought on, but they could not stand alone against the guns of the whites and the 'loyal' blacks, and Nehanda and the other leaders were captured and hanged and the first war of liberation ended.

After I'd been with the Unity Mountain mense about a week, Biani mentioned there was space in his tent. Me, I felt like Daniel when he was hauled out of that lion's den. Escaping that Zipra tent and the cadres muttering about my father Smith was like a one-way all expenses paid trip to paradise. I about got down on the ground and kissed Biani's boots, I chune you.

Noah couldn't figure out why I moved in with those unity blokes, why I was dodging him. He found me eating breakfast one morning, and plonked himself down beside me before I had a chance to escape.

'So you're hanging around with these unity loonies now,' he jeers. 'They've been looking for a pet goffel for quite some time now — but you're the only one daft enough to join them.'

'Well,' I reckon — I didn't want to fight with him, I didn't want enemies anywhere — 'they're interesting to talk to.'

'Interesting — that lot?' he scoffs. 'I've spoken to them too. They could bore a bloody thorn tree to death with all their goddam talk. Come on — just why are you hanging around with them? When this unity business collapses you'll have to go crawling back to your Zipra commander and he's not going to be too charmed.'

I didn't answer. Maybe I was doing the wrong thing. Maybe one of these days I'd end up in the shit for not following the straight Zipra line. But eeh, I couldn't go back to that tent full of bored Zipra cadres

who kept cracking these stale sour jokes about me and Smith. For the
moment I'd rather take my chances with the unity.

Chapter 11

*T*hen, one fine morning when we were all assembled on the parade ground for our daily dose of political education, the She-Devil — the commander of the Zanla cadres in the camp — swaggers up onto the platform. Us cadres, we woke up fast, I chune you; that one, she was notorious. Everyone in the camp was shit-scared of her cos, according to all the stories, she was a witch. One story had it that this Zambian guard who'd spotted her riding a hyena had been struck blind, and according to another story she'd been seen cutting flesh from a corpse at the clinic. And if she touched you with the kierie she carried, this long thick stick of shiny black wood, your thing would shrivel up and drop off. Ya, she wasn't the sort of woman you'd want to tangle with.

She stands on the platform, that mammoth backside of hers

bulging out of the jeans, glaring down at us, and when everyone is
quiet, dead quiet, she starts.

'Muzorewa is a whore,' she roars full volume. 'Him and his ANC
rubbish are trying to sell us to the racist colonialist dog Smith. They
want to destroy Zanla — the only fighting army — the only pride of
the poor oppressed masses of Zimbabwe.'

The ANC ouens jeer, the Zanu cadres cheer and she booms on right
through the racket.

'Zanu will be holding its own political classes in future,' she
announces, 'and all clear-thinking cadres can come.'

An ANC cadre tries to clamber onto the platform to get at her but a
couple Zanu cadres grab hold of him and drag him back to earth with
a thump, and next thing ANC and Zanu cadres are knocking the hell
out of each other.

The Zambian officer, who's supposed to be watching over us, is
leaning against a tree 50 yards away chatting up this Zanu chickie.
When he finally registers that he's got a riot on his hands, he ttoot-
ttoots on his whistle and his troops, who are stretched out in the shade
playing cards, jump to their feet and grab for their gats.

'Back to your tents,' the officer screams at us. 'Back to your tents
— or we'll shoot!'

And, when the cadres saw the troops coming, guns at the ready,
they took one last swipe at their enemies and withdrew muttering.

As the Zambian soldiers patrolled up and down, up and down, us
cadres up on our Unity Mountain rolled ourselves a few reefs and
tried to make sense of the latest developments.

'Got a point, this She-Devil,' blasts off this Comrade Bazooka, ex-
Zanla himself, as he takes a hit. 'This ANC nonsense — all this leader
talk — it gets us nowhere.'

'The talk is a waste of time,' ou Biani interrupts, 'but the unity isn't.
We can't destroy the unity just because we don't like the leaders.' Ya,
there were some things that Biani felt should be beyond all argument.

Us ouens all schemed that the Zambians would put a stop to this
rebellion but quick. Kaunda, the Zambian president, was all for
unity, you check, cos like the leaders of the other Frontline states, he
believed it would scare Smith into a settlement. And Zambia badly
needed a settlement: the country had helped the struggle a great deal
— providing camps and supplies, closing its border with Rhodesia —

but the help had not come cheap, and its economy was in such a mess that there was open talk of a coup.

But the days passed and nothing happened. The Zambian commandant didn't even protest against Zanu's move, and in fact he allowed Zanu cadres to build their own logistics and kitchen, and to take their tents and pitch them in a Zanu-only section down by the Rat River, which then became the Zanu River.

The ANC commanders wrote to their HQ in Lusaka to complain. No reply. Either the letters weren't getting through or else HQ had other things to worry about. Ya, I chune you the main mannes were worried. Was this part of some new political development? Were Kaunda and Zapu fighting? Was the Zambian army about to coup him? In our camp the Zambian commandant and his officers were becoming all very buddy-buddy with the Zanu commanders. They all had Zanu girlfriends — the women in the camp were all Zanu — and they were always taking stew and sadza and stuff from the Zanu kitchen.

In the camp the Zanu cadres were allowed to do whatever they wanted — take the business with the trucks for example. The Zanu cadres, you check, had brought two big green Bedford trucks with them to the Unity Camp. When Zanu joined the ANC, the trucks became ANC also. Quite fine — but when the Zanu cadres at the camp withdrew from the unity, they took the trucks with them.

The ANC complained to the camp commandant who promised yes, yes he would look into the matter immediately. Whether he did or not, I don't know, but one thing is for sure: those trucks stayed parked down by the Zanu logistics.

The ANC continued to complain, but there were soon other things to complain about and the trucks were forgotten.

Then one of the Zambian trucks broke down, and a Zambian officer borrowed the other to visit his sweetheart in Lusaka.

The only transport left in camp were the two Bedfords, and when the week's rations had to be fetched from Kabwe, the camp commandant asked both Zanu and the ANC for permission to use them. After two days of talks an agreement was reached: it was either that or starve.

In terms of the agreement the drivers would be Zanu cos the trucks were in Zanu hands, but the ANC would be allowed to send along an observer. The food would be split up as it normally was: three-fifths to the ANC and two-fifths to Zanu.

Which sounded fine but, when the trucks rocked up back in the camp, the Zanu drivers headed straight for their kitchen where they offloaded all the meat and vegetables and most of the mealiemeal and beans. When the observers tried to object they were beaten up.

Us ANC ouens, we were mal, I chune you. Shouting and jeering we surrounded the commandant's office. He called in his troops but not even the sight of their guns could silence us.

To cool us down the bloke eventually invited our leaders in for talks. Half-an-hour later they all came out smiling. The camp commandant told us there had been a mistake, a big mistake and he would personally see to it that Zanu returned our share of the rations.

To cool us down, he announced that the Zambian army kitchen would issue us a dozen bags of mealiemeal, six sacks of sugar and a box of yeast so we could brew ourselves some beer. Well, once we heard 'beer' we're all very happy, I chune you, very, very happy, and every last one of us cheered that camp commandant as if he'd just announced Zimbabwe had been liberated. We set to work with a will there, scrubbing out these rusty old oil drums and arguing about recipes. Within hours I chune you, we'd built this lekker mix, and set it simmering.

Us ouens, we were as excited as schoolboys who've been given a half-holiday: hell, most of us hadn't touched a dop since they'd joined the struggle. Not a drop of alcohol had passed my lips for a good eight-nine months. Whatever the rest of me thought about the struggle, my liver must've schemed it'd already arrived in paradise.

Come the evening when the brew is ready, I down just one sluk of the muck — and pass right out. My comrades carried me back to our tent and went right on celebrating. Ya, some of those livers were pretty fit, practice or no practice, and the ouens lasted right through until dawn when the beer finally gave out. A dozen of them who were still looking for action broke into logistics, tied up the guard, and scaled two tins of white paint and all the brushes they could find. Carrying their booty they sneaked down to the Zanu tents and proceeded to paint ANC, ANC in large, medium and small letters all over the trucks.

They were still painting their ANCs about an hour later when the first Zanu toi-toi squad jogs past. By that time the trucks looked as if they had come down with a bad case of the ANC rash: every last space on the surface of those things — the cabin, the wheels, the entire body, even the windows — was covered. The Zanu cadres were not impressed.

Then some idiot up on the cabin of one of the trucks — he'd painted ANC all over himself cos there wasn't any other space available — informed them that the ANC had taken back its property. This impressed them even less. According to the ANC cadres a Zanu cadre then insulted their mothers. Whatever, one of them flung what was left of a pot of paint at the Zanu cadres who then grabbed up sticks and stones and stormed over to lodge their objections onto the nearest ANC skull.

The racket roused the Zanu cadres sleeping nearby. They came over to check things out. They saw and were appalled. Dozens of them picked up sticks and stones and charged into the battle.

A couple ANC cadres who were waiting for breakfast drifted over to find out what all the noise was about. When they spotted their comrades, outnumbered maybe ten-to-one, being beaten up by Zanu, some sprinted back to the tents for reinforcements and some began throwing stones.

The first barrage shatters the windscreen of one of the trucks and eeeh, those Zanu cadres, they're as angry as a lion which has just had its kill stolen. Grabbing up tent poles and rocks and knives, this horde charges at the ANC cadres. The stone throwers, they turn and run and don't stop running until they run right into the ANC reinforcements, about 200 of them, streaming up from the tents. One moment there's a bit of a brawl, the next there's a fullscale battle: about 500 cadres are milling around screaming their slogans and laying into each other.

The row awakened me, hungover as I was, lying in our tent up on the Unity Mountain. My head felt as if it'd been dribbled down to hell by a clumsy elephant. 'Water,' I croaked and shut my eyes and hoped for death. Or better, for some kind person to fetch the water jug for me. No answer. All the rest of the ouens had already rushed off. I'd have to organise the water myself.

The fighting awakened the Zambians in their barracks too, and a unit, shirt tails flapping and trousers slipping, charges over to restore order. 'Stop,' pants this officer, his belly bulging out between his underpants and his vest. 'Stop all this fighting.' And, after all that shouting, the bloke catches such a bad stitch in his side that he had to sit down then and there and wait for it to pass.

But when the troops reached the battleground, they weren't so sure what to do. 'Move,' one of the troops shouted at this milling mass. 'Move — or we'll shoot.' But everyone was too busy kicking, punching, pounding, thumping, biting and jabbing to notice. The Zambian screamed again, but the battle continued. Finally one of the sergeants fired off a couple of shots into the air.

Shots! Me, I jumped right out of bed, water or no water, pulled on my trousers, grabbed under my bed for my boots — nothing? Eeh, I chune you, my gut felt as empty as yesterday's beer bottle. Gats or no gats, I couldn't just disappear off into the bush without my boots — my feet would be shredded.

After the shots, most of the comrades cooled off but quick. The battling stopped, the two sides parted and the Zambians moved between them, their rifles cocked. The officer picks himself up off the parade ground and trots over, wheezing 'get moving, get moving' at the top of his voice. Order had more or less been restored.

It's then that the She-Devil swaggers up. When she sees the trucks, ANC ANC all over them and the windscreen of the one smashed, she lets out a roar like a bull buffalo which has just discovered that some creature has run off with his balls.

Everyone stops dead. Me, I stop scrabbling around for my shoes. This is it, I'm scheming, someone's shot — time to get moving. I dive out of the tent — and there, out of the corner of my eye I check tied to the tent pole — my shoes. The comrades who'd carried me home after I'd passed out had done it as a joke.

'What have they done to our trucks?' the She-Devil booms out, and her shout echoes all round the camp. 'Are we going to allow these mangy dogs to get away with this? Let's show these Madzwitis.' And with that she turns and, waving her kierie, she marches straight at the line of Zambians. 'Stop or I'll shoot,' this soldier yells, but she heads straight at him like a truck rolling downhill without any brakes. 'My muti turns bullets to water,' she shouts, 'and when I touch you with this kierie....'

The soldier, he doesn't stick around to hear any more. Mobs and riots are one thing, but a witch who rides a hyena at night and cuts chunks out of corpses is another. He turns and gaps it, and all the rest of the Zambians scatter like birds when a hawk flies overhead.

The ANC cadres watch open-mouthed as the Zambians run. That

She-Devil eeh, she had to be a witch to chase off men with guns. How could you stop her?

And, once the Zambians had gone, she checks us out with a naked eye. 'Let's finish the ANC,' she bawls. 'Forward with the struggle.' And, without a glance behind her she starts off towards this mass of 3-400 cadres, waving that kierie of hers like it's a wand. Not that her Zanu cadres need any second invitation, I chune you. Snatching up sticks and stones they charge straight for the ANC. Me, I just picked up those boots and, with one in each hand, I'm off and running.

I didn't stop to put those boots on until I'd leapt across our Kitchen River and topped the ridge on the far side. There I perched panting with the rest of the ANC cadres as the Zanu forces lined up on the banks of the Kitchen River and taunted us, shouting that we were cowards and sellouts and weaklings.

After an hour the ANC commanders called all the cadres together and told us the situation. They'd sent a note to the camp commandant who'd written back saying he was sorry about the incident but there was nothing he could do as the Zanla troops would not obey his orders.

'I don't have the forces to fight Zanu,' he said in his letter, 'but we are expecting reinforcements from Lusaka in about two weeks' time.'

Two weeks! Us ouens were horrified. Were we supposed to live in the bush for two weeks waiting for the goddam Zambians to get themselves organised? And, hell, if the Zambians said two weeks you knew it was more likely to be two months anyway. Ya, to us cadres the whole situation began to smell like a Zanu/Zambian plot: why else had the camp commandant given us the stuff to make beer — and why else hadn't Zanu complained that they hadn't been given beer too?

'So,' our commander sums up. 'If we want anything to eat, any place to sleep during the next couple of weeks, we're going to have to take it ourselves.'

The cadres cheered him loud and long. 'Forward with the struggle,' they were shouting. 'Down with Zanu.' Hangovers, bruises — alles — were forgotten. The ouens were red-hot keen for a fight.

Armed with rocks and sticks we marched down to the Kitchen River. The Zanu guards soon spotted us, and the rest of the Zanu force was summoned. Within minutes they were lined up three or four deep all along the opposite bank of the river, shouting their slogans and taunting us· for being 'sellouts' and 'Smith's stooges'. We were ordered to stop, to form ourselves up into ranks of three deep, and when our commander roared 'forward' we began our advance. But eeh, long before we reached the river, Zanu began bombarding us with such a burst of stones and spears (tent poles with a nail hammered through them) that our line slowed — stopped — and us cadres were forced to withdraw.

We anchored just out of range, anchored there as our commanders conferred and Zanu jeered. After about half-an-hour the main mannes selected this squad of about 100 cadres to sprint about half-a-kilometre up along the river and force a crossing so's to divert as many Zanu men as possible from the main body of our troops. Another squad, made up of 20 solid, unsuperstitious sorts, was instructed to wait for the She-Devil and, the moment she came within range, to let fly at her with every last rock, spear and kierie they could lay their hands on.

The rest of us — there must've been more than 1 000 of us all told — lined up again as the commanders withdrew to this large rock from which they could comfortably watch operations. Up on one of the neighbouring hills we could check the Zambians, armed with beer and goat stew, taking up positions in the shade of this clump of wild oranges. Later we heard there was plenty betting that morning and most of the money was on Zanu.

The main ANC commander climbs up onto this outcrop, waves his kierie like one of those conductor characters you see on TV, and it all starts happening: the first squad dashes up the river and about half the Zanu army takes off after them, waving their spears and screaming bloody murder. 'Forward,' our commander bellows and the rest of us, all 1 000 cadres answer 'Forward with the struggle', and as the echo of the shout booms off among the koppies of the escarpment, our troops begin their second charge.

All up and down the banks of the stream there was this great shout of slogans and the thwack of stick on flesh as the two lines met. Zanu fought fiercely, lashing and jabbing and shoving, and about the whole of our front rank was knocked, cursing and splashing into the stream. But eeh, so many of us were milling about on the bank that when one went down, two would be pushed forward to take his place. There were just too many of us. Within minutes we'd ripped huge holes in the Zanu lines and our forces were pouring across.

Me, I suddenly found myself across, behind this Zanu cadre who was keeping off two ANC ouens with some fancy stickwork. I belt the bloke a shot across the back of the knee. He yelps with pain, jumps round to deal with me — and the other two blokes bash him across the skull. Down he goes, groaning and bleeding, and all around us there's the crack of sticks and the cries of the fighters. Right beside me seven ANC cadres had surrounded four Zanu cadres. I join in, poking here, feinting there as they swipe out at us. Ya, all up and down the river, the Zanu forces are in serious trouble.

This club is swinging down at me, I jump back out of the arc of the blow and, as I start forward again, 'Forward with Zanu' booms out over the battlefield as if someone's shouting down a microphone. There's no mistaking the voice: the She-Devil, the She-Devil's coming! Us ANC cadres, we all check behind us to make sure our retreat is clear, and the Zanu cadres — it's as if this is the sign they've been waiting for — hurl themselves on us like a pack of mad dogs. Us ouens withdraw back and back, down towards the stream. Then eeh, the She-Devil tops the bank, flanked by her harem, half-a-dozen women almost as large as she is. This is it, I'm scheming, we're finished.

But, as I'm edging back towards the stream, the stoning squad spots her. The cadres rush to the river, blast her with a rain of rocks. She starts yelling something about muti, maybe that she's got muti against these things, and this rock the size of a cup smacks her on the forehead, and she drops like she's been shot.

This great groan goes up from the Zanu cadres. They knew then that they were finished; without her we were just too many. Even as the She-Devil's women run forward to drag back their champion, the Zanu line disintegrates and suddenly the whole Zanu force is gapping it and us ouens are charging, whooping and yelling, after them. The camp is ours.

Us ouens split up into groups to patrol for stray Zanu cadres. Some we chased into the bush, some we cornered, beat up, and threw into one of the camp's boundary rivers. Some were still fighting, and there were several skirmishes.

As we followed the Zanu River, some blokes ambushed us from the reeds. They threw rocks, we rocked them back. We're closing in, closing in when — paaa — this rock flies straight into my left cheek. My mouth is thick with blood, and when I try to spit, my tongue pricks itself on splintered teeth.

Jisis Kiernan, I remember thinking as I staggered off holding my jaw. You've been fighting for how long? You've had rounds smacking into the dirt beside you, you've had mines going off behind you — and you walk out of it all with a few scratches. Then out here in this bloody bush battle....

But, as we saw soon enough, those rocks and kieries and spears weren't children's weapons. Three cadres were killed in the fighting, and nine were hurt so bad that they had to be taken to hospital. Another 200 were treated by the clinic and nearly everyone collected a couple cuts and bruises.

Amongst us Unity Mountain crew there were quite a few casualties. Hendrix, he was the worst: his right kneecap had been smashed by a rock and eventually he had to be taken to Lusaka for an operation. Cos the doctors said he couldn't run anymore he was finished as a fighter, and he joined the camp's administration staff.

Comrade Shungu had the head of a spear stuck in the fat of his backside, Biani had a long deep gash at the back of his head and eeh, my jaw was paining me something shocking. Comrade Lovemore, who'd learnt a little about roots and bark and stuff from his herbalist uncle, made a fire and warmed this pot of water on it. He added a few roots and bulbs and herbs, stirred it once or twice and, when he judged the muti was ready, tore up an old shirt and began his rounds, cleaning and bandaging. He made me wash my mouth out with this concoction — which burnt so much that it was only afterwards I found out how bad it tasted — and then gave me this shrivelled-up stump of root to chew. It looked more like poison than medicine but eeh, the sockets of my teeth were throbbing like a drum and so I wasn't shy to take my chances. I did what he said, tucking the root between my cheek and my good teeth, ignored the weird taste, and gradually the pain eased.

It was only after everyone had been patched up that we realised we were a couple comrades short: not one of us knew where Bazooka and his buddies were. Biani went over to the clinic to ask if they were among the dead or the badly wounded. When he returned he was quiet. 'Not there,' he told us. Then he said his head was paining, and he crawled into our tent and lay down with his face to the canvas for the rest of the day. Ya, we all guessed what had happened: Bazooka and his buddies had crossed back to Zanu. In the face of the fighting we couldn't even hold together a unity group as small as ours.

Next morning the Zanu cadres tried to retake the camp but their spirit had gone from them and we beat them back easily. Afterwards the Zambian camp commandant rocked up and informed us the Zanu cadres had to be allowed back. Our commanders eeh, they were flat I chune you. No chance, they told the commandant, those baboons must live out in the bush until they've learnt to behave, and asked why the Zambians hadn't helped when Zanu chased us out of the camp? Was the camp commandant favouring Zanu when Kaunda and Zambia were for the unity?

The camp commandant, he wasn't exactly charmed. He accused our commanders of talking 'irresponsible nonsense' and threatened us with his troops. 'My men are scared of this She-Devil,' he finishes, 'but they aren't scared of you. You they can shoot without even thinking about it.'

Eventually, after much muttering, our commanders reckoned okay, could we at least have an hour to explain this to our people? The commandant agreed and, when he went to the Zanu cadres to tell them what's what, the ANC main mannes broke into one of the Bedfords. Before the Zambians realised what was happening, they'd roared out of the camp. The truck reached Lusaka the next morning, and that afternoon the commandant was relieved of his duties.

Two days later the new commandant arrived. He was one of those blokes who want to show you right from the beginning that they don't stand for any nonsense. First thing he ordered the Zambian troops to collect every last kierie and spear in the place, and he had them all burned in this huge bonfire beside the parade ground. Afterwards he assembled everyone — Zanu, ANC, the lot — and informed us that anyone caught fighting would be flogged 50, no argument, anyone caught with a weapon would be sent back to Smith. He gave permission for Zanu to leave the unity and pitch their tents down by the Zanu River, but told them that the camp's logistics, clinic and kitchen were all now under the ANC control. 'This is a unity camp,' he reminded them, 'not a Zanu base. This is OAU and Zambian policy and that is how things here will be run.'

The ANC cadres cheered, the Zanu cadres sulked, and for the first few days everything was more or less quiet. Even so, right from the start it was obvious that this new arrangement wouldn't last long. What with only one kitchen, one logistics and one clinic, the ANC and Zanu cadres met every day, and there were often fights. Some blokes were flogged, some were let off, and if you had something for the soldiers who arrested you maybe nothing would ever be reported.

There were always problems at the kitchen. Once it came under ANC control, us ouens were all right as far as graze was concerned. Every morning for breakfast us cadres would be given a mug of tea, a large lump of sadza and a little relish or sugar. For lunch and supper you could have as much sadza and beans as you wanted, and at least once a week there'd be chicken or fish or beef. We weren't exactly eating gourmet but then we weren't exactly starving either.

I don't know what Zanu was being fed, they sent a squad of women to fetch their food and carry it to their tents, but whatever it was they were always running to the commandant to complain.

'The ANC feeds us worse than dogs.'

'They are trying to kill us with starvation.'

'When the ANC is finished with the meat, they throw us the bones.'

But the commandant wasn't sympathetic. He reminded them that they were in a unity camp and that the OAU was supplying food to the ANC, not rebel groups. They were lucky, he told them, to be getting any food at all.

The political situation didn't exactly contribute to peace and quiet either. Towards the end of August 1974, the BBC announced that an agreement — the Pretoria Agreement — had been signed by the South Africans and the Zambians: in their wisdom they had decided it was time for Smith and the guerilla leaders to begin negotiating again. Not that either Smith or the ANC leaders were particularly enthusiastic: Smith felt the talks wouldn't last longer than half-an-hour, and Muzorewa reckoned if that's his attitude, why bother with them anyway?

A good question, a very good question indeed, said the cadres. Why carry on talking, why give Smith more time to organise his defences and buy guns and mercenaries? Why bother to resume these talks at all?

'Let's try fighting.' someone wrote on the wall of the clinic one night, and 'We need new leaders' was scrawled across logistics.

Me, I must've been the only bloke in the camp in favour of talks: hell, as far as I was concerned any settlement was better than none. I just wanted to go home.

The commissars called us all together and explained that Zambia and the OAU would only help us if our leaders tried to negotiate.

From the back some bloke shouted the old slogan that power came through the barrel of a gun. There's a roar of approval from the crowd.

'We can fight if Smith won't settle now,' the commissars told us, but they didn't sound too convinced themselves.

Ya, when the crowd filed off the parade ground that night, they were anti: anti-talks, anti-settlements, anti-leaders. For months they had been sitting round, sitting round, waiting for something to happen and being told next week, next month, maybe tomorrow. Now they were bored and frustrated and angry, and it looked as if they would be waiting around for a long time yet.

'If only there was something to do in this blasted place,' Lovemore moans afterwards as we were sitting round skyfing it up outside our tents. 'If only there were some consolations. Back home you could always find yourself a woman and a drink....'

'Well,' reckons ou Hendrix, 'if you want a woman, we will have to kidnap one of those large Zanu ladies. But we can brew some booze without too many problems.'

Well, everyone wants to know more and ou Hendrix explains that since he's been working in logistics he's discovered this way to sneak into the storeroom.

'If we break in late at night, we'll be able to lay our hands on pineapples — there are thousands of them — and no one will ever notice,' he tells us. 'We can do the brewing in some of these old tin cans that are lying round all over the place.'

'How are we going to hide the stuff?' Comrade Lovemore objects. 'We'll get caught.'

But ou Hendrix, he had all the answers. 'Those caves up on the escarpment,' he tells us, 'that place where Biani goes to smoke his stop sometimes. No one could ever find it there — and, even if they did, how would they ever know that it was ours?'

Biani, he wasn't entirely sure about this business. 'This sounds like stealing from the cadres,' he says.

Ou Hendrix tells him not to worry. 'They've got thousands of pineapples there,' he chunes us, 'a whole truckload. Half of them will go rotten.'

Shungu, he's a practical bloke. 'Are you sure you can brew pineapples?' he wants to know.

But ou Hendrix, he reckons he knows all about it. 'I trained at this camp in Tanzania,' he tells us. 'We had good relations with the peasants and they showed us how to make their kangara. It's just pineapples and water and yeast. It doesn't always taste so good but it's potent, strong like an elephant I'm telling you....'

That night we went to work. Using ou Hendrix's key, we opened up the gate and tiptoed in past the sleeping guard through to the storerooms. Hell, we could've stolen every last thing in that place if we'd wanted, that bloke was sleeping so sound.

But all we took — except for a couple packets biscuits and a few cartons of smokes — was a sackful of pineapples and yeast which we carried up to Biani's cave. At first light we began our brewing.

Our first batch was ready on the night of this huge ANC singsong. Some main mannes had been sent up from Lusaka to tell us not to worry, everything will be sorted out soon, Comrade Muzorewa knows just what he's doing. And eeh, while all the rest of the cadres were slouching towards the parade ground to dry out their throats in honour of the mighty Muzorewa, us ouens were wetting ours with the mighty river of kangara

Like ou Hendrix said, though the stuff tasted like some putrid muti concocted by a nyanga trying to drive the devil out of a hyena, luckily it was pretty potent so you didn't have to swallow too much of it. Just one cup and you're staggering like you've been hit on the head, two and you're on the floor crawling. Me, I downed about three glasses of the stuff.

That night, I chune you, I collapsed into bed like I'd been shot through the head with a mortar. I roll over, make myself comfortable, and — gaa — I jump out of bed, check and eeeeh, there's this big black scorpion waggling its tail in the air. Me, I knock the thing off the bed with my boot and slam it a couple times until it's flattened into the floor.

'Don't make such a racket,' shushes Lovemore. 'The guards'll hear, they might smell the booze and come and investigate.'

'This bastard thing — it stung me,' I explain, picking the scorpion up with a piece of twig.

Lovemore lifts up our scrap of candle to take a closer look. 'O sweet Jesus,' he cries when he checks the scorpion, 'that thing is as good as a cobra — you are going to die.'

And, then I notice that my back is paining-paining, and my mouth is dry — just like when you're bitten by a snake. This is it, I'm scheming, what a place to peg out.

'What's all this about dying?' asks ou Hendrix, who has this idiot grass grin spread all over his face. He lurches over and carefully checks the thing out. 'You only see these on the escarpment,' he chunes us. 'Maybe someone carried it into the camp on a bundle of firewood for the kitchen.'

'A bundle of firewood,' Lovemore shouts, very indignant. 'Your comrade is dying and all you can care about is firewood.'

'First,' yells Hendrix, 'we must establish what's happening.'

'In a case like this. . .' Comrade Lovemore bursts in but before he can get any further ou Biani shoves his head in through the flaps.

'Take him to the nurses,' he says, and with him propping up one arm and Hendrix the other, and half-a-dozen sympathetic cadres trailing along behind, arguing about how long the poison would take to kill me, they drag me to the clinic. It's closed, of course, but the ouens set up such a hammering on the door that the night nurse wakes up.

'What's it now?' she shouts through the door. 'Another one with too much to drink?'

'Our comrade has been stung by a scorpion,' ou Lovemore shouts. 'He's going to die.'

'We'll have a look,' the nurse shouts back. She didn't sound very enthusiastic. 'Bring him in.'

She opens the doors and the ouens half-drag, half-carry me inside. I go sort of slack, the ouens grab hold of me and it's like I'm hovering there in the room, right up near the ceiling, and all of this is happening to someone else.

'Do you know what the scorpion looked like?' asked the nurse. 'What colour was it?'

'It was a scorpion,' breaks in ou Lovemore, very angry now. 'Do you think we do not know what a scorpion is?'

Any moment, I'm scheming, I'm just going to slip loose and float up through the roof.

'It's one of the big black ones,' puts in ou Hendrix, 'the kind you see up on the escarpment. Maybe it was carried into the camp in a bundle of firewood. . . .'

'Firewood! Scorpions!' yells ou Lovemore. 'How can you worry about these things when our comrade is dying!'

The nurse, she begins to laugh. This is sort of strange, I'm scheming, people — or at any rate nurses — don't usually laugh at you when you're dying. What's this woman's case? I open one eye.

'You should have all just stayed in bed,' she tells us. 'This big black one — it's nothing. It gives you a sting like a bee. The small yellow one, it can kill you.'

I stood up shakily, and muttered my thanks. The nurse gave me a Disprin for the headache, and told me to sleep it off. Eeh, I chune you, us ouens were feeling so skaam about that scorpion that we gapped it out of there as fast as we could. All of us except for ou Biani that is: he said he had a pain, and would stay behind for a minute.

'Ya, I know all about his kind of pain,' reckoned ou Hendrix as we're trudging home — 'it's his balls that are bothering him.'

Ya, that was our first glimpse of Nurse Rudiya. And next morning, after Biani rocks up back just as the birds begin to sing, I found out a great deal more about her. Though Biani had been up all night he was in no mood for sleep. He just about drags me out of bed and off we go trapping up the escarpment towards his cave. 'That nurse last night — she's the one who saved my life after the flogging,' he tells me the moment we're out of the camp. I nodded, opened my mouth to speak, but ou Biani was whirling on again. 'We were discussing the struggle last night and she is also strong for the unity. . . .' Me, I was wondering what kind of unity exactly when Biani takes hold of my shoulder. 'What do you think of her?' he wants to know.

Well, hell I'd been too busy dying to notice her overmuch. 'She's got her head screwed on right,' I told him, 'and she's a looker.' What else do you say? He was only interested in talking about her. When your buddy gets wrapped up with a chick you always lose out; all's you can do is make the best of it.

'She talks sense,' ou Biani agrees. 'There's no nonsense with her.' And, when I got to know the lady I found that he summed her up pretty accurately. She was a tough lady that one, she didn't take bull-shit from anyone.

As we're trapping back to the camp, ou Biani he reminds me we must all be cautious-cautious about this story. 'You're the only comrade I've told,' he informs me, 'and you mustn't let anyone else know. Not even the comrades in our tent.' Rudiya was with Zanla, you check, and Zanla did not approve of its female cadres meeting men from the other parties. Biani couldn't risk letting them know.

On the morning of August 25, 1975, Smith and the leaders of the ANC met in this railway carriage on the middle of the Victoria Falls bridge. Though Vorster was there from South Africa and Kaunda from Zambia, they weren't able to reach any kind of agreement. When the cadres heard the news there was cheering throughout the camp — from Zanu, ANC, the lot. Us ouens, up on our Unity Mountain, roared along with the rest. 'Now the Frontline states must let us fight,' ou Biani reckoned, jubilant. 'Smith has shown he's not serious about these talks.'

And, for once, there wasn't a single cadre arguing with him. I joined in the shouting and cheering too, making damn sure that I kicked up as much of a racket as everyone else but eeeh, I felt then as I feel now: the failure of the talks was a disaster.

If Smith had accepted the settlement, the fighting would've stopped at once, and majority rule would have come in three to five years — a reasonable length of time as far as I was concerned.

By then, you check, I supported some of the unity blokes' ideas about how the country should be run— no more race rules, and decent education, housing, food and medical care for everyone — and I felt that with a little practice and some help from the honkies, the guerillas would set up a pretty good government.

But now, with the failure of the talks, there would be war again — at God alone knew what kind of appalling cost — and it would be years before I found myself back in Burg with Naomi again.

Even now, looking back, I scheme Smith should've settled then. His Rhodesia, which he once said would remain white-ruled for 1 000 years, was liberated just five years later, and by then more than 30 000 people had died, and huge areas of the country had been devastated. There was no need for it to have happened.

Within hours of the failure of the talks the camp was rife with rumours: tomorrow we'll be off to the Botswana border; a group of

Zipra and Zanla cadres will denounce the leaders and start a new army; the Zanla cadres are plotting to escape to Mozambique.

But all that happened was that Sithole, who was still officially head of Zanu, tried to hijack the ANC. In a speech in Lusaka he announced the formation of his Zimbabwe Liberation Council and his Zimbabwean Liberation Army. He appointed himself chairman of both of these organisations, and he packed them both with his buddies: Frolizi cadres, cadres who'd fled Zanla after the Nhari rebellion— all the scraps and strays of the struggle. Oh — and he did add a couple ex-Zapu cadres to his list to make this new unity look genuine, but they wouldn't have anything to do with him.

In the camp the ex-Zapu cadres were angry. 'How can Sithole suddenly tell us this and this and this is the case?' they were asking. 'How can he suddenly call himself our leader when there haven't been any elections?' Quite a few were arguing against the unity. 'Why do we have to put up with this nonsense?' they said. 'Why can't we just get on with the struggle?'

Not even the Zanu cadres were pleased with Sithole's new army. They weren't keen on the men Sithole had selected for his committee — there were too many counter-revolutionary Nhari supporters, too many cadres from other parties for their liking. They also wanted to know why Sithole hadn't chosen Tongogara, the head of Zanla and spokesman for the fighters, and they were very keen to find out what happened to the escudos and Rhodesian dollars that Sithole had promised to change for them a couple months back.

The ANC cadres turned to Muzorewa for advice; after all he was still the head of the party. He said all this fuss was just 'a storm in a teacup' and flew off to America on a fund-raising trip.

Nkomo wasn't so forgiving. He described Muzorewa as 'weak' and 'spineless' and denounced Sithole as 'power-mad', a 'runaway too cowardly to return to Rhodesia and face its realities!' (Smith had said he would be arrested as soon as he returned.) The time had come for the new leaders to be democratically elected, Nkomo said, and he began organising elections for the head of the Internal ANC, which he knew he would win as he controlled more party branches than all the other leaders combined.

In the unity camp squads of ex-Zapu cadres beat up members of the ANC, and the Zambians were called out to calm everyone down. The camp commandant ordered us all confined to our tents and summoned the commanders.

The ANC cadres, they were trapped. Their party's tents were all mixed up with Zapu's, and they were outnumbered maybe seven-to-one. The ANC commanders asked for another place to pitch their party's tents, the camp commander agreed and that afternoon, with silent rows of Zambian troops and ex-Zapu cadres looking on, all the members of the ANC struck their tents, and carried them across the parade ground and pitched them on this rise near the Entrance stream which we afterwards called the ANC River.

As it turned out the ANC moved just in time. A day or two later Muzorewa announced that Nkomo had been expelled from the ANC and eeeh, those Zapu cadres they were flat. 'Nearly a year we wait for them to get organised — and then this happens?' they were saying. 'Those ANC dogs, they must be in Smith's pay.' If it hadn't been for the Zambian troops and their guns, they would've attacked the ANC cadres and driven them into the bush.

'I'm leaving, this is enough,' Comrade Shungu announces the next morning as we sat round rolling a reef up on our mountain in the middle of no-man's land. All of us ouens tried arguing with him, repeating the arguments which he knew off by heart anyway.

'I agree with you, comrades,' he kept saying, 'but unity just won't work,' and he went on to explain that if you looked at the problem historically, you would see there was never a unity among the progressive forces in any struggle because the contradictions within the society were reflected among them too. 'It's always been like that,' he finished, 'in Russia, China, here. We must just forget about this unity business now, and get on with the struggle.'

'What about the Zhii riots?' ou Biani almost shouted. 'What about Angola? Is that the kind of thing we want to see after liberation? Without unity we'll tear ourselves apart like a baboon that's been shot in the gut.' Ya, for a moment there I thought Biani would belt the bloke.

We argued and argued until we all finally realised that there was no point in arguing any longer. Shungu and the ex-Zapu cadres had made up their minds. They took their share of our stuff — tents, kieries, traps, stills, stop and alles — and climbed down from Unity Mountain to rejoin their party.

'I'll help you when you need to join the party,' Shungu called back to us and in fact, when the time came, he did.

When they'd gone, there were only two tents left up on our Unity Mountain, and only five cadres — me, Biani, Lovemore, Hendrix and this crazy bloke called Cooks.

Me, I couldn't see much point in sticking around, and I don't think some of the others could either.

'So, what do we do now?' ou Hendrix asks. 'The ANC at least says it is pro-unity but....'

'No,' says Biani, and you can see that he isn't going to listen to any discussion. 'No. All the parties are anti-unity now. We must hope that something else will happen. Maybe the Frontline states will force the leaders to come together again....' But not even he sounded too hopeful.

Ya, in those days everything was party-party. Two, three times a day there were fights, even though the commandant did what he could to keep the peace, confining the members of each party to their tents, flogging all offenders and doubling the number of patrols. But it didn't help much; by then it would've taken considerably more than a couple platoons of Zambian soldiers to keep the camp under control anyway.

It all finally blew up one morning. Me and Biani were helping Hendrix sort through some boxes and things at logistics when there's this screaming over at the kitchen. We look at each other — this is it, we're all scheming — drop what we're doing and race over to see what's what. We push our way through to the front of the cadres crowding into the kitchen courtyard and there in the dust under one of the giant fig trees, half-a-dozen Zanu women are rolling around, moaning and shrieking. 'The doctor,' someone is yelling, 'go fetch the doctor.'

'What's happening?' everyone's asking. 'What's happened?'

'Oooo — oooo,' the ladies are shrieking, 'the ANC is killing us.'

'They came to pick up their rations,' this bloke behind me explains at the top of his voice. 'I was here — I saw the whole thing. They sampled a couple mouthfuls, picked up the pots — and next thing they're on the ground yelling.'

'Ooo — oooo,' the ladies screech. One falls over onto her back, grabbing at her stomach with both hands. Foam drools out the sides of her mouth, bits of dirt and sadza are plastered to her face, and her eyes are staring wide like she's seen the devil. 'Poison,' she yells, 'poison in the sadza. The ANC is killing us!'

Major Ndweo, the Zambian doctor, and four-five nurses — Rudiya was with them — rush to the women. Every time he tries to examine one of them, she starts flipping about and screaming.

That's when I check the She-Devil shoving through the crowd, a horde of Zanu cadres behind her. 'They're trying to murder us,' she booms out. 'First they try to starve us — and when that doesn't work they try to poison us.'

'No one knows what's the problem with these women,' Major Ndweo shouts. 'We've got to get them to the clinic to find out.' He grabs the collar of the blouse of the nearest lady, and begins dragging her down towards the clinic.

'Leave our women alone,' roars the She-Devil as she pushes her way right to the front. 'You Zambian imperialists are with the ANC.' She pulls that black wand of hers out of her jeans, and eeeh, that's when I notice all the Zanu cadres are suddenly carrying tent pole spears and kieries and knives.

Ou Biani, he realises there's going to be trouble and grabs Rudiya and yanks her into the crowd.

The She-Devil sees him. 'The ANC are stealing our women,' she screams at her cadres. 'How can you just stand there and watch these things happen? Are you men?'

Some Zanu bloke answers by belting Biani in the guts with his kierie: Biani grabs the thing; they wrestle for it, and all around the Zanu cadres climb into the crowd with their sticks and spears.

A platoon of Zambian troops charges up. 'Back to your tents — everybody,' the officer shouts. 'Back to your tents!'

Most of the ANC cadres — as well as us Unity Mountain cadres and Rudiya — are only too pleased to obey. But the Zanu cadres, they stood their ground, and more and more of them swarmed over from their tents.

'Disperse,' the Zambian officer shouts again. 'Back to your tents.' He lines his 10 men up, orders them to kneel and cock their rifles. 'If you don't go back I'll tell the troops to fire.'

'Little boys with toy guns,' the She-Devil scoffs. 'We're going to fix these ANC dogs once and for all. If you don't go back to your barracks, I'll make your things dry up and drop off.' She waves that kierie of hers at them menacingly.

But the Zambians aren't budging. 'Disperse,' the officer yells at them again. 'Disperse or we'll shoot.' He draws his pistol and stands there beside his men, pointing it at the Zanu fighters.

'You aren't our leaders,' says the She-Devil heading towards him. 'You aren't Zimbabweans. Get out of our way.'

'Back to your tents — now!'

'You can't stop us.' The Zambians cock their gats, take aim, but that doesn't stop her. She never hesitates, she heads right for him.

That's all I saw. A group of Zanu cadres had sneaked round the Zambians and were coming straight for us. We had to withdraw, and as we were running off we heard the shots and the shouting. I never did find out exactly what happened: according to the Zambians, one of the Zanu cadres speared the Zambian officer and his troops then opened fire. According to Zanu, the Zambians opened fire as they withdrew, killing their own officer. Whatever, when everything was quiet again, there were 13 mense including the She-Devil and the Zambian officer, lying dead among the broken pots and trampled sadza in the kitchen courtyard.

Chapter 12

*A*fter the shooting the commandant suspended all camp activities: all lectures, all parties, all politics, even all sport. The
Zambians took charge of the kitchen and the logistics, and all day
long Zambian troops tramped up and down between the lines of
tents. We sat around and smoked our stop — what else was there to
do? Every night we crowded around ou Hendrix's radio, listening to
the news on Radio Zambia and the BBC, hearing the latest story
about which leader had condemned the others and the latest
Rhodesian claims about their 'mopping up operations' against the
fighters in the north-east — the last freedom fighters in the country.
Eeeh, I chune you, news of that kind didn't make the comrades any
happier. 'Why won't they give us guns and just let us cross?' the
cadres were saying. 'Why are we being kept here in this camp? We left

the country to fight, not to sit here and rot.'

Night after night it was the same. The leaders fought and insulted each other and the Rhodesians announced fresh successes. The comrades were becoming more and more restless. 'I wish I had an enemy I could grab hold of and wrestle with,' ou Hendrix said once. 'I wish this was something that could be finished in one quick fight — win or lose — but finished.'

Ou Biani was the only one who wasn't bothered by all this confusion. He was with Rudiya now and he couldn't concentrate on anything else. After the shooting, you check, she hadn't dared go back to Zanu, and she and Biani scrounged a tent from somewhere and pitched it up on top of the Unity Mountain.

Watching the two of them together, touching when they thought no one was looking, so completely absorbed in themselves, reminded me of myself and Naomi just after we first met, how we spent hours just holding hands and kissing and talking. I began daydreaming about being back in Burg, about us two getting back together again. She'd have been waiting faithfully all this time and when I opened the door she'd collapse sobbing into my arms. All of this even though I realised at the back of my mind that there wasn't much reason for her to sit around and wait.

All of us except for Biani took to smoking stop fulltime. There wasn't much else to do. Day by day it became hotter; the dry season was on us. Clouds of dust blew up with every breath of wind, and swarms of flies buzzed around us, stinging and biting. Even before we rolled out our beds in the morning, we passed round a reef or two and as we slouched over to breakfast we would find time for another. For the rest of the day we could do nothing but catch flies and complain and smoke.

Ou Hendrix was our champion flycatcher. That wound on his knee had never quite healed and even though he missed half the time, it was such a popular fly shab that he had more chances than all the rest of us put together. He'd lie there with his eyes half closed except for that hand of his stuck out stiff as the dead. And then — whack! — quick as a snake his hand would strike down on his knee, and then he'd pull himself up to examine the extent of his victory. 'Four imperialist CIA-sponsored fighters shot down by the noble forces of the revolution while feeding on rotting Africa,' he'd announce. 'Another great victory for the struggle.' Or: 'In spite of the heroic efforts of the freedom fighters the imperialist forces managed to escape this time with only a few injuries when they were surprised on one of their plundering raids on the unhappy body of Africa.'

One morning he killed so many flies we decided ya, this comrade was a Hero of the Fight against Imperialism. We must give him some special recognition. After this long debate, we issued this declaration that he would have the honour of the last hit of all our reefs for the next 24 hours.

Then next day Comrade Lovemore, who was so quick that he could catch flies even in the air, splashed sugar water all over his leg and showed that when it came to killing imperialists, he too was a hero of the revolution, first-class.

Ya, it became quite a game there for a while, with us comrades working out all the strategies and tactics of fly killing. Then one afternoon Comrade Hendrix complained there weren't enough flies around and he went out and got this heap of stinking shit which he puts right in the centre of the tent.

No, no, man, the rest of us ouens decided. This nonsense has gone too far. We told Hendrix to take that shit away and we drifted up to the kitchens to see if lunch was ready.

While we were catching flies, the comrades at Mgagao, a Zanla training camp in Tanzania, summed up how everyone felt in a declaration. There were two or three copies in circulation at the Unity Camp and ou Hendrix managed to borrow one from a connection in logistics.

First thing, these cadres 'strongly, unreservedly, categorically and totally' condemned any more talks with Smith.

Secondly they called for a front of all the fighters to resume the struggle.

'Hear, hear!' reckons Biani when he reads this lot, and there's a murmur of agreement all around.

'We are the freedom fighters, and nobody under heaven has the power to deny us the right to die for our country,' the document went on, appealing to the Frontline states and the OAU to allow us to continue the struggle.

And, if they couldn't, the cadres kindly requested to be deported to Zimbabwe, 'where we will start from throwing stones'.

'If we cannot live as free men,' it concluded, 'we rather choose to die as free men.'

The document became very popular, and within a few days half the camp knew it by heart. But, of course, in spite of a new rush of rumours, the leaders ignored it, the Frontline states and the OAU ignored it. The struggle was going nowhere. Nothing was happening.

We smoked so much that we ran out of stop. Us Unity Mountain ouens had our private patches of it up on the escarpment, and whenever supplies were short we'd sneak out to pick more. But, cos the cadres in the camp had nothing better to do than sleep and smoke, every night groups scoured the slopes in search of the weed. Our patch was discovered and stripped, and one fine morning we woke up to the realisation that we only had 24 hours' supply of the stuff left. The situation was serious. Comrade Lovemore suggested rationing, and ou Hendrix suggested buying some from the Zambian privates.

'With what are we going to buy it?' Lovemore wants to know. 'These rags?' — he plucks dramatically at his tatty shirt — 'not even a Zambian would wear this.'

'There's the radio,' I put in hopefully.

'Never,' says Biani, 'we need to know what's happening.'

While the comrades were scratching their heads Hendrix comes up with one of his fancy ideas: why not just borrow a couple trousers or jackets from logistics and swap them for stop. 'There's a mammoth shortage of clothes here in Zambia,' he tells us, 'the privates will go for it, no problem.' Well, everyone's congratulating him on how nicely he's solved our problem when Biani interrupts:

'This will be stealing from the cadres. We can't do it.'

'Ag no man,' ou Hendrix protests. 'It's not like that at all. Comrades, logistics is piled to the rafters with bales of clothes. There's a whole shipment of jackets from Sweden, and not one has ever been distributed.'

'It doesn't matter how much there is,' Biani tells him. 'It will all be necessary — and more — when the struggle begins again.'

'If the struggle begins again,' Lovemore butts in.

'Those jackets they're all too heavy for bush warfare,' ou Hendrix argues. 'And anyway the party didn't pay a cent for them. They were donated.'

'The party could sell them. They could be used to raise party funds,' Biani argued.

'Come on comrades,' pleads Hendrix. 'How much do you think one jacket is going to mean to the struggle? Is it going to slow the victory of the masses by even one minute? How much have you done for the struggle — and how much have you been paid? Don't you deserve something?'

'If they catch you,' Lovemore warns him, 'they will shoot you.'

'They wouldn't dare,' says Hendrix. 'They know damn well I can tell any court martial exactly who has been taking what.'

We debated for hours about those goddam jackets and as we argued, we just about finished the last of our supplies. Finally Biani got the hell in and called for a vote: only Biani and Rudiya were against it. I voted with them cos I didn't want to end up on the wrong side of Biani.

That night, after Biani and Rudiya retired to their tent the rest of the crew — me included — sneaked down to logistics past the Zambian guard (who'd been presented with our last jar of kangara just before he went on duty), unlocked the door and removed a bale of jackets which we hid up in our caves on the escarpment.

Then two days later ou Hendrix rocks up from work one afternoon carrying this big green Zambian kitbag and grinning like a kid that's been given the largest box of chocolates in the shop. Once we're all inside he opens up and eeh, the rucksack is packed tight with these tender green heads, as sticky as if they've been dipped in syrup.

Us ouens, we figured, hey you know, we must make a celebration. Ou Hendrix, he tears another page from *Lenin Vol IV* which he'd nicked from the camp library, and rolls us this mammoth reef. And aaah, once you'd had a pull on that thing you felt the smoke seeping through to your brain, your face relaxing into a grass grin.

Hendrix tears another page from the volume and breaks off a chunk of a head to crush for the next reef. 'Smokers of the world unite,' he proclaims, giggling.

'You have nothing to lose but your struggle,' puts in Biani, refusing a hit.

'That's just colonialist nonsense,' reckons ou Hendrix. 'The people of Africa have been smoking this stuff for generations. The Bushmen smoked it, the Zulu took a few hits before going into battle,' — he breaks into a high maniacal cackle — 'it's authentic Africa. But whitey he didn't like seeing people just sitting around enjoying themselves so he tried to ban it. When you guys finally have the sense to crown me Emperor of Africa, I'll make sure you get your ration of stop every day.' More cackling.

'Pamberi ne Hendrix,' shouts crazy Cooks. 'Smokers of the world unite.'

Biani and Rudiya, they duck out of the tent.

'Gone off to save Africa,' scoffs Hendrix. Me, I just sat there staring down at my boots.

A few days later Private Chumba, this shiny black bloke with piglike rolls of fat on his neck rocks up at our Unity Mountain with another rucksack of stop: big brown cobs which had been wrapped in banana peels and buried deep in the manure of a sheep kraal until they were brown and hard and crystalline — rather like that sugary dried fruit that Katz sometimes passed round at his bakery. Those cobs were so solid you couldn't just crush them up and smoke them, you had to mix in quite a quantity of tobacco else the stuff wouldn't burn. Eeeh, I chune you, it was potent; one reef and you lie back and watch your big toe for the rest of the day.

About a week after that Private Chumba rocked up with another kitbag and a few days later with two more and suddenly we found ourselves with more stop than we knew what to do with. Some we gave away, some we sold cheap and the blokes who came to visit us got to smoke as much as they wanted. Cadres from all the parties sneaked over to join us — ANC, Zanu, Zapu the lot. Quite a number brought their tents with them. Soon, instead of the six of us camped there, there were 50, 60 mense up on our ridge. Ya, Smokers' Inn was much more popular than Unity Mountain ever had been.

Now all this smoking wasn't exactly popular with the party commissars. They complained that we were stealing their cadres away, that we were destroying morale in the camp and turning the cadres into drug addicts. All three parties denounced us to the Zambians, but the Zambians never did anything about it. Maybe ou Hendrix organised something; more likely the Zambians felt it at least kept our minds off politics.

Meanwhile ou Chumba kept bringing us more and more stop. Our hideaway up on the escarpment was jampacked with the weed, and our tents up on Unity Mountain were practically sandbagged with the stuff.

One time someone asked where do you find so much and so cheap? Chumba explained the setup: him and his buddies borrowed one of the camp's trucks and drove out into the bush until they found a kraal. 'Got stop — mbanje — to sell?' they asked the locals, and offered such a high price that the locals brought out every last scrap of the stuff. Chumba and his buddies then confiscated the lot and fined the villagers a couple goats for possession. What with the profits they were making from the sale of the jackets and the goats and the surplus stop in Kabwe, those privates weren't doing too badly at all.

Eeh, us ouens we were shitting ourselves when we heard this lot. What would happen if the authorities found out about this racket? We figured it's best to get rid of all the damn things at once.

So next time ou Chumba rocks up we sat him down and explained hey, thanks very much, but.

Chumba didn't seem to care about being caught, but he was worried about losing his supply of jackets. They were selling well, very well, on the black market, he told us. Would we prefer, in future, to be paid in kwachas instead of stop? Maybe that would be safer. No, well then why can't you sell me the rest of your jackets? If you leave them lying around someone can find them. Say 20 a jacket or 25 if that wasn't enough. What about — and you wouldn't do better than this — 30?

Well, we couldn't do anything with the jackets and if we'd been caught with them we would've been deep in the kak. The best thing, we figured, is get rid of the damn things at once. After an hour's bargaining we settled on a price of 65 kwacha a jacket, and sold the bloke our last dozen. Chumba, he took this wad of notes out of his pocket and counted off 780 kwacha just like that.

Hendrix shared the coin out among us Unity Mountain ouens. Biani and Rudiya, though, wouldn't take their share and so of course I had to refuse as well. Not that the stuff meant much anyway — in the camp there was nothing you could do with all those wads of notes. The stuff was like Monopoly money: we used to gamble with it — bam, bam — 10 kwacha win, 10 kwacha lose. You couldn't take it seriously. Some blokes used to pin the notes to their clothes, some used them to roll reefs, some collected every kwacha they could lay their hands on and hid them away.

Ya, those days everyone was a little strange. One comrade, I remember, was always asking for his lost cattle and if you'd give him half a chance he'd describe them all in loving detail. Comrade Shave believed he turned into a baboon and every night he went scampering around the camp on all fours. One bloke stopped talking, stopped eating — and then set his tent alight. The Zambians took him off to Lusaka, and we never saw him again. Another bloke threw himself off a cliff and broke his back. He died a week later.

Comrade Sputnik, who'd added so many wires to his hair that he looked seriously in orbit, decided that he was the man to lead the struggle and walked round the camp trying to persuade the comrades to send him off to speak to Comrade Vorster or Comrade Nixon.

Around that time quite a few cadres deserted. Some the Zambian police brought back; most we never saw again. A couple, I heard later, managed to organise themselves graft and papers, and made lives for themselves in Lusaka. There were also stories that some died out in the bush as they trapped toward the Lusaka road.

'You blame them?' Noah said when we were discussing it one afternoon. What with the free stop and all Noah was spending a lot of time at our Smokers' Inn. 'Hell, they're the only ones with any sense. This struggle's going nowhere — why should we rot along with it?'

'Sooner or later the struggle will begin again,' I said — it was what every commissar was saying — 'it's just a matter of time.'

'We'll all have grey hair before these houties get to square one. We should get out now while the going's good. I chune you, it'd be easy man. I've got it all planned. We just walk off.'

'Me?'

'Relax man, hear me out — we just walk off into the hills and keep going straight. Sooner or later we've got to hit the Lusaka road. Hell, you couldn't miss it. We flag down a bus — I've got 200 kwacha — and before anyone realises we've gone we'll be there — in Lusaka.'

'So what do we do once we're there,' I said, despite myself. 'Sit around and wait to be arrested by the Zambians?'

'Fix ourselves some papers, get ourselves some graft or cross to Botswana and then back home.'

I told Noah he was just bullshitting but eeh, I couldn't put that plan of his out of my mind. It would work, I knew it would work; it probly wouldn't be as easy as ou Noah made out but with luck I could be back with Naomi and the lightie within days. I pictured myself there in the shab downing a dozen cold beers and spinning all these stories of my great escape from the terrorist camp. Why not?

I was still thinking through his offer the night when a couple of us Smokers' Inn guys went off to a celebration thrown by Private Chumba. Half the blokes were already smashed out of their minds when we rocked up and the others were battling hard to catch up. There's a wall of beer crates in the bungalow and pots of sadza and goat stew simmering just outside the door.

'You guys know how to celebrate,' I chune Chumba as he shoves a bottle of lukewarm beer in my hands. I take a sip, savouring the bitterness. Hell — I hadn't had real beer, I hadn't had a drink out of a bottle for at least a year.

Chumba — he's quite pissed — slings a piggy arm round my neck.

'In Zambia there can never be a shortage of beer,' he declares. 'Anything else — quite fine. Smokes, rubbers, clothes and no one will complain. But beer — a shortage of beer and there'd be revolution.'

'Sounds as if Kaunda's at least got his priorities right,' I say, trying to back away so's I can sample the goat stew. My nose has these suspicions that there are chillies — and ginger — bubbling away in that pot, and after months and months of the blandness of boiled sadza and beans, eeeh....

But, as I turn to grab my share, Piggy Chumba grabs me by the arm. 'Zambia, Zambia is a fine place,' he informs me, holding on tight. 'But I can't understand you Zimbabweans. You're always fighting. Here we are two tribes and we are at peace.'

Well, I'd heard different but I wasn't going to argue. I wanted that stew. 'That's how it should be,' I agree, downing another sluk of beer.

'Ya, I can't understand it,' chips in one of Piggy's buddies. 'Why do you Zimbabweans fight so much? You all want to chase out whitey. Why can't you forget your differences and get on with the struggle?'

'Ask the commissars, they're the only ones who can explain.' I try to pull away but it's too late: two of them were gripping me, one on each arm.

'But how do you see it?' they keep insisting.

Me, I play kaffir. 'It's all Smith and his agents,' I chune them. 'He causes all the divisions.' I'm battling to stay polite, I chune you. The other Smokers' Inn ouens are already lining up for their second helpings.

'Why do you stick around then?' Comrade Chumba asks as he steers me over to the wall of the bungalow where half-a-dozen of his buddies sat in a row. I take another sluk of beer to dampen my sorrows. 'If I was in your position. . . .'

'What do you mean by that?' But I knew, of course, I knew. Why was I, a goffel, fighting in a black man's war?

'Have another beer, man. Now why do you have to stick around in this mess? This isn't really your problem. If I was you I'd have left them to fight it out — long ago — hell, they're not your people.'

'Ya,' said one of the other boozers, leaning over to grip onto me too, 'don't you want to go home?'

I was getting worried, I chune you. The conversation was beginning to sound like an interrogation. They couldn't know that I was considering gapping it, could they? Did they think I was a spy because I stayed?

'Everyone thinks about going home,' I said, trying to sound sensible like Biani. 'But we are freedom fighters: if we go home now Smith will hang us.' Except in my case he probably would've given me a medal and my back salary.

'You could stay in Zambia,' Private Chumba said, tightening his grip. 'A few kwacha in the right pocket, a few jackets — and you could get papers saying you're a Zambian citizen. Comrade Hendrix says you were a baker — I'm sure they need such people here — why should you stick around and suffer? Have another beer.'

And all the other privates around him were asking, 'ya — why should you stick around here? — and suffer? — have another beer.'

When I was finally able to stagger out of there I was still trying to figure this little lot out. 'This isn't your war, Muzukuru,' they were telling me, 'wake up now. The fun is finishing, it's time to go home.'

Who did they think I was anyway? A spy? Or did they just want me to steal them more jackets? What did they know about my story? But, me, I didn't want to catch a spook everytime I walked into a bar and saw a couple of crazy honkies. I didn't want to be turned away from restaurants, swimming baths, I didn't want to be told where to sit in a cinema, I didn't want to be told where I could live, I didn't want to take any more insults from any more stupid honky troops, kowtow to any more racist officers. I didn't want any more coloured wages, coloured jobs, coloured battalions with their green meat and antique gats. I wanted some say in my own life. I wanted Zimbabwe to be like

Unity Mountain. All right, so my grandmother was a houtie and my grandfather was a honky but it wasn't my fault I'd been born that way and I didn't have to apologise to anyone about it. It was my war as well, it was my struggle no matter what any comrade, honky, goffel, houtie or Zambian thought. It was my struggle and I was going to see it through.

Chapter 13

*F*or months we'd been hearing that the fighters were forming a front and the war would soon start again. But, after we'd heard this rumour for the third or fourth time most of us just yawned and schemed it was one of those stale camp stories which survive only cos so many cadres were praying it was true.

Then, one afternoon in mid-November, the camp commandant assembled us on the parade ground, announced the formation of Zipa, the Zimbabwean People's Army, and told us we'd be fighting again within weeks.

The parade ground exploded into cheers — 'Pamberi ne Chimurenga!' — 'Forward with the Struggle!' — 'Pasi ne Smith!' — 'Power to the People!' The cadres were whooping and dancing, shouting and singing. At last, after almost a year of waiting the struggle was on again!

When we'd all quietened down, the commandant explained that we were all now members of this Zipa, the new military wing of the struggle. Zipa, he told us, had absolutely nothing to do with any of the political parties or political leaders; Zipa was only a military front for fighting the war.

One of the Zipa main mannes explained to us that the front had been formed after Comrade J.Z. Moyo, head of Zipra, visited Comrade Tongogara, head of Zanla, in the prison where the Zambians had him locked up for his part — or rather what they said they believed was his part — in the murder of Chitepo. Both Moyo and Tongogara wanted the struggle started again, both knew the Frontline leaders would not allow any party thing, so they decided on a unity of the fighters. 'When the country is liberated, the people will decide who the true leaders are,' he told us. 'Now we must co-operate and smash Smith and his settlers.' And, in this spirit of co-operation, Moyo and Tongogara had agreed that half the Zipa big shots would be selected from Zipra and the other half from Zanla, and all the posts in the army right down to unit level would be divided equally between them.

Wonderful — the war is on again — but as we are walking away from the parade grounds the squabbling starts. 'I can't see why you are so happy,' this sourfaced ANC commander, Comrade Samson, says to Biani who is prancing around yelling 'Forward with Zipa! Forward with the unity!' 'The ANC has been totally ignored in this Zipa business.'

'The ANC is only a front,' Biani tells him. 'It's the struggle that matters,' and off he blasts again: 'Forward with the unity of the struggling masses of Zimbabwe!'

Ya, ou Biani, he was suddenly his old self all over again: arguing, explaining, sloganeering, lecturing — always pushing the Zipa line. As far as he was concerned this new Zipa army was a step towards genuine unity, a step towards restarting the struggle, a step on the long march to victory.

But few cadres were as keen as him. Though the cadres were pleased that the struggle was finally starting up again, most of them were anti Zipa itself. The ANC cadres were furious cos their party had been ignored; the Zanu cadres were upset cos though they were in the majority, only half the main mannes would be chosen from their party; and the Zapu cadres schemed that as they were better trained and better armed, they should control the new army.

In spite of the complications the day the first convoy left for the front was like the first day of school holidays: as the truck trundled out the camp the comrades cheered and sang, shouting to us that we would all meet up in Salisbury for the Victory celebrations in just a couple of months' time. 'If we do,' throws out one of the Zapu cadres, as the truck wheezes up the hill, 'it'll be thanks to Zipra weapons.'

'But Zanla fighters,' cuts in this Zanu cadre.

Ya, what with the rainy season and the dirt roads and the trucks breaking down, we were nearly a week on the road, and by the time we reached Chingodzi, the main Zipa base, the bickering was so bad that the cadres from the three parties were travelling in separate trucks. The conditions at the camp didn't improve anyone's temper either: there weren't enough tents, the supplies hadn't arrived, and neither had the cadres from the training camps in Tanzania. We were sleeping eight to a tent meant for four, and ate only a handful of plain sadza a day. The drizzle never stopped and a mist of mosquitoes hung over the place. We were all sick. Worst of all, no one had any idea how long we'd be stuck there. 'Is this just another Unity Camp?' the cadres were asking.

For more than a month we perched there waiting and arguing, arguing and waiting. If there hadn't been so many Frelimo troops around the parties would've clashed again for sure.

When the troops and supplies finally arrived, us cadres were assembled for this Frelimo main manne to address us. He spoke in Portuguese, halting after every sentence for his interpreter to English it. 'Frelimo has liberated Mozambique,' he told us, 'and now the people of Mozambique are assisting their Zimbabwean brothers in their struggle against imperialism and colonialism. But, though we have given you bases along our borders, though we have reached out our hands to help you in your struggle, you have not done much fighting. Your politicians have been too busy arguing with each other. But now, with the struggle beginning again, you must forget these old leaders. Remember, leaders are only a product of the struggle, and new leaders will quickly emerge from amongst you — the fighters. That's what happened here in Mozambique!'

'Why isn't there one ANC cadre in this Zipa leadership?' yells a voice from the back. 'Why are you forgetting the ANC?'

I turn, trying to see who's spoken.

The ANC's Commander Samson is pushing his way to the front. 'Some of us here are ANC cadres... the ANC, do you remember? The ANC, the front of all the Zimbabwean parties — the ANC, which Mozambique and all the other Frontline states recognises! Our leaders are accepted throughout Africa! You can't just push us to one side!'

The crowd begins buzzing and it looks like the Zanu and Zapu cadres are going to start with their complaints as well, but before anybody else can make himself heard, the Frelimo commander bellows 'Silencio!'

'Aqui Mozambique, ne Zimbabwe!' he shouts angrily. 'This is Mozambique, not Zimbabwe! Here you do what we tell you!' He checks Commander Samson out with a naked eye. 'And — if you don't you go to prison.'

Well, that shut up the commander for the moment, but he wasn't finished. After the Frelimo commander stomped off and the crowd dispersed, a bloke ran up and whispered to us that the ANC was holding a meeting outside.

Ya, by then the ANC was a lame duck in a lion's den. There was no way round it: all but a handful of cadres had deserted, and no one — not Frelimo, not Zipa — was prepared to give us any kind of hearing.

Biani argued that we should now just forget about the party. 'Zipa stands for unity now,' he argued. 'The ANC isn't unity anymore; it's just one extra party.'

Most of the members didn't like what they were hearing. 'Capricorn sellout,' someone yelled.

'Nonsense,' he blasted back. 'I'm not any kind of agent — but we must change our tactics. You'll have more luck getting a fart out of a dead donkey than a fight out of this ANC.'

That night we had a visit from an old buddy, Comrade Shungu. (Actually he was now Comrade Commander Shungu: he'd been promoted since he'd rejoined Zapu.)

'You two better disconnect yourselves from the ANC,' he warned us, 'and you'd better do it soon because the ANC cadres will be locked up any day now.'

'What's going to happen to us?' I asked. 'Where do we go now?'

'Zapu,' he tells us. 'You, Muzukuru — you are still officially Zapu. And you, Biani, I could speak to the big fish about you.'

So Shungu sorted things out and two days later we joined Zapu. Or rather, Biani joined and I followed, sticking to him like a tick to a tortoise. even though I wasn't too happy with his decision. Me, I chune you, I'd had enough of Zapu for this lifetime and the next.

'I can't go back,' Biani told me when I pestered him about rejoining Zanu. He said it like a fact of life: the world is round, my skin is black, I can't go back.

'But why?'

'Think,' he told me, 'Zanu must have a file on me this thick — the big fish didn't like my questions about Chitepo, they didn't like me crossing over to the ANC, they didn't like me talking unity and they didn't like me fighting against them. How can they trust me now? I'd always be a capricorn to them, they'd always be watching. Rather we find another party.'

Two days after we crossed over, the ANC cadres who insisted that they had a party and a leader were marched off to a farm and ordered to grow food for the struggle. Most of them tried to sneak back to Zambia and, according to the stories, got lost on the way and landed up in Malawi instead. There the Young Pioneers, the youth wing of the ruling party, caught them, beat them and locked them up in a camp for political prisoners. They were only released when Muzorewa and his UANC came to 'power' about three years later.

On December 1, just two-three days after we'd switched, Smith and Nkomo announced that they were talking. Though Nkomo insisted he was only interested in majority rule, and though Smith insisted majority rule was completely out of the question, somehow they found something to say to each other.

The announcement set the camp stirring. The Zanu cadres were outraged and everywhere they were shouting that Zapu was set to sell out to Smith. In fact, some of the Zapu cadres were no longer keen to fight. 'Why should we die now when a settlement could be signed any day?' they asked. But most cadres argued that talking would not affect the fighting as politics was a separate front.

Then we're called to this secret Zapu meeting where one of the big fish informed us that Zanu was plotting to destroy all the dissidents in Zipa — ie us. 'We are too few to resist,' he told us. 'So when you cross back into Zimbabwe you must desert and head to Botswana — and collect all the recruits you can along the way.'

Somehow Zanu found out about this meeting. They complained to Frelimo, which sent one of its big shots to threaten us with prison if we didn't stop inventing differences. But when the Zapu commanders tried to tell him about Zanu's plotting, he wouldn't listen and threatened to lock us up if we didn't stop causing confusion.

Then the cadres from the Tanzanian training camps arrived. Overnight, preparations became serious. We were split into three groups of 130 each, and every day there was toi-toi. After a week the groups were transferred to their border camps.

I remember watching two-three of the nurses and their boyfriends, Rudiya and Biani among them, hugging each other goodbye as the truck drivers hooted for them to finish and the comrades yelled advice and encouragement.

Me, I looked down at my boots. Naomi. Hell, I realised I hadn't thought about her for — what was it? — two days. When I'd first been captured, she'd been in my mind every day — every hour, almost — and I'd spent every spare minute trying to work out a way to get back to her. But, over the months, without even noticing it, I'd thought less and less about her and Burg, and now all of that felt thin and faded, like a book I'd read a long time back, and could hardly remember. I added up the months we'd been apart — 18, 19. More than a year-and-a-half. Ruthie would be nearly six — she wouldn't recognise me. And anything could've happened in that time: I'd been away just a few months before, and I'd come home to find mammoth problems. She could've married again, could've produced another lightie even. Hell, what would she want to stick around for? She'd had to put up with the fuckup I'd made of my life, the dopping and the stopping, not finding another job and then selling myself out for Smith's measly salary. But eeh, in my gut I couldn't believe she would leave me, and somewhere at the back of my skull I'd cached the notion that if I survived we'd get back together again when the struggle was over.

About 130 of us cadres were taken to a spot near the Rhodesian border just across from the Melsetter area. We trekked a couple kays off into the gwashas, cached our supplies in the nearby gomos, and built a base on the side of a bushy hill, digging deep bunkers for the radio and the HQ and throwing up a couple huts in the local style as camouflage for the kitchen. For ourselves we dug shallow trenches, which we hid with branches and grass, all around the camp's perimeter.

We were issued with AKs and, since most of us hadn't had a gat in our hands for about a year, we were put through a couple retraining sessions — dismantling the gun, cleaning it, that kind of thing. We also fired off two rounds of ammunition each: we were short of supplies and there was no more to spare.

A day or two later we were divided into units, and me and Biani managed to work things so that we ended up together. He was commissar, I was medic. The logistics, Comrade Gondodema, and the commander, Commander James, were also Zapu. Comrade Gondo, this stubby, brainless Kalanga from the Gwelo district, was about 17 years old and he knew nothing, nothing but Zapu, and he was always complaining that the other cadres were trying to make a fool out of him.

Commander James was a Tswana; his parents had left South Africa while he was a child, and he'd been a catechist for the Catholic Church until he joined the struggle. He was a nice sort of bloke, maybe too nice; and he could never get the cadres in his unit to listen to him.

Our deputy, Killer Mabhunu — Killer of the Whites — was a real rebel. Killer made it plain that he wasn't happy serving under a Zapu commander, and the other three Zanu cadres followed him no question.

Biani preached unity but it was like trying to pick up water with a wire bucket. 'Zanu/Zapu, Ndebele/Shona — forget those divisions,' he told us. 'To be sure of victory we must stand united against the imperialists.'

'That might be the Zapu feeling,' reckons Killer, 'but our Zanu feeling is we can manage by ourselves.'

'You lot are like my grandfather,' Biani says, shaking his head. 'When I went off to work in the city, he told me: "If you marry an Ndebele girl — don't come back home." He could not understand we must bury these old grudges if we are going to live together in the new Zimbabwe.'

'You should listen to your elders,' says Killer. 'The Ndebeles drove us off our land, massacred half our people, stole our women and cattle — and then when whitey came along, they sold the country to him.'

'That's a lie,' cries Comrade Gondo. 'No Ndebele ever sold an inch of this country to the whites.'

'This is an old man's fight,' Biani interrupts. 'What matters is the struggle now. What....'

'You say that cos you're with Zapu,' Killer cuts in. 'But just watch how these madzwitis treat you — you'll come crawling back. With ı's you'd be a big fish; with them you'll be nothing.'

'That's enough — that's enough,' says Commander James finally. 'Any more tribalist nonsense, and I'll take you all to the camp commander.'

But there was one thing all of them, Shona and Ndebele, agreed about: they didn't trust me. For a start, most of them schemed goffels were Smith's sons, just like whites, and then, on top of that, I'd once fought for Smith. I could see what those blokes were thinking: once we've crossed, this goffel, this 'ex'-enemy, he's going to head straight to the nearest cop shop and call in the Fire Force. Not even ou Biani was 100 percent sure of me. He tried to hide it, but you could see what he was thinking — and actually I can't blame him. Just a few months back he would have been right. Hell, in their place I would've been suspicious too. But, I chune you, all this suspicion didn't make my life any easier. Everybody had their eyes on me, everybody was looking for a sign that I still carried the security force in my heart. One slip and there would be a knife in my back. It was as bad as training all over again, so bad in fact that I started to believe that if I wanted to survive I would have to cross back to Smith.

One day, out of the blue, the camp commissar announced that we were crossing into the country that evening.

'Pasi ne vadzanyiriri! Down with the oppressors! Forward with the struggle!'

When we were quiet again, he told us fighters had crossed to the north of us and another column would be crossing to the south.

'You are crossing back to carry on the struggle which began when the whites first occupied our country,' he told us. 'You are following in the paths of our ancestors. They were defeated and it is up to you to carry on the struggle, to keep fighting until the last of the colonialists has been driven from the country.... Remember — there isn't a single brother, a single sister in Zimbabwe today who hasn't suffered from this racist, murderous settler regime. Thousands of our people have been massacred — and every day more die. All of us, each of you, have been insulted and humiliated by this regime. . . .'

'Down with Smith! Zimbabwe must be free!'

That night, red-hot and ready, all 130 of us started for the border. Come first light, we camped on this koppie just inside Mozambique, and all that day we lay awake among the rocks, stiff and sweaty from all that trapping, waiting for evening and the crossing.

When we reached Rhodesia, about an hour after sunset, we were quiet, hardly whispering amongst ourselves. Ya, you couldn't stop yourself wondering how many of us — who? — would be coming back.

Now we were in the country we moved through the night as cautious as chameleons, freezing at every strange grunt and whistle and shadow.

Once we'd crossed through the white area into the TTLs, the column split up into units. We moved northwest towards the river up around Wedza and eeh, it wasn't exactly easy going I chune you. It wasn't just the bush, though that was bad enough — us cadres were all out of shape after those long, slack months in the unity camp. The baggage on our backs — mines, food, guns, rounds, pots, medicine, clobber — didn't improve things either, and after just the first night's trapping our feet were blistered, our legs swollen and our backs aching. To lighten the load we grazed our cans of reserve food within the first day or two, and after that there was nothing else for us but plain porridge.

Ya, after a couple days of porridge us ouens were on the lookout for anything edible — especially meat. But there wasn't much chance to catch anything — we trapped all through the night, and by morning we were too buggered to do anything except doss out.

Then as we're making camp one morning when the birds are just starting to call, Biani unearths this tortoise, this huge reddish monster which dribbles piss all over the place, out from under a tussock of grass. 'Aah,' he says with a grin, weighing the thing in his hands. 'Kamba! The spirits have been listening to us. Today we eat better than whitey with his steak and chops and eggs!'

At first I schemed he was joking. Hell, I'd never actually heard of anyone grazing tortoise before, and as a confectioner you come across some pretty bizarre things. I watched how the other cadres were taking this lot, and I wasn't surprised to see that a couple of them were looking dubious too. At least I wasn't going to stick out as Smith's son, the weak-gutted goffel.

But when Biani began to axe the thing with his combat dagger, I wasn't just dubious, I was sick. Blood trickled from the beast as he hacked and sawed at its shell. Finally the tortoise makes the mistake of sticking out its head — and Biani lops it off with a stroke. The neck stalk sways about squirting blood all over, the legs scramble in the air. Biani pulls, pulls, prises open the flat undershell, and there inside the animal is this quivering mass of orange and green guts. To top it off, he reaches into the middle of this mess, feels for the heart, rips it out, and goois it off to one side.

'Dear Jesus,' says Gondo, eyeing the pulsing lump, 'it's alive.' And he was right: the heart lay there in the dust pumping away like something out of a horror movie.

'Ya,' grins Comrade Killer, winking at the other main mannes. 'You eat one of those things, and it carries on beating right in your stomach. You can feel it thumping away for days.'

Gondo looks as if he's about to puke.

'S'true,' agrees Biani. 'It's the one part of the tortoise you can't eat.' He scraped the rest — liver, kidneys, head, feet, lungs, bits of flesh — into a pot and went off to look for roots and herbs to add to it.

Well, after the graze in the unity camp and the security force, I schemed I had a stomach like a hyena's and could swallow anything, but eeh, right then, I couldn't have eaten a spoonful of that kamba if somebody'd promised me steak as second course.

'You'll change your mind,' predicted Biani as he set the pot cooking on a smokeless fire.

Me, I was sceptical and what with the way those comrades were winking at each other, I began to scheme the whole thing was a put-on. 'I'd like to see you try it first,' I said. This wasn't going to be a joke at my expense.

The cadres laughed; even Gondo was laughing. 'No more bacon and eggs for breakfast now,' Killer chunes me.

'You're not with Smith any longer,' Gondo joins in.

'Same difference,' reckons Killer. 'Nkomo and Smith, they're drinking their tea together these days.'

'It's called negotiations,' breaks in Comrade Gondo, very

sarcastic. 'Zapu can fight on two fronts: one military, one polit....'

'I see, I see,' says Killer, mock-apologetic. 'And when they sign their agreement they'll make you teaboy to one of Smith's units....' The Zanu cadres laugh. The Zapu cadres are quiet. 'Ya, maybe,' Killer continues, 'maybe cos you're such a good kaffir they'll even let you have some tea too — if you bring your own tin can.'

Gondo swings at Killer, and next thing the pair of them are rolling in the dust.

'Stop it! Stop it!' yells Commander James, but those two are not hearing anything. 'I'll have you court-martialled if you don't....'

Biani drags the two of them apart. 'There could be security force....'

'What's this famous Zapu discipline you cadres are always boasting about?' Killer pants.

'You were asking for it.'

'I'll report this,' Killer threatens, 'I'll report this — a Zapu cadre attacking without provocation, without reason.'

'You're the one who should be reported.'

'Lies!'

'Everyone's at fault,' begins Commander James, 'let's just....'

'Rubbish!' Killer breaks in. 'This is Zapu provocation.'

'Listen... we can sort this out amongst ourselves... no need to report....'

'A Zanu cadre is assaulted and you're saying....'

'Shut up!' shouts Biani. 'Your commander is talking.'

'Zanu....'

'I SAID SHUT UP!'

Killer finally shut up. Commander James cleared his throat and began telling us that we needed each other if we were going to succeed in the bush. 'Think about it,' he kept pleading. 'I would like every one of you to think about it carefully.'

But come sunset, when we woke up, the only thing on our minds was graze. The old mannes of the unit headed over to the pot, and quick-quick they were sending that tortoise, gulping it down, grabbing for more.

'Give it a try,' Biani chuned us new blokes between mouthfuls. I looked away, but just the smell of that stew sent me dreaming of those chicken-and-mushroom pies I used to bake, Naomi's chicken curry. Eeeh, my mouth was watering like Victoria Falls. It'd been a while since I'd tasted even halfway decent graze and, well, the more I thought about it, the more I figured I had to prove that this bacon-and-eggs business was bullshit. So, finally, trying to push away this picture of quivering orange and green guts, I take a lump of sadza, roll it in my hand and dip it into the pot. I nibble at it, taste. . . and you know, it's not bad, it's not bad at all, sort of like chicken, but even lighter. Well, I send the rest of the lump and grab for more. 'Next time,' says Biani, amused, 'next time you'll believe me, hey?' My mouth's too full to answer.

Soon after the kamba, we reached this white farming area which we had to cross to get to our operational zone. As the crow flies, it was maybe 25 kays wide, but on foot, what with the gomos and alles, it was quite a ways longer. We cut through a field of cotton, climbed a fence into a paddock where a herd of maybe 100 Friesland cows lay quietly chewing their cud. There were herds and herds of cattle in the area and on the flats near the river the fields of mealies and cotton and lucerne stretched off for miles.

'Good farming area,' someone remarked when we took a rush.

'Yea,' reckoned Biani. 'All this probably belongs to just one or two whiteys — while up in the hills there our people are crammed together on tiny patches of land so poor that even the goats are starving.'

'These whites want to own the whole world,' says Killer, agreeing with a Zapu cadre for a change.

'A gun is all whitey can understand,' says Gondo, joining in the chorus.

'Oh?' asks Killer, all very innocent. 'And what about tea? Last time you were telling us they can understand tea very well too. I thought you were planning to swop that AK of yours for a kettle. . . .'

Gondo aims a kick at Killer, misses and falls flat. The Zanu cadres are howling with laughter. Gondo grabs for his gat, squeezes the trigger.

Everyone freezes. He squeezes the trigger again. Nothing. Biani grabs the barrel and rips the thing away from him. Luckily the bloke had left the safety catch on; if he'd fired he'd probly have wiped out the lot of us.

'What in hell do you think you're doing!' yells Commander James.

'This guy's crazy!'

'. . . Jesus!'

'He's out to assassinate us!'

Gondo shakes his head as if he's waking up. 'It was a joke,' he says desperately, 'it was a joke.'

Biani cracks the guy one across the back of the head. 'A joke! That's the kind of joke that gets people killed! You don't point a gun at a fellow cadre — not ever! Whether it's empty or what — whether the safety's on or what — you never!'

'That was no joke,' shouts Killer. 'He must be taken back to Mozambique — court-martialled.'

'It's your fault also,' Biani yells at him. 'You should be up for court-martial too.'

'He tries to murder us — and now it's our fault!'

'Just stop — all of you,' cries Commander James. And for a moment everyone does stop, waiting for his pronouncement. 'This is a serious situation.'

'You can't let him get away with trying to murder us,' Killer breaks in. 'It's a conspiracy, a Zapu. . . .'

'Don't interrupt your commander,' Biani bellows.

'No one is getting away with anything,' Commander James says. 'I'll decide on the proper punishment.'

'He must be court-martialled — in Mozambique.'

'DON'T INTERRUPT.'

Yea, if the security force had been within earshot we would've been in big trouble.

Well, we took Gondo's gat away from him and gave him extra supplies to carry, but Commander James never did get round to deciding on the punishment, even though Killer kept pecking at him, pecking at him.

'If you can't decide about this, how can you make decisions whilst we're fighting?' he asked one time. The rest of us stopped in our tracks; you don't go asking commanders questions like that. If Killer had tried that with any of the other main mannes he would've been lucky to escape with his life.

But Commander James wasn't even angry. In fact he tried to reason with the bloke. 'This is a more difficult kind of decision than one about, say, deployment and positioning of troops,' he explained in his schoolmasterly way. 'Everything will be reported of course, and if Comrade Gondo does anything again. . . .'

At dawn me and Biani were sent out on a recce. 'This one he is useless, he can get us all killed,' ou Biani chuned me while we're perched up on top of this koppie surveying miles and miles of motionless green gwashas. 'Commander James couldn't lead a soccer team — let alone this unit.'

'He's too weak,' I agreed.

'Right in the beginning he should've smashed some bloke — then none of this would've happened. Out in the bush a comrade must obey his commander — no question — else you get this confusion.'

'What can you do?' But short of couping him, which would have been impossible with Zanu around, there was nothing. All we could do was wait.

As we're trapping along a few nights later, the scout stops like he's heard something, holds up his hand and looks off into the shadows. My heart heaves. I click off the safety and crouch down with the others. But there's no sign of the enemy.

'We are here,' the scout announces in a whisper. 'We are here. This is our operational area.'

Biani beckons us to him. Further instructions, I figure. We're standing round in a rough circle while he fishes down the front of his jacket and finally hooks out this small, shiny black duiker horn.

'Your children are home,' he says. 'We are here to finish the struggle Chaminuka and Nehanda began when the whites invaded Zimbabwe. We ask you, the spirits of our ancestors, to help us in our fight.' He unstops the horn, taps out a little snuff for the spirits, takes a pinch for himself and passes it on to the next bloke.

As the horn heads towards me, I try to look casual, but I chune you this wasn't the sort of thing I'd been taught in training and I'd never been one for spooks. But, hell, I don't want to be the goffel who didn't know what to do, the goffel who'd fought for Smith, so when the horn lands in my hands, I take a pinch of snuff — a big one, to show that I mean it — and I sniff and sniff and eeh, it's like a pair of red-hot knitting needles have been rammed up my sinuses.

I try to stop, to hold, to swallow the sneeze — but AAAaattchoo! AAaatttschooo! — my nose just about blows up. Aaatchoo! Every few seconds there's another spectacular explosion — like an armoury going up — and the cadres, they're laughing so hard, they can hardly stand. Aatchoo!

'One sniff of guerilla life,' laughs Killer, 'and look what happens to him.'

'Maybe it's a signal — a secret signal for Smith's men,' cracks one of his buddies.

'Or maybe the spirits are trying to tell us something.' One of the Zanu cadres was suddenly getting serious.

'I'd like to hear you sneeze after you'd swallowed that much snuff,' Biani says. 'You'd have blown your nose right off your face.' Ya, you could rely on ou Biani: he would always stand up for you. He was a real comrade.

Next evening we made contact with our link man, Comrade Cletus, and just after midnight we rendezvoused with him on the banks of this river. The spadework had been done, he told us; the area had been organised, his network kept an eye on every enemy movement in the area. 'What's happening to the unit here now?' he asked when he'd finished. 'Are you relieving them or reinforcing them?'

'Unit?' said Commander James, very surprised. 'No one told us about any unit.'

Cletus explained that the unit hadn't withdrawn at the time of the ceasefire, and hadn't been in contact with Zanla HQ since.

'Zanla?' Commander James exclaimed, 'there is no more Zanla or Zipra, only Zipa,' and went on to explain about the fighters' new unity front.

Comrade Cletus, he was listening carefully. 'You must discuss this thing with the cadres here,' he said. 'They will want to know about this Zipa too.'

Well, of course, Commander James was keen to tell them about Zipa, and Cletus agreed to organise a rendezvous with the Zanla unit and to keep us fed in the meantime.

We climbed to the top of a hill, and took cover in a thicket of thorns. Then, late the next afternoon, when we're lying around wondering what to do next, what do we check but there, waaay off in the distance, this military truck chugging slowly along this stretch of road passing directly beneath us.

Comrade Gondo, he's dead keen to go out — there and then — to ambush the thing. 'Let's hit them,' he shouts. 'Let's show them the power of the people.'

But before Comrade James can begin to explain that this isn't such a good idea, that we didn't have rounds to waste and these things have to be planned, Comrade Killer breaks in. 'We're not going to fight alongside this criminal. He's already tried to exterminate us.'

'Sons-of-your-mothers'-tapeworms!' cries Gondo, 'you're too scared.'

'Let's see who's the coward,' cries Killer, jumping up. 'You Zapu — you're nothing but talk.' — he turns to his cadres — 'Come, comrades — come — let's finish this truck.'

'It's too late now,' bleats Commander James. 'These attacks must be prepared —'

But by then Killer's charging down the hill with the rest of the Zanu cadres right behind him. Commander James curses but there's no way of stopping them short of ironing them out.

'Come on, come on.' Gondo stops halfway down the hill, and turns and yells at us. 'We must show them.'

'Ag, let them kill themselves,' says Biani, but Gondo doesn't hear cos he's already off haring down the hillside, the RPG he's carrying for punishment jiggling around like a live thing.

Me, I charge right after him: I want to prove to the others I'm no son of Smith.

Commander James must've figured he'd better make the best of it. 'Don't waste your rounds,' he shouts behind us. 'Don't anyone fire till Gondo stops the truck with his RPG.'

By the time we're halfway down the hill, the truck is still two-three kays off. There's this long straight slope in front of us — not the best place for an ambush. You're supposed to hit a vehicle as it's climbing a steep hill, as it crawls around a tight corner, so it's chugging along lekker slow and you've got time to aim. But that truck came burning along the drag like the driver's trying to make the pub before closing time.

When it's still maybe 500 metres off, Killer kneels and opens up. His eyes close as his gat jerks heavenward sending the rounds rocketing off in the general direction of the sun. Gondo, just behind him, kneels too, and the RPG loader, a Zanu cadre, throws a rocket into the barrel nose-first — the truck's there — Gondo fires — the rocket somersaults off a few yards — lands right next to Killer. Ya, if that item had exploded, half the unit would've been blown to smithereens.

Now, when the truck driver hears all this commotion, he slams his foot to the floor and the truck just about takes off. As it speeds past, a bloke on the back sticks out his FN and opens up.

Everyone dives for cover — everyone that is except me. Standing there like a target at a shooting range, I blaze away at the disappearing truck. It's quite a way off and moving fast, but a couple rounds connect, rattling across the rear like rain on a tin roof. I don't reckon I did more than chip the paint, but a minute later, when the thing's out of range and the other cadres begin crawling out of the grass, I stand there waiting to be congratulated on being a genuine freedom fighter with plenty guts, a serious hardcore ouen.

'Now you see why you have to plan these things,' Biani yells at Killer. 'Wasting rounds, exposing yourselves. . . .'

'You — sticking at the top of the hill — too damn scared. . . .'

'Make your facts straight!'

Me, I just stood and listened, the forgotten hero.

Recognition — of a kind — had to wait until that evening when I was picked for the detail to collect graze from this nearby kraal. Eeeh, as we trapped out of the bush, Comrade Cletus up in front, the mense crowded about us singing songs and shouting slogans. The lighties swarmed all over us admiring our gats. 'We must do what we can to help our fighters,' says this fat old queen with a wink as she put a pot of beer into my hands. Then came the food: roast mealies, chicken stew, the haunch of a goat, bowls and bowls of sadza. I'd never seen anything like it. From my security force days I was used to the lighties racing off as we arrived, the mense standing stiff and sullen as we searched their huts. I'd thought the mense were welcoming back in Binga but eeh, looking back, I realised they were just being polite. This was another story completely. It made you understand better than 1 000 commissars that the fighters were heroes to these people, and that they were crying for an end to oppression. Well, that's how it struck me at the time. Now I can't help wondering if the people hadn't been told to convince us that we were welcome.

Cos, just a little later that same evening, we received another kind of welcome altogether when Cletus led us off to the rendezvous with the Zanla unit. As we were trapping over this neck between two koppies — 'DROP YOUR GUNS — ZAPU CADRES — DROP YOUR GUNS OR YOU WILL DIE'. The voice came from everywhere and nowhere, and me I chune you, I dropped my gat no argument, and I stuck my hands up over my head like they do in the movies so whoever it was could see that I wasn't bluffing. Out the corner of my eye I saw that the other cadres had thrown down their gats too.

We had no chance, there was no doubt about it. But who then had trapped us? The Rhodesians? Zanla?

Comrade Cletus clarified matters. 'Co-operate,' he says as he picks up the AK at Commander James' feet. 'Co-operate with Zanla, and you'll all be fine.'

Commander James, man, his jaw was hanging wide open. 'Let's talk about this,' he says.

Cletus ignored him. 'Get their guns,' he tells the Zanu cadres.

For a second there I schemed there'd been some trick, that Cletus had pulled off the whole thing himself, but then eeh, high up, maybe 30 feet up the koppie, I spotted this bloke crouching with his gat aimed right at us. Eeeh, I chune you, my guts about dissolved on the spot.

When the Zanu cadres in our unit had put all our gats to one side, their comrades stood up from behind their cover. They were only four.

'You are Zanla cadres now,' Cletus told us. 'Zanu is the only party in this area. . . .'

'Zanla is now part of Zipa,' begins Commander James. 'I was appointed commander of this unit by the Zipa high command — the cadres here will confirm it.'

The Zanla commander came over. Eeeh, but he was skinny that bloke, his eyes were red and his clothes were ragged. He looked like a tramp but from the way he walked you could tell he was one of the main mannes. He looked us up and down, glaring at us as if we were shit on his shoes.

'This Zipa business is rubbish,' he informs us. 'Zanla has been fighting in this area long before anyone was talking Zipa, and Zanla will still be here when this Zipa is rotten in its grave.' No one had anything to say to that.

'If you are with us, you are comrades; if you are against us, well. . . . Any questions?'

There weren't. The bloke had a way of putting things very clearly.

He took Commander James' Tokarev, stuck it in his belt and handed out our AKs to four of his own mense. Eeeh, those cadres they were very pleased with our gats: our AKs were almost new —

we'd only fired a few shots with them. They began to pull them apart, fiddling with the various mechanisms, explaining the latches and catches to each other. When we were handed their old gats, I could understand their excitement: they'd been carrying Seminovs, a Czech sniper's rifle which fires only one shot at a time. Now, it's a good gat, accurate over quite a distance, but not much use in the bush where you hardly ever get a clear shot. What you need is an AK, an automatic, something which can spray an area where you spot a movement.

Those Zanla cadres might've liked our gats, but they weren't so keen on the cadres who came with them. 'You the one who tried to massacre your Zanla comrades?' the commander asks, checking me out with a naked eye. By the sound of it we had been discussed in some detail already.

'No — no,' I tell him, panicky, 'not me — him!' I point at Gondo.

But the bloke isn't keen to be the centre of attention either. 'He's the one who was trained by Smith,' Gondo chips in, pointing at me.

Worse was to come. Because of all the new 'recruits' the commander decided to split the unit: Biani and Gondo land up in one half and me and Commander James in the other. Me, I was terrified I chune you. How was I going to handle Zanla without Biani around? He'd been giving me cover, he'd been the one saying, 'Okay, he's a goffel, he once fought for Smith but....' Commander James on the other hand would be no help at all: he might say 'Let's speak about it...' but that's as far as it would go. I was in the shit, in the middle of a whole sea of shit. I tried to catch Biani's eye: maybe there was something he could do, something he could tell me, but he was staring fixedly at the ground, and he didn't look up, not even when the Zanla commander told me and Commander James to join our new comrades.

The unit I was in set out, trapping and trapping through the night. No one told me where we were headed. At first light we camped among some rocks at the base of a koppie. Each of us was given a lump of cold sadza to eat, and when I smiled at one bloke he glared at me like I'm the cockroach in his cake batter. Commander James was quiet, not talking to anyone. I camouflaged my kit under a bush and tried to doss out.

Then I was dreaming and in my dream I heard this fly buzzing and it got bigger and bigger and louder and louder and someone was shouting and I heard the ba-ba-ba-ba-ba-ba-ba of a Browning opening up and eeh the sky is full of choppers! real choppers these, no dream machines. Out of the corner of my eye I check a Zanu cadre whipping round in a spray of blood as the rounds catch him — me, I grip my gat and take off. There's this spurting line of dust in front of me — I dive into a heap of boulders, dodge amongst them — slide into a riverbed.

It's wide and open and sandy, and there's only a thin trickle of water among the rocks. I sprint up alongside the sandbars — pa-pa-pa of an FN to my right — throw myself down and wriggle for the bank, but it's too high, too crumbly, they'll get me if I try, and I slither on and on, it seems forever, waiting for the bullets to strike like a stick across the back of a snake. Then there's this thick tongue of bush where the bank has collapsed to the water, and I crawl, crawl up it, into the bush, until there's this massive boulder with a huge crack, I duck inside, and lie there panting, the small black balls of dassie shit digging into me, expecting the tramp of boots at any moment, listening to the pa-pa-pa of the FNs off in the distance, and the thumping of my heart.

I anchor there, anchor there, waiting and hoping, and finally, there's the whirr of choppers taking off, one, two, but me, I don't budge, I stay there beneath the boulder all the rest of the afternoon. Maybe there's a security force OP nearby, maybe soldiers are sweeping the area. I'm not taking any risks. And besides, I had no idea what to do next.

Before we'd made camp, the commander had pointed out a rendezvous point, this koppie shaped like a nipple. Now, if anyone had been captured, the enemy would already be perched up there, waiting for stragglers. No ways. What to do? After this disaster, the cadres would accuse me of selling them out anyway: they'd scheme I was security force. Go back to Biani? Well, the commander of Biani's unit — supposing I could find it in the first place — would be seriously suspicious if I rock up the solitary survivor.

What to do? I scratched my balls, picked at this cut on my palm. My old queen, she'd known about palmistry, could tell you how many kids you'd have, how long you'd live. In the right hand she'd see what was most likely to happen, in the left other directions your life could take. I wished I could read what was written there, what my chances were, what the best plan would be. Cross back to Smith? I considered it for quite a while. What with a story about waiting for a chance to gap it, I'd be a hero in Burg. I saw myself back there, Naomi smiling and smiling, the old man clapping me on the shoulder, some stiff and shining honky presenting me — what a good boy you've been — with a medal. No. No. Though I wanted Burg so bad I could kill for it, no. I couldn't ever be a good boy, a yes baas, a sellout again. Since that afternoon when I'd first seen the barrel of the AK behind the thornbush, I'd learnt too much; I'd changed too much. I couldn't ever do those things again. If I ever returned to Burg, I'd swagger back, a freedom fighter marching into a liberated city. One way or another, I would see the struggle through.

Quite fine. But I still didn't know what the hell to do next. Come the dark, I'd have to do something. Then it struck me: the sun sets in the west, rises in the east: Mozambique is in the east. In fact, if you head east Mozambique is impossible to miss. Why not head back, explain what happened and next time make sure I end up in a unit going to a Zipa area? Me, I was so relieved to have some kind of plan at last I didn't think about it too much; in fact I didn't think about it at all. Come sunset, I eased myself out from under the rock and started out for Mozambique, trapping slowly, cautiously, keeping to the shadows, aiming myself in the opposite direction to the setting sun. It was scary moving through the dark on my own. I kept thinking about leopards and lions and snakes, as well as the enemy, and at every shift of a shadow, every noise, I'd grip my gat and the shivers would slither down my spine. I was used to moving through the bush at night with a unit; on your own it's another story. Either my ears had grown enormous or the creatures of the night were having a party: chittering, cheeping and caterwauling. I was crossing through rough, broken country and often I couldn't see my landmark up ahead and I just had to keep going, putting one foot in front of the other, hoping like hell I wasn't going around in circles.

During training we'd been taught to read the stars but what little I remember only made me curse myself for not having concentrated. I knew where the Southern Cross was, but couldn't remember whether it was the long arm or the short arm you have to extend to find south. I kept moving until, round about midnight, stiff and sore and exhausted, I collapsed onto this pile of leaves in the middle of a thicket and passed out.

I woke up just before sunrise. Me, I was hungry then, cold and very hungry, but it was too dangerous to move about during the day so I curled up again and tried to get back to sleep. My gut wouldn't settle down: it was growling and burning and within 10 minutes I was up again and looking for something — anything — to eat. I found this bush with whitish berries but I didn't know whether they were poisonous or not. I broke one over my fingers. It smelt sourish so on I went. Then — aah — there in the riverbed I spotted a clump of muhacha trees with a few orangey-yellow fruits high up in the branches. Not caring, not even thinking about Smith's men, I scrambled up the first tree like ou Chico and perched there in the branches grazing all the fruit I could reach — not that it took me so long. The fruit quietened my gut but made me thirsty and I emptied my water bottle.

Come evening my guts are burning again. All that night I trapped and trapped watching-watching for anything that might possibly be edible. Nothing. At dawn I came to this stream and drank and drank but not even all that water could still my stomach. I knew I should take cover and sleep but I was just too hungry — I decided to keep going till I got something to graze.

That morning when the sun was high, I was still searching. Smith, Zanla, I'd stopped caring. All I was interested in was food. Then I hear it: this weird noise, wheezing off in the grass to my right. I freeze, grip my gat, and then aaahhh, there down among the rocks I check this lekker fat puffadder, a huge item, nearly four foot long. While it's wheezing away there, I lop off its head with my bayonet, and then skin it and clean it, wedging out the thick black line that runs down its back. Once I've hung the bleeding pink body on a thorn to drip, I make a small fire — I don't even consider who might spot the smoke — and cut up the snake, skewering the pieces on thin green twigs and then roasting them. But eeh man, I'm so skraal I don't even wait for the snake to cook properly; I'm grazing puffadder tartare there, I chune you, sending the first couple pieces so quick, I didn't even notice the taste. The last couple pieces got braaied a couple minutes longer and eeh, they were lekker, really lekker. It had the taste and texture of crayfish.

Well, after that puffadder, I was ready for anything. The ouen who couldn't face kamba, he was another somebody. When a locust flew into my face, I didn't even stop to think: off with the spikey bits — head, legs, wings — pop out the guts, and gulp down the rest. Those things weren't bad either, not bad at all. Locusts, grasshoppers — I kept my eyes peeled for them and grazed all the ones I caught.

Ya, I was nothing but a walking stomach; graze was all I thought about, all I dreamt about. I'd forgotten the explaining I was going to have to do to the Zipa big shots when I got back. I wasted hours stalking lizards among the rocks, but the few I caught only made me hungrier. I spent whole mornings looking for nests, eating the eggs and the young birds, I searched under stones for grubs and crickets, I stopped passing by berries and fruits I didn't recognise — anything the birds grazed, I grazed. When I crossed the main road between Salisbury and Umtali, I walked for about a kay along the tar, hoping to find food that somebody'd thrown out of a passing car. Pretty soon I came across a squashed hare and, sheltering behind a thornbush as the cars whizzed by, I ate the thing almost raw.

I lost track of the days, but I reckon I'd been trapping maybe a week, maybe a little longer, when one morning early-early, I checked a cluster of huts up ahead of me. I was seeing chicken curry with pumpkin shoots in peanut butter sauce; I was seeing tripe and onions, sadza and matimbes with a little rape relish on the side. I didn't stop to make any recce, didn't try to find any OP, didn't begin to even consider what the mense there would do when they saw me, a lone goffel in tattered camouflage with a story guaranteed to make you suspicious. I could just feel the burning in my stomach.

But there's no movement in the village, no roosters crowing, no women bent over pots, no cattle, no kids, no fires, no dogs — nothing, no trace of the mense, no sign of what had happened to them. The huts were empty and some had collapsed and weeds were growing out the thatch. You could hardly make out where the fields had once been. Down by the river I found the remains of a bed of spinach, a clump of sugar-cane and a patch of sweet potatoes. That was all. The bush was growing back and in a year or two it would cover everything, and even the earth would forget that people had ever lived there.

I slumped beside one of the huts and watched this line of ants disappearing into a crack in the wall. A fly lit onto my arm, and sat rubbing its feelers. What if I died out here in the bush? What would happen if as I was trapping along in the middle of nowhere, a mamba bit me, or if, light-headed from hunger, I slipped down a koppie and broke a leg? The hyenas would eat my bones and no one would ever know what had happened. I'd just be one of the thousands who'd vanished, swallowed up by the bush and the war. Biani might ask after me for a while; he might remember me as I remembered ou Headlights, but there were always other comrades, other stories. My father would probly be relieved and he'd scheme I'd been respectably murdered by the terrs, Naomi'd probly found her consolation already, and Ruthie, well, she must've forgotten me by now. It would be as if I'd never existed at all, as if nothing that I'd done mattered or could matter. In an odd kind of way the idea was a relief: the worst that could happen would be that I'd die. Then it would all be over.

Chapter 14

*A*fter the village I remember only a few things: a flat, brownish tortoise which tasted so foul that even I couldn't graze it; a nest of mice, an old queen and her seven pink lighties, which I stuck on a stick and kebabbed; a treeful of ripe wild oranges; a young vervet monkey which I brained with a lucky throw; a lemon tree, loaded with fruit, growing in a riverbed miles from anywhere; a lame wildcat which I bludgeoned to death with my gat; the mealie field near a village which I plundered one night, devouring almost a row of milky, half-ripe cobs. I remember spotting a patrol— I didn't bother to find out whose it was — and burrowing deep into a thicket of reeds; I remember catching myself talking to myself and scheming this is it, I've flipped, I'm crazy. I remember singing to myself and humming scraps of old songs — everything from 'Tungamirai Hondo' and

'Silent Night' to 'Jack and Jill', 'Pack Up Your Troubles', 'When the Names of the Heroes of Zimbabwe Are Called', 'Rhodesians Never Die', 'God Save Our Gracious Queen', 'Eight Days a Week', 'Jumping Jack Flash', 'We're Carrying an AK, We're Carrying an AK'....

Then one afternoon, round about dusk, I hear singing way off in the distance, too far away to catch the words. Either I've got a screw so loose it's dropped out or there is a choir somewhere in the middle of the bush. But every minute it's getting louder, I can make out the words, but not the language — spirits? Then the singing ends and the voices begin chanting, 'Viva Frelimo!' 'Viva Machel!'.... Mozambique! I'd reached Mozambique.

I push frantically through the elephant grass to the road — and there, marching off into the distance, I check a troop of Frelimo soldiers. Shouting and waving my arms I chase after them — 'Comrades-Camarada-stop-help!' And, finally, they did.

'Camarada-Muzukuru,' I pant when I reach them. 'Camarada-Zimbabwe-Zimbabweanos — hey, you don't know how pleased I am to see you guys — aluta continua.'

They took me back to their camp where a comrade who spoke Shona and a few words of English translated for the others. I told them about the choppers, the massacre, and eeh, those Frelimo troops, they were sympathetic. There are quite a few goffels amongst them, and they don't just check your colour and start calling you son of Smith. Graze was brought to me — lekker graze — fish and macarao and beer — and eeh, I gulped it down, and talked and talked. Eeh, but I couldn't stop talking. I told those blokes the whole story of my trek, the whole story of my life, practically; I told them what good people the Mozambicans were to help us Zimbabweans in our struggle, and how thankful we were for their help. They listened and smiled and downed their beer, and gave me more graze, and me, I sent it, sent it, and then I began to puke, and eeh, I chune you, I puked and I puked for hours, I couldn't stop puking. But even that didn't shut me up, and I talked and talked even while I was puking. Ya, I reckon I must've still been babbling even when I passed out.

Next morning I was sent under escort to the nearest Zipa camp. We trapped for about three hours and then, right out in the middle of nowhere, the Frelimo cadres stopped and began jabbering amongst themselves. Finally one fired two shots off into the air, there were two answering shots and about 10 minutes later this Zipa unit emerged from the bush, AKs cocked. After a quick talk to my escorts they took my gat, and blindfolded me and led me off to this underground bunker — the prison.

Just routine, the camp commander assured me, nothing personal. I dossed out there all afternoon until the radio man managed to get through to HQ and confirm my story.

HQ ordered me to report back to the base camp I'd crossed from — easier said than done, I chune you. It was over a week before I finally caught a glide to the main Zipa base at Chingodzi near Tete and by the time I rocked up there I was puking and puking, I couldn't stop puking. They shot me up with antibiotics and put me in hospital and after a few days my gut quietened down. I asked about Rudiya and the nurses told me ya, she grafted there at the hospital but she'd just been sent off to Maputo for further training.

When I was well enough to be sociable, I was moved into this recovery ward, a mouldy old bungalow with room for four people. Altogether there were 10 of us, two to a mattress, and all of us Zapu. According to the nurses, the arguing never stopped when the parties were mixed.

First thing, the comrades filled me in on the news of the struggle: Nkomo had pulled out of his talks with Smith cos he'd come to the conclusion Smith wasn't interested in change. Zapu and Zanu had clashed again: 50 unarmed Zapu trainees had been massacred by Zanu at the Mgagao training camp in Tanzania. There'd been reports of clashes at some of the other camps too, and three of the Zapu big fish in Zipa had mysteriously disappeared.

Ya, it was obvious to all of us that Zipa wouldn't last much longer, and the cadres often discussed deserting and crossing to Zambia or Botswana.

Me, I kept quiet about my unit's troubles. I figured there had to be a spy or security somewhere in the ward, and I didn't want any further complications. Without Biani to back me up, my position felt pretty dicey. Getting friendly with the Zipra cadres didn't work; they were all suspicious of me. Should I cross to Zanla and hope they'd heard nothing of my time with Smith? I wished I was sicker so's I could stay in hospital another couple weeks and sort out a strategy.

When I was eventually discharged, two weeks after I'd been admitted, I was put on a supply truck heading to the forward camp and, when I arrived, I was taken straight to the administration bunker where the commander and his deputy were waiting. The commander was Zanu, the deputy Zapu.

First thing the deputy asks about my gat. 'So where's this Seminov come from suddenly?' he wants to know.

Well, I'd planned to say nothing about that, but now this guy's talking like I'm a sellout or something so I start from the beginning and tell them everything and just when the choppers are ascending, the deputy interrupts. 'This must be reported,' he says, looking at the commander, 'an incident like this . . . .'

'We'll discuss it later,' says the commander. 'This is serious. This is very serious. The medic deserts when his comrades need him. Perhaps some comrades were in desperate need of those medicines you were carrying. It was your duty to get those medicines to them.'

Me, I caught one hell of a spook. Was the bloke out to get me or what?

I began to babble: those cadres hadn't trusted me, they'd threatened to kill me; it was fine, perfect in the first unit, but the cadres who'd ambushed us didn't want to check my buzz, were threatening me something bad. . . on and on until the commander raised his hand and I stopped and he told me all that didn't change anything. 'The point remains that you deserted your comrades.'

He was going to have to spend some time deciding what to do with me, he said, and in the meantime, I'd better show some of the loyalty to the struggle which had been so conspicuously absent on the battlefield.

The Zanla ambush — he didn't want me spreading my version of that around, did I check his buzz? Stories like that would only cause division in the struggle, and I'd done enough harm already. The problem, such as it was — and he said he was sure I'd exaggerated it — would be dealt with by the right people.

'You can't believe what someone in that state says,' I heard him tell the deputy as I finally slunk from the bunker.

It was almost midday and most of the cadres were lounging around playing draughts and cards. I knew a couple of them from before, and since I was just from the front they were keen to hear my stories. Now that was more like what I'd been expecting. I left out the Zanla ambush of course, but brushed up the best of the rest — you know —

my heroic stand against the truck for example. I was just starting on the choppers, when somebody calls out, 'Ask him about his biggest battle, eating kamba!' I swing round and hey! it's Biani.

If I'd seen Smith striding out there amongst the bunkers with a golf club in his hand I don't scheme I would've been more shocked.

Eeh, man, I chune you I grabbed hold of the bloke and clapped him on the back and shook his hand till it about dropped off. 'Hey, hey, hey — good to see you again,' I chune him. 'I feel safe again.'

'I didn't think I'd ever see you again,' says ou Biani, shaking his head. 'I didn't think I'd ever see you.'

'Why?' I ask him but eeh, I chune you, to me the answer was pretty obvious: even ou Biani, even my buddy suspected I was one of Smith's men at heart.

Well, ou Biani, he checks me out, realises what's what, and tries to explain: 'I thought you were dead. A helicopter flew a netful of bodies over the kraals.'

As we walked around the camp I told him my story. 'So what about you?' I asked when I'd finished. 'Where did you get' — pointing to this gold watch on his wrist — 'that thing?'

He'd taken it off a whitey he'd ironed out in an ambush. 'But then Smith's men came after us, and we couldn't lose them. There was a skirmish and we were scattered. Three of us regrouped. We couldn't find the others and we were too few to operate so we came back here.'

'You looked for the other cadres?' I was surprised.

'It was all right,' Biani said. 'We were all fighters.'

'And Comrade Gondo?'

'Comrade Gondo is a fool. He's lucky to be alive.'

I told Biani about the camp commander and his threats. 'He tried the same tricks with me,' Biani said. 'He threatened me with court-martial — for desertion and undermining morale too. But the thing is, you can understand his position: if this gets around the Zapu cadres won't want to stay and fight.'

I pointed out that, what with these clashes and massacres and disappearances, not many Zapu cadres wanted to stick around anyway.

'These things are only rumours,' he says tiredly like he's argued out the issue 100 times without getting anyone to listen to him. 'Nothing is proven yet. We can't destroy the unity just because of rumours.'

Well, I agreed I'd follow the commander and not say anything about the ambush but, as it happened, the Zapu cadres in the camp heard the whole story soon enough. That evening, at a secret Zapu meeting, Comrade Gondo spilt it all, including the commander's threats, and there was nothing me and Biani could do except confirm the whole story.

'Zanu is trying to exterminate us,' bellows Comrade Mortar, this giant from Bulawayo.

'We must escape,' squeaks his buddy, Comrade Trigger, a tiny bloke, maybe just five foot. The two of them were about the same age but together they looked like a father and his son. If their bodies were different, their feelings were identical: they were both hardcore cadres, Zapu through and through, and all they cared about was the party. 'We must escape back to Zambia and rejoin Zapu.'

Biani tried to defend Zanu: 'How much of this talk is just rumour?' he wanted to know. 'Some Zanu cadres may be causing problems but it's not their party policy to murder us. For the sake of the struggle we must give it one last chance. . . . The big fish know what's going on — they'll put a stop to it.'

'After they've put how many more of us in our graves?'

Well, by the next morning Comrade Gondo had gone either to his grave or to Zambia. At first roll call we discovered he and another Zapu cadre, Gumboitaya, had vanished. Patrols were sent out to look for them, and Frelimo was alerted.

Us Zapu cadres met to discuss the situation.

'The commander is responsible,' shouts Mortar. 'Comrade Gondo was killed for telling the truth.'

'You're jumping to conclusions,' put in Biani. 'Maybe they're heading to Zambia — Comrade Gondo talked about it often enough.'

'Why didn't he tell anyone he was leaving then?' squeaks Trigger.

'Maybe he was scared the commander would come to hear of it.'

'It's fine for Comrade Biani,' says Trigger, very bitter. 'You're Shona, you're okay. The Maswinas here aren't gunning for you, but they're after us Ndebeles.'

'We've got to sort out the facts,' argues Biani. 'We can't start accusing the Zanu cadres here before we've got all the facts.'

'Maswinas,' sneers Mortar. 'You can never trust them. By the time we find the bodies — if we find the bodies — how many more will be dead?'

'Ya, how do we know you aren't a Zanu agent?'

'Nonsense,' says Biani. Eeh, he was very angry by then. 'Hate me or what, for being Shona or what — but I am a Zapu cadre and you are Zapu cadres. If you want to battle me, quite fine, but wait until we are back in Zambia amongst our own people.'

'Forget all this nonsense,' says a Zapu commissar impatiently. 'We have bigger things to worry about. Are we going to stay here to be picked off one by one or are we going to clear out?'

'If we leave we will all be shot for desertion.'

'If we stay we'll be shot anyway.'

'Let's go to Chingodzi — now — this afternoon — tell the big shots just what's happening here.'

In the middle of this, the camp commander rocks up, two cadres with AKs behind him. 'Disperse immediately!' he shouts. 'Disperse or there'll be trouble!'

'We're going to headquarters to tell them how you are murdering us,' the Zapu commissar yells back.

'To leave camp is mutiny and you know what the penalty for that is,' the camp commander warns. 'I suggest....'

'You just want an excuse to kill us!'

The commander looks like he is more than ready to oblige, but you can't shoot 25 mense just like that, especially when they've got gats too. 'Nobody has been murdered,' he tells us. 'Nobody has been killed — this is all your invention.'

'Then give us Comrade Gondo.'

'Where's Gumboitaya? Where's Comrade Gondo? Give us Gumboitaya! Gumboitaya! Gondo! Gumboitaya! Gondo!'

Behind the administration bunkers, the Zanla cadres were taking up their positions.

'Comrades Gondo and Gumboitaya have vanished,' the commander tells us. 'I've sent out three patrols to look for them. Frelimo is also looking for them. When we find them, we will bring them....'

'You'll bring their bodies back here and tell us that they were caught crossing to Smith.'

'Death is the penalty for desertion,' says the commander stiffly.

'Why did you order Comrade Gondo not to tell us what Zanu is doing to Zapu cadres? Do you want us to be wiped out?'

'Gondo — Gumboitaya — Gondo — Gumboitaya...' the chant drowns out the commander's reply. 'Gondo — Gumboitaya — Gondo — Gumboitaya....'

And whilst the commander backs off to the radio bunker to tell his story to HQ, us Zapu cadres, still cursing and shouting, split off to pack our kitbags for the long walk to Chingodzi.

Next day, while we were trapping along, we were picked up by an empty Frelimo supply truck and taken to Tete where Frelimo soldiers were waiting for us. They disarmed us, and escorted us across the Zambezi bridge to the Zipa HQ at the Chingodzi base, where we were put under guard and confined to barracks. We never did get to speak to any of the main mannes or find out what happened to Gondo and his buddy. There were rumours of graves being found, of unidentified bodies out in the bush, but nothing definite. Years later, in Zambia, I heard another comrade talk of a Comrade Gondo, but I don't know whether in fact it was the same bloke.

We sat around for days in Chingodzi base, squabbling and sulking, cursing Zipa and trying to bum smokes from the guards. Biani was restless, pacing up and down, up and down, eyeing everyone going past and once in a while there'd be this confidential conversation with the guards, which usually ended up with the guards either yawning or snorting with laughter. One day I check him hand over his watch, so I corner him behind the barracks and ask what's happening.

'Rudiya,' he tells me and eeh, he's looking worried. 'She's at the Chingodzi hospital. I've been trying to get somebody to take a message to her, but he's saying he can't find her. I don't know... hell, maybe she's taken up with someone else....'

I reminded him that when I'd been in hospital she'd been off in Maputo and said she probly wasn't back, but eeh, I couldn't quieten him down. Next day as we're perching there in the sun, playing cards and patching up our kit, I check this mammoth mamma heading in our direction, suck in my cheeks for a whistle... and then, hey! I check again; I don't believe it.... 'Rudiya! She's here!'

Biani charges across the courtyard to her. As they embrace the rest of us ouens whistle and cheer them on and the guards come running over to see what all the commotion's about.

Rudiya had news — big news. She's pregnant and eeh, when ou

Biani announces it, he's smiling like Zimbabwe had just been liberated.

'When's it due?' I ask him.

'In about four months she reckons,' and, as he goes on about how she'd been and what she'd said, me I'm doing some quick calculations there. Five months back — where'd we been then? The Unity Camp — ya, it was Biani's kid for sure.

'She'll be back tomorrow,' he's telling me, 'and she'll be bringing smokes and stuff for us.'

But when Rudiya came to the barracks the next day, she found we were gone. First thing in the morning us Zapu cadres were split up into groups of three and four and shipped off to prisons up and down the country. Me and Biani, along with Mortar and Trigger, ended up at the Tete prison. There we were shoved into this tiny stinking cell which already housed four other Zapu cadres — including ou Lovemore, our comrade from Unity Mountain days.

'They're leaving us here to die,' ou Lovemore informs us before we can even say howzit. Him and his buddies had been in the cell for three months and no one had spoken to them the whole time.

Eventually, we managed to calm him down and extract the full story. Him and his buddies had all been locked up for refusing to cross into the country. 'All the big shots in the unit were Zanu,' he told us, 'and they were so fresh-from-home they didn't know the working end of a gun. We refused to go with them.'

For the next few weeks it seemed as if we'd been forgotten too. There were eight of us in that cell, and only just enough room for us all to lie down. High up in one corner was a window, our only source of light, and the walls were mottled with dark splashes of dried blood from the days when the building housed the Portuguese security police HQ.

The only people we saw were the cleaners. They were prisoners too but, cos the prison was so overcrowded, they only spent the day there, and at night they went home to their families. Biani, who had picked up some Portuguese, tried to get chatting to these blokes, but they barely bothered to answer. They just did their graft, removing our slop pails and handing us our food and water.

The second meal, which we ate at about 5.30 in the afternoon, was the high point of our day: we were given macarao, Portuguese macaroni, and fish from the Zambezi. The graze wasn't too bad actually — what there was of it.

The meal was our reveille cos during the day the cell was so hot and stuffy you could do nothing but sleep. Sometimes the air was so bad that we battled to breathe. At night though, when the air was cooler, we'd sit cracking lice — the cell was crawling with them — and sing or talk, sometimes for hours. Ya, we'd talk about anything — unity, the struggle, Zapu and Zanu, Ndebele and Shona, women, drink, soccer, why whiteys were like they were, the future of Africa, Pan Africanism, socialism — hell, anything that came up.

After a month of this, we had a visitor, this Frelimo secretary, a short fat bloke with a bright pink handkerchief, which he kept stuffing in front of his nose as he spoke to us through the grille. He told us, in English, that we could go free if we joined Zanla.

'Zipa is dead,' he informs us. 'There is only Zanla now.'

'We are Zipra cadres,' Trigger counter-attacks. 'We will not fight for Zanla.'

'It's your decision.'

'We just want to get back to Zambia, to our own people,' pleads Comrade Lovemore.

But the secretary doesn't argue. 'If any of you change your minds,' he says, 'speak to the guard.'

We spent most of the night debating. 'Why not?' schemed one of the cadres. 'At least we'll be out of here. And first chance we get, we can foot it back to Zambia.'

'It's a trap,' said Mortar. 'If your enemy invites you to supper, he's going to poison the food.'

'Do you want to live here in the dark like a worm for the rest of your life?'

Next morning three cadres called the guard and told him they wanted to join Zanla. They were led off and we didn't see them again. We were five then: Trigger and Mortar, Lovemore, me and Biani. Me. if I'd had my way, we would've all joined Zanla — hell, I reckoned, one party was as good as another. I wasn't charmed, I chune you, with Biani and Lovemore: they were always talking unity but, when it came to the push, they refused to switch parties. The way I saw it, we'd be of far more use to the struggle out in the bush than rotting in prison.

'So how long you planning for us to wait here?' I asked.

'Make your own decision, Muzukuru,' Biani told me. 'Nobody's telling you to put your foot where I put mine.' Which was true, of course but, angry with him or not, I wasn't going to let Biani out of my sight. He was my buddy, and the only bloke I could count on to stand up for me.

A couple weeks later the Frelimo secretary returned. He must've figured we'd had time to do some thinking. 'Nobody in Zambia wants you,' he informed us.

'Nonsense.'

'Let us write to them.'

'Look, comrades, Frelimo sympathises with your struggle. . . .'

'Let us go back to Zambia then. We'll fight from there.'

But the secretary just repeated his offer and when he left, us cadres weren't feeling so happy, I chune you. For all any of us knew, we were going to be left sitting there in that cell for months, years.

Days passed, weeks passed and one afternoon when it was hot-hot, ou Lovemore began to wheeze. He wheezed and he wheezed until he collapsed. We beat on the bars of the cell, yelling and screaming, but no guard or cleaner came — they must've been on lunch or something. We thought Lovemore was going to die. Finally Biani told me to take our food pot and, standing on his shoulders, I smashed out the glass in the cell's window. We hoisted Lovemore up and held him gasping against the hole, his face in the fresh air, until he could breathe again.

When a guard finally came, Biani demanded to be taken to the prison commander. The warder probly schemed we were finally ready to join Zanla so he took Biani off to see him right away. Biani put our case to the bloke: we were freedom fighters; we were prepared to do anything for the struggle; we were ready and willing and we wanted to be useful. If he couldn't send us back to Zambia, then at least he could let us help where we were. The commander sympathised, gave him a pack of smokes and said he'd see what he could organise, and the next afternoon, for the first time, we were allowed into the courtyard, into the sun.

The light blinded us and, blinking like owls, we perched in the shade beside the building. The breeze off the bush was scented with muboa and frangipani. As our eyes adjusted to the light we saw that about 200 mense were crammed into that courtyard, jamming themselves into every tiny patch of shade. Ya, it was almost as cramped as the cell, but at least we were out in the wind and the sun.

A week later we began grafting as cleaners at a Frelimo barracks on the other side of town. Every morning, escorted by a single guard, we'd march to the barracks and in the evening we'd march back again. It'd been years since I'd seen a town and eeh, it was something just to walk down streets again, klanking the graze cooking in the cabins, watching the chicks stroll past with their buckets of water and bundles of firewood on their heads. Everywhere the walls were scrawled with Frelimo slogans and every room we could see into had a picture of Machel stuck to the wall.

Our job was basically cleaning up after the colonialists. Like just about everything else in the country, the barracks had been smashed up by the Portuguese as they pulled out. Frelimo had repaired about two-thirds of them, and it was our job to fix up what we could of the rest. We scraped the muck and dead leaves out of the buildings, scrubbed floors and walls. All the windows were broken, but there wasn't any glass to fix them with. Mortar, who'd once grafted for a plumber in Burg, began working on the bunged-up pipes. Once in a while we'd spend a few hours in the laundry washing uniforms or in the kitchen gutting fish or scouring pots.

Sometimes we carried supplies from the barracks across the river to the Zipa HQ at Chingodzi. Biani always wangled himself a place on these expeditions and soon as we were there, he'd start asking if anyone knew the nurse Rudiya. He had no luck, but he kept trying. Ya, those days, all Biani could think about was Rudiya and that baby. He'd already decided on the lightie's name, Unity — whether it was a boy or a girl.

'You might as well curse the kid as give it a name like that,' Mortar told him. 'We all know what's happening to unity in the struggle. Why don't you call it Victory or Freedom or something?' But ou Biani was set on Unity.

After about a month, the bloke who'd been escorting us around gave us a pass — gia de marche they called it there — to present to patrols and told us we had to get ourselves from the prison to the barracks by seven bells every morning. No more escorts, he told us; we were only five and Frelimo had bigger things to worry about. Us cadres, of course, began seriously trying to work out an escape plan. It was simple: wait till we're sent to Chingodzi, cross the bridge and vanish. But we had a couple problems: none of us knew how to get to Zambia and Biani refused to leave town till he'd seen Rudiya and his kid.

The second problem was solved when we delivered some uniforms to Chingodzi. With no escort to control him, first thing ou Biani barges into the hospital grounds and asks the nearest nurse about Rudiya.

'Yes, I know her,' the nurse says. 'She works with me.'

'Which ward? How can I get there?' Before she's finished explaining, he's off.

Rudiya was fine, he chuned us when he returned. The baby still hadn't come; she thought it'd only be another week or so. Quite fine. But Biani's not finished: 'Rudiya and the baby are coming with us — to Zambia.'

For a minute us ouens just looked at him.

'You're mad,' says Mortar. 'You want to bring a baby with us?'

'We've got enough problems without any screaming brat announcing our position,' put in Trigger.

'Are you sure she's going to want to go along?' I put in. This lightie business didn't sound to me like one of ou Biani's brighter ideas. 'She's still Zanu and she'll have the baby, and it's one hell of a long haul to Zambia.'

'She'll come.' The way he said it I knew there'd be no point in arguing.

'I don't believe this,' Mortar tells us. 'I can't believe cadres — cadres — could even be considering this nonsense.'

'This baby, it's not even born,' ou Lovemore pointed out. 'We can argue when it arrives.'

Well, that shut us up for a bit but it wasn't long before Lovemore had to find another excuse to stop us arguing. A week later when we carried a couple parcels over to Chingodzi, ou Biani sneaked off into the hospital. No Rudiya. She'd been taken to the maternity section of the Tete hospital across the river. It wasn't far from the barracks so on the way back we made a detour and stopped there. The rest of the ouens waited under these palms round the side whilst me and Biani slid past the orderlies and clerks, down the corridor into this ward where we spotted Rudiya lying in a bed asleep. Me, I faded away as ou

Biani took up her hand and started whispering sweet nothings.

I rejoined the cadres under the palms. As the minutes crawled by Mortar and Trigger began worrying someone in the barracks would notice that we were late. Just as Mortar suggests we leave Biani to find his own damn way back, he's escorted through the hospital's front door by about a dozen orderlies.

'He's a boy,' he shouts to us as he comes down the stairs. 'Unity — he's a boy — but so tiny — like this —'

'Are you still calling him Unity?' Trigger wants to know.

'For sure.' Ya, not even Mortar and Trigger could bother him then.

And as we're tramping back to the barracks, he just can't stop talking: he told us when his son was born, how long the labour had been, how heavy the child was, what a large pair of balls the thing had, how you could hear him shouting from one end of the hospital to the other, which didn't make Mortar and Trigger look any happier. Also he told us about this chick on the bed next to Rudiya: she was from Zimbabwe, Rudiya had known her sister slightly, and she's married this Frelimo big fish, a general or something. Her baby had died, and she'd given Rudiya clothes and bottles and stuff.

We made several trips to the hospital during the next few days, us ouens anchoring outside in the shade whilst Biani talked to Rudiya. Later, much later, I discovered that it hadn't just been sweet nothings the pair of lovebirds were whispering about. Biani was telling her to pocket any medical supplies she could — especially malaria pills — for our trip to Zambia.

But there were still big problems. Though every day we had a dozen chances to disappear, we weren't willing to risk it without a map. Even if we dodged Frelimo and ducked out of Mozambique, we'd be locked up if we landed in Malawi and blown up if we wandered into the minefields along the Rhodesian border. Biani quietly began asking locals questions about the route: where's this town, how far is the next one, what's beyond that? His tactics didn't alert Frelimo but they didn't get us very far either, and though no one we spoke to really knew the route it didn't stop them explaining it to us. We needed a map — or someone reliable who knew the whole route and could direct us.

One afternoon whilst we're still picking our teeth over that one, we rock up at the hospital and Rudiya — she's not there. Ou Biani, he's frantic, threatening to tear the place apart unless she's produced, when along comes this nurse who slips him a note from Rudiya telling us that she's been discharged and has gone to stay with her friend, the one married to the general.

Now, the general's house is on the other side of town in the compound of Frelimo HQ. We take a chance, flash a couple of old gia de marche to the guard at the gate and next thing we're knocking on the general's front door. Me, I feel like a lightie playing tok-tokkie; every nerve, muscle and tendon is yelling jump and run. The general himself opens the door, Biani explains who we are and we're invited inside. First thing Biani disappears to visit Rudiya leaving us ouens sitting there in the front room. The general smiles. We smile. He smiles. Finally Biani reappears, and the general pours us all a glass of wine in spite of our protests, no, none of us drink, and they both sit back and discuss the struggle. Another glass of wine. Gradually we begin to relax. Another glass of wine. The general proposes a toast to Zipa. Biani tells him Zipa is dead, that it's Zipra and Zanla all over again.

'Zipra is fighting from Zambia now,' Biani says. 'And we want to go back and rejoin the party. We're tired of cleaning toilets and washing floors. We are fighters.'

'It's a sad situation,' the general agrees.

'Well, then — can you help us?'

Ou Lovemore, he just rolls back his eyes. Here was Biani, a prisoner, asking a Frelimo general to help us escape. Me, I was scheming we were going to be locked up back in the Portuguese torture cell but quick.

But the general didn't seem at all worried. He sipped his wine and shook his head slowly. 'I sympathise with you cadres. But there's nothing I can do to help you. Officially nothing can be done.'

'Unofficially?' Biani asked. Eeeh, I was expecting to be locked up for 10 years for sure.

The general poured himself another glass of wine. 'I can't give you guns, if that's what you're after.'

'All we need is a map. A map of the way from here — Tete — to the Zambian border. That's all.'

'That's all?'

We're all nodding as the general picks up an empty cigarette box and draws the map on the back. 'It's not so difficult,' he says. 'You follow the road north and when you can't go any further north, you turn west.' Ya, it sounded very simple in the general's house but out in the bush, with hundreds of tracks turning off in all directions, it wasn't quite so easy.

Once we had the map, there was still one more problem: crossing the Zambezi. Round about Tete the river is almost half-a-mile wide, a slow green soup thick with sharks and crocodiles. You can't exactly swim across. There were canoes, but if a couple foreigners asked the villagers to ferry them across, Frelimo would be there waiting at the far bank. Besides, stealing canoes wouldn't have got us far either; they're delicate items and, unless you know what you are doing, they roll easily. We could also have followed the river all the way into Zimbabwe and then crossed into Zambia but the border was thick with enemy troops and lined with minefields.

Biani came up with a plan. Like I said, we sometimes carried supplies from the battalion over the bridge to Chingodzi. The gia de marche we used for the bridge were dated, but as we crossed quite often, the guards on the bridge had come to know us and though they'd check our passes, they didn't look too closely. 'If we could get into Frelimo HQ using old passes, we should get across the bridge,' he schemes.

'What happens if some bright spark checks the dates?' asks Lovemore. 'If we're caught....'

'So what can they do to us? We're already in prison.'

'They probably can't read anyway,' schemes Trigger. 'If Smith and his army had a piece of shit paper with a Frelimo stamp on it, those guards'd let them through.'

'And what about these?' says Lovemore, pulling at his prison uniform. 'How are we going to cross from one end of Mozambique to another wearing these? The first person who sees us will turn us in.'

'It won't be easy,' agrees Biani. 'But do you want to sit here for the next few years cleaning toilets?'

Lovemore scratches his head, still doubtful.

'We can scale some Frelimo uniforms next time we work in the laundry,' suggests Mortar. 'I reckon we can get five no sweat — how's that?'

'Six,' says Biani. 'One for Rudiya.'

Well, we socialised the uniforms, waited until the weekend when

Frelimo would be most disorganised, and then went into action. Biani left first, sneaking off into the bush behind the barracks. He circled round to the general's house where he collected Rudiya and the baby. An hour later, one by one, the rest of us ducked away, rendezvousing in this burnt-out house on the outskirts of town. Biani was carrying Unity in a Zambian kitbag — it'd somehow survived all the way from Smokers' Inn — which he fixed up lekker with these soft blankets. The baby was fast asleep. Trying to act casual, we marched down to the bridge.

The Frelimo soldiers on duty recognised us, hailed us as camaradas and waved us through. They hardly glanced at our passes. Me, I felt like doing cartwheels all the way across.

As soon as we were out of sight of the bridge, we ducked into the elephant grass, changed into our Frelimo uniforms and then hit out along the main road, greeting all the mense in the proper comradely fashion, clenching our fists and shouting 'Viva Machel!' A couple kays further on we turned off into the bush, when we checked this platoon of genuine Frelimo, come marching towards us and followed this path more or less parallel to the main drag. It was hot-hot and humid and the bush was thick; not exactly your Sunday afternoon stroll. Every couple kays we'd sink into the shade for a quick rush. When there was a stream nearby Rudiya would go over and clean up the baby. Sometimes a couple of us would head off into the fields to scrounge these spiky orange cucumbers that grew round there — once you'd peeled the spikes off those things they were like your usual cucumbers, cool and full of water. Ya, we didn't have much problem scaling whatever was around — beans, pumpkins, spinach — from the local farmers. What with our Frelimo uniforms no one was going to argue. Besides, I don't know if it was the season or what, but we hardly ever saw any mense in their fields. By the look of it, the local farmers just stuck in the seeds and came round every once in a while to see how the battle with the weeds was going.

Three days out we came to this river with Frelimo guards on the bridge. We weren't so sure we could pass for Frelimo any more so we sneaked up the bank about a kilometre until we came to this bend where the river seemed shallow. We looked around for crocs — no sign — and then Mortar, who'd been taught how to swim properly, went across to check the scene out. The water was about chest deep and the current wasn't too bad, except close to this rock near the other bank, so we all stripped and, holding our clothes and whatnot on our heads, waded across in Indian file.

We were nearly there when Lovemore screamed and slipped and began thrashing about like he was being attacked. The rest of us, I chune you, we jumped out of there but quick. Mortar, who was waiting on a rock, saw that he was just panicking, and dived in and pulled him out, no problem.

Except that he'd lost all his clothes — and a box of anti-malaria pills. Lovemore, man, he looked green.

Biani, he was furious. 'This could be comrades' lives,' he told the bloke. Though none of us were too keen to stick around after that scream, he made us poke around in the reeds to see if we could find the pills. All we found were Lovemore's trousers.

Rudiya brought out her own supply of pills which she'd kept separate. She counted them out. There were just 14. 'There's not enough for prevention now,' she told us, very much the nurse, 'but we can try them if anyone gets sick.'

One afternoon, I remember, we stopped for a rush cos Rudiya said she was thirsty. She gave Unity to Biani to hold and went off to pick us some cucumbers. The rest of us sat around and smoked, fending off the flies and the mosquitoes. It was hot and we were tired and she didn't come, didn't come.

'We'd better go find her,' says Biani eventually.

'She's probably just stopped to eat a couple,' yawns Trigger.

But, finally, after another few minutes, Biani and Lovemore go off to check out what's happening.

Next thing the three of them reappear — Biani carrying Rudiya, Lovemore with a kitbag full of cucumbers.

'Must've been the sun,' says Biani as he lays her down under a tree. He squeezes one of the cucumbers, letting the juice dribble onto her forehead. 'She'll be all right in a couple of minutes.'

Rudiya moaned and began to shiver, and it was then we realised she had malaria.

Biani pulled her into the sun and we all sat around waiting until the shivering had stopped. She came round, sort of, and asked Biani to bring her one of the anti-malaria pills from her kitbag. He squeezed a couple of the cucumbers into a pot and gave her a pill and the juice to drink. She managed to get the stuff down well enough, but five minutes later she puked it all up again.

Sick as she was, she still gave us instructions. 'Boil some water,' she told him. 'Dissolve two pills in it, and inject it into me.' She closed her eyes and began to shiver again.

After Biani'd stuck in the needle, she went to sleep and us ouens walked off a few yards and discussed what we were going to do next.

'We'll have to wait around for a while,' said Lovemore. 'She should be fit enough to travel in two-three days.' The poor bloke, he was looking pretty bad. You could see he was blaming himself.

'I'm not going to stick around here waiting to be captured and taken back to prison,' Trigger informed us.

'She'll be fine in a day or two,' Biani assured him.

'It's fine if they capture you — a Shona. You can always go back to Zanla, but us they'll wipe out.'

'We are Zipra comrades and we stick together,' Biani said. 'Anchoring here for two, three days won't be such a big thing.'

'Leave her for Frelimo now — at least they've got hospitals,' Mortar argued. 'She'd stand some kind of chance.'

One by one Biani caught our eyes, checked us out. 'A comrade isn't just another person in the struggle. He is like your father and your mother: he or she is your family because out in the forest none of us have families. If you are hurt, he is the one to help you; if you are in a fight, he is the one to cover you. There is no one else you can ask. You can go on if you want, I'm staying here with Rudiya.'

So we anchored there for three-and-a-half days, just sleeping and smoking. When Rudiya was well enough we started out again, weaving our way through the thick tangled bush. It was hard going, humid and hot, and I was always exhausted. The baby got sick and cried and cried. I began to scheme Mortar'd been right; we'd been crazy to bring the kid, a little kid like that, he should have been somewhere warm and clean and dry with mense who could look after him properly. I was sure he was going to die, but what could we do? Eeh, I couldn't even care about myself some days. I'd wake up weak and tired and just want to sink back into the dirt and never get up. Somewhere along the line I must've got sick myself, and I remember that time through a kind of feverish haze, a hot green hell with the sun beating down and our clothes damp and heavy, sticking to our backs, and clouds of mosquitoes and ticks and mopane flies and the dust that dried in our eyes and throats. Our uniforms were rotting by then and even the mense out in the bush could tell we were refugees, not Frelimo.

Every evening me and Mortar and Trigger went foraging for graze. One time when we were walking through these patches of pumpkins and beans down near a stream, I heard this gurgling and thrashing about just a couple yards off in the bush. Me, I scheme the locals have ambushed Mortar and Trigger, and I duck into the bush there and snake over to check out what's what.

As I wriggle round this rock eeh, I spot them: Mortar lying between the legs of this girl and pomping away, one mammoth hand so tight around her throat that her eyeballs are bulging out. A rag had been stuffed into her mouth, and Trigger's gripped her wrists. She was squirming about, pounding her heels against Mortar's back, but it didn't seem to bother him any: he pomped away like a piston.

As he's finishing he spots me. 'Take a turn,' he says, pulling up his trousers as he straightens up. The girl kicked out wildly, tried to roll away, but Trigger held her tight. 'We can all die any day. This can be your last.'

The way the two were looking at me there, I knew damn well that if I didn't accept their invitation there'd be complications. Zipra executed all those guilty of rape, and those two weren't going to live at the mercy of any goffel. Also, hell you know, I was excited — it'd been more than a year — two years almost — since I'd been with a woman.

So I went over and took down my trousers and knelt there. She could've only been about 14 years old. There was blood there, and the spunk from the other guys, all oozing out. I closed my eyes and stuck it in while Mortar held her head and arms and Trigger took her legs.

But as I pomped away there I couldn't you know, stop thinking of how open, how vulnerable your back is, and all that blood, and the girl, and I felt myself going soft. It was sort of like peeing in a shit-house full of blokes when I was a lightie: the harder you try, the worse it gets. I tried thinking of sexy things but that didn't work so I pretended to finish, and Trigger took over.

I waited there with them until they had both had another turn and then reminded them that we'd better get moving. Mortar said he'd 'take care' of her.

'Why...' I began, but Trigger just pulled me away. 'You want Frelimo to come looking for us?' he says as we head back to camp.

Mortar caught up with us about five minutes later. None of us said a thing to the others.

One morning Lovemore collapsed. As we were close to the road at the time, me and Biani carried him into a thicket. He was shivering — malaria. But there was nothing we could do about it; we had no more pills. The last one had been shared between Rudiya and the kid. Well, we took a rush, rolled a reef. I reckon everybody knew what everybody else was thinking, but no one said anything. We just perched there, slapping at the mosquitoes, watching Lovemore sweat and shiver.

Finally, around evening, Biani stands up. 'Look,' he tells Lovemore. 'There is no point in us waiting around. We've got no medicine. We can't help you. You are going to die.'

Lovemore, he just lies there and looks at him.

'There's no one to carry you on their back,' Biani says, 'You're too big for that. And if we wait here until you die, either Frelimo or the mosquitoes will get us. We are only the weapons of the people. We must think: how many can I save from this?'

Lovemore nods. Biani lets out his breath. 'We'll take you to the side of the road. Maybe someone will find you and take you to the hospital. If we get back to Zambia we will tell your family.'

So we carried him to the road and, since he was sweating, we put him in a patch of shade. There was no one about. 'If Frelimo interrogates you,' Biani told him, 'say that you were all alone. Say that you were trying to cross into Zambia, but you got sick. Okay? Do you understand, comrade?'

Lovemore nodded, turned away and closed his eyes.

And we put foot. We pushed on through the mosquitoes and the haze and the ache in our legs, putting one foot in front of the other, one foot in front of the other. The path seemed to go on forever, my head spun, and I was scared I would fall cos I knew that if I went down I wouldn't be able to get up again.

When the morning came and we finally stopped I dreamt I was trapping on and on through this valley of thick rustling bush full of shadows and cries. The bush seemed to close in front and behind, and I picked up this sickle and began to hack out a path, slashing and chopping. I cut and I cut though my hands were all blistered and the sickle was blunt until at last I came to this still, small pond. All around there were reeds, and I pushed my way through and planted myself on the bank. The pool was clear all the way to the bottom, and swimming around in it were these silver fish, not your ordinary fish, but shining and so quick you could only half see them. I began to catch the fish and when I'd caught them all, I sat back. All around me it was still and peaceful and all the tiredness, the fever, the ache, the worry. . . it all left me then.

The next day I remembered my dream. That feeling of calm stayed with me. I told Biani about it and he didn't laugh or make a joke out of it like my goffel buddies would have done. It was a sign, he said, and a good one. We were trapping from Furancungo up to the border then and the road wound through hills and it wasn't as hot as it had been earlier. Whether it was the coolness or whether I was over my fever, I don't know, but I felt like I was waking up after a bad dream.

Not long after that we were trapping along when we saw some soldiers down below us — in uniform, but not in Frelimo uniforms.

'Hey!' says Rudiya. 'We can't be in Mozambique anymore — we must be in Zambia!'

So we make for the nearest village and ask the way to Katete. The old queen, she scratches her head and says that she's never heard of any Katete. But there's this town, this Dezda, just down the drag and a Young Pioneer camp just over the gomo. Maybe they would know where this Katete is. Do we want her to show us the way?

Young Pioneers! We'd ended up in Malawi. Well, we had to change direction fast, or else we'd be locked up like the ANC.

'Don't worry,' Biani chunes her. 'Don't worry about those Young Pioneers.' He explained that we were from Mozambique, but that we didn't want Mozambique anymore. Frelimo had stolen all our land and our houses, and now we wanted Zambia.

She shook her head, clicked her tongue very sympathetic and gave us a potful of sadza.

Once we'd eaten we backtracked to Mozambique and checked the general's map again: he'd drawn a road with a fork in it, left to Zambia, right to Malawi, but out there in the bush there was this whole spaghetti of tracks twisting off in every direction. Fortunately ou Biani had picked up basic navigation somewhere along the line so we waited for evening. He took his bearings from the stars, and led us in a south-westerly direction. Three days later we flagged down a

Zambian police Land Rover just outside Katete.

'We're Zipra cadres,' Biani told them. 'We've come to rejoin the struggle.'

The police took us to a customs post and the customs officer phoned Lusaka. Two days later a Land Rover arrived to pick us up.

'You four will be taken to the base camp,' the driver informed us. 'Your wife and the baby, they'll be taken to one of the refugee camps.'

On the way to Lusaka, Biani made Rudiya learn the address of his father off by heart. 'When the struggle is over, you must go to my father's house,' he told her. 'Even if I am finished my grandfather's spirit must see the child,' and every few hours he made her repeat the address again and again and again.

Chapter 15

*W*hen we reached the camp the first thing we heard was that Kissinger, the US Secretary of State, had been on safari in Africa. After organising America's retreat from Vietnam, and after patching up a settlement of sorts in the Middle East, he now wanted to bag Zimbabwe for capitalism.

He'd flown to Tanzania to speak to Nyerere, and then on to Lusaka for discussions with Kaunda. South Africa was next on his schedule, and there he'd met with Smith and Vorster before flying back to speak to Nyerere again.

For a while it looked as if he would collect his trophy. Smith, who'd been talking about a 1 000 year empire just six months back, went on Rhodesian television and told the whites that majority rule was inevitable — and that was the end of the stumbling block which had tripped up all the previous talks.

But times had changed. The conditions Smith was offering — majority rule of sorts in two years, a say of sorts in the interim government — would have been tempting just a few years back, but now that the leaders of the struggle had their new guns and new armies, they reckoned they could win a settlement on their own terms.

Then it came out that Kissinger had sold one set of proposals to the Rhodesians and another to the struggle. Smith had been told he could have the Defence Ministry and the Ministry of Police in the interim government, which meant he could coup the new government if it didn't happen to suit him. The guerillas and the Frontline states pointed out that Kissinger didn't have any right to negotiate such details, and that was the end of that.

Nonetheless, the British began organising a conference at Geneva to see what, if anything, could be salvaged. Zapu and Zanu united (on paper at least) for the occasion, and all the main mannes from the various parties flew off to Switzerland.

The Geneva conference opened at the end of October, and the first item on the agenda was the date of Independence. That's it, me and Biani were scheming, the discussions will go on for months and months, and we'll be stuck here in the camp. But, next thing, the two of us are assigned to this unit about to cross back into the country. Quite a few units crossed around that time: maybe the big fish at the conference wanted to prove to the world that Zipra was a force to be reckoned with, maybe they realised Smith wasn't ready to surrender after all.

We rendezvoused with the rest of our unit at a camp near the Zambezi and there we found we were replacing two cadres who'd vanished off into the slums of Lusaka just a few days before. Biani replaced the deputy commander, and I was made medic. Zipra security couldn't have trusted me much: they switched the bloke who'd been trained as medic, Comrade Fidel, to munitions logistics.

Comrade Mamba, our commander, had crossed into the country twice before, both times as a commander. Because he'd trained in Russia, he'd gone right to the top. He was a big bloke, Mamba was, and when he talked, I chune you, mense jumped, no argument. He had fighting in the blood, he told us, being one of the descendants of Mzilikazi. Already he had killed two of Smith's men, and wore two watches on his right arm to prove it.

Comrade Todzo, the commissar, had grown up not far from our zone. The bloke didn't look like much — bent and shuffling, his clothes all baggy, and when you spoke to him his forehead always twisted up as though he had to concentrate hard, real hard, to understand you. But when he started talking you realised eeh, this one, he's no fool. He had a sweet tongue, did Todzo, and his duty was to explain the struggle to the masses. To us cadres he was a kind of mother, listening to all our complaints, advising us, putting our side of the story to Comrade Mamba when we landed in the shit. Even though I was officially the medic, he did most of the doctoring.

Ya, he was hot with herbs, was ou Todzo, and when you cut yourself or had a cold, he'd disappear off into the bush and show up 10 minutes later with a couple of leaves or a root. He'd put the leaf on your cut, tell you to chew the root, and in an hour or so you'd be feeling better, and in a day or two you'd be fine.

The other main manne, our security, was Russia, an Ndebele from round Tjolotjo. He'd gone to Salisbury when he was still a kid to find work to pay off his bride's lobola. 'I've paid two cows — the deposit,' he was always telling us, 'so she'll be waiting when I get back.' Whilst in Salisbury, he'd become a member of Zapu, an active member, and he'd had to skip the country after firebombing the house of a sellout. From Zambia, he'd been shipped off to Russia and Algeria for training. As far as he was concerned, he knew more about the struggle than all the rest of us put together. Any chance he got he'd tell us about his training, about how when he'd finished the course in Russia, they'd quizzed him about the exact number of stairs to the dining room, the names of the people who'd met him at the airport on his first day.

Well, ou Russia might have been able to answer all his classroom questions, but whether it was bad leadership or just bad luck or what, both sections he'd led into the country had been wiped out and, for this, his third crossing, he'd been demoted to security. His graft was to pick up what he could about enemy operations in the area; also at the end of the mission — and he never let us forget it — he'd be putting in a report on each of us. He was always watching to make sure we stuck to the straight and narrow of the party line, no matter whether it made sense or not. If Nkomo had announced — as he once did — that all us fighters immediately had to drive every last enemy soldier out of our operational areas, he would've obeyed orders even though he knew as well as the rest of us that it would've been crazy even to try. Ya, if the party had announced that the moon was red, Russia was the kind of character who would've reported everyone who argued against it. He was also our bazooka man, and carried the barrel of the gat.

Koshkosh, the logistics, carried the shells. We called him Koshkosh cos he was a hunchback, and when he walked, the legs of his trousers rubbed against each other koshkosh-koshkosh.

Koshkosh's people were from Malawi, but they'd moved to Harare when he was still a boy, and there he had picked up Shona, Ndebele and English, and quite a few other things besides. Ya, ou Koshkosh, he was a town boy, a joller. He was for the struggle for sure, but he didn't see why it had to interfere with his other activities. He liked his stop, did Koshkosh, and always carried a big bag of it around with him. And food — eeh, Koshkosh had the stomach of an elephant: if there wasn't anybody around to stop him, he could polish off a whole pot of sadza, no sweat. Chicks too he was always chasing. Ya, that one he was always tripping over trouble.

Our scout, Comrade Nyoni, a Shona from the Lupane area, was the opposite — quiet and reliable. He'd grown up herding in one of the TTLs, and had never gone further than the nearest village until one day he upped and left his wife and three lighties to join a guerilla unit. Nyoni knew the bush like the back of his hand; he knew how to set traps for birds, how to make birdlime, how to hook mice from their holes, how to poison fish — and how to find them — and how to tell what fruit and roots you could graze.

Comrade Fidel — he'd been named in honour of Comrade Castro — was also a farm boy. He'd grown up on some whitey's farm near Bulawayo, and went off to the city looking for graft when he was about 14. He didn't find anything, and after a month or so, he'd been recruited by Zapu and sent to Zambia for training. He was young, only about 17, and he tried to show what a big shot he was by imitating the rest of us, especially Koshkosh. He was crossing for the first time.

Once we'd been given our mission, we were taken by truck to Fuella, a small town near the Zambezi. Just outside town a guide met us and led us to a camp near the crossing point. It was quite a trek, a whole day's tramping through the bush. The camp was well camouflaged and no fires or shooting were allowed for five kays around cos Zipra didn't want to attract any attention to the area. That stretch of river was crawling with crocs, really big ones, monsters, some of them 30 feet long. A Zambian nganga had given the guards muti to keep these items well-behaved and, to make sure they stayed on the right side of the animals, they fed them the head and the skin of all the buck they shot. The blokes reckoned their tactics were successful: during the past year or so the crocs had only taken one fighter.

Our unit anchored in the crossing point camp for a couple of days listening to tales of crocs and cadres until, late one afternoon, the guards decided that it was safe to cross. They ferried us across the river, two at a time, in this tiny rubber dinghy. We didn't see any crocs but, out in the middle of the river a herd of hippos floated half-sunken. One of those things steered over towards us and yawned; hell the thing's mouth was as big as an oven, and its teeth, man, they were serious — it could've chomped us in half, no problem. I cock my AK — 'don't shoot, don't shoot,' the guard whispers — and the thing snorts and sinks back under water and vanishes.

Once we landed we took up defensive positions and anchored there, already sopping with sweat, and waited for the rest of the unit to cross and disembark. Up ahead of us, through the trees, we could see the slopes of the Zambezi escarpment stretching off into the whitish blur of the heat haze. When we were all across, we moved inland, watching every step, cos Smith's men had mined and booby-trapped the bank. The minefields weren't a problem; the guards knew where they were and it was easy to pick our way through them. But after the minefields there were booby-traps and eeh, with those things around, you didn't dare move an inch.

We were lucky though. We'd crossed into a game reserve and the animals had cleared the trails for us: as they came down to the river to drink, they walked right into the traps.

We crept along till we spot two dead waterbuck — a cow and a calf. They're humming with flies but they haven't begun to smell yet, they can't have been dead long. We check and check the path from us to the nearest waterbuck and — aah, I see it, a thin strand of gold across a patch of sunlight — a piece of fishing line about knee high. One side is tied to a tree stump; the other leads to an explosive. We'd had a close shave, I chune you; that line'd been tied so tight that if we'd so much as brushed against it, we'd have been blown back across the

Zambezi.

We chopped out the bucks' hearts and livers and tramped on, following this game trail which wound up through the thick river bush. It was getting dark; the darkness seemed to ooze out of the bush and coil itself, hot and sticky, around you, and sweat dripped stinging into your eyes and clouds of mosquitoes settled on every scrap of bare skin. The moon came up and ahead of us the steep rocky slopes of the escarpment were smooth and gentle in the soft light, and beyond them, looking as close as if you could reach out and touch, you could see the hills of Zimbabwe.

Gentle as those slopes looked, having to lug yourself and your gear to the top was the worst part of the crossing. According to Zapu intelligence, all the valleys — all the easy routes up — had been mined and booby-trapped for about the first 10 kilometres, so Comrade Mamba led us straight up, and we scrambled over those rocks like third-rate baboons. Even at night the Zambezi valley was hot-hot, and dragging your webbing, loaded as it was with rounds and supplies for the whole mission, was sticky, bruising graft. Our hands were quickly cut and battered by the rocks, our feet blistered and our shoulders rubbed raw by the straps. Every half-hour we had to take a rush: Mamba would whisper the command, and we'd all collapse onto the first flattish patch we came to, and lie there panting, sipping water and maybe sharing a smoke, until Mamba told us to get climbing again.

There were plenty animals around. The baboons bared their teeth and shouted, 'waurrh-waurrh' as we passed; herds of impala, zebra and wildebeest faded off when they checked us coming. Lions roared all around us — not what you could call a comforting sound — but they kept their distance. The only lion we actually saw was loping along a game path just before first light. The moment it checked us the thing about fell over backwards it disappeared so fast.

The only animal which caused complications was a rhino. We'd heaved ourselves over the steepest section of our route, and climbed down into this valley. Just before dawn, when the birds began to sing, we spotted this rhino and her calf in a small swamp thick with reeds and arums. Mamba decides 'divert', so we turn off onto a game path climbing up the side of the valley. The rhino spots us, snorts, and rushes off. Quite fine. On we trap. Next thing though, the animal turns and circles back behind us and charges. Mamba, who's in the rear, fires a shot into the air, but the thing just keeps on coming, barrelling towards us like a goddam tank. A second later, Mamba opens up and the rhino goes down grunting and squealing.

We circled back to check the thing out. It was one massive animal, man, and fat and muddy as a pig. 'Let's cut a couple of quick steaks,' suggests Koshkosh. 'Rhino?' schemes Mamba curious. 'Won't it be too tough?' 'It's meat,' says Koshkosh, and taking off his shirt he gets down to work, sawing away at the thing's thigh with his bayonet. He hacks off a couple lumps of meat and wraps them in leaves. When we cooked the meat that day it smelt more or less okay while it braaied over one of Koshkosh's special smokeless fires, and we were all set for a lekker graze. But eeh, when we tried to eat the stuff it turned out to be so tough and rubbery and musty that not even ou Koshkosh himself could finish it off.

Once we'd reached the top of the escarpment, the going became much easier. We crossed from the game reserve into the TTLs but, as the security reports reckoned that the villages were infiltrated with spies, we avoided all contact with the locals and trapped on towards our operational area.

At dusk one day we stopped just below the crest of this koppie while Mamba and Nyoni checked the map. They puzzled over it for a couple of minutes and then informed us ya, we're here, we're already in our zone. Comrade Todzo brought out a horn of snuff, and we passed it around. Down below us, in the villages, you could see the glow of the fires among the huts, the thin loops of smoke hanging in the still air. Mist was rising off the river, and the cattle were bellowing in their kraals. We could smell the sadza and relish as it cooked, even the tobacco of the men at their pipes. Everything seemed so quiet and peaceful. A woman shouted for her child, a dog barked, yelped, and barked again.

Mamba folded up the map, we cached the heaviest of our supplies and, carrying only our gats and a little food, we began the long climb down.

There was a beerdrink at the first kraal we came to, the people had just finished weeding their mealies. Comrades Mamba and Todzo went down to make contact while the rest of us waited in the bushes, AKs at the ready. They came back about an hour later, smelling slightly of beer, and informed us we would hold a meeting now. We positioned ourselves around the kraal as the locals were all assembled: about 30-40 mense from all around the area were gathered there, most of them women, old men and lighties. There was hardly anyone the right age to recruit; all the young people had left, presumably to look for graft in the cities or on the white farms just across the river.

'Do you know who we are?' Comrade Todzo began when he had everyone seated. The audience shook their heads.

'We are the freedom fighters. We are here to help you, the people, liberate yourselves from the settlers — to chase them off and to return your land to you. Now Smith and his black dogs have told you many lies about us: the enemy is telling you that us freedom fighters are short and hairy — some kind of wild animal that they tie up in their sack. They say we have tails — eh,' — he turned round and waggled his backside at the people. 'Now tell me true: do I have a tail?'

The mense laughed. Ya, he had a sweet tongue, did ou Todzo.

'These white liars tell you we are foreigners, Russians who want to steal your land. What kind of fools do the mabhunu think you are to tell you such rubbish stories? Mothers, fathers, you can see and hear we are not the enemy — we are your children. We are all Zimbabweans, and we want the same things you want. We want to take back our land and our cattle which the white settlers stole from us. We want to be free, we want to rule ourselves — we don't want to be beaten and robbed and murdered by these white thieves any longer.

'We don't like having to leave our homes, we don't like living in the forest. We don't want to die. But our people are suffering, and when a son sees his parents suffering, he cannot just lie like a lizard in the sun. When a brother sees his sister insulted, he cannot just smile and say, "yes, my baas".' The mense, ya, they were nodding to each other: they liked what they were hearing, that was for sure.

Then he handed out pamphlets about Zapu and taught them one of the Zapu songs.

> Chaminuka lead us against the enemy
> Musaruwa lead us against the enemy
> Chinamano lead us against the enemy
> Monomatapa lead us against the enemy
> **Nkomo** lead us against the enemy

Give your children power to win the struggle
Help us liberate Zimbabwe

Then he went on to explain that Nkomo was the father of the struggle, that Nkomo had been leading the fight against the settlers for over 20 years.

'Who is the father of the struggle?'

'Nkomo!'

'I can't hear you,' — cupping his ear.

'NKOMO....'

'Now the people can only be victorious if we all fight — if you all work with us. We freedom fighters are the spear of the struggle — but a spear cannot fight by itself. We cannot fight without you, the people, helping us.'

Comrade Todzo told the people what we expected of them: the kraalhead, Comrade Clever Maradza, was now our eyes and ears in the area, and if anyone found out who the sellouts were, or picked up any information about Smith's men, or spotted them out on patrol, then they must tell Maradza at once, and he would pass it on to us. 'You see — you the people will be on the front line of the fight for your own liberation,' Todzo told them.

But the people they just sat there. They certainly weren't as enthusiastic as they had been when we'd started.

Then Comrade Todzo called for recruits. No answer. It was getting embarrassing. Finally he tries another tack. 'So how do the whites treat you?' he asks. One old bloke, this Titus, totters to his feet, steadies himself on his stick, and starts on about this mabhunu impounding his cow and about the shocking way the cops beat up, lock up and fine drunks. He hopes, he tells us very serious, that when this Nkomo rules the country, he'll treat drunks better than the mabhunu do.

Comrade Todzo really checks this bloke out. You can't quite tell whether he's performing or whether he's actually a bit mad in the head. One or two of the mense are sniggering among themselves, but most are looking so worried ou Todzo decides to play it straight. 'What about the cow?' he asks and I chune you there's no doubt they're genuine about that one. Ten, 15 mense jump up and start shouting all at once.

Ou Todzo quietens them all down, lets them all speak one at a time. This mabhunu, they tell him, this Makhaki (he always wore khaki clothes) impounded any animal that strayed onto his land and sold it and kept the money. He was always whipping his workers and, if they made mistakes, he kicked them and docked their pay.

Todzo asked who would help us punish this exploiter of the people. 'I'll help,' this Titus volunteered. 'I am old and I must die soon. But I want to ask you one question.'

'Yes?'

'How can you beat these whites and their guns?'

'We have guns too,' Todzo told him, raising his AK with its long banana magazine. 'We have guns stronger even than Smith's.'

'But these whites they have lived with guns all their lives. Their ancestors knew guns. What can fly better than a bird?'

Todzo explained that we had been trained to use guns, that our ancestors would protect us and defend us. But Titus didn't look convinced. 'I can see you don't believe us,' Todzo told him. 'Remember deep pools become crossing places.'

Then Todzo warned the people not to tell anyone, not even their relatives at the next village, that the boys were around, and warned them that we had a special magic to smell out traitors. 'And if we catch a sellout, we are going to burn down his huts, we are going to kill him and his family and his cattle. We will leave his body to rot for the dogs to eat, and his spirit will roam the earth and never rest.'

Back in the bush we discussed the situation while we downed the sadza and relish and beer the mense had given us. 'These people are for the struggle,' ou Todzo reckons, 'but they are still suspicious. We will have to show them that our words aren't empty.'

'That farmer — we'll kill him,' says Mamba dipping a fistful of sadza into the relish. 'That should do it.'

'Yes,' reckons Biani, 'and we must also ask for the blessings of the mhondoro.'

'What's all this spirit nonsense,' scoffs Russia. 'This is what we must believe.' He pats his AK, and launches into this long story about materialism and the struggle.

'My grandfather's spirit spoke to me once,' says Biani.

Russia is not impressed. 'A Zipra cadre — a deputy commander — and you believe that? Aaeeeii, the party should've cleaned all that nonsense out of your head long ago: Zipra cadres are materialists, not idealists. We believe in what we can touch and what we can see.'

'I believe in the spirits in a bottle,' cracks Koshkosh, but no one was listening to him.

'This isn't nonsense,' says Biani, and eeh, I can check he's boiling. 'I'm not your liar — or your idealist or materialist either. I heard the spirit of my grandfather speak.'

Russia, he shakes his head. 'Hallucinations — we are supposed to be the new brooms sweeping the country clean — and you are spreading superstition like a farm boy — if you'd been to Russia like me. . . .'

'Superstition or what,' breaks in Todzo, 'truth or what — it doesn't matter. What does matter is what the people here believe. And I tell you one thing: if we offend the mhondoro, no one here will ever help us.'

Comrade Russia isn't exactly convinced, but before he could open his mouth, Mamba puts his rubberstamp on Biani's suggestion. 'Comrade Todzo grew up here,' he tells us. 'He knows the feelings of the people. First we must win them over and then we can teach them.'

Next evening, a couple of cadres went to the kraal to collect Titus. Comrades Mamba and Todzo cross-questioned him about this Makhaki, what his habits were, how many guns he had. He told us though Makhaki was a farmer, he spent a lot of his time piloting his small plane around the area on the lookout for 'terrs'. His house was protected by a security fence and a pack of dogs, and he owned about a dozen gats including an Uzi.

'If you want to catch him,' Titus told us, 'Friday is a good day. He drinks with his friends and comes back late.'

Mamba then sent him off with Nyoni to recce the farm and check that he had the geography straight. When they returned the next morning Nyoni reported that the old man knew what he was talking about: the dogs, the security fence, the aeroplane were all there exactly as he had described them. Even so, Nyoni didn't scheme it would be too hard to hit the place. 'We could either rocket it or ambush the bloke when he's returning home,' he said.

'We'll hit this one while he's coming home,' Mamba decreed. 'We'll show these people how to fight the mabhunu.' We would meet Titus at Maradza's village on Friday afternoon, and attack in the evening.

Next afternoon we paid our respects to the local spirits. Wearing our civvies — shapeless black trousers and torn khaki shirts — us cadres trapped along in broad daylight as if we're your ordinary locals off to a beerdrink. One of the lighties from the kraal led us along this path which rambled round the koppies near the river. The women were in their fields, bent over weeding, and up in the koppies the herdboys and the goats and cattle lay panting in patches of shade. We followed the bed of this stream for about two-three kilometres until we came to a cluster of six or seven huts tucked away in the middle of this clump of muhacha trees.

Mamba nods. Three cadres take off into the bush to give cover. A thin yellow dog yaps, ducks away between the huts. A rooster cackles. We anchor there, anchor there. Me, I'm not quite sure what to expect: bats, hyenas, owls? Whatever, I was not going to make a fool of myself like with the snuff. Finally this lightie rocks up, your usual snot-nosed seven-year-old.

'We want to consult the mhondoro,' Todzo tells him, and then the bloke himself finally appears. He's short and paunchy, maybe 40 years old, barefoot, and wearing only baggy black trousers tied up with a piece of string. He looked ordinary, just like any of the mense round there except for one thing: he carried a thin metal rod, maybe three foot long, which had a knob on the end of it. I figured he'd come to lead us to the svikiro, the medium, but Comrade Todzo recognised him at once.

'We are the boys,' he says with a sort of bow. The guy eyes us all for a moment then claps his hands, and a woman peers round the wall of one of the huts. 'Beer,' he shouts and then leads us to this ring of stones, the dare, in a clearing under the muhacha trees.

Well, once we've all settled ourselves down, the svikiro claps his hands, picks up the pot of beer his wife has set in front of him, tastes it, and passes it to Mamba who's seated beside him. Each of us takes a sip and passes it on, while Todzo begins talking about the weather, how well the cattle are doing, what the harvest looks like—anything, it seemed to me, but what we'd come to talk about.

Anyway, as the svikiro was going on about the crops, an old man who also carried a steel kierie hobbled over. Ou Todzo, he stood up, greeted the bloke as 'muzukuru'. Ya, me, I was taking a swig from the pot of beer right then and I just about dropped it. That old man was a houtie to the core — nothing white about him at all. 'What's this?' I whisper to Biani. At first he doesn't check what I'm on about, but then he grins and explains that 'muzukuru' doesn't only mean goffel. The bloke who helps the svikiro while he's speaking with the spirits is also 'muzukuru'.

Me, I've never been too comfortable around spooks and stuff, and this other meaning of my name gave me goosepimples. While Todzo and the muzukuru talked, and the medium wandered off to his hut, I perched there trying to sift this lot for significances.

When it grew dark, we went to the svikiro's hut and found him waiting for us there, sitting outside on a mat.

'I want a goat,' this weird high voice coming from his throat informs us.

'Chirinduka wants a goat,' repeats the muzukuru helpfully. 'The spirit wants a goat.' So off we go to find a goat. The old man led us to a nearby kraal and there, for a couple of dollars, we bought the goat, a large black-and-white billy which we led back to the svikiro's hut and tethered to a nearby tree.

The svikiro vanished inside his hut, and his muzukuru who sat outside the door with us, pulled out a mbira and began to play. It was dark by then, and the thin twanging of the strips of metal made a spooky, lonely music. Todzo began to clap his hands and the rest of us joined in, clapping and swaying, waiting for the svikiro to show.

After about an hour the door of his hut swung open and he stumbled out, his face set and strange, his eyes out of focus. His wife came over and put a bowl of water, with a smoking piece of charred stick floating in it, down in front of him, and the muzukuru draped this black cloak over his shoulders and handed him a short wooden kierie. He sat down, anchored there for five minutes unmoving, staring right through us as though we didn't exist, and all the time his lips moved as if he were arguing or praying, but no sound came.

Then, with a grunt, the svikiro leans forward and sucks his face full of water. For a moment he just sits there, swollen-cheeked and blinking. Me, I just wanted to get up and run — this lot was all too weird for me. Next thing this svikiro spits the water out, sprays it all over us.

'I, chief Chirinduka, fought against the invaders with Nehanda and chief Mayashayamombe,' the svikiro suddenly began in a high sing-song. He spoke quickly, in what Comrade Todzo told me was old-fashioned Shona, and I could only catch snatches of it. The others were leaning forward, puzzled.

'It's the spirit!' says the muzukuru.

'Ask him about the struggle,' says Todzo. 'Ask him how the spirits feel about the struggle.'

Which he does, and as the svikiro goes on in his high voice, the old man translates. 'Chaminuka says now is the time to fight the invaders! Nehanda says now is the time to fight the invaders! Changamire says now is the time to fight the invaders! Now is the time to take back what the invaders have taken from us; now is the time to take our weapons and win back our cattle, win back our land, win back what is ours and drive the invaders from our country!'

The svikiro stopped talking and looked beyond us into the night, his eyes still wide and vacant. The muzukuru handed him a horn filled with snuff and he took a pinch, then began muttering again, almost to himself. 'Chaminuka has begun to fight. Chaminuka will lead us as we chase the evil from the country.'

'What about the boys from the bush?' Todzo whispered.

'Our children are the sons of the soil,' came the mhondoro's answer. 'They have taken up our spears and they are continuing our fight!'

Mamba nods at Todzo. We had our message loud and clear. 'Tell the spirit that his children thank him for his words,' says Todzo. 'Then ask him — will the struggle succeed this time?'

The old man leaned over and muttered our question to the svikiro, and for a moment there none of us breathed. It was a big question, a very big question — with all our weaknesses taking on the Rhodesians sometimes seemed to be nothing short of lunacy. The svikiro sat there unmoving and it seemed like forever before the spirit began to speak again.

'The sons of the soil will overcome the invaders,' we heard at last. 'Chaminuka and Nehanda will chase them from the land!'

Well that, I chune you, had us just about cheering.

'Your children thank you for your words, great spirit,' said Mamba. 'We will fight to help make your prophecy happen.'

Next day we began, visiting the kraals and villages in our zone, holding meetings where we explained Zapu and Zipra and the mhondoro's prophecy. Our zone was a rough triangle: its southern boundary was a stretch of river, maybe 30 kilometres long; and a section of road about the same length, which bridged the river en route to the border, made up the eastern side. The river and the road were linked by a chain of koppies — the third side.

According to Zipra intelligence the road was being repaired and widened, and a platoon of RDR goffels guarded the bulldozers and other equipment. There was also a district commissioner's camp of sorts at a village which had accumulated round the trading store next to the road.

It was poor farming country, except for some of the land near the river, and the best of the river lands were across in the white farming area. In our zone — on the TTL side of the river — the country was broken and hilly, and beyond the hills was a flat dry plain covered with mopane scrub. Beyond the plain were the koppies bordering our zone. Among them were these two huge and blackish gomos which the svikiro told us were the homes of the spirits of the old people, the people who had lived there long before Monomatapa had ruled or Zimbabwe had been built.

But, even with the mhondoro's blessing, we didn't have much joy at the kraals. After Todzo had spoken to the assembled mense, telling them who we were, why we'd come, explaining how the mhondoro had prophesied our victory and ordered them to help us, he'd ask for food and information. The villagers would tell about a DC patrol three weeks back and they'd feed us sadza. But when he asked for recruits, there was only silence; when he asked for Zapu party members or Nkomo supporters at the kraals, not a single person would ever admit having heard of us. It should've made us suspicious, I suppose, but we swallowed all the stories we were told, and at every kraal Mamba made the headman our link man.

'I can't figure these people out,' Todzo kept saying. 'You'd think they'd help us. They understand why there's a struggle, yet. . . .'

'There's Titus,' Fidel put in. 'He's eager enough to help.'

'He's also been drunk everytime we've seen him.'

'Maybe they don't trust us,' suggested Biani. 'Maybe they think we're Sku'zapo — Selous Scouts.'

'They want to see if we can fight,' said Mamba. 'When we've finished that farmer, then they'll come forward — just wait.'

Come Friday we rock up back at Maradza's village. Titus is waiting for us there, half-drunk as usual but ready and willing. With him as our guide we crossed the river into the white farming area, and followed this path across Makhaki's land, through his fields of tobacco and groves of oranges, on towards the lights of his cabin up on the koppie above us.

Quiet-quiet, we sneak up the koppie, sticking to the path. Nyoni's up front with Titus. The wind's blowing toward us, so we don't have dogs to worry about. Everything's going according to plan but eeeh, my stomach melts. Silly, cos the farmer's a soft target, but you can't argue with your gut. When we stop in the moonlight for final instructions, I barely make it behind the bush to do my business.

'If the wind was coming the other way,' schemes Koshkosh sarcastically, 'they'd smell us coming.'

'Sssssshhhh!'

We move on again, listening to all the noises of the night, eyeing every shadow. Two hundred yards, 100 yards. The house is quiet and still. 'This is going to be easy,' I tell myself, but my guts are cowardly, they're beginning to melt again, and pa-pa-pa-pa-pa-pa the night is suddenly ribboned with the red of tracers — I throw myself down, spin round, and I'm off, sprinting back down the koppie, jinking and dodging through the trees.

'Come back, you cowards!' this honky is shouting. 'Come back and fight like men!'

But we were far too busy gapping it, splintering off in all directions. Not a single one of us cadres even returned the fire.

We regrouped, panting, back at the gathering point — a small koppie across the river. A quick count: all present and correct. Our only casualty was Fidel's AK; he said it'd been shot out of his hands.

'The spirits must've been with us,' panted Todzo. 'If they'd waited till we were in the killing ground... if that bloke hadn't opened up too soon....'

'There must be a sellout somewhere,' Biani was saying, 'has to....'

'Cowards!' said Russia, 'that mabhunu called us cowards. We should circle back and show him — cowards!'

'We fight only when we can win,' Biani reminded him.

'There's got to be a sellout!'

'What about him?' Russia pointed to Titus, who'd thrown down his stick and run like a lightie. 'What about you, old man? You, hey you? Did you go telling anybody what we were up to?' He grabbed him by the collar, but the poor bloke was so spooked by the shooting, Russia would've found it easier to shake sense out of a stone.

'He would've been wiped out first,' schemed Todzo, 'so he wouldn't have done it. And anyway, if he sold us out, he wouldn't have stayed with us.'

'Listen,' put in Biani, 'there'll be security force choppers after us tomorrow.' Choppers! For me the word was like an electric shock.

'We've got to withdraw,' I broke in. 'Tomorrow Smith's going to be sweeping the area. . . .'

'Let Titus go,' ordered Mamba and pushed the guy toward the path to Maradza's village, 'we can sort this out later.'

'Traitor,' muttered Russia. 'He might be the one for all we know. . . .'

'Later,' said Mamba. 'Let's move!'

And we began to trap. After a couple of kays, we split up, rendezvousing further on, and then trapping again, trapping right through the night — no rushes — trying to fiddle the trail so that no one would be able to follow. We trapped for miles that night. By the time the sun rose we'd crossed the road bordering our zone and we'd hidden out in a cave in these koppies just a kilometre or so beyond it.

Eeeh, but I was so exhausted, so exhausted that I couldn't sleep. When I closed my eyes the trail was there in front of me, shadowy and twisting and I was plunging along it, not daring to look up for a moment in case I stumbled and fell. I shook myself awake, told myself not to be an idiot, it was only a dream, and dozed off again. Then I'm lying in this bunker and all around me are Smith's men, FNs at the ready. It's just as I start to scream that I realise I've been dreaming. Everyone shushes me and moans and groans and goes grumbling back to sleep. I try to doss again and this time I hear buzzing. I shake myself awake scheming it's the chopper dream, but even when I'm awake it doesn't stop, and I stick my head outside, my eyes crinkling against the late afternoon sun, and what do I check but this chopper cruising along down the valley.

I duck back inside but quick. 'There's a chopper — they're after us.'

'May the balls of these mabhunu rot,' moans Koshkosh, 'I want to sleep.'

'It's probly just a routine flight,' mumbles Todzo.

'We'd better get moving,' cries Fidel, who is wide, wide awake.

'Calm down,' Russia tells him. 'The helicopter can't see in here.'

Me, I figure Russia knows what he's talking about so I settle down again and close my eyes, whilst all the other blokes, grumbling and shuffling, rearrange themselves.

But after that no one can sleep and next thing, the chopper is backpedalling, sweeping past us again. They were after us for sure. We must've left some trace: footprints or signs that we'd wiped out footprints — probly there when we'd crossed over the dirt road. Whatever, it was too late for tears.

It was Nyoni who spotted this patrol just as it crossed the road and continued up the valley towards us. They were obviously following our spoor, the tracker bent over like a guineafowl as he trotted forward. Well, there was no particular reason for us to stick around to say howzit, so we gripped our gats, and sneaked off down the slope.

'If we have to split up,' Mamba told us, 'we'll rendezvous at the gap over there,' — pointing to the neck between these two huge blackish gomos — 'there between those two mountains where the svikiro said the old spirits live.'

Just as we hit the dry riverbed in the floor of the valley, the chopper roars overhead again, and we all dive for cover. The thing eases down about a kilometre up ahead of us — and a second stick jumps off and starts casting around for our trail. As us ouens are huddling there among the rocks and thorns trying to pretend like we're part of the scenery, the chopper lifts off again, and this new patrol starts sweeping up the valley away from us.

'If one of these honkies spots us now,' Biani breathes, 'we're going to be the polony on Smith's sandwich.'

Well, there's nothing for it but to crawl along, keep our heads well down, and hope hard. Then someone spots a gap in the koppies just up ahead, a gap leading through to the plain and, beyond that, the spirit mountains.

We duck into the gap and take cover. The patrol behind us sticks to the bed of the stream, and marches right on past us just 50 yards away. We lie there, gats cocked, pressing ourselves flat against the rocks and thorns and eeh, just when we're scheming we're safe, and just as we're beginning to crack jokes about Smith's stupidity, there's the buzzing overhead again.

We dive for cover, but eeh, that pilot, he spots something, and comes over to have a look. The dust whips up in devils around us as we cower down, flattening ourselves into the earth. The chopper fires, circles, fires. It seems as if he doesn't know where we are exactly and he's aiming to keep us pinned down until the patrols get within range and flush us out. Down come a couple of grenades which explode just about 10 yards off, showering us all with sand and splinters.

'Stay down, stay down!' screams Mamba.

When the dust clears ou Koshkosh is rubbing blood and dust out of his eyes, and blood is blotching Biani's shirt high on his right arm. Another grenade explodes, closer. We flatten ourselves even further into the dirt. Me, I'm wanting to jump and run. 'We're going to die, we're going to die,' Fidel is muttering beside me, 'we're going to die. . . .' Mamba and Biani each fire off a magazine skywards and the chopper backs off a bit, then — pwwwaaa — another grenade hits nearby, flattening a thornbush, and there's the rattle of FNs from the patrols. The chopper backs off and disappears. Its fuel must've given out or something.

'Come on! Move!' yells Mamba. 'Move or you're dead!' Koshkosh jumps to his feet, groaning and swearing. 'Russia — Muzukuru — cover fire! The rest of you — move!' Me, without thinking, I roll behind this sugarbush. It's like I've been switched to automatic. I fire — roll sideways — fire — roll again. For a second I anchor, trying to figure where the enemy fire is coming from. A couple of rounds tear up the spot I'd been a moment before and me eeh, I flip myself sideways — roll — fire — roll — fire whilst behind me, Mamba's yelling the orders as the unit withdraws.

Russia ducks down beside me. 'Over there,' he pants, nodding toward a heap of rock about 50 metres from us as he clicks another mag into his gat. 'Go — and cover my back.' Me, I didn't need any second invitation. I'm off before he's finished. Russia fires a burst here, a burst there and the rounds are rattling all about as I dash to the rock, snake up the side, crouch in the thicket of aloes.

Then eeeh, I check something: a glint of metal, shaking grass. Part of the patrol is trying to outflank us, they're working their way round on the right and cutting off Russia and me. 'Watch it!' I scream, opening up in the general direction of the movement. Soon as I open up, there's a chorus of gats answering back. No ways is Russia going to follow in my footsteps, not with that guard of honour waiting for him.

Ducking among the boulders and tangles of thorn Russia vanishes off to my left. They fire a couple of quick bursts, but it's too late: he's gone. He's safe. But now Smith's men, they're closing in on me. From the way they moved forward, keeping well behind cover, revving up every likely hiding place, it was obvious they were good troops, experienced troops, and they were just waiting for me to panic and run.

Then I clicked; it was like someone had turned on a light in my skull, I knew what I was going to do; I had a plan. Smith's men were waiting for me to run, wanting me to panic — well, here goes. I picked up some small rocks, gooid them down the koppie and fired my AK up into the air. Experienced troops hearing that lot were sure to figure I'd lost my head and was gapping it. And ya, these blokes on the right they're smart enough to take the bait. I check four of them bobbing up and down, trying to spot this panicky 'terr'. Ya, whitey, I'm scheming, I'll show you. You're always figuring us goffels are too dumb to catch what's going on, but I'm gonna show you — I'm gonna screw you. I rolled another couple of rocks down to encourage them.

One of the soldiers wriggles out onto a flat piece of rock. He's checking and checking, trying to spot me, and that's when I hit him. The gat jumps in my arm, he's picked up by his legs and swept off the rock. 'They've hit me!' he yells. 'Fuckin' gooks've hit me!' On the rock there's his gat and a big red splash.

The other blokes are poking their heads up, looking about for their buddy, and I let them have it too — kkkkkkkk — then I dive off to the left across this patch of open ground, flinging myself behind this boulder, and leopard crawl, leopard crawl.

'They've hit me! My leg... they've...' the whitey shouts. There's this sudden flare up into the dust in front of me, I throw myself to the side into a clump of grass, roll behind a rock, fire a burst in the general direction and take off again, zigzagging through the thorns and mopane.

Buzzing fills the valley, fills my head and I launch myself into the dust, try to lie like a rock, a log, but the chopper doesn't even bother to look for me. It heads straight over to the middle of the plain where the rest of the unit are putting foot, racing for the spirit mountains.

There was this huge roar and the grass flattened as the chopper shot off towards a reddish smudge of dust out in the middle of the plain. That's when I lost my head: I jumped up and raced right after it, too panicked to bother with strategy or tactics. I could see the gap between the gomos that Mamba had pointed out, and that's where I was going — irrespective. The chopper rose and dipped as it revved up patches of mopane scrub, and clouds of red dust whipped and whirled around it. Then it began to descend slowly, and for a moment I thought that the thing'd been hit but, instead of toppling over or bursting into flame, it dropped slowly-slowly as if it was being lowered on invisible ropes, and there, black against the red dust, I saw Comrade Mamba holding his gat high above his head with both hands — in surrender.

Me, I kept running, I ran all the way to the spirit mountains. As I reached the foothills I spotted the rest of the ouens disappearing up a gorge. I put foot and caught up with them as they stood in a circle.

'Mamba,' I pant, 'Mamba — they got Mamba.'

'Dead?'

'No — surrender — held up his gat — chopper landed — took — him.'

'Get moving, we must —'

Biani took the gourd from his neck and sprinkled a pinch of snuff on the ground. 'We are the sons of the soil,' he intoned. 'We are fighting to free the soil and the mabhunu are chasing us and we need a place to hide. Spirits, please help us, hide us on your mountain.'

'We don't have time for this rubbish,' Russia muttered in my ear. I was inclined to agree with him, but I didn't dare say anything in case it delayed us. We hung in there, all of us cadres, all through this long moment of silence, until Biani finally looped the gourd round his neck again, and we carried on up the mountain, picking our way among rocks, up and up, scrambling through banks of thorn and thickets of aloe, until finally we came to the top, and there in front of us was this cliff. The only way down was the way we had come, and already the Rhodesian army units were probably halfway up. Exhausted, we collapsed behind this heap of rocks, the only possible place for a defensive position. Around us, for about 50 metres, there was no cover at all.

There was nothing to do but take up positions. If we could hold off the Rhodesians until darkness fell, we'd be able to sneak off. If they spotted us while it was still light and called the bombers down on our positions, well.

'Comrade Mamba, he was very brave,' puts in Nyoni when he's got his breath back. 'Last time we crossed, he saved my life: there was a skirmish, and I was shot in the leg. He stood there firing — stood upright like a man while the rest of the comrades helped me withdraw. I can't see why he would surrender.'

'Was he wounded?' Todzo asked. He'd found some mupembere leaves which he'd crushed and was now plastering over ou

Koshkosh's cuts. 'Could you see? Perhaps he was wounded and knew that Smith's men would get him, and waited to blow them up with a grenade.'

There was a murmured assent. That's what must've happened.

'But the chopper flew off okay,' I objected. 'And anyway he didn't look injured to me.'

'Maybe it didn't go off, maybe there was a struggle,' Todzo put in. 'And he was so far off, and there was so much dust how could you know if he was hurt? Maybe he wanted to blow up the helicopter when it landed.'

Todzo had a point, everyone agreed.

Then, there way below us, we heard the rustling of bushes. A stone rolled down a slope. We stiffened, cocked our gats. Biani swore under his breath. In another 40 minutes or so, it would be dark and we would be as easy to catch as a black cat in a coal mine. But, in the last light, we're very vulnerable, very vulnerable indeed. 'Quiet,' Biani whispered. 'Wait till I fire. Koshkosh, Fidel — you two cover — everyone else break to the left —' On the left there were about 50 metres of open ground, bare of all cover. We were trapped.

The security force climbed up the slope towards us. One hundred metres, 50 metres, 30 metres. We lay with our safety catches off, still as a stone.

'This is useless,' one of the soldiers was chuning his buddy, '... getting dark, leading us on a wild-goose chase....' They weren't shouting or anything, but what with the acoustics up there, sound carried like the smell of a smoke on a still night.

'It's getting late,' — same voice again. They seemed to have stopped. '... waste of time... ask me. Cooper's crazy to send us up here.'

'Ya, let's go back, man. We've got the one. This place gives me the creeps.'

'Those rocks up there... could be there... spoor goes straight up.'

'Ag, nobody could hide up there. Tracks go right to the edge, then stop. I've seen it before. Their idea of a joke.'

For a second there was silence. Then one of them said something we couldn't catch; it must've been some kind of joke though, cos we heard them laughing and a minute later, like in a dream, the honkies had turned and were shuffling down the mountain.

'They had us,' breathed Biani about five minutes later. 'They had us in their palm — all they had to do was close their hand. . . .'

'It's the spirits,' said Todzo staring down the darkening slope. 'The spirits are looking after us.' Biani unlooped the horn from round his neck and dropped a pinch of snuff onto the ground. Right then I scheme not even Russia felt like scoffing.

Chapter 16

'We better get moving,' reckons Biani. 'Mamba knows where all the arms caches are. If we're going to save anything, we'll have to hide it before the security force gets moving in the morning.'

'Mamba is a Zipra commander,' says Russia angry. 'His blood is the blood of kings. He'll never talk.'

'When those bastards start on him,' reckons Koshkosh, 'he'll forget all about commanders and kings.'

'Never. Not Mamba. He'll die first.'

'Well,' says Biani, 'we can't take chances. Comrade Koshkosh: what's the position of the food caches?'

'There's very little food — rather we go for arms first.'

Comrade Fidel then tells us that all the arms caches were right over on the other side of our zone in the koppies above Maradza's village. Mamba knew where they all were so we would have to move them. 'I don't know if we can get there and find them and move them tonight,' he says, and adds hopefully: 'if the mabhunu find the caches, there'd be no point in sticking around. With what we've got we can hardly fight a week — we'll have to head back to Zambia.'

Ou Biani checks him out with a naked eye there, and he shuts up fast. 'We're not going back just yet,' Biani informs him. 'In fact we are not going back until we have completed our mission.'

We put foot all the way to the koppies behind Maradza's village. Ou Biani, he kept us moving, cursing anybody who slowed down or stumbled. I was so exhausted I hardly knew what I was doing, hardly noticed it when Biani clapped me as I fell out of line, almost asleep on my feet. All night long he went up and down the line. 'Come on, faster!' he kept yelling at us. 'Was your father a snail or a tortoise?' — encouraging us, swearing at us, anything to keep us putting one foot in front of the other.

It was still dark when we reached our first cache. We reccied the area and, as there was no sign of the enemy, we collected our weapons and hid them. We reached our second cache too, but by the time that we had finished moving it the birds were beginning to sing and there was no time to save the third arms cache or the emergency food supply. Smith's men captured them in the morning.

At first light we found ourselves a cave and slept. Not even my worst dreams could keep me awake. We didn't even bother about the enemy finding us; nobody could've even pretended to stand guard.

It's late afternoon when we finally wake up. As we perch round waiting for the dark, Biani reminds us that now Mamba has been captured, he is the commander.

We all nod. No problem.

'We need a deputy though. . . .'

Now, Russia, he'd been trained in Russia and alles, he'd been commander before and we all figured he'd be chosen; so did he — the ouen was leaning forward there, nodding, ready to hear his name.

'The cadre I've chosen,' says Biani, 'he's crossed into the country a couple of times. I've watched him in action and he's a good fighter. He never loses his head and he never gets excited: Comrade Nyoni. . . .'

Russia shakes his head like he's not hearing correctly. 'What's this now?' he demands. 'The commander is now Shona, the commissar is Shona, and now the deputy is Shona too!' Ou Biani, he'd landed in the shit plenty of times for fighting against tribalism, and he wasn't happy to be accused of it now.

'I chose the best one,' he says, very quiet. 'He might not be Ndebele, he might not have trained in Russia, but he's the best bloke here. This tribalism you talk is only fit for Smith.'

That shut Russia up all right, but after that him and Biani never liked each other.

At dusk we went down to Maradza's village and found the headman leaning against the wall of his hut. Beside him was a gourd of beer. 'Sit! Sit!' he cried when he saw us, and clapped his hands. 'Beer, beer, beer for the boys.'

We stood. 'We haven't eaten since day before yesterday,' Biani told him. 'We want sadza and relish — now!'

'Come — come, sit!' Maradza jumped up, flapping his arms round hospitably. 'I'll get you food — Rudo! — Rudo!'

A dark, dumpy woman scuttled round the side of one of the huts, stopping dead when she saw us. Maradza rattled off an order and she vanished back in the direction she'd come.

'Smith's men were here looking for you on Saturday,' Maradza told us, spitting spectacularly. 'Smith's dogs. . . .'

'Did you offer them food too?' Biani didn't wait for an answer. 'Call your people together.'

And so they assembled, every last person in that village, even the children who were big enough only to cry. 'We were ambushed outside Makhaki's farm,' Biani told them. 'We were ambushed by the enemy and we could have been killed: if it wasn't for the spirits watching over us, we all would have walked right into their guns. Afterwards the enemy attacked us with helicopters and one of our comrades was captured.' Biani paused. Everyone was quiet. 'What we want to know is, how did the enemy know where to find us?'

'Everyone here knew we were going to ambush the farmer,' said Todzo. 'Everyone here could have told them that. But only one person knew *when* we were going to ambush him — Titus!'

The other mense turned to look, waiting as Titus pulled himself to his feet, shaking his head, protesting that he hadn't told the enemy we were coming. 'Why would I tell them? You said yourself — I would be the first to die.'

The people nodded to each other, agreeing. The old man was making sense.

'So how did the enemy know then?' demanded Biani.

'Somebody told them — but it wasn't me.'

'Who then?'

'Well, people in the village knew. . . .'

'Is this true?'

There was a chorus of agreement. Yes, they had all known, every one of them.

'But,' said Todzo, 'how should they know? How should they know something that is a secret between us and you?'

'You didn't tell me it was a secret.'

'How could you be so stupid?' Biani went over and cracked him one across the face. 'Do you think we will let you kill us with your not thinking?' Clap! 'You think Smith hasn't got ears everywhere? Maybe we didn't tell you to shut up, but we expected there was something in your head except bone. Think!' — Clap! — Clap! — Clap!

Some bloke volunteered that Titus had been drunk and in the midst of his drunkenness had thundered on about how he was a big man, just the man to kill Makhaki. Just wait till Friday night, he'd told everyone who cared to listen. I'm a big man now, you'll see.

When Titus lay bleeding and snivelling in the dirt, Biani turned to the mense. 'So, one of you told the security force? This dog here told the village — but he didn't tell the enemy. Who did?'

Silence.

Biani grabbed Titus's ear and yanked him to his feet. The bloke screeched with pain. 'A comrade has been captured!' Biani shouted now. 'Somebody will die for it. Is it going to be you?'

'I don't. . . .'

Biani twisted harder.

'Mlambo — it might have been Mlambo. . . .'

'Might have been?'

'It was — it was.'

'Why didn't you say so before?'

'I wasn't think. . . .'

Biani left off the ear and kicked him one in the groin. The bloke fell to the ground in agony.

'Mlambo?' Biani asks the mense. 'What do the rest of you say? Is this dog still not thinking? Was it Mlambo?'

'Lies,' squeaked this greybeard near the back. 'Rubbish, lies.'

'It was him,' a woman called out. 'It was him. His son was here afterwards with the police — and he gave the old man money.'

'My son always gives me money,' Mlambo protested as the crowd shoved him to the front. 'He is a good son and every month he gives me money so I can buy cows for his bride price.'

'A good son?' Biani roared. 'A good son who works for his people's enemies?'

'No — no — he is not good by being with the government, he is good to me, his father —'

'How can he be a good son for you when he is not a good son of Zimbabwe?'

'How can an old man have so much money?' this woman cried.

'He has many cows,' put in the bloke behind Mlambo. 'He is allowed double the cows of the rest of us.' The number of cattle that you could keep in the TTLs was restricted to prevent overgrazing, you check, and the mense were very bitter about this.

'My son, he is a big man with the district commissioner. . . .'

We searched his hut and, tucked away in the thatch, we found a cache of about 60 dollars.

'Look at this money!' Todzo held it up for them all to see.

'My son. . . for his bride price. . . .'

'Or was it your bride price when you married the enemy?'

'Never! I never. . . .'

'I saw him!' another woman shrilled. 'I saw him take the money from his son!'

'And he was showing him one of those papers you boys gave us. . . .'

'Lies! Lies!'

But suddenly it seemed like the whole village had seen him for certain and everybody remembered it.

All of them had seen him take the money and, when they thought about it, most of them realised that they'd seen him showing his son the pamphlets. Mlambo was the one with connections to the enemy, it must have been him. Everyone agreed.

Mlambo went down on his knees. 'My son does not listen to me,' he pleaded, cringing like a dog that knows it's about to be kicked. 'I only keep cattle for the bride price —'

'You're a sellout, you're betraying your people — your own people

— for money. He is a Judas to you all, this son of Mlambo, and his father has been helping him.'

'No! No!'

'What do the masses do with sellouts?'

'Hit him,' the people were shouting, 'kill him — hit him!'

'As he is a spy, first we must cut off his ears.' Todzo handed his bayonet to the woman who'd first denounced Mlambo, a huge lumbering old aunty with this fixed wide grin. She grabs the bloke's head and, just as if she's slicing off a piece of pumpkin, she lops off each ear with one neat stroke. She threw them at him, and he just looked at her, his face blank, as the blood floods down his neck, and gobbets on his shirt and shoulders. The ears, lying in the dirt, looked like little rubber toys. You couldn't imagine how they'd ever fitted onto him.

'Hit him,' roars Todzo, 'kill him.'

But the mense just stood there for a moment, as if not quite believing what they'd heard.

'Come on — pick up your sticks and hit him.' Mlambo put his arm over his face and began to whimper. 'Come on — you judged he was a traitor.'

The aunty with the grin snatches a kierie from someone's hands, and fetches the kneeling man such a clout across the back of the neck that he collapses, screeching like a dog that's been run over. She storms in, smashing him over the head and neck and arms as he lies there wriggling, and another three or four women grab sticks and shriek and climb in too.

'Kill the sellout,' yells Todzo, 'harder, harder,' but what with the thwack of sticks on flesh you can hardly hear a word he's saying. Suddenly the whole crowd's joining in, and everyone's pushing and shoving in this circle all around him, and we can't see what's happening anymore.

Mlambo stopped screeching, and after a minute or two some people pulled back, looking sort of sick. Through the screen of legs you could see the body, still now and twisted, and the sticks, some splashed with red, smashing down on him again and again.

When we were sure it was all over, Todzo shooed the last of the villagers from the body, and Biani spoke to them, telling them not to bury it. The mense there eeh, they went quiet cos, you check, if a body isn't buried properly, if it is left out for the witches and hyenas, then the man's spirit can't leave the earth and rejoin his ancestors, but must roam through this world on its own forever.

Not to bury someone, even a sellout, was a serious move.

That night me and Biani went on a short recce of the area. After we'd trapped a ways, we stopped and smoked a reef and I started rambling, telling Biani about my days in the security force, about the time we'd hit the landmine near Chipinga. 'Ya, this honky lootie, he blew away two mense just like that,' I told him, 'and meantimes, they were always chuning us how we were fighting to 'protect' the people.'

Biani really checked me out there. He knew what I was getting at. 'Sometimes we do have to beat people up,' he said, 'and sometimes we have to kill them. But we are killing for a good reason; we are killing for the struggle.'

'I didn't mean it was the same....'

'The sooner the struggle is victorious, the fewer will die,' he says, staring right at me. 'Pity now will cause more deaths later. We can't worry about just one person at this stage, we can't allow liars and sellouts.'

Eeeh, from the way he said that, I caught a spook then, I chune you, and I remembered Stinker, the cadre I'd turned in to security in training cos I thought he was out to trap me. You have to be so cautious; you never know how people will hear things. Before that night, I would've told Biani anything — how I felt about the unity, about Zipra, the struggle — but afterwards, for a long time after that, I never discussed a thing with him.

Ya, once he'd become a commander, he'd started sounding almost as Zipra-Zipra as Comrade Russia. He wasn't exactly keen on anyone questioning him, and if you questioned the party, you were just about a sellout. He was still my buddy and alles, but he was also a Zipra commander, and I knew if I slipped, if I gave him the wrong impression, he would quietly take me out on patrol with him and there'd be a shooting accident.

All this worried me, bothered me. I remembered those honky blokes I'd overheard way back in — where was it? — ya, after we'd captured that 'terr'. They'd had a few dops and one was telling his buddy and the rest of the camp how he wasn't fighting for the civilisation and democracy crap the officers were always on about. He was fighting for what was *his* — his farm, his wife, his kids, his country.

But the comrades — blokes like Biani, Todzo, Nyoni, Russia — they had nothing of their own any longer, not even their names. Everything they'd had, they'd lost when they'd taken up the struggle. They couldn't contact their families, so they didn't know if their parents were alive or dead, if their wives had run off, if their kids were begging in the gutter. Any property they might've had, would've been confiscated. If a comrade died, we'd bury him, if he was lucky, somewhere out in the bush — and forget about him. We had to worry about ourselves. His grave wouldn't be marked and it would be as if he'd never existed. Ya, some of those blokes, they had nothing, nothing but the struggle.

Oh, I'm not saying there weren't plenty ouens who'd strayed into the struggle or who fought for what they could get out of it — the car, the job or whatever some sweet-tongued commissar promised them — but there was also a core of cadres who were fighting not just for themselves, but for freedom, for the people, and their future. And if some of the people had to get beaten up or killed you had to understand it, because we were fighting to put an end to all the fighting, we were fighting to put an end to all the suffering and misery caused by Smith's government. We were fighting so that the people would be able to rule themselves.

We woke up slack and tired as if we had the babbelas. We made ourselves some tea, ate a couple handfuls of cold sadza, and tried to figure out what we were going to do next.

'We must knock some more sense into these villagers,' reckoned Russia. 'When they're convinced we're dead serious, they'll cooperate.'

'A guerilla moves through the people like a fish through water,' cautioned Todzo. 'If you separate the fish and the water, the fish won't survive. We have to get the trust of the people. So far we've shown them that we can hit them — now we must show them that we can help them.'

'What are we supposed to do then?' scoffed Russia. 'Tell them naughty-naughty? Next time we'll smack your hand? But if you're a good boy, we'll give you a sweetie? Do you think anybody will listen to that? If we tell them do, they must do — else they die — finished. That's what they told us in Russia.'

'They'll sell us out.'

'Somebody down there's already sold us out. They must be more scared of us than of Smith.'

'We must show them that we can help them against Smith,' reckons Todzo. 'We must hit an enemy target.'

Comrade Fidel suggested we hit Makhaki's farm again. Russia informed him Makhaki was now ready and waiting, hoping we'll be just dumb enough to come back. Todzo wanted to hit the DC's HQ. There'd been a couple of complaints about the bloke and it seemed like a good idea. But, that evening when we reccied the HQ, we saw that hitting the place wouldn't exactly be easy: there were forests of barbed wire, troops of guards. Without mortars all's we could do was creep up close and snipe. Worse, we'd be risking casualties, and Biani wasn't at all keen on casualties, especially as we'd been sent to recruit, not to fight.

'Well, there's always that RDR camp,' I joked. 'You couldn't find a target any softer than that — those goffels probly need a visit just to remind them that it's a war they're fighting.'

Me, I hadn't meant it seriously, but Biani decided ya, it was worth checking out. So, come the next evening when we split up, me and Russia were sent to check out the goffel camp while the rest of the cadres either scouted the road for an ambush site, or visited the neighbourhood kraals to pick up what intelligence they could.

There was no moon that night so we were able to crawl within yards of the wall, this giant sand castle pushed up by a bulldozer — the kind of set-up I knew from my Binga days — and judging from the racket, the goffel scene hadn't changed that much over the years either: what with their radios blasting and the reek of their dop and their stop, you'd have schemed there was a celebration on, not a war. They'd been braaiing an impala and, aah, I chune you, when I klanked their graze, I wanted to knock on the gate and chune them — hey — hey — hey it's me — Muzukuru — Kiernan — Donk — one of your own mense. And they'd let me in, and I'd perch there with them, sample the roast impala sprinkled with soom, down a couple slugs brandy, roll a few reefs, and catch up on the scene in Skies and Burg, what's the hot gossip, how's Naomi?

Those sort of guys all seemed to believe the cadres who painted 'Wake up Wazukuru — this isn't your war' back in my security force days. 'Ag, roll a reef and forget all that political bullshit,' they'd chune you, 'what can a poor goffel do?' For a moment there, I chune you, I hated every last loop in their goffelguts. I wanted us to hit them, to rattle them until they had to face facts: there was a war on and you couldn't pretend that it was none of your business.

But Russia wasn't too keen on attacking the goffel camp: without mortars he reckoned, we wouldn't be able to do much more than waste ammunition, and when Comrade Nyoni said he had found a first-class ambush site just a couple of kays down the drag, our strategy was settled on the spot. I was surprised to find that I felt slightly relieved.

That night a couple of cadres fetched a mine from the cache and come morning, when the world was still grey and misty, we all rendezvoused at the ambush site, this stretch of road which zigzagged sharply as it struggled up over the top of this koppie. Todzo climbed to the top to keep watch, while the rest of us did our best to lay the damn mine. The road had been cut through rock, and in spite of all our hacking and prying and scratching, we weren't able to make enough of a hole to disappear the thing. Finally we gave up and as the sun rose, we buried the mine in the dirt on the shoulder, and positioned this boulder on the inside wheel track so's the driver would be forced to swing further out than usual.

Biani positioned us behind this ridge about a 100 metres from the road — well out of range of shrapnel from the explosion.

Only the RPG gunner, Russia, and the loader, Koshkosh, were down near the road, lying hidden and protected in a donga. If the vehicle somehow missed the mine they had to stand up and try to stop it with their RPG.

I squatted behind a boulder, picking my teeth with a thorn, anchoring, anchoring as the sun rose up from behind the hills. The security force trucks would be leaving their base, speeding toward our ambush. The drivers could be goffels, could be buddies of mine.... eeeehhh, that was the worst of the waiting, just sitting there, no one to talk to, nothing to stop your mind ticking. Some old buddy burning down the road and all's he's thinking about is 10 days R and R and here I am waiting to kill him. But then he would be with the enemy, and those fighting for Smith had to be prepared to pay the price.

Todzo barks like a baboon — waaurrrh-waaaauuuurrrrh — twice, the signal that the vehicles are approaching — two of them. I check and eventually waaay in the distance ya, there's this thin brown string of dust winding down the road towards us. The buzzing of the trucks' engines is faint at first like the drone of a mosquito and, as they begin the long crawl up the koppie, the growl of the engines grows deeper, lower, as the drivers change. Listening to those trucks battling up the koppie, it all became familiar again: the hot, dusty cabs with their lumpy seats, the exact moment when, from the whine of the engine, you knew you had to change down. A few twists and it could've been me there driving.

The trucks seemed to crawl up the koppie as slowly as shit through the gut of a constipated snail. Russia knelt, carefully balancing the long tube of the RPG on his shoulder and Koshkosh picked up a shell from the stack behind him.

The jeep swings round a corner — he must've missed that mine by inches. Pwaa — the RPG opens up and the rocket just skims its roof and smashes slap into the windscreen of the truck following along behind. The rocket blasts right through the cabin, right through into the back where it explodes — BWWWAAA — so loud that it about blows out our eardrums, and suddenly the air is thick and dirty with fluff and dust. The truck skews across the road, bashes into a boulder. Us cadres all fire together — KKKKKKKKKK — and the driver of the jeep, he jams his foot so hard down on his accelerator that the thing about takes off, and as it skids away round the bend, another rocket screams off overhead, whooshing over the valley.

It all couldn't have taken more than a minute. As the jeep vanishes down the koppies, the driver on the radio yelling for help, us ouens grab our gats and race down to the truck. The left fender's buckled where it smacked the rock, and water's dribbling out the radiator. Tufts of fluff sift down onto us, and chunks of mattress lay in the middle of the road. Up in the cabin of the truck was this goffel, dead. His head flopped against his shoulder at this funny angle, and his face chewed raw and bloody. It wasn't anyone I knew.

Comrade Russia grabbed the driver's arm and tried to drag him out, but his legs were wedged in under the dashboard. He pulled and he pulled, but he couldn't get the bloke free.

'We can't stick around,' I shouted, 'the choppers will be after us.'

Russia quickly unstrapped the watch from the guy's wrist and strapped it onto his own and Koshkosh wrestled off the bloke's jacket.

'Stand back!' yelled Biani, and then blasted a couple of rounds into the petrol tank. The truck flared up and within seconds it was aflame, this thick black cloud of smoke barrelling skywards. Nice and easy for a chopper to spot. I was getting panicky.

'We'd better get moving,' I said. 'We better get moving.'

We headed up the side of the koppie, climbing for about a 100 yards until we came to a stony slope where tracking would be about impossible. We made a few marks there, as if to disguise the trail, then backpedalled along the way we had come, all the way to the other side of the road, Nyoni dusting out our spoor with a large branch. He dusted for nearly 50 yards, wiping out every footprint, every trace, and just as we heard the first faint buzz of a chopper in the distance, we put foot, we really put foot, ducking down into this valley, sprinting along this gorge. We took cover in a stand of reeds and anchored there, anchored there, as the choppers crisscrossed the area over on the other side of the road. Koshkosh rummaged through the pockets of the bloke's jacket and found a box of smokes — Madison — with eight left. One for each of us and one to share; a lekker change from our usual pipe tobacco wrapped in odd scraps of paper.

Then this military convoy charges up, the trucks as tiny as beetles in the distance. Next thing there's this almighty bang echoing off among the hills and us ouens eeeh, we dive for cover. What's the enemy opening up with now? bombs? mortars? And then eeh, we click: it's not the enemy, it's us — one of the Rhodesian trucks had hit our mine!

We laughed, I chune you, we laughed — it seemed like the biggest joke in the world. Later when we heard two RDR soldiers had been seriously injured and their truck wrecked, we realised we'd actually won quite a victory: two of Smith's trucks destroyed, one of his men killed and two injured — and all at no cost to ourselves.

As we trapped back through our zone, stopping at all the kraals to announce our victory, we heard from the headmen that security force patrols had swept the area, searching all the huts and interrogating all the mense. If they persuaded anyone to confess that the boys had been visiting the entire kraal was fined half their cattle.

There was one thing we couldn't work out though: we hadn't been anywhere near most of the kraals that had been fined. Finally we figured that the enemy's interrogation tactics had to be responsible; hell, those blokes could make you admit to flying to the moon every

Saturday night if they wanted to. We couldn't see what else it could be.

Ya, the security forces' tactics didn't win them many friends. Everywhere we went the men complained that they had been pushed around and made small in front of the women and children. The soldiers had stolen cash while they searched huts, a woman had been raped, and they had helped themselves to beer and fowls. As Todzo used to say: anyone we couldn't convince, Smith's men would convince for us.

But though these mense damned Smith's men, though they made us sadza and sang our songs, they didn't seem too keen on us. We had no recruits at all and the local headmen were telling us only just enough about security force movements to stay out of trouble.

'Zapu looks after its people well,' Comrade Todzo told the mense. 'Many cadres are sent to Russia for training as teachers and doctors. And, when we rule Zimbabwe, all those who were with us in the fight will be rewarded. They will have cars, good jobs....' But not even cars and jobs could tempt anyone to ask about maybe joining.

'Something's wrong,' reckons Todzo after we'd visited our dozenth village. 'These people — they understand the struggle, they support the struggle, but still they aren't with us. On my last mission, after a victory, the people cooked us chicken and brewed us beer. But here they do nothing.'

'But what else can we do?' breaks in Biani, angry. 'We've shown them we aren't children with toy guns, we've shown them the spirits are with us.'

'Knock some sense into them,' reckons Russia.

'No, no,' Todzo shook his head. 'Then they will think we are just like the Rhodesians. Let me talk to them again — maybe I will hear what is worrying them.'

We were back around Maradza's village by then, so that evening we visited there first.

'We had to bury the body,' Maradza bursts out when he checks us. 'The soldiers came, they made us. They hit us.' Ya, and in the firelight you could check that his face was a mess of lumps and cuts.

Todzo calmed the bloke down, calling him 'father' and telling him that we were not there to punish the people but to help them. Maradza then told us that the killing of Mlambo had reached the ears of the security force the next day. This patrol arrived, wanting to know how the bloke had died and why exactly he hadn't been buried. No one would speak, so the security force took the mense into the donga one by one.

'Someone here told them,' Maradza confessed. Eeeh, but that bloke, he was shitting himself. 'I can't say who — anyone could have. They hit us, they hit us hard. Then the next day the DC's people came and took away half of our cattle.'

Well, Todzo assembled all the people, told them about our victory and began exercising that sweet tongue of his.

'We are your children,' he said. 'But sometimes parents are angry with their children. And if parents are angry with their children, they must not hide this anger in their hearts; they must tell their children why they are angry, so that their children can make things right. So, then if any of you know of anything wrong — let him speak out now. We will not harm anyone who speaks. . . .'

After a long silence — I'm sure they're all reliving the killing of Mlambo — old Titus pulls himself up, leans on his stick there and begins to speak. 'Yes, my children,' he says. 'Yes, you have sinned; you have sinned grievously and my heart is heavy, very heavy, and I don't know whether I can find it in my heart to forgive you.'

I lean forward. The old man has the spirit of a lion, I'm scheming. Pissed or not, I wouldn't have dared to open my mouth.

Ou Todzo he's very polite, very encouraging. 'Yes, father,' he says. 'Tell us our sins then. We will not harm you. You must help us help you and we cannot help you if there is bad blood between us.'

'Well,' says Titus, very solemn, 'it's my stop.'

'Your stop?' repeats Todzo confused, 'your stop?'

'You and your comrades have been stealing my stop.'

Hey, you should've heard those mense laugh. Even us cadres, we were pissing ourselves. It was true too. Koshkosh and some of us others had been looking after our supplies. But eeeh, when we checked Todzo's face, we shut up but quick. He was flat, I chune you, no mistake. He just stood there waiting till all the people were quiet again, and then he told Titus to come to us after the meeting and we would sort out payment.

The old bloke grinned and sat down. He schemed it was all a great joke.

'Has anyone any other complaints against us?'

Nobody had, or nobody was talking, so after a couple more slogans and a song, Todzo dismissed the meeting.

Shouting to his friends that now he was going to be rich, Titus hobbled after us happily, but as soon as we were into the bush, Todzo gripped the guy's stick and laid into him. 'This is your payment!' he shouted. 'This is your payment for insulting us in front of the people.'

'I'm just about finished with these people,' says Biani, looking down at the bruised and whimpering old man. 'I'm sick of this. Maradza is going to tell us now. If he won't tell us what's going on — he won't go back.' Two cadres are sent off to fetch him and by the time the bloke arrives, he's shivering like it's midwinter.

Biani sits him down and puts our problem to him: we do everything we can and still the people aren't with us.

'You aren't sons of the soil,' Maradza comes out finally. 'You aren't our sons and daughters. You are Madzwitis — Nkomo's people.'

'Lies!' argues Biani. 'That is lies. We are not only Ndebeles. We are three Shonas, two Ndebeles, one from Malawi and one muzukuru. All of us are Zimbabweans.'

Maradza flinches as if he's been clapped. 'That's what they say,' he mumbles.

'But where did you hear these things?'

Maradza looks down at his shoes. 'From Zanla,' he says apologetically, 'from the Zanla comrades. At first they thought you were Skuz'apo — but now they know you are Zipra — Madzwiti. You are not our children.'

And when we heard that eeeh, everything clicked into place: the speed with which the people had understood the struggle, their reluctance to be our 'eyes and ears'. The svikiro had told us that the sons of the soil would be victorious, and in their eyes we weren't the sons of the soil at all. We had been prophesying against ourselves.

Ya, as Biani cross-questioned Maradza about Zanla's activities, it began to sound as if we had arrived in the area far too late. Zanla had an intelligence network in every village and kraal, and the security force — us too probly — couldn't make a move without them hearing about it. Dozens of recruits had already been sent off to be trained. All the local traders and even some of the white farmers were paying them protection money. They had the area organised.

'But why haven't they tried to contact us?' Biani asked him. 'Why haven't they let us know that they are in the area?'

'They don't trust you,' Maradza mumbled. 'They told us stories about the Skuz'apo. As soon as they saw you were here, they told us to say nothing in case you were Skuz'apo.'

'This is how Smith divides us against each other,' Biani cried. 'Us Skuz'apo!'

'So are you for Zipra or Zanla?' Russia asked the bloke.

'I support all the fighters — all the comrades are my children.'

'You must have been very busy,' cracked Koshkosh. No one laughed.

'Do you think the Zanla comrades would speak to us?' Biani asked.

'I don't know about these things.'

'Well,' Biani reckoned, 'it's worth a try.'

He tore a page from his war diary and wrote:

> To the Zanla Commander
> Zipra and Zanla are both fighting against the racist Smith regime. We can co-operate while working for our common aim. Let us meet to discuss by the muhacha tree outside Maradza's village at two o'clock on Sunday afternoon.
>
> Yours in the struggle.
> Comrade Commander Biani

Biani gave the note to Maradza, telling him to get it to the Zanla comrades as quickly as he could. Two days later we checked and found that the Zanla commissar had already sent a reply agreeing to the meeting.

Not all the comrades were too keen on the idea. 'We don't have any instructions to negotiate with Zanla,' Russia informed us once we'd heard the reply, and from the way he said it you could check he was getting ready to add another page to his official report. 'Only the politicians can talk.'

'We don't have instructions not to talk,' said Biani very stiff.

'Our orders say "spread Zapu" and Zanu is in our way. Invite them to a meeting, that's fine, but ambush them.' Ya, quite a few cadres were nodding as he spoke.

But Biani was commander, and Biani was for unity. 'Zanla is not the enemy,' he told us, 'Smith is.'

'These Zanla have tried to kill us before,' Russia argued. 'Who else told Smith's men we were going to attack Makhaki's farm? You are taking us into a trap.'

'Where's your proof?' Biani challenged him. 'Come on — this is just nonsense.'

'I know this truth here,' Russia banged his chest — 'here in my heart. No one else could have done it.'

And, come the day, Biani was cautious with his instructions. He himself would go to the talks alone, but with all the rest of us giving him cover, and if anything happened to him Nyoni was to lead the unit straight back to Zambia.

At noon we began climbing down from the gomos, openly making for this koppie overlooking the muhacha tree where we were to take up our positions. Moving during the day was chancey, but Biani wanted to demonstrate our good faith.

But good faith or not, we'd just about reached the koppie when somewhere over on the left maybe half-a-dozen gats open up. We hit the deck, roll, fire, roll and then — they've gone. The whole contact couldn't have lasted more than 30 seconds.

'Don't waste your fire,' Biani yells. 'Advance.'

Moving forward I heard this gurgling off to my left, and then Koshkosh calling for us all to come. He'd found this Zanla cadre lying in the grass; the bloke had been hit in the gut and there was blood all over. You could see he was pretty near finished. 'Water,' he was saying, 'gimme water....'

Biani knelt down beside him and held up a water bottle in front of the bloke's eyes. 'How many Zanla cadres in the area?'

'We are 10 — just one platoon.'

Biani poured a lidful into the bloke's mouth. 'How many guns?'

Sweat stood out on the bloke's face and he was raving, raving, he'd forgotten all about us and Smith and the struggle, he was talking about some woman, and it was obvious that nobody on this earth was going to extract any further information out of him. We looked around for his gat, but it'd disappeared, along with his rounds. One of his comrades must have taken it.

Then he was quiet. 'The people must leave him unburied,' said Russia. 'That will scare them.'

'He was a comrade,' said Biani looking down at the body. 'He was with the struggle, even if he fought against us. We will leave him for his people to bury.'

In the days that followed, we began to counter the stories Zanla spread about us. 'We are the strongest,' Comrade Todzo told the mense, 'we have beaten both the security force and Zanla. We are the strongest because our party is the party of all Zimbabweans, not just one tribe.' He'd point to me and ask: 'Is he now Ndebele?' — then pointing to himself — 'Am I now Ndebele? Not even Father Nkomo himself is Ndebele. . . .' But not even these new stories of his could win the people over.

Us cadres began to feel that we were just wasting our time. The mission was a flop: the people didn't want us, what was the point of sticking around?

And, just to make sure that we were comfortable, the rains were very heavy just then, and we were always wet and muddy and itchy with mosquitoes.

After a week of this we rock up back at Maradza's kraal. Comrade Todzo spoke to the people and we were given chicken and beer.

Biani and Todzo looked at each other. You could see they were thinking hey, what's this, are the people beginning to listen to us? Then Maradza asked if he could hold a church service. It was nearly Christmas, he explained, and at Christmas everyone who was off working on white farms or in the city came back to their kraals. For years there'd been a service and then Zanla came and burnt the church cos the minister had not supported the fight for freedom. Only the walls were still standing.

'Won't it be wet?' Biani asked.

'We'll pray for a dry night.'

'Hold your service then,' Biani told him after a couple moments consideration. 'This religion is your own business.' In the background Russia was muttering about the opium of the masses. 'But what about Zanla? What do they say?'

The Zanla unit hadn't been seen for a couple of weeks, Maradza admitted, in fact not since we fought them, and many people were saying they had gone back to Mozambique for supplies.

Back at our camp we discussed the situation. Had Zanla really withdrawn, or were they trying to trick us? After we'd been arguing for an hour ou Koshkosh yawned and asked what did it all matter anyway? 'There's nothing we can do here but wait for malaria,' he schemes. 'Even if Zanla isn't here, the masses still support them.'

'Ya, let's go back and get ourselves deployed someplace dry,' puts in Comrade Fidel. 'Some place along the Botswana border where no one talks about Madzwitis.'

Biani informed them that there was no shortage of anti-malaria pills. 'If we stay here maybe we can get a chance to convince the people,' he added. 'If we go back now our mission will be a failure.'

Ya, ou Biani, he needed that chance all right; since he'd become commander we hadn't done enough to balance the complaints that would be written up in Comrade Russia's report, and he knew that unless we managed to pull off something spectacular, next time out he'd be just an ordinary cadre again.

But Biani wasn't just your ordinary cadre, and he wasn't going to go back to being an ordinary cadre without a fight. 'Now what if we could round up some recruits?' he threw in.

Comrade Russia lost no time in pointing out that was exactly what we'd been trying to do.

It was then that Biani explained he was thinking of recruiting with the barrel of a gun. 'Many of the sons and daughters will be back for Christmas,' he said. 'They will be the right age, and we can catch them all together in the church.'

The people's prayers must've worked. Come the night the sky cleared. Hiding in the bush we watched the people troop into the church, dressed up in their best clothes and a little shaky from celebrating.

The service started with a long prayer by Maradza. We took up our positions and, as the congregation began the first hymn, we slipped in, gats at the ready. The mense in the back saw us, and went quiet, and when the mense in the front heard the singing stop, they looked round to see what was happening and when they saw us they stopped too. For a moment Maradza battled on alone, but finally he gave up as well, and peered off into the church, which was lit by only a few flickering paraffin lamps.

'What is this?' he asked, his voice shaking as if we were the devil or something. 'Who are you? Why are you disturbing us?'

'Brothers, sisters, we are the sons of the soil,' said Biani. 'The revolution needs recruits — and you are coming to Zambia with us.'

Eeh, there was wailing and weeping as we went through the congregation picking our recruits. 'You — here. You — here — and you three — over there.' One recruit, a bloke in a fancy suit, went to Biani and said, 'Look, comrade I'm all for the struggle, I'll give you plenty money, but I can't go to Zambia at the moment. My business....' Biani just shoved him back into line.

'If you call Smith's men they will send planes and bomb us all to death,' Biani told the rejects. 'If you want to see your children again — keep quiet.' Then we began to trap.

We put foot, I chune you we put foot that night, making those mense trap like they'd never trapped in their lives before. It'd been tough enough for me when I'd been captured — and I'd been a soldier and reasonably fit. Ya, those mense, they had to battle, they really had to battle to keep going. At one point the fat bloke, the one who'd tried to buy his way out, decided he'd had enough and flopped down in the mud. When I told him to move it, he just said, 'Rather shoot me, rather let me die,' so I borrowed Biani's Tokarev — the noisiest gat we had — and fired off a shot right next to his ear. That bloke he was up and on his feet in an instant. 'Hey, hey,' I chuned him, 'now you've got so much energy you can help the struggle,' and I gave him my pack to carry. He carried it, without so much as a bleat, all the way to Zambia.

Right through the night we kept moving, and in the morning the rain began again, hard and grey, and everywhere there was mud. We trudged on, on until dusk when Nyoni shot two impala, and Biani decided that it was time for a rest. As there was no way to cook the buck, we butchered them with our bayonets, and ate the meat just like that, raw and bloody. Half the mense wouldn't look at it, not that first day anyway, but later they all gulped it down like chocolate. That night we took shelter under a big tree with wide branches and all the mense they just flopped down in the mud, all their fancy clothes wrecked, their suits and white dresses torn and filthy.

We were all dossing there, with the rain trickling down through the leaves when out of nowhere came this flash, a huge bang and we were all lifted an inch or two off the ground. For a second I schemed we'd been bombed — that Smith's men had found us — I grabbed for my gat — but alles was still quiet, so I just lay there in the mud, shivering and shaking and wondering if maybe I hadn't dreamt the whole thing.

It hadn't been my imagination though; next morning everyone was discussing it. 'It's magic,' the cadres were scheming. 'It must be witchcraft.' 'It's just lightning,' scoffed Russia, but Todzo went over to the recruits. 'Do any of you have any relations who are ngangas?' he asked.

A chick in a muddy white dress sticks up her hand. Ya, she tells us, her father is a nganga. 'I'm not supposed to leave him,' she tells us. 'He's very angry. If you want to survive, you'd better take me back home.'

'If we die because of your father's bloody muti,' Biani informs her, 'one of us is going to survive and he will go to your father's kraal and he will shoot your father, your mother and everyone else he can find and then he will burn that place down to the ground. It's better you talk to your father right now — you tell him to stop this nonsense, because if he doesn't we are going to turn around right now and finish him and his people before we cross the Zambezi.'

Well, the lady promised to try. She went over to one of the trees and spoke in this singsongy way, sort of like the svikiro. Ten minutes later, she came to tell us we could carry on. 'I talked to my father,' she said, 'and he says you'll be quite safe — provided you don't touch me.'

And, I don't think anybody did, but eeh, with all those chicks around you couldn't help feeling things. I mean you're herding a dozen of them through the bush there, never letting them out of your sight, their torn dresses plastered flat and transparent against their bodies by the rain, you're going to get ideas, You can't help it. One night I remember, I wandered off from the column to catch a piss and heard noises behind this bush and eeeh, I got one hell of a spook. I duck down, release the safety and I creep forward and peer through the leaves: there behind the bushes is Koshkosh's arse. His trousers are down round his ankles and beneath him there's this chick, her skirt up around her waist and she's trying to shove him away.

'Stop,' she's telling him. 'No.'

With a sigh he stops. 'Listen, comrade,' he says, 'why don't you try it awhile before you decide?'

She frees her arm and swipes at his face, but he just laughs and grabs hold of her wrist. 'Stop it,' she cries. 'Let me go.'

'It's your duty to the struggle,' Koshkosh informs her. 'You've been sitting all nice and comfortable in town while I've been out here in the forest risking my life for the people. Now you can share some of your comfort with a freedom fighter.' And with that he began pump-pumping away.

What with the rain and the mud we moved slowly slowly, reaching the escarpment five days after Christmas. It took us another three days to reach the river. Biani and Nyoni went on ahead to the bank to one of the secret signalling places where they managed to make contact with the comrades at a crossing point. A dinghy came over to collect us, a tiny thing that could only take three passengers at a time, and it was nearly three days before everyone had crossed.

Chapter 17

*W*hen we finally rocked up in the camp, we lay around in our tent, playing cards and dopping this homebrew Kosh-kosh'd bought with these Rhodesian dollars that he'd pocketed somewhere along the line. Eeeh, but it was lekker just to sit back and have a smoke without worrying about choppers and ambushes and the enemy, lekker just to be able to lie down and doss without having to keep half an ear open in case the security force suddenly rock up.

That afternoon the unit's main mannes — Biani, Russia, Todzo — went off to file their reports. They must have had a lot to say for themselves cos it was only at sunset that they came strolling back.

'So what's our next mission?' ou Koshkosh shouts to them as they rock up. 'Guarding the women's camp?'

'Almost as good,' says ou Biani once he's safely inside our tent.

'Tonight we're off to Lusaka.'

'What's the story?' asks Fidel, puzzled. 'The rules say we can't leave the camp.'

'This is an unofficial mission,' says Biani with a grin. 'Hey you — Muzukuru — we must go now — there's some organising to do.'

As we head through the camp there I ask ou Biani what's happening but he just chunes me it's all classified information, he's not at liberty, etc. Then we sneak into logistics round through the back and, ya, there in a room packed with boxes is ou Hendrix, the chief chimney of our Smokers' Inn days, all very smart in a brand-new uniform, reading a newspaper as he sits sprawled in his chair with his feet on the desk. He jumps up when he sees us and after much slapping of backs and shaking of hands, he rolls us a reef and we sit back and smoke and talk about the good old days. The stop is potent, man, and after just one hit you can feel your thoughts ricocheting off the walls of your brain.

'Where's it from?' I ask, one connoisseur to another.

'Angola.'

'Angola?'

'This comrade that I was helping — he went there to check out the new training camp.' And from the state of Angola, our discussion moved to the state of the war, and ou Hendrix filled us in on all the news: the Geneva conference had stuck on the first item on the agenda — the date of majority rule — and then it collapsed. Now Nkomo was speaking of a short sharp conventional war to finish Smith once and for all, and Smith was saying well, if Zapu and Zanu wouldn't settle with him on his terms, he'd just find other parties that would.

Just before five — suppertime — we stood to go, and ou Hendrix nodded at this large cardboard box. 'A little help for you blokes,' he said, opening it up.

It was packed tight with beans, mealiemeal, cigarettes, a couple pairs of trousers, and a small packet stuffed with stop. 'In Lusaka you could sell it all for 80, maybe 100 kwacha,' he says. 'Enough for an evening's celebration.'

'Where's this stuff from?' Biani wants to know.

Comrade Hendrix grins. 'Ask no questions and you'll hear no lies.'

'It's not stolen is it?' Ou Biani, he was looking so serious there that for a moment I thought he was going to refuse the box, like he'd refused Hendrix's stop back in our Unity Camp days.

'What things do you think about me?' Ou Hendrix, he was indignant. 'If you try nonsense in a place like this, they'd catch you in a week. This is Zipra, not the Unity Camp.'

'Okay — okay — sorry. But where does this stuff come from?'

Hendrix explained that sometimes a unit went off to the bush without being able to carry all the rations allocated to it. 'To put it back on the books would be such big trouble it's not worth it,' he told us. 'You know what the red tape is like here.'

We nodded understandingly, though to tell the truth, neither of us had the faintest idea.

'So when fighters come back from the front, we let you have these awkward things. The comrades really appreciate it — that's why my friend brought me the stop. Others have given me ivory, even emeralds.'

Back at our tent the rest of the unit admired ou Hendrix's gift with caution.

'Nice,' says ou Koshkosh eyeing the graze. 'But we don't have any passes. We can't get out — this place is like Salisbury Central. Let's just cook ourselves something here.'

But Biani wouldn't have any of it. 'We are freedom fighters,' he reminds him. 'If we don't have, we improvise.'

So just after dark we sneaked down to this quiet stretch of fence at the rear of the camp and, while the guards were busy grazing their supper, snipped our way out. Ten minutes later we were in the nearest roadside store bargaining a bag of beans into a lift to town.

Well, Lusaka wasn't exactly one of the sizzling hot spots of the seventies. Most of the shops were empty but there were plenty peddlers roaming round the streets. Everything they had was Russian-made and expensive: smokes at a kwacha a pack, a bar of soap two kwacha. About the only cheap item in the whole of Lusaka was beer.

Which suited us just fine. After we'd sold off our supplies we headed straight off to the nearest bar — there were a span of them around, small, dark, dirty places mostly. We perched there and dopped, and when the beer wasn't helping as fast as we wanted, we tasted some homebrew. I don't know what that stuff was called but eeeh, it was potent — one sip and you were gone. Koshkosh swallowed four glasses, but the rest of us only managed two or three.

As we're downing that stuff, three ladies from the Lusaka night totter in on high heels, a gent in a fancy suit marching behind. Koshkosh whoops with joy. 'Pretty ladies!' he yells to them, frantically wiping the seat of the bar stool beside him. 'Beautiful ladies... come sit by me.'

The chicks consider the room. Koshkosh's seats are the only ones free, so over they teeter. Koshkosh throws his arms round the nearest. 'My chicken leg,' he croons. 'My honeycomb.'

'I want a drink,' Chickenleg says, snuggling up to him. 'I want a whisky. My friends want whisky — hey, buy me a bottle of whisky.'

Whilst he's buying her a solitary glass of the local poison, I sidle over and buy a beer for Honeycomb, skinny yellow lady, with a wild afro, and pretty soon she's telling me all about her old queen, how she's so sick and all, and I put my hand on her thigh to console her and she brushes her hand across my crotch as she reaches for a smoke. My cock is about breaking through my fly and we're negotiating a quick trip to the back when — urrrgggghhh — urrgggghhhh — Koshkosh is puking all over Chickenleg.

'Rhodesian baboon!' she screams, jumping up and belting him over the head with her handbag.

'Daughter of your mother's tapeworm!'

The pimp grabs Koshkosh by the collar and demands money, much money, and not just kwacha either, to buy the lady a new dress. Koshkosh, he shakes his head and spits out a last mouthful of puke which spatters all over the pimp's shiny black shoes.

The pimp yells, goes for his knife, but ou Koshkosh is quicker. He grabs the bloke's wrist, twists it until he drops the knife and then flings him onto the floor.

'Son of a syphilitic hyena and a leprous pig,' the chick shrieks.

'Zambian pus from a rotting cow's arse.'

At which point all the Zambians in the bar stand up to defend their national honour. But you can't forget your comrade in his hour of need: us cadres grip whatever weapons we can find — ashtrays, beer bottles, chairs — and charge over to reinforce Koshkosh.

A beer bottle explodes against a wall, an ashtray knocks a hole in a window. 'Police!' screams the barman. 'Help, police!' The Zambians retreat into a corner. Koshkosh breaks loose and lays into the crowd with a chair. Biani picks up two beer bottles, smashes their bottoms off against the bar, and seizes the door, threatening any Zambian who comes near. 'Withdraw,' he shouts to us, 'withdraw. We've got to get out of here before the cops come.'

We gap it through the side streets and by the time we stop running, the noise of battle's far behind us and we're hot and thirsty. Beer, beer, us ouens want beer. Biani counts our coin. 'Okay, okay,' he informs us, 'we can afford one more beer each — and then it's back to camp. Come morning, they'll find the hole — we'll be trapped outside.'

So we went into another bar and that barman, he fished out some special poison that about burnt the skin off our throats. Last thing I remember is Fidel coughing his guts up. I passed out and next thing I knew there was this crocodile chewing away at my heel. I'm trying to draw myself up onto the bank which is swaying from side to side, but the thing is chewing at me — it's got quite a grip on my ankle. I pull. It pulls. I open my eyes and eeh, there's this bastard trying to pinch my boot. I let out a mammoth yell that must've been heard up and down the street and the bloke, he gets such a shock that he about somersaults out the door.

Me, I struggled to my feet and staggered out the door after him. By the time I reached the street he'd vanished. Most of the others were already there, perching on the pavement, heads in hands, feet in gutter. I dumped myself down next to them. Two blokes dragged Fidel out of one of the bars and abandoned him on the pavement. He lay right there where they left him.

'Something for the babbelas, comrades,' moans Koshkosh, 'or I am going to die.' We all search through our pockets and manage to scratch up a single kwacha which isn't much help at all.

Just as Biani was promising him a good funeral, I came up with a bright idea. 'Why not sell Fidel's boots?' I scheme. 'We can just say they were stolen. Mine nearly were.'

'It's stealing from the struggle,' Russia objects automatically.

'Ag, Zipra can afford to give us one pair of boots,' reckons Koshkosh. 'The Russians give us all the boots we need.'

So we took a democratic vote, all of us except Fidel that is, and booze carried the day. Ou Biani was too busy holding his head, too desperate for another beer to even argue. Me and Todzo eased the boots off Fidel without waking him and Koshkosh held a quick street auction, pointing out how well the boots had worn, the quality of the leather, the strength of the stitching, and the anti-imperialist genius that went into making them. Ya, he managed to raise about 30 kwacha on those boots; it turned out there was a shortage of shoes in Zambia too.

We staggered off to the nearest bar and bought beers and, whilst we drank, soothing our dry throats and aching heads, we counted the change and calculated that we had enough for smokes, breakfast — and one more beer — as well as for our ride back to the camp.

As we crawled back through our hole in the fence, the guards rocked up. Biani chuned them we'd all lost our passes, they'd been stolen off us, and offered them the few kwacha we had left if they'd keep quiet about it. The guards pocketed the coin, no problem, but instead of letting us go they marched us straight to the camp commander's office.

'What's this?' he wants to know. 'Where's your dedication to the struggle? What are these decadent bourgeois habits? Are you revolutionaries, reactionaries or what?' As he's carrying on, he notices that Fidel has no boots. 'And what happened here?'

'They must have been stolen,' poor Fidel begins apologetically. 'When I woke up this morning — they were gone.'

'Stolen?' scoffs the camp commander. 'These are children's stories — who can steal the boots off a freedom fighter?'

'I did have something to drink,' Fidel confesses, 'perhaps. . . .'

And that's when the commander sees red, green, blue and yellow. He storms up and down that office of his bellowing like a bull hippo that's had his whole herd of cows stolen, and us ouens we stand there trying to pretend that we're only a block of wood while he swears and rages and roars. 'What do you mudfish take me for? A fresh-from-home? Do you think I joined the struggle yesterday? I know damn well that you — you drunkards, reactionaries, dog filth — I know very well that you sold those boots for drink.'

Poor Fidel, he was too terrified to say anything. He just stood there, his mouth opening and shutting like a cow chewing the cud while the camp commander raved at us, threatening to have us flogged 50 and tied to a tree for a week.

But come to think of it, this commander said, we hadn't just been profiteering at the expense of the struggle — which was pretty bad just by itself — we'd also committed treason. We'd cut a hole in the fence of the camp, and any saboteur who happened to be roaming about, any stray Smith supporter, could've sneaked straight through and laid his mines — or just had a look round — and in fact, maybe one had. How did us comrades feel now, having placed the lives of a whole campful of comrades at risk just so that we could go get drunk and catch the clap? What kind of commander would lead his men on such a mission, what kind of security would go along without reporting him, and why didn't the commissar point out the implications? Ya, I chune you, by the time that bloke was finished there, I was expecting a public execution.

But, he went on, because we were fighters, just back from the bush, because this was our first offence, this time our only punishment would be to cut down the bush growing beside the fence — he wanted it down because the guards were using it as their excuse for not seeing us.

So we slouched over to the guards to collect some axes but eeh, what with the babbelas and alles, the only thing us ouens wanted was sleep. 'Why couldn't he just have had us tied to a tree for a day or two?' Koshkosh was complaining. 'Why couldn't he give us a comfortable punishment?' En route we spotted a dozen recruits dozing in the shade. 'What are you doing here?' Biani shouts, and they all spring to attention. 'Why aren't you working?' He doesn't listen when one of them tries to stutter out an answer and informs them that they all have punishment parade — now. We marched them to the bush and set them to work with the axes. Ya, I chune you, we had them so terrified that they cleared that bush in record time.

Biani managed to wangle a pass to visit Rudiya at the women's camp. I went along to see him off, and while he was waiting there in the back of this empty truck — it'd just delivered a load of uniforms to logistics — Biani talked me into hopping aboard too. It was easy enough to manage: ou Todzo, who was with us, agreed to cover for me in camp, and ou Biani changed '1' to '2' on his pass and added my name.

Now the women's camp was a mammoth place; we didn't know where to begin looking for Rudiya. The pair of us just checked these acres of tents and looked at each other. 'Ask somebody,' I suggested. 'Brilliant strategy,' said Biani, and went up to a group of chicks, none of whom had heard of our Rudiya. So we ask again and again and again, and when Biani's begun to scheme she's run off with a

Zambian or something, we meet this Comrade Sebbia, this bulky, talky chick with tits the size of soccer balls. No, I couldn't keep my eyes off them as she tells us ya, ya of course she knows Rudiya, in fact she's Rudiya's big buddy, and sometimes even looks after the baby — and isn't he such a fat, such a beautiful child? And so well-behaved too....'

'Okay, okay,' says Biani, who looks as if the chick has been yakking away for 7 000 years, 'let's see the child now.' Sebbia leads us off through this tent town. We turn this corner and there's Rudiya sitting on a rock outside her tent and suckling little Unity.

Not quite so little as I remember him though: he'd about doubled in size since we'd seen him last, and with all of us jabbering away around him, his face scrunches up like he's about to cry. Biani picks him up, tickles his chin and charms him into a smile. But, just when he's got the brat enthusiastically trying to pull his nose off, he mutters something about wanting to fetch some smokes, hands it to me and disappears with Rudiya.

Well, Unity he takes one look at me — 'howzit, fatface,' I chune him — decides I'm a serious threat to his personal security, and lets out a howl that must've been heard halfway to Lusaka. Half-a-dozen concerned mothers turn round to witness my cruelty. 'Shut up,' I tell the lightie, trying to rock him quiet. 'You'll give our position to Smith.' But that lightie, he's not at all interested in Smith — I'm the enemy right there in front of him. He's got a fine pair of lungs and he's making it clear that he's going to exercise them just as long as I'm holding him. 'Help me, comrade,' I say to Sebbia as the brat howls louder. 'Rescue me.' She takes the brat from me, cuddles it and whispers so much nonsense that the thing finally squeaks and burps and falls asleep.

'He can save the camp the cost of an air raid siren,' I said with relief. 'Just belt him one whenever you see a plane.'

'It's only that you are a stranger,' Sebbia explained. 'He's a good child.' And she went on to tell me that he never cried at night, always ate his sadza and beans, and how her child — he's turning six next month — was pretty good too, usually, and how he wanted to be a freedom fighter, and always carried this wood-and-wire AK with him.

'He'd like to hear about the bush from you,' she said, adding that he hadn't had a chance to speak to many fighters, cos most of the blokes at the camp were unfit for military service, and with so few of them around and so many women, it could get pretty lonely sometimes. I nodded, very sympathetic, and she went on and on, telling me about the camp and the cooks and the cleaners and the kids. She had a jaw that chick, but I wasn't complaining; I was enjoying myself there, letting her charm me up something stupid. She sewed uniforms, she said, and told me how a new shipment of sewing machines from India had doubled their production. I wanted to know if there was any chance she could've made my uniform and she asked if I'd been lucky. 'Why's that?' 'Well, you see,' she told me, 'whenever I'm sewing a uniform, I ask the spirits to make it lucky for the comrade who will wear it.' Then she ran her hand along the seam of my shoulder to check if my shirt was well-made and I stopped listening and suggested a walk.

By the time me and Biani revived the next morning Rudiya and Sebbia had already gone off to work. We lay around for a couple hours and then got up and drifted around checking the place out. We got talking to one of the commissars. When he heard we were fighters he took us off to his office and gave us tea and told us he'd very much wanted to be a fighter, but he'd come down with a bad case of malaria just before being sent to the front. The doctors decided he was too weak to fight and he'd been assigned to the refugee camp where he explained the news to the comrades and tried to keep their morale high.

After about half an hour or so he had to go to a meeting, but he let us stay in his office and look through the books and newspapers and magazines he had lying around.

There were piles of *Zimbabwe Review*, our Zapu magazine, stacks of the usual Zambian stuff — and two Rhodesian papers, a *Herald* and a *Chronicle*. I grabbed the *Herald* first.

The front page was full of the Geneva conference and its failure, so I flipped to the sports page and read all about the Rhodesian cricket team's chances of winning the Currie Cup, and then worked backwards, through the smalls, the death notices — no one I recognised — features on coups in black Africa, a Rhodesian general on the imminent end of the terrorism menace, an article about breastfeeding. There was a list of divorces — I skimmed through and hell, what's this — Edward Adrian Kiernan and beside it, Naomi Ruth

Kiernan née Reddy.

'What's the problem?' said Biani looking up from one of the Zambian rags. 'One of your buddies catch it?' To me he seemed to be saying that I was mourning one of my security force buddies, he seemed to be questioning whether I had in fact crossed over.

'My wife — she divorced me,' I told him. 'It's in the paper. Are you happy now?'

There was a bloke behind it; for sure there had to be some bloke. But who? Vyvyan was always hanging around. She was always telling me how helpful he was when I was off on callup. The bitch, she'd been a flirt — right from the first. God alone knew what she'd been getting up to even when I'd been around. There'd been that look of hers, that come-to-bed look she'd flashed those honky troopies in the bar. There'd been the time I'd heard her boasting to one of her girlfriends about how her boss, a sweaty slob with a gut the size of a cement mixer, had propositioned her. There was probly some honky bastard behind this. I shut my eyes and my hands were round her neck and I was squeezing, squeezing. How the hell could she do this to me when I was so far away out in the bush? Maybe she kept getting into shit cos the enemy'd found out I was a freedom fighter; maybe she had to do it just to survive. No, knowing her, she'd probly divorced me cos the army had stopped the monthly payments and there wasn't anything more she could get out of me. Always thinking of herself, of keeping her nest well feathered — septic little bitch. I was probly lucky I hadn't caught sif from her. Ya, I told myself, one day when this struggle's over and us cadres march into Burg and her boyfriend is dead or gapping it to South Africa, she'll come wanting me back, trying to charm me up — and I'll make her beg and then I'll spit in her face.

'Why worry?' schemes Koshkosh back at camp. 'You should be relieved. You're rid of her and it didn't cost you a cent. Why bother with wives in the first place? All they're good for is spending your money. First they want food and when they've got food, they want clothes. Then it's curtains, stoves, radios, TVs — always something. You can slave for the rest of your life just to keep your woman in junk. You should be like me: I've got my substations. I visit each one every week or so, and cos they are always trying to catch you, they make you nice food; they try to look after you.'

What happens when you find a substation occupied?' asks Russia.

'You can't trust a woman anyway. Not even if you give her all the junk she wants,' he retorts. I nod enthusiastically. He's right about women, ou Koshkosh, I'm scheming.

'Even a dog is better than a woman,' agrees Fidel.

'You've tried both then?' chunes Koshkosh. 'I've never seen you chase a woman, but weren't you fondling that dog in the bar the other night?'

Great shouts of laughter. Todzo and Nyoni tackle and disarm Fidel before he reaches Koshkosh.

'It's the modern woman you can't trust,' pronounces Russia. 'Those ones in the Lusaka bar — even the ones in the camps. Touch any one of the ladies in the camps round here and you'll end up with a dozen kinds of clap. But the old-fashioned ones, like the woman I paid my two cows deposit for just before I left Salisbury. . . .'

'Well,' says Nyoni, 'I hope my wife's hearing this about old-fashioned women. She grew up very old-fashioned and we've got five children but last time the comrades visited my village she wasn't there.'

'All women!' I put in, mildly hysterical, 'all women!'

'Smith must have locked her up,' Russia says. 'Those women from the country, they're the only good kind. They know how to look after a man. Ya, Muzukuru, when this struggle is over, you must come into the country and find yourself a decent wife, not one of these corrupt city women.'

'I thought you were a new broom sweeping the country of all the old-fashioned ideas,' puts in Biani. 'What are you going to do when your old-fashioned wife wants to visit the nganga?'

'My wife will do what I want; the country women know who is boss.'

'Some of these new women are all right,' says Biani, who must have been thinking of Rudiya. 'At least you can discuss with them. Maybe your wife didn't run off. Maybe she had to get a divorce cos she couldn't get work; you are a freedom fighter remember.'

'Don't give the bloke false hopes,' cries Koshkosh. 'If she managed for so long without divorcing him, why'd she need to do it now? There's some bloke somewhere.'

'Forget the whole business,' advises Todzo. 'When you become a comrade, you must forget about women.'

'Tell that to your cock,' scoffs Koshkosh.

'Worrying isn't going to help anyone,' Todzo goes on. 'And that's all you can do from here. What matters now is the struggle — and your comrades. Your comrades are your family now.'

I got to thinking about Todzo's words, and I realised they were the truth, nothing but the truth. My comrades were my family. I talked with them, grazed with them, lived with them, fought with them. Even though I'd been captured in the first place, I was now one of them and they were the only real family I had. Naomi well, she was too busy screwing around to bother much about me, and anyway, I was finished with her, I'd been finished with her for such a long time I couldn't figure out why I was getting so excited. We'd done nothing but battle each other from way back and, if it hadn't been for her old queen, we probly wouldn't even have married in the first place. My old man and me — well, we'd never had that much to say to each other, and now we were on opposite sides. What kind of respect could I have for a bloke who'd sold out to Smith? My lightie — hell, she must've had her head infected by all the rest of them, and anyway we wouldn't recognise each other if we passed in the street. I didn't want anything more to do with any of them.

I wasn't Salisbury's, Naomi's Kiernan anymore. Me, Muzukuru, I'd finished for good and all with Kiernan and his Rhodesia, Kiernan who'd murdered a freedom fighter and who'd been ashamed to be the cousin of a comrade, Kiernan who'd wanted most of all to be white and all right. I wanted to throttle that character and leave his body out in the bush for the hyenas to feast on. I wanted to wipe myself clean of him and his doings. Ya, for me whiteness was a disease like those stinking white peelings of skin between your toes during the rainy season. If I could have cut off all my whiteness from me by chopping off my right hand I would have done it, no sweat.

I was frantic to get back to the front, desperate to get another white bastard in my sights. The other cadres were enjoying the rest but me, I got more and more restless. I kept thinking of that enemy soldier I'd shot the day they captured Mamba. Swinging the AK into position, the heft of it, the sights hovering a moment before I touched the trigger. Tricking him like that had been like solving a maths problem, when you suddenly see how all the parts fit together, how to twist and turn them to get the answer exactly right. I kept replaying the moment over and over again, watching all the various lieutenants and sergeants who'd tormented me being swept legless from the rock. One time Naomi had a sudden starring role. That made me feel slightly sick. I just wanted to be out in the bush, after the enemy. I just wanted to kill the bastards.

But us comrades perched round doing nothing, and I cursed the camp's bureaucracy which digested us at the speed that a python digests buck. I stomped around complaining that the struggle would be over before we were sent back to the front. I wanted to fight, not rot in camp.

I told them I wanted a chance to kill the enemy. I told anyone who would listen. Mostly the cadres just laughed at me. 'Maybe we should call you Comrade Killer Mabhunu now,' cracks Koshkosh. 'If you can kill like you can talk, this struggle is going to be over next week Wednesday.'

'Rather call him Comrade Words,' jeers Russia. 'All he's ever done is wounded one of Smith's men, and here he is talking like he's a hero of the revolution.'

But even with everyone laughing at me, I carried on just like before. Biani and Todzo gave me this amulet and a hollowed-out duiker horn filled with a special muti for the spirits. 'Should keep the ngozi — the evil spirits — off,' Comrade Todzo told me as he hung them around my neck. Him and Biani were quite worried about me.

'Can it melt whitey's bullets to water?' I cracked. 'The only evil spirit I know is the white man.' And I began telling them just what I was going to do next time out.

'You just wear these,' ou Todzo told me. 'And cool down, Muzukuru — you'll get all the fighting you want.'

But I chune you there was no ways I could cool down.

Finally, when all the reports had been signed and filed, when we'd all been cleared by security again, we were marched to logistics and issued with our kit. First thing they handed us our civilian outfits: just one shorts and one pair of trousers each. Before we'd had two. 'The packs were getting too heavy,' ou Hendrix explained. 'It'll be easier for you to find your own clothes in the operational area than to lug them all the way there.'

While everyone was busy he took me to one side. 'That box of goodies and all,' he says. 'That was a nice present wasn't it?' I nodded. 'Well — maybe — you could pick up something for me? Say, if you run across some ivory or emeralds or rhino horn or Rhodesian dollars?'

'If we find anything,' I said, 'Biani will hand it over to the party.'

Hendrix, he shook his head. 'You know what happens to all that stuff? You think the party sells it for the struggle? Not a chance — the Russians finance us well enough anyway. One of the big shots nicks it and then....'

Ya, I was glad when the logistics staff called me over to find out my shirt size. Hendrix's stories weren't the kind of thing I could think about just then.

I ran back to the others, who were getting their stuff together. When we were all kitted out, we were led across to HQ for a briefing. Some big shot commander who'd had so much Russian training that he was too valuable to risk on the front, congratulated us on the success of our last mission and told us we were going to be sent back into Zimbabwe soon — I let out a cheer — and we would be operating in the same zone as before but this time our mission would be to liberate the area, not just win recruits. Biani would be our commander and a new comrade, Goliath Khumalo, would be our deputy. For the rest, our unit wouldn't change, but we would now come under the command of one Commander Advance, the regional commander, who would synchronise our activities with those of the other units in the area.

Chapter 18

*O*nce we'd crossed, we rendezvoused with Comrade Advance. Biani gave him a parcel from HQ and he gave us a long lecture on how we should all work together. The main thing, he said, was to keep in touch: every week a runner had to bring him a report and fetch his instructions, and Biani and Nyoni were shown this secret spot, a rock with a hollow beneath it, which was now our postbox.

Comrade Advance then transferred Khumalo, our new deputy, to a unit whose commander had just died of a gut infection, and made Comrade Russia deputy in his place. Quite a few of us cadres weren't exactly happy with this, and it was now the turn of the Shona cadres to mutter 'tribalism'.

Comrade Biani wasn't at all satisfied with this new setup. 'Russia, he could wipe out a kraal for sneezing too hard,' he told me. 'Nyoni at least knows how to handle the people.'

Biani wasn't too impressed with the zone system either. 'All this messaging and what,' he kept saying, 'it just gives Smith extra chance for catching us. The commander in the field, he's the one who can watch what's happening. He must be the one taking the decisions. . . .'

Loaded down as we were it took us three nights' trapping from Comrade Advance's hideout to reach our operational area. It was nearly dawn when we finally rocked up, and to celebrate we took a rush and shared a smoke up on this koppie above Maradza's kraal.

Even from up there we could see the tracks of the war: the burnt-out church, the charred rings of huts where the kraal had once stood, and next to it, mixed up among this stand of muhacha trees, the new huts, some only part-built. Smith's men had obviously been through the area.

'We must be cautious,' ou Todzo reckoned as we surveyed this lot. 'These people can think we are the ones who brought the trouble.'

'These people should have some sense knocked into them,' said Russia.

Only Biani was optimistic. 'They must be with us now,' he said. 'We have their children.'

But down at the kraal there didn't seem to be much reason for optimism. The assembled mense huddled together like a flock of frightened sheep, and gave no sign that they were pleased to see us. Ou Todzo at once began trying to win them round with that tongue of his, while Biani looked round for the headman, Maradza, wanting to question him about the damage. He checked the crowd, double-checked, but there was no sign of the bloke anywhere, so he called over Maradza's brother, Phineas, who filled us in on the news.

Phineas told us that just after we led the congregation off to Zambia, security force patrols had searched every hut, every dura along the river. They'd found some pamphlets and a couple AK rounds in the thatch of one of Maradza's huts, so they'd burnt the whole kraal down, all 20 huts, and they'd taken the mense into the bush one by one and interrogated them. Someone — no one knew who — had told the security force that Maradza and Titus had been helping us. The two of them were then taken to one side and thrashed until they confessed. They were then handed over to the police, and tried and sentenced to five years each for 'aiding and abetting terrorists', and the kraal was fined 10 cattle for not reporting our presence.

Among the cattle taken was a red-and-white bull which'd been given to the spirit of their grandfather. The animal was almost holy. It had never been used in the fields, or to pull a sled. The ancestors, Phineas said, were enraged.

'I have spoken with your children,' Comrade Todzo was saying when we returned. All the wriggling and scratching and nosepicking stopped. 'They are with the struggle now. Some are training to fight, some of the women are training to be nurses. Pius Makombe, the teacher, is now working at a school in one of the camps. Before we left he sent us this letter.'

The mense were dead still as Todzo took the letter out of his pocket, lit a candle, and began to read. This Pius character, he sent his greetings to his father, mother, grandmother, uncles, aunts, cousins, sweethearts and buddies, and didn't forget to give details of what had happened to each and every one of the people that we'd marched off to Zambia.

'I am well,' he finished off. 'I teach at a camp for refugees in Zambia. Many of the masses are fleeing Zimbabwe because Smith's army is killing them. When I hear their stories I feel the rage of a lion inside me, and I want to take up a gun and fight. But the camp commander tells me I am most useful to the people here, teaching the children of Zimbabwe. Help our Zipra comrades because their struggle is yours also. Forward with Father Nkomo.'

That night the people brought us pots of beer and chicken relish. You could tell that we were doing something right.

'They've realised we're on their side,' says ou Koshkosh with a very satisfied burp.

'About time,' reckons Comrade Russia.

'Ya,' says ou Biani. 'At last we can begin.'

And begin we did. Two days later this lightie chases his flock of goats up near our hideout and starts waving frantically. Security force, we're scheming and eeh, I chune you we caught one hell of a spook. Grabbing our gats we skid down the slope to the lightie, this skraal kid maybe 12, 13 years old, with a toy AK — made of wood and wire — slung over his shoulder. 'Where the soldiers? Where Smith's men?' we want to know. 'Do they know we're here?'

'No-no-no,' the lightie tells us. 'No Smith's men, nothing to worry about.' It's just he saw us heading off into the hills to hide this morning when he took his goats to the river, and now the district commissioner's people are coming, they're visiting the kraals — do we want to do anything about it?

'Let's hit them,' I butt in. Eeh, but my trigger finger is itching. All's I want is to get those puppets of the white man, those pawns of Smith, nicely in my sights and blow them right off the face of this earth.

'The people don't like the district administration,' puts in Comrade Todzo. With good reason: the officials checked that they only had so many cattle, pulled up their stop and taxed them and fined them whenever they had the chance.

'How many of these people are there?' Biani asks the lightie, who'd told us his name was Special. From the way that lightie was checking us out you could see us freedom fighters were his number one heroes.

'Just 10,' Special tells us, 'and only four with guns.'

'Are you sure? If you are wrong we can all die.'

But Special says no, no, he's sure, he's certain — absolutely. 'I always won full marks for Arithmetic at school,' he informs us.

'It could all be a trap,' Russia points out, and me I tell him, hey, you're much too cautious. It's like trying to put out a fire with a can of petrol: next thing all seven of us are yelling at each other. Me, I'm all for fight, fight, fight, Russia is calling for caution as in the regulations, Todzo wants to take a chance and co-operate with the masses and Biani is yelling at us all to quieten down so that he can think.

I'm just about dancing on the spot, I'm so impatient. Why are we wasting time with all this bullshit? Why can't we just wipe out Smith's dogs before they sneak out of the area?

When ou Biani decides okay okay we'll take a chance, I just about burst into cheers.

The lightie led us off to this kraal about three-four kilometres away. Leaving Todzo stationed on a koppie to watch our rear, we set up an ambush on the path to the next kraal.

Ten minutes later two blokes — both blacks — carrying G-3s come strolling down the path laughing and chatting as if they're prom-enading down Rhodes Avenue. The rest of the party follows, maybe 50 yards behind, and the whole crowd of them head straight for us. It happened like these things happen in dreams: it was so perfect you couldn't quite believe it. Forty yards, 20 yards — and then the blokes up front stroll right into the ambush killing ground.

Biani opens up, we all open up, and the two topple over like skittles. The others, man, they don't even return fire — they just spin around and gap it.

Me, I jump up and run down to the bodies. The guts of this one bloke are protruding, all torn and bloody, through this hole the size of a football in his side. There was this stink, shit and blood and vomit mixed. The other bloke, man he was minced.

The first bloke's watch is smashed, the second doesn't have.

'O shit,' — I start cursing there — 'my first kill and I smash the fucking watch.'

'Your kill!' says Koshkosh indignant. 'I had the pair of them perfect in my sights.'

'Me too,' chirps someone else, and ya, I chune you, there was quite a chorus of 'me toos'.

Not that all our fighting mattered much anyway: there wasn't any booty to share out. All's we'd picked up were the two G-3s. One was so badly shot up that we dumped it, and the other we gave to Comrade Special for tipping us off. Eeh, that lightie, he was crazy about his gun even though Biani wouldn't let him have any ammunition cos he was scared the kid would start fiddling with the knobs and accidentally discharge into somebody's back. His wood-and-wire AK was forgotten and that G-3 never left his hands, not even when he slept. He spent hours swaggering up and down, up and down with it in his hands, daydreaming of heroic and bloody massacres. Ya, ou Special, he was just like what the commissars told us a freedom fighter should be.

After that last ambush of ours, Smith's men did what they could to finish us. They offered the locals a 1 000 bucks for any information which assisted them in tracking us down, they set up ambushes, they tried to talk some of the headmen into giving us poisoned food and clothing. They were always around, and you couldn't forget that if you had just a little bad luck you'd be finished.

So one fine afternoon when we're all snoring away and someone starts screaming 'Smith's men, Smith's men!' eeh, I chune you, we jump. We grab our gats and dive for cover, and this bloke's still screaming 'Smith's men! Smith's men!' We lay flat there behind our

cover checking, checking for some sign of the security force —
nothing. Then Nyoni spotted the problem: ou Koshkosh, still fast
asleep, is rolling round screaming in this thicket where he had hidden
himself.

Someone grabs his throat, cuts off his screaming, and next thing
he's surfacing.

'Mabhunu, mabhunu! There's no mabhunu.'

'Smith's men, they were killing us.'

'It's just this filthy stop of yours,' scoffs Russia. 'It rots your brain.'
Us ouens eeh, we just pack up laughing.

Koshkosh, of course, wasn't so keen on this interpretation. 'It's not
a rubbish dream,' he says very serious as he hauls himself to his feet,
and brushes himself down. 'It was a strong dream, a *power* dream —
you lot, you'll see.'

But we're all laughing so loud he stops protesting and tells us what
with all the racket we're making, we'd better shift camp. Which only
makes us laugh all the more.

Koshkosh wasn't exactly keen to be on the receiving end for once.
'It's a strong dream,' he repeated, very serious. 'You'll see.'

And he was right. We did see. Two-three days later while we're
trapping through this section of our area that we'd never got round to
visiting before, he spots these hills up ahead.

'I've been here before,' he declares. Us ouens we're all scheming it's
a big joke.

'You,' reckons Russia, 'you're such a city tsotsi, you couldn't tell
one hill from another.'

'No, no,' ou Koshkosh is very serious. 'I know this place.'

Russia paraded the old stop-rots-the-brain crack again, and eeh ou
Koshkosh lights up like someone's hit the switch.

'Ya, that's where I saw it: in my dream,' he says. 'The security force,
they were just over the other side — a patrol of them.'

Well, we weren't exactly convinced — Biani was muttering about
knocking some sense into him — but still we took cover well-hidden
behind some rocks, and Nyoni and Special went forward to scout out
the scene.

Next thing they came scuttling back: Smith's men were up ahead, a
whole platoon of RAR sauntering up the valley like they're on the
parade ground. Well, there were far too many of them for us to fight,
so we lay where we were and watched them march on past not a 100

yards away.

Ou Koshkosh, that one he could hardly keep still he was so excited. 'Me — I dream power dreams,' he whispered. 'When I dream you comrades better listen. You better make sure I've got plenty stop so I can dream what the enemy is up to.'

After that, I chune you, we kept him well supplied. But though he suddenly had quite a crop of his power dreams, he was never spot-on like that again.

Nyoni was sent off to report our ambush to Comrade Advance. He returned with orders for us to take the war into the neighbouring white farming areas. Some sort of directive had arrived from higher up, Nyoni told us, and Advance was just passing it on. 'If you can chase a farmer off his land,' Advance wrote us, 'you will be damaging the economy of Smith's regime which will have less to sell, and therefore less money to buy arms. You will also be damaging white morale; because of the many attacks of this kind, many whites are leaving the country — and every white frightened into leaving is one enemy less.'

Biani wasn't impressed. 'We don't even know any targets,' he said.

'Farmer Makhaki,' says Fidel promptly. 'Let's get our revenge on him.'

'According to Zipra policy, we hit the enemy when and where he least expects it,' Russia informs him. 'After that last raid of ours Makhaki's ready and waiting.'

'Makhaki must've been waiting so long he's forgotten all about us,' argues Biani.

'Ya, the whitey must be so relaxed now he's lying back with a beer and listening to cricket,' schemes Koshkosh.

Which, when we considered it, made sense, and so we decided to hit farmer Makhaki again.

Me and Nyoni reccied the place to check out the security. As we're circling the farmer's cabin, the wind swings and the dogs, three huge ridgebacks, jump up against the security fence barking and yowling. On come the lights, these mammoth spotlights which illuminate every rock and bush for yards around as though it's midday. What with the glare us ouens can't see a thing, and we cower back under cover hoping like hell that the farmer can't spot us either. We lie there until the wind swings again, and the dogs calm down and whoever is watching decides o shit, another goddam false alarm, and switches off the lights.

When the night was still again we sneaked off and rendezvoused with the others. Next on the agenda was the compound, 20 huts ringed by a security fence in a valley about a kilometre from the farmhouse. Skinny yellow mongrels yapped and snarled as we circled the place looking for an entrance but when we lobbed a couple rocks at them they yelped and slunk away. We took up positions beside this small gate and anchored there, anchored there until finally this old bloke crawled out of his hut and went off to piss against a thornbush.

'Hey, old man,' Todzo calls softly, 'come here — or I'll shoot.' We weren't expecting co-operation. The permanent workers on the farm were Malawians, and Malawians had a reputation for being difficult to handle cos they were loyal to their boss and suspicious of the struggle.

The bloke comes up to the wire, and eeh, he's shaking.

'We are the boys,' says Biani. 'Let us in or we'll kill you.' We didn't want to cut our way through the wire; we didn't want to leave any clues for the farmer to find.

'I-I-I-I haven't g-got the k-keys,' the bloke stutters. 'The b-bossboy, he's got.'

'Get them,' Biani tells him, 'if you want to live.'

Next thing the bossboy is there fiddling with the lock.

Half the unit anchor outside in the shadows while the rest of us go in. First thing, Biani orders the bossboy to get his wife to make us sadza, a span of sadza, enough for 20 men. 'And once you've organised her, call the rest of the people together,' Biani says. 'We have something to discuss.'

Two minutes later everyone in the compound — men, women, lighties, the lot — is standing outside the bossboy's kraal. Todzo explains to them that the white men had stolen the land and it was time to do something about it.

'That's fine, we agree,' ventures the bossboy, 'but we are Malawians, this isn't our country. . . .'

'You can't sidestep the struggle,' Todzo tells them. 'You are either exploiters or exploited, oppressor or oppressed. You'd better decide pretty quick where you belong.'

'We just work here. . .' a woman bursts out.

Todzo realises that he'd better begin right at the beginning. 'Now you,' he says, pointing to the bossboy, 'now you tell me what kind of man this Makhaki is.'

The bossboy, he stares down at his toes. 'Not so bad,' he begins.

Todzo, he checks the bloke out with a naked eye. 'What are these lies you are telling me?' he says. 'We know about this man, don't try to bullshit us.' Russia begins fiddling with his AK. He was always heavy with his hints.

The headboy gets the idea. 'When we cut the tobacco, if we don't do everything just right, he beats us and he won't pay us....'

Then up stands this bloke and tells us about this goat, a big black billy with a crumpled horn that he'd been keeping to sacrifice for his father, but it'd strayed into the farmer's vegetable patch, just once or twice, and hadn't eaten that much anyway, just a few beans and one or two tomatoes, and the farmer had fined him and forced him to get rid of it, and he'd had to take it to his brother at the farm over the ridge and leave it there with him, and....

And so on and so on. 'Now can you see how this white man treats you badly?' Todzo asks eventually. 'Can you see how he is getting fat from your labour — and from the land and cattle stolen from your brothers here in Zimbabwe?'

'Yes, but....'

'Yes, but??? Are you men???' He launches into yet another long explanation, but it doesn't seem to help much either. Those blokes had cemented themselves into their worries and you'd have needed dynamite to blow them loose.

While all this is going on we take the cook behind the huts for questioning. After a little poking and prodding, he tells us that Makhaki's wife is a teacher, that she gets a lift home from school and is usually home by four. Makhaki himself spends his day out on the lands, and he carries this big, elephant-sized gun, but he was always back for lunch at 12.30.

After about 15 minutes, we take him back to the meeting where ou Todzo is now carrying on about sellouts, asking the mense if they know what sellouts are, if there are any sellouts in the kraal. No one is saying anything, so Koshkosh tells the bossboy to stand and pokes him in the gut with the barrel of his gat, and he eventually manages to stutter out that this one bloke, one Beans had once wanted to join the police reserve.

Beans is requested to please stand and explain himself. It's the old bloke who we'd ambushed in the middle of his piss, and eeh, his legs are knocking together. 'All lies,' he manages to stutter out finally. 'All lies.'

'Good,' says Biani. 'Pleased to hear it. So you won't mind helping us then.' He gives the sadza, wrapped in newspaper, to Beans. 'You're coming with us.'

'My legs,' stutters the good Beans, 'my leg — it's lame.'

'Do you want me to kick it better?' Biani threatens. 'You're coming with us.' And so Beans, limping loudly, carried the sadza for us for part of the way.

'That's fine,' Biani says eventually. 'You can go back now. Don't forget though — if you tell the police that you've helped us — they'll shoot you.'

The next morning we waylay the cook as he strolls out into the backyard with his lunch, a few slices of bread and marg and some cold meat that he'd liberated.

Chapter 19

With our AKs in his back, he calms the dogs down, holds them while Nyoni and Koshkosh nip through the gate of the security fence into the house. They check the place out, signal all clear. The cook drags the dogs inside and locks them in the toilet, and the rest of us troop in behind him. As we're heading through the kitchen, Koshkosh flings open the fridge. 'Aaie, look at this lot,' he says, deeply impressed. 'Just look at this!'

There's a leg of lamb, hardly touched, half a roast chicken, cheese — three kinds — Vienna sausages, a row of eggs, a jug of milk, cream, a slab of butter and a pack of bacon. Next thing we're all snatching and grabbing and filling our faces, gobbling up the graze like a plague of locusts.

'Hey, hey,' the cook says, very worried. 'The baas — he's going to be angry.'

Us ouens, we just pack up laughing. 'How many are eating here?' asks Todzo, pointing at the fridge with a chicken leg.

'Just Makhaki and his wife.'

'Only two,' ou Koshkosh burps. 'They must have the stomachs of elephants!'

The cook stares down at the floor, but Todzo wasn't going to let him off so easily. 'How often does the farmer give you meat?' he wants to know. 'Once a week? Once a month?'

'He gives us an ox at Christmas,' the cook says, 'and the cows that die.'

'How often does the farmer eat meat?'

The cook he just hung his head. 'Answer — you are the cook. You must know.'

'All the time — with every meal,' the cook admits.

'Now — do you see? That's exploitation,' says Todzo, 'his dogs probably eat better than you do.'

'He probably throws better food into his dirt bins,' puts in Koshkosh, starting on the sugar pot with a tablespoon.

'Okay, okay, you blokes,' Biani shouts. 'Time to get moving. We've got plenty to do. You — Muzukuru — check out the kitchen and keep an eye on the cook.'

As the rest of the ouens left, I grabbed a Vienna sausage that had miraculously survived the onslaught. 'Any shit from you and you'll be frying your balls in butter,' I told the cook and, to make sure he got the message, I had him sit on a high stool, face to the wall, hands held high over his head. 'Just keep quiet and don't move.' I sounded so much like those hardcore ouens in the movies I started to laugh. Keeping my gun trained on him, I rummaged through the cupboards. Plates and tea sets — not quite what we were after — pickled cucumbers and peach jam — not particularly useful either. Then, in the freezer, beneath half-an-inch of frost, I found three-quarters of a sheep. A feast, I chune you, a real feast. I set the cook to work: he heaved the sheep out and dumped it in the sink, and began chipping off the ice. Meanwhile I ransacked the rest of the kitchen, going through the food and sorting out what we could use — rice, mealie-meal, salt, sugar, tea. I sneaked a small pack of curry powder into the pile as well, but eeh, there was all this confectionery stuff too, stuff I hadn't seen for years: nutmeg, cinnamon, vanilla, almond essence, sultanas, candied cherries.

By then the cook had bashed the bulk of the ice off the meat, so I had him stack up all the pieces — legs, ribs alles — in the oven which I turned up as high as it could go. We didn't have time for fancy cooking, and me, I prefer my meat well done.

'I used to be a confectioner,' I found myself telling cookie. 'I used to be a good confectioner too. My wedding cakes were famous.' Which was something of an exaggeration, but then I never did have any complaints.

The cook didn't turn to look. He probly didn't care.

'Might as well keep my hand in while I've got the chance,' I added very chatty.

I dug through the cupboards until I found sugar and flour and baking powder. Off to the fridge for milk, eggs, shortening. I gooid all the stuff into a bowl, added a handful of sultanas and a pinch of cinnamon for luck, found an egg beater and told the cook to get on with it. He thrashed away at the mixture as if he was paddling for his life.

Next —icing! Me, I'd always been an expert at icing, but I was very nervous you check, and out of touch, so I figure I'd better not try anything fancy. It'd have to be quick and simple — confectioner's icing! I collected butter, milk, sugar and vanilla, poured them all together and when the cook was finished with the batter, I shoved him the bowl of icing to keep occupied. When it was all done, I had him grease a pan, pour the batter into it and push it into the oven which we turned down to medium. Cook turned to his corner and I went back to the cupboards.

When I reckoned the cake was done, more or less, I opened the oven and prodded it with a fork. Ya, it wasn't a bad cake at all, actually, just a bit charred round the edges. I was still employable. Keeping one eye on cook I iced it, decorating it with a whole box of bright red cherries and a fistful of hundreds-and-thousands. When I was done, I ordered the cook to get started on the tea, and out he brings this silver teapot, cups with pictures of a bloke in a red jacket and black cap perched on his horse jumping a gate, milk in a jug with a special net to save the flies from suicide and a silver sugar pot with a silver spoon. I was impressed, I chune you: he'd been well-trained. He carried the tray through into the lounge like a hotel waiter and I followed behind with the cake in one hand and my gat in the other.

Makhaki's cabin had style, I chune you, just like you see in magazines. The lounge carpet was thick and green and the curtains and the lounge suite were brown and leafy. On the TV was a soap-stone head of a worn-down, beaten-down old tribesman, the kind of thing that honkies are particularly fond of. There was this huge stereo and a stack of records, 'Rhodesians Never Die' at the top — and on the wall above the mantelpiece, there's a painting of some grey-haired honky, very fierce, with a whole row of medals all across his chest.

I shouted to the comrades that tea was being served in the lounge, and, one by one, they began to drift in. 'Can't find any money,' said ou Biani, dumping a bundle of stuff into the middle of the floor. 'Where does he hide it?' he asked the cook who just shook his head.

'Not a drop of booze in this whole place,' complained ou Koshkosh, staggering down the stairs with an armload of booty. Not even the sight of tea and cake could cheer him up.

'Baas finish drink,' said the cook unhappily. He looked like he could do with a quick dop himself.

The others came down one by one and gooid all the stuff into this pile of plunder in the middle of the floor. Then and there us ouens began stripping off our clothes — they were crawling with lice and falling apart from the sun and wet and the thorns — and trying on selections from Makhaki's wardrobe. Eeh, he was a big bloke, was ou Makhaki, and the skinny scrawny blokes like me fell right out of his clothes. As we're scratching around for something our size, ou Todzo uncovers this pile of Rhodesian T-shirts.

'Look at this!' He picked up one, holding it away from himself as if it's a rotting rat or something. 'GET YOURS WHILE STOCKS LAST', the thing announces in large black letters and on the back there's a picture of half-a-dozen comic book guerillas turning tail as the Great White Hero charged in, gat at the ready.

'We should probly keep it,' Koshkosh put in. 'With that thing on no one would ever suspect you were a freedom fighter.' But, even in the interests of camouflage, there was a limit to what we were prepared to do.

Then someone uncovered a heap of Makhaki's son's clothes. Though he was only a youngster they were more our size, and we forgot all about the T-shirts as we scrambled for a share of the booty.

When, after much arguing, the clothes had been more or less evenly distributed and we were all decently dressed once again, we began sorting through the rest of the stuff.

It was like Christmas, I chune you. Within minutes I'd collected quite a heap: a bottle of Makhaki's aftershave, a pair of takkies only three sizes too big for me, a bar of white soap specially for 'oily skins', a radio that worked when you shook it, a pile of pill bottles from the medicine cabinet (Makhaki seemed to suffer mainly from constipation and piles), as well as all the food from the kitchen, and a pack of cards. Ya, I chune you, I was pleased to have those cards — all those days when we were hiding out, waiting for evening, I'd roll myself a reef, clean my gat, and sit in the shade and play Patience.

Taking them from the pack one at a time, I laid out the lines of the cards as they came up, never cheating once. Ya, those afternoons were so big and endless you felt you had all the time you could ever want for them to come out right. They were good to have around those cards, they were another world, a world apart from the war; you could get into the game and forget everything else. I've still got them, actually — that same pack. One or two are missing, and all the rest are torn and dirty but I've always hung onto them. Except for the clothes I was wearing and a yellow T-shirt with a couple of holes in it, they're the only things I brought back from the war.

But that afternoon in Makhaki's house I grabbed enough to stuff a junk shop, and the rest of the comrades didn't do too badly either. Which was quite fine — except when we tried to get everything into our packs we found we had problems, big problems.

Those who did manage to stuff all their booty into their packs battled to lift them, but most of us — me included — eventually had to admit that there just wasn't room for everything that we wanted. Biani — with his mammoth pile of whatnots in front of him — eventually reminded us that it wouldn't be easy to run with a rattling collection of rubbish on our backs. Point taken. With a sigh I emptied out my pack, and rummaged through the pile again, throwing out the radio and the alarm clock, the takkies and the aftershave, most of the pills — a whole heap of stuff. I kept two changes of clothes, a jersey, some of the graze, the soap and the cards. Nothing more.

When we finally had all our baggage organised we flopped onto the chairs and the settees in the lounge, and the cook, who'd been watching the goings-on as if he wasn't there, poured us all a cup of tea.

'Hell,' says ou Koshkosh settling back. 'This is better than the

Ambassador Hotel.'

'When we've liberated Zimbabwe, us comrades must all drink a cup of tea at one of those fancy places,' puts in Fidel.

'You'd better start practising right now then,' said Koshkosh very serious. 'You drink tea like a tramp. If you try that in any fancy hotel — even after we've won — they'll chuck you out, no question. I was a waiter once, and I know about these things. Now the first thing you must learn is to hold your cup by its handle — like this.'

Which Fidel promptly copied. The rest of us, we just packed up laughing. Ou Fidel, he looked at us sort of bewildered, and began to scratch behind his ear.

'What you gentlemen need is a couple of lessons in tea drinking,' said Koshkosh twisting his voice into this imitation of a crusty British accent. 'Comrade Muzukuru — no — don't take yourself to the teacup. Sit up straight and bring the teacup to you!'

Without thinking, I found myself obeying him. Great laughter. 'Blood, you see,' cried Koshkosh, 'blood counts. Even our great killer of the whites here is half-way to being an Englishman already — while the rest of us have to work hard and practise.' A great roar of laughter.

'Not enough sugar,' I announced in what I hoped was an English accent, and tipped the entire pot into my tea. The tidal wave splashed across the table drenching Koshkosh's shoes.

'There's still a lot of wild kaffir in you though,' he said, shaking his head. More laughter.

Fidel, having got the idea, took the milk jug and downs the contents in a gulp.

Ou Koshkosh shook his head sorrowfully. 'I've known monkeys who are more civilised than you lot,' he said. 'Look — don't carry on as if you are an elephant slurping the stuff up your trunk! Come on — sip it, sip it gently, sippppp it. Come on, comrades now — all together.'

Russia blew a stream of bubbles through his tea.

'What's this?' cried Koshkosh, throwing up his hands in horror. 'Blowing bubbles in your tea like a farting hippopotamus? Your tea is too hot, you cool it like this.' He blew a small tornado into the cup, spattering us all.

Twelve fifteen. 'Time to get moving,' Biani tells us and, after locking up the cook in the pantry, we file out into the garden, and take up our positions. If all went according to plan the bloke didn't have a chance: the moment he got out of his truck to open the security gate we would blow him away. I anchor behind the bougainvillaea, sweating and scratching. There's no sign of him. The minutes crawl by. Maybe the bloke had had a breakdown — or there'd been an accident and any minute the cops would arrive to inform his wife. Finally, though, there's the drone of an engine off in the distance and in the valley you can check this small white truck zipping along towards us.

The bakkie pulls up in front of the security gate and Makhaki, an FN slung over his shoulder, jumps out to open it. First thing he shouts for his dogs. 'Delville, Churchill.' Locked in the toilet they can only bark and whine. Something's up, the bloke realises. He jerks up his gat, ducks back toward the truck but he's hardly taken a step when Biani fires one quick burst — kkkk — from behind this trellis, and the bloke's knocked spinning to the ground. That's it. End of story.

Me, I'd never seen anything quite as white as that bloke as he lies there: he's footrot white, frogbelly white, wedding cake white, dripping come white, white white, and his face is set in a sort of smile as if he's sneering at us, as if somehow even in our killing of him we hadn't quite managed to get everything entirely right. Me, I don't know what happened: I take a kick at his face, his smile, his whiteness, and all the hate I felt for Smith and Salisbury, for the whites who'd tormented my father, the whites who'd broken Naomi's jaw, and for the white lunacy that'd wrecked the country and was eating at my life, for the whites who swept us their crumbs and acted like they were Jesus, all my own stupid wanting to be white — all of that boils over and next thing I'm kicking and stomping at the body, smashing at the whiteness. Koshkosh, Fidel, Russia, Special — they all pile in too and the body flops around as if it's still alive, and someone catches it nicely in the ribs and over it flips and there in the bloke's back is a bloody great hole — you could've stuck two fists into it, no problem, a bloody great bleeding hole.

'That's enough now,' Todzo said. We stopped kicking.

Koshkosh rolled the body over and started feeling through the pockets. The bloke's thigh had been all smashed up too: I spotted the car keys — they'd been slammed into his flesh by one of the rounds.

'Get the cook,' Biani ordered. 'Show him how the struggle treats its enemies.' When the bloke saw the body he pissed himself. No joke. Pee was running down his legs.

'Go now,' I told him. 'Let the mense know what happens to sell- outs.' The bloke didn't need any further encouragement. He ran.

It was time to get moving. 'Everyone over here,' Biani yells. 'You — Russia — take the paraffin and set fire to the house.'

'Smith's men will see the smoke; we'll have to move quick,' he shouts back.

'I can hotwire the truck,' I put in.

'Get moving then.'

I fiddle, fiddle with the wires, and finally the engine catches, wheezing and sputtering. Ya, that was about the one useful thing I learnt at reform school.

'Ready,' I shout to Biani, who yells to Russia to get moving. As Russia ducks inside Biani jumps into the front with me and the rest of the blokes all climb into the back with their booty.

I'm already easing the truck down the drive when Russia comes belting out, and already behind the lounge curtains there's this orange glow. He catches up with us, pulls himself aboard, and me, I hit the accelerator and we're off, tearing along the drag there. Ya, it was something to be behind a wheel again, feeling the power when you put foot, the swing of the car as you round a corner. Then eeh — right in front of us — there's this jeep. 'Security force,' I yell, slamming on anchors. 'Smith's men.' The truck skids to a stop on the shoulder of the road, and all the blokes in the back are thrown on top of each other. 'Calm down,' someone screams. 'It's only the Malawians.'

God alone knows what the Malawians thought they were doing. Maybe they figured we were coming after them. Maybe they'd just had enough of struggles and bosses and were heading straight back to Malawi. Whatever, there must've been almost 20 people crammed into that Land Rover, and, from the way it was skidding and sliding all over the place, you could check that whoever was behind the wheel hadn't had too many driving lessons. The driver spots us, accelerates and, as the Land Rover rounds this corner, he loses his nerve, hits the brake, skids off the road, and topples down this embankment and lands upside down in a field of mealies.

I pull up beside them as they scrambled out bruised and wailing. One of the lighties is dead — he'd broken his neck as the Land Rover rolled. The bossboy — he'd been driving — is standing there, his one arm was flopping about sort of loose.

'So why were you running?' Biani demands. 'Are you scared now you know we can use a gun as well as a white man?' The bossboy doesn't move. 'What have you been doing that you think we want to shoot you? Have you been informing on us?'

Still no response. Biani leaves the bloke looking down at his arm and puts a couple rounds in the Land Rover's petrol tank. It flares up at once, barrelling out great black clouds of smoke. Up on the hill, smoke is beginning to seep out the house and flames are jumping at the curtains. It's time to get moving. When Biani jumps back into the truck, I put foot I chune you, I put foot.

We're eating up the kays, bouncing and sliding along these dirt roads, and every turning toward the bush seems to twist back and lead us deeper and deeper into the white farming area. We're speeding past farms with names like Hereford and Sussex, and me, I'm shitting myself, scheming that any moment some lumbering army truck, bristling with RLI rifles is going to swing out onto the road just in front of us. And the gauges are all on empty, the truck can cut any moment. Another side-road — it swerves off into the bush too. Any moment, I'm scheming, we'll run out of petrol, someone will spot us, and next thing, the fire force. . . . Then we turn a corner and suddenly we're in the middle of this tiny dorp — service station, store, two three houses, a sign 'POLICE: ONE MILE'.

'We've got to get petrol,' I yell to Biani. 'We've got no choice.'

As I brake on the platform, I shout to the attendant to fill 'er up.

The old bloke, he hobbles over. 'Coupons please, baas,' he says. I'd completely forgotten about petrol rationing. Biani takes out his Tokarev, and the bloke blinks and forgets about it too. 'How much petrol you want?' he says.

When he was finished, he came to the window. 'That'll be 21 dollars.'

'No,' says Biani, 'you give me your money,' and waggles his gat to prove his point. Once the bloke hands over his takings, Biani tells him to jump in the back of the truck. On the double.

'Smokes,' shouts Koshkosh from the rear. 'Let's grab some smokes.'

Me, by then, I'm about half-dead with fright. Any moment I'm expecting an army truck to come trundling round the corner or a police van to pull in next to us. 'Let's get moving,' I yell.

'Fine,' says Biani, who doesn't seem at all worried. 'And if you can find any chips. . . .'

'We could die for your goddam chips,' I moan, but ou Biani, he isn't listening to me, he's too busy counting the cash in the attendant's satchel.

'There's about 300 dollars here,' he says, 'we're not doing too bad.'

Me, I'm not listening. 'That Koshkosh — why's the son of a slug taking so long?'

'Relax,' says Biani soothingly. 'Complain when you're enjoying his smokes.'

'O shit.'

'Now what?'

'The mutton — I forgot the mutton!' I explained. 'It's still in the oven. It'll burn.'

Koshkosh staggers out with a cardboard box loaded with smokes, chocolates, cakes, aspirin, soap, chips, peanuts and whatall, and dumps it into the back. 'Kachase,' he shouts over to us — the attendant, he had his own private stock there in the back — 'you want?'

Biani nods. 'Okay, but hurry up.' From his voice I can tell that he's finally starting to worry too.

Seconds later ou Koshkosh appears brandishing his bottles like a football star with a new trophy.

'Forward with the party,' he yells and jumps, grinning, onto the back of the truck. And me, eeh, eeh, I put foot and that truck rockets out of the service station with a devil's screech and the stink of burning rubber.

We drove off, dodging down the side roads, trying to find a turning which led into the TTL, but by then we had absolutely no idea where the hell we were anyway. For all I knew we were riding round and round in circles. Around dusk, we decided to abandon the truck, and to head back to our area cross country. I drove the truck into the bush as far as it would go, the rest of the ouens following, trying to camouflage the tracks. We left it in the mud beside a stand of elephant grass. There was also the problem of the pump attendant: though, in the course of the ride, he'd insisted that he was with us, we didn't want to leave him loose in case he suddenly developed doubts and decided to tell his story at the nearest police station. Finally, we tied his ankles to a tree. By the time he'd worked himself free, we would be miles away.

As we're leaving, the bloke asks for his money back.

'What money?' Biani wants to know. 'The money we liberated wasn't yours. It was the money your boss stole from the people.'

'There's eight dollars of mine,' the bloke cries, 'and 75 cents. It's my pay, my tips.'

We gave it to him. 'You tell your friends that the boys from the bush don't steal from their own people,' Todzo said as he handed it over. 'We only take from the rich, the exploiters.'

The old bloke was so pleased to have his coin back, tears were dripping from his eyes. 'You are the true friends of the people,' he kept saying, 'may the Lord bless you.'

Ou Todzo was so pleased the old man was happy, he gave him a blanket, a cooldrink and a pack of smokes. After those Malawians, we were glad to meet someone who appreciated us.

The next day eeeh, we all felt sort of weird: though we'd done far more damage to Makhaki's farm than we'd ever expected, we all felt in need of a blessing or two. For starters, we weren't sure where we were, and not even Biani and Nyoni could pinpoint our position on the maps. Ya, losing our road like that, after so much had gone so right for so long, left us ouens sort of uneasy. You couldn't help yourself thinking, there in the back of your mind, that somewhere among those twists and turns, we'd lost the road of our luck, that we'd skidded back into all the usual confusions of the world.

So we celebrated our victory quietly, in spite of the kachase and the chips and all the chocolate, lying low and listening for choppers and spotter planes. All morning, all afternoon, there was nothing. 'They must've got lost too,' Biani joked, but you could see he wasn't easy either. Me, I remember at one point, unsteady from too many sluks of that kachase, I staggered out of our hideout, propped myself against this rock and felt for my fly, and looking down at the plains stretching off into the heat haze, the untouchable bleached whiteness of the sky, I put my fingers to my cheeks, felt the flesh of my face. Kiernan the drunken Irish bum who'd fucked my grandmother — I'd got his nose, his cheekbones. Eeeh, for a moment there, I wanted to shove my nails into my face, tear at my flesh until thick, dark drops of blood welled out the wounds. Me, I closed my eyes, jammed them shut, and eeh, for a moment there, I was wishing hard that everything was already over, and I could lie down and sleep and sleep and sleep.

Just before dusk we climb down to the bed of this stream to fill our water bottles. We're working down toward the water, moving in indian file among the banks and boulders and clumps of reeds when, at the top of the rise, Nyoni halts, holds his gat across his body — something funny. We freeze. Special sneaks forward to peek. Nyoni waves him back, and as he turns to look again — KKKKKKKKKKK — and the pair of them are grabbed up — twisted and spun — and smashed down and the rounds are ricocheting among the rocks, throwing up sprays of dust in the path. Fidel, turning to run, crashes down like he's been tackled and screeches and screeches, and the rest of us scramble back between the rocks, trying to figure out where in hell the firing's coming from.

Todzo reaches out for Fidel — jerks back — looking at his hand all mangled and bloody. Fidel claws his way back to cover, screaming and bleeding.

'Muzukuru — Koshkosh, give cover,' Biani cries, yanks Fidel to his feet and drags the bloke out of the line of fire.

Keeping my head well down, I blast off a mag into the general direction of the racket, duck behind another boulder, shove in another mag, fire again. To my left Koshkosh opens up high and wild. The security force — there must've been at least two sticks of them — begin to sweep forward, revving up every patch of shadow, throwing a grenade behind every boulder. A stick of troopies try to outflank us on the left but us ouens we backpedal, backpedal, keeping our distance, firing a couple of rounds here, a couple there, just enough to keep them cautious.

The troopies came up to the bodies of Special and Nyoni, and fired a quick burst into both of them to make sure they were thoroughly dead.

Special eeh, Special was just a lightie, and like any lightie he'd been wowed to find himself in the middle of a war story. For him it'd been a game of hide-and-seek, very exciting, but he hadn't quite realised that mense died when gats were fired; he hadn't yet smelt the stink of the fright and blood. He hadn't known anything really, he'd hardly put away his wood-and-wire AK for the real thing.

Nyoni dead. He was a big loss to us. I'd never really known the bloke — he was quiet, kept to himself, but he was a comrade, the kind of comrade you can rely on, the kind you can trust behind you. He'd spoken about his wife once, said that after he'd joined the struggle, she'd vanished. I wondered where she was, what she was up to, whether she would ever hear what finally happened to him, if his kids would ever know what kind of man their father had been.

The one troopie tried to pull Special's gat free, but even in death ou Special wouldn't let go without a battle, and the troopie had to prise his fingers off it one by one. Carefully I lined the Rhodesian up in my sights and, as he finally freed the gat, I squeezed the trigger. 'Company for you, comrades,' I'm scheming, but the gat didn't jump, there's no noise, and with his boot the troopie flipped Special over onto his stomach, knelt down and began to search his pockets. Jammed! I grabbed hold of the mag, jerked it backwards and forwards, trying to force it loose so's I could get a shot in before the troopie disappeared. But next thing Koshkosh sprayed a few rounds in the general direction of the bodies, and the troopie dived for cover. Me, I was so mal that I took that goddam gat and thumped it against the nearest rock. That did it: the mag snapped out. One of Smith's men over on the left opened up, and I had to take cover. I withdrew a couple yards, fired off a burst, withdrew again.

The sky darkened from white to purple, and the air thickened by the moment. When night fell, the security force would withdraw to their camp, and we would be able to disappear. More firing on my left. I withdrew, fired, withdrew again. The first star appeared.

Out of the corner of my eye, I spotted this shadow flitting among the rocks and then a troopie ducking down the bank, back towards the river. They were withdrawing. Next morning, though, they would be back to collect the bodies: they'd throw them into a net which they'd hang from a chopper and parade up and down over the kraals along the river telling the people that this is what happens to all those who fight the government, and Special and Nyoni would then be buried by enemies, in unmarked graves.

When it was completely dark, I withdrew too, circling back behind the rocks where I expected to rendezvous with Koshkosh and patrolled up and down, up and down, howling like a jackal. No answer. I was getting worried, I chune you; maybe he'd been hit, maybe he'd panicked and had taken off without me. Keep calm, I told myself, and took a deep breath and sat down and tried to figure out what to do next. I could either try the day's rendezvous, even though the security force might find it, or I could try to make it to Commander Advance's koppie on my own. I decided to check out the rendezvous.

I was used to having my buddies about me as we tramped along, I was used to putting my feet where they had put theirs. What with the darkness of the night I could hardly see my hand in front of me, and I kept slipping and stumbling over bushes and rocks. The spoor I was leaving would be as obvious as a main road to an experienced tracker. Hell, I was scheming, this is hopeless. I might as well just sit and wait for Smith's men to find me. But I kept going anyway — there was no point in making things easy for them.

Then just before 3 am it rained, and cold and damp as I was, I about jumped for joy: my trail would be washed away.

I reached the rendezvous point at dawn: I tramped round and round in the bush and howled and yowled like a jackal until my throat was sore. No reply, nothing. The unit, or rather what was left of it, must've headed straight for Advance's koppie. The sky was lightening fast. I couldn't stay where I was in case the security force captured one of the others and persuaded him to talk. I had to hide — and quick.

The koppie nearby was the obvious place: a heap of round, reddish boulders with wild olives and umsasas growing in the cracks. Somewhere up on top I'd reckoned I'd find a cave or a thicket. Pulling myself up over the last of the boulders, I saw a ring of black rock about ankle-high that looked as if it might be the remains of an old cattle kraal. Beyond the ring was another wall, almost knee-high in parts, and beyond that, on the far side of the koppie, 50 yards away, almost hidden by a clump of umsasas and euphorbias, I saw, black against the dawn sky, a stone citadel.

I went cold then, I chune you. The branches of the umsasas creaked and groaned in the wind like the spirits were talking, and my gut was whispering make a duck, make a duck. But it was getting light fast and I needed cover quick. With my gat cocked, I checked the place out: part of the wall of the citadel had collapsed, and on the rubble grew these bushes with tiny white flowers. The ruin must have been ancient, centuries old, some kind of outpost of one of the old

Zimbabwe empires. My history teacher during my reform school days — old Scab — once explained to us that Zimbabwe had to have been built by the Arabs or the Phoenicians or the Egyptians — or perhaps even the Queen of Sheba — cos the 'kaffirs' just didn't have the brain capacity for it.

Pushing through the bushes I went into the citadel. With those blackish granite walls rising sheer around me the hair stirred on my spine. The world here was silent, still: and the sky was like a small patch of blue cloth up overhead. What kind of place had it been back in the days of Monomatapa — altar, watchtower to keep an eye out for Portuguese bands, beacon, cattle kraal? The koppie itself must have been fortified. There must have been soldiers here. I tried to picture them: ordinary blokes like us, and all of them dead now, and the stones still standing.

What did we know of them, all the thousands that must have died as kingdoms rose and fell, as the Portuguese, the Madzwiti and Rhodesians invaded, hundreds and thousands of them, all in their unmarked graves out in the bush?

It struck me that we couldn't remember the names of the comrades. We remembered their struggles, their leaders. We sang their names, asking their spirits to lead us in the struggle. But, if you thought about it, the names of all these struggles, all these leaders, were really made up of thousands and thousands of cadres, the way dots make up a newspaper picture. Even if I was only one among all the nameless at least I would have been part of something worth fighting for, and whatever happened to me, even if I just vanished into the veld or ended up being flown along the river in a net dangling from a helicopter like Nyoni and Special, the struggle would continue and be remembered.

The last stars faded. Smith's men would be out in force at any moment. I crawled into the bushes at the base of the citadel, and tried to sleep.

All day long the spotter planes droned overhead, and bursts of firing echoed off in the distance. I lay down in the thicket, and it was only late-late that night, when the guns and the choppers had been silent for several hours, that I climbed down the koppie. My throat was dry as a dust road in October, and when I came to a stream I forgot all about strategy and security force and knelt down and drank like an animal. When I was satisfied, I filled my bottle, and with my gut groaning hungrily, headed north to Advance's koppie. It was dark that night, dark as the inside of an elephant's arse, and I trapped and trapped, yipping and yowling, tripping and stumbling. God alone knew where Biani and the others were. Then, around 3 am waaay off in the dark a jackal howled in reply, and howled again when I howled back. Comrades? Keeping my fingers crossed round my trigger, I headed for the howling, hoping that it wasn't just some lonely female jackal, or some troopie playing werewolf in his bivvy.

I stumbled through the dark after the howl, yammering away whenever I wasn't so sure where I was heading. The howl seemed to float through the night like a ribbon of sound: I couldn't tell exactly where it was coming from. I kept zigzagging towards it for what seemed like hours, never seeming to get any closer when suddenly out of the dark from everywhere and nowhere all at once, like the voice of Chaminuka himself, someone orders me to stand still and hold my gun over my head. I do what I'm told. If it's a trap, it's too late for tears anyhow.

'Is it him?' Koshkosh asked, and me I said, as if I was speaking to a friend at the other side of the room, 'Don't be such a fool. Of course it's me.'

'Finally.' Russia stepped out of the dark, gat at the ready. 'Have you got the medicines? What took you so long?'

'Sure, sure I've got the medicines. Jisis man,' — I was babbling — 'what the hell happened to you ouens? I thought you were dead — couldn't find you — figured they'd got you too.'

'We thought they'd finished *you*,' said Russia. 'Until we heard the howling. You sound like a Salisbury mongrel with a bellyache.'

Even with all his nonsense eeh, I was pleased to see that long-faced lout. I could have fallen to my knees and licked his feet. 'I was beginning to think I'd never see any of you guys again.' I was beginning to babble once more. 'And where...?'

'Did you dump any of it?' Russia broke in.

'Dump any what?'

'The medicine.'

'Hell — no — it's all here.'

'Our supplies have finished,' he told me. 'We can't stand here all night gossiping like girls fetching water. Come.'

Just before sunrise we caught up with the rest of the unit. With Todzo out of action I was now medic, and the wounded were my responsibility. First thing I got out the kit and made sure they were patched up properly. As I unwound the shirt bandaging Todzo's hand I was just about sick. The hand looked like a headless rabbit: red and raw and oozing. The thumb was gone and the finger next to it too.

'Let's get some herbs,' I suggested, shaken. 'Tell me what to look for.'

'No good,' he told me, and even in that light I could see that he was grey with pain. 'Whitey's guns need whitey's medicines.'

We took cover in the nearest cave, and I unpacked the unit medical kit and gave him a shot of morphine. He quietened, closed his eyes. I wanted to make a fire and boil everything, like we'd been taught in training, but it was too dangerous. So, when the morphine had taken hold, I swabbed the mangled flesh, cleaned off the muck with cottonwool soaked in antiseptic. When the hand seemed more or less hygienic, I crushed a couple penicillin tablets, mixed in a little water, and then smeared the paste across the wound. I got him to swallow a couple tablets and bound the hand up. That was all I knew to do.

As I was cleaning up the hand, Biani told me his half of the story. While me and Koshkosh had been firing, him and Russia had dragged the two wounded — Todzo and his smashed hand, Fidel with his calf blown off — to shelter behind this small koppie. There they patched up the wounds as best they could and, after dumping about everything they'd been carrying, Biani and the wounded cadres headed east to Mozambique.

'I reckoned our best chance of shaking off Smith's men was to make them believe we were Zanla cadres heading home,' Biani explained. He sent Russia to rendezvous with me and Koshkosh. The two of them bumped into each other but, in the darkness and panic, they missed me and, when I didn't show, didn't show, they schemed I'd been ironed out and withdrew.

When they caught up with the others they all changed direction, heading straight for Comrade Advance's koppie, except for Koshkosh who took the spoor due east for another two hours.

He faded his false trail on a rocky hillside, doubled back and, just before dawn, caught up with Biani and the wounded comrades again. All that day the group lay low in a thicket of reeds, listening to the spotter plane overhead and the rattle of gunfire in the distance. They were convinced then that I'd been finished.

Fidel's leg was next. He was lying deep in a cave moaning quietly to himself. His forehead was as hot as the barrel of an AK after a contact. I shot him full of morphine, tried to put myself in neutral as I peeled off the shirts and field dressings wrapped around his calf. As the wadding fell away, the stink hit me, and eeh, I stuck my head out of the cave and was sick. That leg eeh, it was a mess, a real mess. The calf had just about been blown away, and though the bone hadn't actually snapped, there were chips of it floating around in the flesh. Me, I just didn't know where to begin. We tried to clean it up — all us cadres took turns swabbing at it — and finally, when none of us could stand it any longer, I smeared the wound with penicillin paste and bandaged it up again.

'If I'm ever like that,' I told Biani as I came out of there, 'you better shoot me.'

'The medic at Advance's koppie — he might be able to help,' Biani said. But we all knew that Fidel couldn't be helped by the advice of Advance's medic or anyone else for that matter. He needed to be in hospital. He needed his leg amputated, he needed blood transfusions and drips and fancy antibiotics and rest. All he had, out there in the bush, was me and a medical kit.

For the first day or two, we took turns helping him, half carrying, half propping him up as he lurched along on his one good leg. But by the third day, he was too far gone to help himself and we had to carry him. To make matters worse, the leg'd gone green, and it'd begun to stink, and the smell was so bad that, when we stopped, we left him downwind. He stank so that I stopped changing the dressing — I couldn't handle it. Secretly, I stopped the penicillin tablets too. If he was going to die, better he die quickly. Meanwhile, I kept up the morphine, I kept pumping it into him like air into a leaky tyre. If he was going to have to endure a couple more days of being bundled through the bush, rather have him too high to notice.

The miracle was that he'd lasted so long. He hardly drank and he'd pretty much stopped eating. I tried to tempt him with canned beef and spinach — the cans of beef we reserved for the wounded — but I couldn't get him to swallow much.

The rest of us had to eat spinach. The stuff had to be boiled three, four times cos it was poisonous, and though we always started off with a huge potful — there were acres of it around — by the fourth boiling all that remained were a couple handfuls of green slime.

We were always hungry, and in the mornings when I sawed off the top of the can with my bayonet, and the smell of beef flooded the camp, the blokes went quiet. The smell of that stuff eeh, it made you think of braais where you could eat yourself thick with steak and wors and drink yourself silly with Castle. I remembered those curries, thick with cubes of beef and reeking of chillies and garlic, that Naomi used to cook in winter, Katz's steak-and-kidney pies, with lots of meat, a thick salty gravy and a heavy, doughy crust, and the Rhodesian army bully beef which we ate straight out of a can.

Once I had the can open, I'd warm it on the fire, if there was one, and take it to Todzo. He was always hungry, but he'd take only his half, and that half was exactly measured. When Todzo was finished, I'd take what was left to Fidel. He'd be lying where I'd left him, right out of it and, taking good care to be downwind of him, I'd begin feeding him like a child.

'Open up, open up,' I'd tell him, holding a teaspoonful of meat in front of his lips. Ya, it was like being back in Salisbury, and trying to feed the lightie — 'and the choo-choo train goes ooohhh into the tunnel' — at which, when she was good, she'd swallow the train and smile like a crocodile.

Fidel was never so enthusiastic. He'd open his mouth slowly, like the hinges were rusty, and I'd stick the spoon in and turn it over. 'Come on, comrade,' I'd tell him, 'swallow. It's your duty to the struggle. Eat your beef.' And he'd try. He did try. 'Get strong.'

And during this, me, I'd be trying to watch out the back of my head to see what the rest of the cadres were up to. If they were all watching the pot of boiling greens very carefully, trying to forget Fidel and the smell of the beef, then — quick — I'd sneak a spoonful for myself, sticking it in my mouth and keeping up my story all the while. 'Come on now, comrade — you can do it. Open your mouth just a little wider, wider — try' — and gulp — the beef'd go skidding down to my stomach.

What with the mood of the comrades, it was quite a risky business sneaking those spoonfuls. Ya, those blokes, boiling their spinach for the third and fourth time, must've hoped and prayed for Fidel's death so we could share out his half — on one night at least.

A day or two later we're trapping along just before sunrise, when everything is still misty and silent — CLANG — 'Take cover,' Biani yells, and us ouens, we don't need any orders, we've already hit the deck, flattened ourselves against the ground, and we're checking, checking, AKs cocked, trying to figure out what's what. But all we can check is Comrade Koshkosh standing at the bottom of the hill.

'Take cover!' Biani yells again. 'Koshkosh take cover!' Me, I'm expecting him to crumple up any minute — but Koshkosh pauses a moment and drops to the ground. It's then that we check this tin can glittering in the grass.

Biani'd seen it too. He knew what'd happened. 'Finish up,' he tells Koshkosh. 'We'll speak to you once we have made the camp.' And, later that morning, as we sat waiting for our spinach to boil, the whole story came out. According to Russia, the rearguard, Koshkosh had dropped from logistics' place in the centre of the file to a position right at the rear.

'He said he was feeling sick and it was so near dawn I didn't think it would make much difference,' Russia apologised. Ya, ou Russia always did things Zapu-Zapu, and he wasn't happy to be caught out.

Biani then asked how many cans of beef we had. Koshkosh, being the logistics, had to answer. 'Three,' he said.

'Why three? Why not four?'

'The other one, it's gone,' Koshkosh said.

'Gone?'

'I ate it,' Koshkosh admitted. He'd let the rest of the unit pull ahead and had sawed the can of beef in half and fed himself. One half of the can he'd pushed into a bush as we'd trapped along, the other he'd dropped, and it had hit a stone.

'So — now you are all right?' Biani asked him.

'Yes — I am all right.'

'And what about all of you?' Biani gestured to the rest of us, then turned back to Koshkosh. 'What about your comrades?'

'We are hungry,' we said.

'But we have one comrade who is all right,' said Biani, stressing 'comrade'.

'I'm sure that with all that extra power, he will be able to fight for us all today,' Russia said.

'He can carry Fidel too,' Biani agreed. 'With all of that beef that he has eaten he won't notice. And when we faint from hunger he can carry us too.'

Now, by Zipra law Koshkosh was supposed to be shot, but it is difficult to shoot one of your comrades.

'That mouth of his never stops,' Russia reckoned. 'Cut out his tongue.'

Koshkosh went sort of greenish.

'Sew up his lips,' I put in. 'Then he won't be able to eat any more.'

Todzo had the last word. 'He has eaten his share for two days — so for two days we give him nothing.'

Quite fine — except it wasn't his food that he'd eaten, but the food for the two wounded comrades. Biani gave me the rest of the food to carry and told Koshkosh that, from then on he'd have to carry Fidel full time.

For two days we trudged on, eating only our handfuls of spinach and giving Koshkosh nothing. Finally, eeh we just couldn't stand it any longer and one afternoon we decided, hell, forget Smith's men, we're going to cull a couple of the impala grazing near our hideout. Me and Biani went after them, circling downwind until we got within range. When we were still about 300 metres off the impala started sniffling the air and pricking up their ears, so Biani blasted off a mag at the thickest huddle of ewes and fawns. When we got there we found two dead and one badly wounded, which I slagged with my bayonet. We slit open their bellies, cut out their livers, and hacked the hindquarters off the biggest.

Back at camp, the blokes were salivating like a pack of starving mongrels. No one even thought about the security. Quick-quick there was a fire on the go — but none of us could wait for the meat to be properly grilled and we were all grabbing for it while it was still raw and oozing blood. One precaution we did take: we removed Koshkosh's gat.

While the rest of us were filling our faces, Koshkosh sat downwind of us and stared out over the plains. When we'd filled our guts, when we couldn't stuff another scrap down our throats, we stretched out in the shade burping and picking our teeth. Russia grabbed a greasy piece of gristle and went and waved it in front of Koshkosh's nose. Koshkosh was as still as a stone. Russia rubbed the gristle against the bloke's cheeks, his lips, until he couldn't stop himself, he snapped at it like a dog.

Russia snatched the gristle away with a shout of laughter. 'Down, doggie, down — come on — if you want to be fed — you must beg like an old white woman's dog — come on.' Koshkosh licked at the fat smeared on his lips.

'Beg.'

Down on his knees went Koshkosh. And eeh, by then, we were all laughing ourselves sick. Koshkosh held out his hand.

With a triumphant yell Russia stuffed the gristle into his mouth. 'That's what you are — a dog,' he yelled. 'You're not fit to be a comrade. You're a dog.'

Koshkosh, he just turned his back on us again.

That evening, when I went to shoot some more morphine into Fidel, he was dead. During the afternoon I'd taken him this lekker piece of liver; his eyes had been closed and his breathing shallow, I figured he was asleep, and left the liver next to him. By evening the juices of the liver had congealed to fat, and Fidel was as stiff as a board. I ate the liver and called the others. Biani said a few words about comradeship and struggle, and when the names of the heroes of Zimbabwe were called, Comrade Fidel's name would be called also. Russia took Fidel's boots, as the sole of one of his had come off, but his clothes stank so badly no one would take them. We shoved his body into an antbear hole and rolled a stone over the top.

That night we really ate up the kays. Moving without Fidel was one hell of a lot easier. While we were climbing this koppie, Koshkosh keeled over and collapsed. He'd fainted. Biani slapped his face, gave him a mouthful of water and this hunk of roast liver that he'd saved.

'Comrades,' says ou Koshkosh once he'd eaten and drunk. 'Comrades — I swear — I will never do that again.'

'You'd better not,' Biani told him, 'because next time we will shoot you.'

Three days later we rendezvoused with Comrade Advance. Todzo's hand was all swollen by then, and he was always very tired. Their medic took a good look at him, but he wasn't able to help. 'Take him to the mission hospital,' he said. 'The doctor there, he's from Germany. He's with us.'

So late-late that night we took him over to the hospital, woke up the duty nurse and told her to call the doctor.

The doctor — a whitey, this mammoth blond bloke who looked as if he should be out in the bush brandishing an FN rather than in a hospital — ambles in rubbing his eyes and straightening his coat. Without thinking my hands felt for my gat.

The doctor took Todzo's hand and prodded at it. He shook his head, and led the bloke straight to the operating theatre. The other medic went along to watch and learn, but me, I'd had enough of wounds during the past few days so I hung around outside.

After about half-an-hour they emerged, the medic looking sort of greyish and the doctor all concerned. 'Your friend is very sick,' he told me in his funny accent.

'He must leave for Botswana tomorrow,' I said. I wouldn't tell anyone our true destination just in case.

'Is there not any way that he can stay?'

I shook my head.

The bloke sighed. 'Okay, but he is sick. There was a cup of pus in his hand. I give him pills, dressings — and when you reach Botswana, take him straight to hospital.'

Which we did. He was rushed to hospital in Lusaka, and the doctors immediately removed his hand.

Chapter 20

*A*fter that lot all we wanted was peace and quiet, a place to lay
low. We didn't even try to sneak off to Lusaka for a jol, and
when Biani wangled himself a pass to visit Rudiya in the women's
camp, he went off alone. Us ouens just sat around skyfing it up,
playing cards and stuffing ourselves with sadza. We were so quiet that
the camp commanders just about forgot we existed. It was only after
we'd been there for about a month that new comrades, four blokes
who'd just finished their training, were assigned to our unit, and a few
days after that the whole bunch of us, plus a platoon of about 20 other
blokes, were all trucked down to this camp on the shores of Lake
Kariba.

We spent more than a year there, a quiet year. For hours at a time
we anchored in these observation posts — OPs we called them — and

watched and waited. All there was to look at were grey-green hills over on the eastern side, and the waters of the lake, blue with distance. Once in a while you'd spot a boat — fishermen? security force posing as fishermen? — puttering among the islands and the rafts of Kariba weed, but no matter how you screwed your eyes up, how carefully you focused your binoculars, you couldn't say for sure. Sometimes a spotter plane would drift past, and once at sunset I saw a chopper, flying just above the water, vanish into Zambia.

Our camp was almost directly across the lake from Binga, where I'd been stationed back in my security force days. Looking across the water towards Rhodesia — as it was then — I couldn't help remembering the Rhodesian army — the RDR camp where I'd been sent on my first call-up, Headlights, my monkey ou Chico, Lootie Beauty, Soaps, and the Donkey-killer of Binga, Donk for short. Me, I'd been so pleased to get away from Naomi's nagging, and Katz and the confectionery and the kid. Ya, as that truck turned off the tar onto the dirt, I'd schemed I was such a hardcore bloke, a real soldier, a real man.

The whole of the lake seemed to lie between what I'd been in those days and what I'd become. But what would I have been like if I hadn't been captured and marched to Zambia at gunpoint? Would I have just limped along like all the other ouens, bitching and complaining about the army, about Smith, always discussing gapping it to Botswana with my buddies in the shab? Would I ever have crossed on my own? And was I really any different to what I'd been back then?

Around this time we began hearing more and more about Smith's internal settlement. After the Geneva talks and the Anglo-American proposals flopped, Smith had reckoned if these houties wouldn't settle on his terms, well then he'd find some who would. He didn't have far to look: there were plenty stray politicians around who'd fallen out of favour with their parties and the people, politicians who'd tasted power once and who were prepared to do anything to get a taste of it again. Sithole, who'd once been leader of Zanu and who still claimed to lead the freedom fighters, accepted Smith's terms. So did Bishop Muzorewa, who'd once been head of the ANC, and Chief Jeremiah Chirau, an Ndebele who had been a stooge of Smith's since way back.

Smith tried to lure Nkomo along as well, but after a secret meeting in Zambia, Nkomo rejected Smith's proposals, and denounced those who'd accepted them as 'vultures feeding on our kill'.

The internal settlement talks between Smith and his puppets began in December 1977. On the radio we heard how Muzorewa had boycotted the first session in protest against massacres by the security force — but come the second session he was talking again.

That was the pattern — once in a while Muzorewa walked out, and Smith and Chirau and Sithole told him what a naughty boy he was until he came crawling back, scared that the others would all settle without him.

By February '78 Smith's puppets had agreed to everything he wanted. There would be a show of handing the country over to black majority rule: a year of transitional government in which a black and a white minister would share each portfolio followed by a one-man one-vote election, a black majority in parliament and a black prime minister.

Which sounded fine until you realised the whites still controlled the police, the army, the administration and the economy — as well as having enough seats in parliament to block any inconvenient con-stitutional changes.

Nkomo summed up our feelings. 'I want to come home,' he said in a speech on Radio Zambia. 'But after all these years I can't come home to a shadow of what I'm fighting for.'

Smith and his puppets began this huge campaign to persuade the comrades to stop fighting, and even us blokes way out in the bush got to hear of it. One time, I remember, we were rushed to a Zambian village to check out this story that there'd been a bombing raid. The place was white with pamphlets, they were everywhere, trampled into the shit of the goatkraal, caught on the bushes, flapping about among the huts. Apparently a plane had dropped them the day before.

'Zipra fighters,' the pamphlet read. 'Why fight? You have been given what you want. Majority rule has been granted and, early next year, one-man one-vote elections will be held. COME HOME BEFORE IT IS TOO LATE!!' If we came back, the pamphlet said, we would be given amnesty, we would be allowed to keep our gats and we would be given work defending villages against 'the terrorists'. But if we did not return, if we refused to see the truth, if we went against 'the will of the people' we were 'CERTAIN TO DIE'. **Our** comrades were 'DYING EVERY DAY', our leaders were corrupt and wanted to carry on fighting not because they were interested in their own people but because they were making so much money out of it. 'You have little food, but your leaders eat well,' the pamphlet ended. 'They live in Lusaka in big houses and drive big cars. COME HOME BEFORE IT IS TOO LATE'.

'Who can believe such rubbish?' scoffs Russia as he crumples his pamphlet up and throws it down into the mud. For once most of us agreed with him.

Then one fine evening while we're listening to the BBC news, we heard Nkomo might join Smith's internal settlement. The two of them had been talking secretly and now, according to latest reports, were on the point of signing an agreement.

'Hell, I thought the big shots were supposed to be making so much from all the fighting that they would never settle,' cracked Koshkosh.

No one laughed. Some comrades muttered 'sellout' to each other. A little corruption was one thing, you helped yourself when you had the chance, but selling out the struggle was something else altogether.

Comrade Russia stood and turned off the radio — not that any of us were still listening to it — and informed us that this talk about Nkomo selling out was treasonable and irresponsible, and reminded us that disruptive elements could get themselves locked up. And, he added, us comrades weren't supposed to be listening to such a reactionary station anyway: things were always twisted and some of the comrades became confused — as we'd been hearing.

Ya, you had to admire the guy: he was so completely convinced that whatever Nkomo did was right that quite a number of comrades began to nod in agreement ya, ya, this one is talking sense, and the blokes who didn't really care one way or another soon began nodding along too.

The rest of us kept quiet. When someone from Security began talking about locking people up you didn't fool around.

Comrade Russia then went on to remind us that Smith and Nkomo had talked hundreds of times over the years, recalling each and every occasion just in case we'd forgotten exactly how many there'd been. 'And even with all this talking Nkomo has never sold out even one piece of the struggle,' he told us, very sarcastic, like a schoolmaster who is struggling to get a very simple point across to a stupid class.

'So why does Nkomo keep talking to Smith then?' the dumbest of the new members of our unit asks, very puzzled. 'Can't he just say well, Smith old chap — you can surrender now — fine. Otherwise: we fight.'

Russia trundled out this old story from Zipa days: the struggle had two fronts, one military and the other political, and the political front wasn't always exactly what it seemed.

'Let's hope you are right,' said Biani, when Russia finally finished. You could hear in his voice that he wasn't too charmed with all this threatening and speechifying. 'Our comrades did not die for Smith's internal settlement.'

Russia went through all his explanations one more time, and eeh I chune you, he was checking ou Biani with a naked eye there.

Me, I was so goddam scared that I closed my eyes and there were the comrades from Security grinning at me. Russia was just the kind of hardegat bastard who would turn a comrade in. One day Biani'd just disappear — and me along with him cos, as sure as shitting, they'd scheme that if he was up to something then his goffel buddy, the bloke who'd once fought for Smith, had to be involved too.

For a moment there I found myself thinking that, you know, if Biani was going to get himself and me locked up, maybe I should get in first, go to Security and prove to them that I'm no traitor by informing on him.

But eeh, suddenly I felt very tired, and sick, sick of all this scrabbling to survive. Hell, like Biani said, we were fighting to be men. If Security was going to take me, that was just too bad.

But the next day I went to Biani. 'Eeh, you know, you must be careful,' I said. 'We are at war now. The first thing is to survive.'

He checked me out with a naked eye there. 'I am a freedom fighter,' he told me. 'I can say my own thing.' But after that he was more cautious.

Luckily the Smith/Nkomo talks didn't last too much longer. One moment Nkomo confirms that Smith flew to Lusaka to meet him, and while us comrades are wondering just what kind of settlement this is going to be, Zipra guerillas shoot down an Air Rhodesia Viscount with a heatseeking missile and blow up the talks as well. According to the Rhodesians, there'd been mostly civilians on the aircraft and the fighters shot up most of the survivors. Our commissars told us that there had only been troops on the plane, and that some of the survivors were so bad they couldn't live. Whatever, 48 people died on that aircraft and afterwards the Rhodesians weren't in any mood to talk to Comrade Nkomo. They called him a 'callous barbarian', they compared him to Atilla the Hun. From the way those Rhodesians carried on about the Viscount, you'd think they were all shining angels of Mercy and Justice and that all these massacres of civilians at Nyadzonya, Gutu and Mashonganyika and at thousands of kraals around the country had happened somewhere deep in the bush of Never-Never Land.

Soon after the talks collapsed, our unit was transferred to the Freedom camp near Lusaka. There were rumours that we were going to be trained as conventional troops for the third, the last phase of the war, the assault on the cities. By that stage the bulk of the Zipra cadres had been given this training, and some of them had been perched in their camps for years, waiting for this final assault. Us guerillas weren't exactly fond of the conventional troops: they waited safely in Zambia, well-fed and comfortable, and boasted about how well-trained they were, while us ouens crossed into the country and fought and starved and died. Still, when we heard we would be given this conventional training, none of us complained too loudly. We weren't really that keen on crossing back into the country and risking our necks again.

There was the usual disorganisation in the Lusaka camp. The HQ was in the process of moving elsewhere and our files were scattered up and down the country. No one knew our orders. For a week we perched outside offices waiting for papers and commanders. One day, as we were waiting to see this big shot, ou Todzo ambles past. 'Comrade Todzo! Hey!' Ya, I chune you, it was good to see that ouen again. We all sneak off together round the back of logistics for a chat. He's a camp commissar now, he tells us, quite a big shot. His left arm — no hand at all — just the flaplet of skin, like at the end of a sausage.

We told him about Kariba, about conventional training. 'We're not complaining,' reckons ou Koshkosh, trying hard not to look at the stump, 'but after that last crossing of ours I reckon we saw enough action for one war.'

'Me, I'd go back into the bush anytime,' says Todzo.

'We know you're a bigshot commissar now,' Koshkosh chunes him, 'so you don't have to sell us the story too.'

'I'm not selling you any stories,' says Todzo.

'Come off it.'

'But it's the truth. The comrades who've been here in Zambia for a while, they've forgotten that their people are suffering — but back in Zimbabwe, you can see it all the time.'

Someone asked about conditions in the camps, and we all began talking about other things. I forgot the conversation until a couple of days later when I bumped into Comrade Hendrix while I was taking some forms to be signed. He'd also risen in the ranks, and was now a senior logistics officer. He'd been to Russia on a six-month training course, and his uniform was new and crisply ironed, and his boots shone. 'How was your last crossing?' he asks, 'what did you bring back?'

'No crossing,' I told him. 'We were at Kariba — there's nothing down there but bush.'

'A fellow I know got hold of some ivory down there,' he said, hopeful.

'Well, what can you do with comrades like Biani around?'

'True,' he agreed with a sigh. 'Remember — he was the one who wouldn't even smoke the stop we swopped for those jackets.'

'He always puts the struggle first.' I felt obliged to say something in the bloke's defence.

'What about hyena hearts then? You wouldn't be stealing from the struggle if you brought me a few hyena hearts and you'd be doing me a big favour.'

'Hyena hearts??'

Hendrix explained that ya, they were very popular among some of the big shots. Apparently it's very rare for someone to find a dead hyena in the bush, and cos of that its heart was regarded as strong survival muti.

'I'm sure Biani wouldn't mind getting an old friend a couple. A dozen or two would be plenty.'

'I'll try to convince him,' I said. There didn't seem to be much point in arguing. Ou Biani would never take the chance of blasting hyenas while we were in the bush. It would just be too damn risky. Hendrix then hauls a flask of brandy out of his back pocket, takes a swig, passes it to me, and launched into this long story about the car he'd bought with the profits of the shop that his wife, the daughter of the major in the Zambian police, has opened in Lusaka. Ya, after five minutes with Comrade Hendrix, I understood Todzo's point of view perfectly.

Within the next couple days the missing commander surfaced in Lusaka hospital with a bad case of the clap. He signed our papers and someone found our orders in a desk that'd been trucked over to this camp way out in the gwashas by mistake. The bureaucrats had to admit yes, you're in the right place, and no, we're not quite sure where you're off to next.

One morning — we'd been in camp nearly two weeks by then — a commissar announces that the morning parade will be late cos the main mannes from Lusaka are coming to address us. Well, we anchor, anchor there in the parade ground for half-an-hour, an hour, and when they still don't rock up us ouens, we get the hell in and sneak off to see if we can grab some graze. We slip into this queue — all the blokes who are sick or lame — grumbling and cursing as the line shuffles slowly forward. The last of a convoy of trucks, loaded with desks and files, noses out of the camp. 'Sadza, always goddam sadza,' ou Koshkosh is complaining as he watches the cooks dole out lumps of the stuff. 'They could've at least cooked us a decent meal to show the big shots that we eat well.' As he's going on there about how well his mother could cook, her sadza was always light and fluffy, way off in the distance there's the whine of a jet.

'These things, they're not MIGs,' I blurt out.

'Ag, calm down,' says Koshkosh. 'We're right near Lusaka, Smith would never attack us here. And, as for the muck which the camp cooks have the cheek to call relish. . . .' He was off again.

As I'm telling myself to calm down, stop worrying, you're not in the bush, there's this roar, this shriek so loud it blows everything from your brain, and I drop my bowl and clap my hands to my ears and — gggggwwwwaaaahhhhhpppp — everyone's screaming, running, the ground's shaking, and there's so much dust you can't see your hand in front of your face.

I dive to the dirt, the fig tree's a pillar of flame, splashes of fire burst up all over this bloke next to me and he screeches as he flares up like a match.

I rip off my vest, it's bright yellow — dangerous — throw it on this fence post and hare off, sprinting towards the perimeter of the camp. This group of recruits chase after me, running when I run, ducking when I take cover.

'Disperse!' I scream at them. 'You're going to get us all killed — we're a group target — they'll hit us!'

'What must we do, tell us what to do!'

Then there's this rattling, this whirring, and just over the treetops rises a wave of choppers, four of them, all in a line, and heading straight at us. It was like my own death was riding with them. I was absolutely certain I would die. I'd heard my father and his buddies talk about the one with your name on it, and now it was heading for me. 'What must we do!' the trainees were screaming, 'what must we do!' This shell bursts nearby showering us all with earth, and I'm pitched over sideways, rolled over into this escape trench, and crawl, crawl, elbows and knees, twisting through the zigzags like a worm as the choppers roar firing overhead. I slide out the trench, slither through the grass, through to this patch of bush, and I burrow in, right in, flattening myself against the ground, eyes closed and hands over my ears.

When it was quiet again — when it had been quiet for a long time — I crawled out and went back. Everything was ashes, ashes.

With all the smoke you couldn't see the camp. The farmhouse which HQ occupied was burning, and there wasn't a single leaf left in the orchard of mango trees beside it.

For a moment I thought I was dead, already in hell.

A foot still in a boot. The camp was wrecked, everything flattened. There were bodies all over. This bloke with eyes gone, nose gone, face still smoking, asks for water. Another's crushed underneath this huge pole and he's calling for someone to free him. Some bloke is sitting and staring at the stump of his wrist, and the blood is still dribbling out, and he's saying 'do something, do something, or I'll bleed to death'. One guy has his arm covered with watches, watches from his wrists to his elbows, and he's searching all the bodies, collecting more watches, smashed or cracked or bloodied or what and strapping them on. 'Come here, come here,' a bloke shouts to me. 'Come here and help me look for my cousin. He's here somewhere.'

And he's rummaging through the bodies, bodies that are ripped up, bodies that are smouldering, bodies that are all broken but still breathing, shoving them this way and that, trying to figure out the faces.

I sat down. The cars started coming, and people who gave orders. There were party cars, buses, fire engines, ambulances, farm trucks. I helped carry.

While I was helping this bloke along, I found my yellow vest. Bullets or shrapnel had punched holes in it. I felt as if I'd accidentally tricked death, as if the vest had collected all the rounds meant for me. I picked the vest up and kept it. I've still got it now.

A caterpillar dug a pit for the dead. We stacked them in, one on top of the other, like sacks in a warehouse. There must have been hundreds of bodies, maybe even a 1 000. As we worked, my legs began to hurt. I felt behind, and there was a tear in my trousers, and my thigh was damp with blood. A piece of shrapnel, just a splinter, had gone into my leg. I pulled it out and carried on.

A few days later Kenneth Kaunda gave a press conference. He condemned, he condemned this aggression against Zambia and the Zimbabwean people in the strongest possible terms, and when he'd finished his condemning he said he felt he owed the nation an explanation. He had to come up with some kind of explanation cos the Zambians, they were shaken. 'What kind of defence has this country got?' they were asking. 'How is it that Smith can hit us anytime he wants?'

KK explained that in the days just before the bombing he'd seen intelligence reports indicating that Smith was up to something. Unidentified planes had been spotted near Lusaka, and helicopters had been seen near Kafue Gorge. He said he'd had the reports the day before the raid and even mentioned the time — 10 am. The first raids were at about 8 am the next day, which meant he had 22 hours — plenty time to organise some sort of defence.

And according to KK he'd taken all the necessary steps. He'd immediately put the Zambian army and air force on the alert, issued orders that guards were to be posted around all vital installations, and informed his old friend Nkomo that there was trouble on the way.

Hey, you should've seen us cadres when we heard this lot. Our camp — wasn't that a vital installation? Why hadn't we been guarded? Why hadn't we been issued gats? Why didn't anyone tell us about a possible raid?

KK, of course, had his answer for that one too. Military targets okay, he said, he had expected that — but no one had expected even a devil like Smith to attack camps housing innocent refugees. That's when he started to cry and eeh, I chune you that bloke can cry very noisily.

I don't know at which camp those refugees were — and neither do any of the other comrades I've spoken to. There weren't any with us. All those who were wiped out at our camp were either cadres or recruits. They were fighting for the struggle, they died in the struggle, and we all felt that their deaths should've been announced with the proper respect.

There were cadres who argued ya, KK has a point: there hadn't been any big raids into Zambia before, Smith has never come this close to the capital. Zambian intelligence probably spots Rhodesian planes and choppers on this side of the Zambezi at least once a week.

But other cadres argued no, this KK knew damn well that Smith was capable of pulling off these raids — his men had hit Mozambique a couple of times. Either KK or one of the other big fish was negligent or else he'd sold out the struggle.

In fact there were some cadres who reckoned the Zambians were behind the bombing. They pointed out that coincidentally KK had opened the train line to Rhodesia just before the bombing, and hadn't closed it afterwards. These cadres argued that there had been a deal: the Zambians knew Zipra was bigger than their army, and they were scared that we might try a coup so they'd organised Smith to deal with their problem for them.

Others schemed that there had to have been a sellout inside the Zipra high command itself. They pointed out that in a camp there's always a fixed routine — reveille, parade, exercises, breakfast, and afterwards classes or duties or whatever. But that morning the parade was delayed about an hour as we stood round waiting for main mannes from Lusaka who never did show. Ya, some of the cadres reckoned that the camp had been set up for the bombers.

Those cadres also wanted to know more about that convoy of trucks which left the base just moments before the Rhodesians struck. A span of main mannes were on those trucks, and there were rumours that they had all been warned to get out. But Zipra was moving its HQ at the time, and the trucks were carrying office equipment and files.

Some blokes believed the camp had been destroyed cos the majority of the cadres had become strongly anti-Nkomo cos they weren't happy with the official version of the death of one of the main mannes in an explosion near the border. But then our unit was at the camp for a couple days before the raid, and we only heard about this story afterwards.

Then of course there was the official Zipra version of the raid, the version which the commissars told us: the Rhodesians heard that we were about to launch an invasion and so they decided to crush us before we struck.

Well, most of these rumours are probably just nonsense, but mixed up with it there are things that could be true, exaggerated maybe, but underneath true.

Whatever happened, plenty comrades were so shaken by the raids and all the bullshit that they ducked into Zambia and disappeared. Some went to live with Zambian friends or relatives, others lived off the land. That's why, just after the raids, there was so much rustling and raping and robbery that Zambia's last white farmers threatened to destroy their crops and leave the country.

Chapter 21

*A*fter the bombing we anchored there, anchored there, waiting
to be told where to go, what to do. On the second day we
were taken to another camp, and there I met up with ou Russia.
Koshkosh showed two days later: he'd hidden out in the bush until he
was sure the Rhodesians were gone. There was no sign of Biani
though, and we began to think that he had been ironed out. Then one
afternoon when I was sitting round near the camp gate watching this
truckload of stragglers debus, I check this bloke shuffling along in the
crowd. He seems sort of familiar. I double-check — ya it's Biani.

But eeh, the bloke had changed: he was all bent and bandaged, and
we were all shocked to see how worn, how shrunken he looked. To me
ou Biani had always seemed huge, twice the size of most of us ouens,
and there he was bumbling along like any ordinary bloke.

He just stood there as we surrounded him, hardly said a word as we jumped around asking hey, hey, where've you been, hey, are you okay? He'd been wounded in the raid, but not that seriously: his left arm had been burnt by a spot of napalm, and a chunk of shrapnel had sliced open his back. He'd been stitched up and his wounds were healing, but he'd changed. He was always a little tired and without the enthusiasm he'd had back in the days when he'd forced us to march all night even though we were exhausted.

About two weeks later the camp commander called together all the survivors who'd been trained as guerillas, and informed us that we would be crossing again soon. 'Your mission will be to disrupt these so-called free elections,' he explained. 'If Smith manages to force enough people to vote, he'll claim the masses support him and his puppets, and then the imperialists will give him all the guns he wants.'

We were organised into units. Me, Biani and ou Koshkosh we all stuck together, but Russia went off and next thing we heard he'd been made commander of his own unit. Well, we were glad to see the back of him, but we weren't so happy that he had left us just like that, without even a goodbye. His unit crossed into Matabeleland a few days later, and that was the last we ever heard of him.

Four new comrades, all fresh from training, were assigned to our unit. Two of them, Comrade Everestus, the new commissar, this lanky Shona from the Fort Victoria district, and Comrade Norest, the new security, a short, dumpy Ndebele from around Bulawayo, could only see the struggle through commissars' speeches. They both had this idea that us cadres could just stroll into a village and snap our fingers and eliminate 50 of Smith's men, 10 tanks and half-a-dozen choppers — all without any loss to ourselves.

The other two, comrades Lucky and Shakemore, both of them Kalangas, Nkomo's people, could have done with some of that confidence. They seemed to believe that when we crossed an entire Rhodesian regiment would be there waiting to deal with each of them individually, and we would all be shot to pieces inside five minutes.

Comrade Shakemore was so terrified he made the mistake of sneaking up to Biani late one night and imploring him to lead the unit into one of the game reserves. He knew a general, he said, who would look after us if we gave him a couple rhino horns.

Biani beat the bloke up and then dragged him to Security. Security beat him up again, told him, hey now watch it, don't be such a shit-eating mongrel, and sent him back to us.

Ou Biani, he was so pissed off he marched into the offices of the camp commander and told him, hey, we won't have any characters we can't trust in our unit.

But the camp commander wasn't interested in his complaints. 'This comrade has promised to be sensible,' he informed ou Biani. 'If we locked up everyone who did something stupid we would only have half an army.'

Ya, morale was bad then, and the authorities had quite a number of cases like Shakemore to deal with.

Next thing Comrade Shakemore chunes the medic that he's pissing blood. Now it could've meant that he had bilharzia pretty bad so the medic sent him to the hospital for tests.

Ou Biani, he's as happy as a hyena finding a dead elephant: if Shakemore had bilharzia we would cross long before he was cured.

Then a nurse catches the bloke nicking his foreskin with a razor and dripping the blood into his urine specimen. Security had him publicly flogged, told him he'd be crossing even if he had to be floated across in a coffin, and sent him back to us.

'Any problems once we're across,' ou Biani informs this Shakemore, 'just one more piece of your nonsense and — bwa — one shot and you'll never bother anyone again.'

We crossed into the Mana Falls Game Reserve, and began the long climb up the escarpment. The rains had just started, and we had to battle the mud and the heat and the mosquitoes as we scrabbled over the rocks, slipping and stumbling like a tribe of two-legged baboons. In no time we're all hot and muddy and sweaty and exhausted. Shakemore complains that he's tired and, as half the comrades are new, Biani agrees ya, okay, rush. We flop down in the mud, roll a quick skyf and, when Biani pulls himself to his feet again, Shakemore says he needs a couple more minutes.

'We can't laze around all day,' Biani tells him. 'We're not Zipra hunters.'

'Just a few minutes,' the bloke whines. 'It's not going to make any difference.'

Biani, he cracks the bloke a hot one. 'We don't tolerate slack in this unit! Get moving.'

Shakemore, he flips. Then and there he pulls off his knapsack, goois it down — and the thing rolls over this ledge, and rolls and rolls about 200 metres back down the slope.

Biani cracks the bloke again and again. 'That's equipment for the struggle — if it's damaged you are going to suffer. Go fetch your goddam bag.'

Shakemore turns his face away. He's starting to cry.

'Baby wants his mummy?' pokes in Koshkosh.

'For the struggle,' says Comrade Commissar Everestus very concerned, 'pull yourself together for the struggle.'

'This is the worst part,' I chune him. 'Once we're over this it's easy.' Eeeh, as he stands there with his head down to hide his tears you can check he was one of those who'd joined up without really thinking about what it would be like to be a fighter, without realising he was going to be hungry and thirsty and shouted at and exhausted half the time, and when he'd found out he just couldn't cope.

'Go fetch your bag. Move!'

'They'll shoot you all — the whole bunch of you,' Shakemore cried.

'Plug up your arse and fetch the bag!'

Wiping back the tears, he slithers down the gomo. The rest of us, we settle back, light up another quick skyf and then — KKKKKKK — we're down behind cover, gats in hand, checking, checking. It's Koshkosh who spots what had happened: Shakemore had stuck the barrel of his gat into his mouth, and had blown off the top of his head.

Me and Everestus climbed down to collect the kitbag and the gat. We threw out our spare uniforms, and the civilian clobber and a span of graze to make room for the APs — anti-personnel mines — grenades and rounds that he'd been carrying. Comrade Lucky started trembling and stammered out that with this bad luck maybe the spirits were signalling for us to head back to Zambia straight away.

Biani informed him that as we were fighting the struggle of our ancestors, their spirit would protect us from any curses, and Everestus, a well-trained commissar, reminded him that Zipra cadres weren't supposed to believe in curses and ngangas anyway. We put foot then, put foot. That was the last time we spoke about Comrade Shakemore.

A couple days into the country we rendezvoused with our regional commander, Comrade Katusha. We were taken to this hut that he'd fixed up like an office — he had a radio, and a desk and benches from a school that they'd burnt down, as well as a giant map of the USA which he'd found at some mission.

This Katusha, a young bloke with dark glasses and a blue jean jacket, told us that Muzorewa's men, Pfumo Re Vanhu, had moved into the area two months back, and they were trying to force the people onto their side. All the mense had to buy their party cards, and if anyone ran a business — or just wanted to visit a relative out of the area — they had to make a donation to the party.

'But they have support somewhere,' he reckons, 'in your operational area anyway. The last unit we sent in there was sold out and ambushed and about exterminated.'

As we left he assigned one of his men, this Comrade Message, a local bloke who'd picked up some sort of training while moving around with a unit, to be our guide. Comrade Message also carried notes between us and Katusha, and kept an eye on us for him.

When we reached our area, we visited Chombo, the main Zipra contact. He lay moaning on this grass mat inside his hut, so bruised that he could hardly move. Half his body was patched with leaf poultices concocted by an nganga and eeh, I chune you, the stink in that place was worse than a hyena's fart. His wife and his daughter, a pretty girl about 18 years old, ducked away as we arrived.

'They came and told us we must vote for Muzorewa,' ou Chombo croaks. 'When I said I did not like the Bishop, they hit me.'

Ya, as we trapped from kraal to kraal, we heard the same kind of story time and time again: the auxiliaries had beaten up all those who wouldn't give them money, they'd dragged a couple women off into the bush and raped them, and they'd forced the mense to feed them goats and chickens.

Comrade Everestus explained to the masses just how the sellout puppets, Muzorewa, Sithole and Chirau, were being used as hunting dogs by the imperialist hyenas, and how under the smokescreen of these black stooges, Smith was propping up white power. 'But we the toiling masses,' he was fond of saying, 'we won't be tricked by these sellouts. We won't stop the liberation struggle just because these liars beg us to. We will continue to fight until we have crushed them and their colonialist paymasters.'

At which point he'd heroically raise his AK to the sky and roar,

'Down with imperialism! Power to the People!' He looked like he should've been on a poster.

As we moved through the area a lightie, about 14-15 years old, attached himself to us. This Vuso, he was full of shit. He was always arguing, always refusing to take orders, especially from the new comrades who, cos they'd been trained, schemed they were now main mannes, and tried to force him into doing all the washing and cleaning. Even so he was useful: he knew his way round the area, he knew the people, and he was scared of nothing and no one, not even Biani.

One day Vuso came running to us with a message: there was a shopkeeper who was telling the people that he wanted to see us. Biani figured well let's check this lot out, and he sent me and Everestus along to talk to the bloke.

We arranged to meet him right out in the bush, waited till he came to the rendezvous point and made sure he was alone before we introduced ourselves.

'I was at one of your meetings,' this bloke says to Everestus. 'There at Chombo's village. And when I heard the talk, I knew here in my heart that I was a Zapu man and that I have always been a Zapu man.'

Me, I'm wondering what this bloke is up to.

The eager Everestus, he puffs up and launches into this long speech about Father Nkomo and the glories of Zapu and how one day the party will overcome and rule Zimbabwe and alles and alles, and whilst he's talking I'm checking out this bloke, this Elisha Manyara. He's quite an old guy, greying at the top there and wearing this fifties blue suit which is bagging out all over. He's sweating like hell, nodding and smiling and sweating like hell, even though it isn't that hot.

'Here,' says this Manyara when Everestus finally pauses. The bloke took out his wallet and counted out five 10 dollar notes. I couldn't figure the guy's buzz. This guy, I'm scheming, this guy isn't the kind who'll give us 50 dollars just for charity. He's up to something; is he with the auxiliaries? I'm checking, checking the bush there, looking for some sign of a trap and Everestus goes on and on, thanking the guy, thanking and thanking, on behalf of the party, the unit, the struggle, the toiling masses. And then it all comes out.

'I would like to give the party even more money,' this Manyara finally tells us. '. . . make an even larger donation. I would like to give you boys 100, 200, even a 1000 dollars.'

'My heart feels happy when I meet someone with such a commitment to the struggle,' says Everestus enthusiastically. 'It is good. . . .'

'What exactly,' I break in, 'is blocking any larger donation?'

Everestus turns and checks me out like I'm trying to pickpocket the bloke, but Manyara himself looked pretty relieved. Before Comrade Everestus could get rattling again, he told us his story: 'It's Muzorewa's men,' he chunes us. 'They're causing all the complications. In the old days, just so long as you looked after the DC's assistants every once in a while, everything was just fine.' Everestus was frowning. '— you had to,' this Manyara explained quickly. 'Out here you have to do these things just to stay in business. But always I was helping the boys — the last unit that was here, they ate my meat, my sadza. Without me they wouldn't have lasted. Food is scarce here in winter. You need connections. . . .'

Me, I nodded. Things were beginning to connect.

'The problem,' Manyara told us, 'it's this other bloke with a shop. *He* gives cigarettes and beer to Muzorewa's men and *he* listens to everyone talk and picks up information for the auxiliaries. And because the auxiliaries know that *I'm* a Zapu man' (at this point he thumps his chest) 'they tell everyone not to buy from me. That's why I can't give the party more.'

'We must help you,' says Everestus.

'It's a terrible injustice,' I put in. 'You must discuss this with our commander.'

Next evening Manyara gets together with Biani and the two of them organise themselves a deal.

'Fifty dollars,' says Manyara. 'And a carton of corned beef.'

'It's a risky business,' says Biani. 'We'll be wanting regular supplies. We'll be wanting beef next month too and mealiemeal and cigarettes; we'll be wanting you to tell us who Muzorewa's men are. . . .'

'Whooo,' Manyara waves his arms about. 'You'll be eating all my profits!'

'You think we'll wipe out your competition just to make you rich?'

The bloke, he groans. 'No wonder the people call you the eating army,' he says.

'We fight for the people,' says Biani quietly, checking him out with an eye like the barrel of a gun. The bloke agrees, no further argument.

To prevent the imagination of the unit overheating, Biani kept the plan quiet until an hour or two before the big moment. When he finally told them, Comrade Everestus declared that this was the greatest moment in his life and Norest proclaimed that he wanted to wipe out at least one of Smith's men on this, his first time out. All this heroism must have gone to Lucky's head cos he loudly denounced the forces of imperialism and swore to attack them and fight like a lion even though Smith's men had many big guns and bombs and choppers and planes.

It wasn't long after he'd told us just how potent the forces of imperialism were and how tough the battle was going to be, that Lucky came down with pains in the back. Being medic I had to investigate this lot: there he was lying on his stomach — he couldn't sit upright — moaning and grimacing and grinding his teeth. I tried to feel around a bit, and everywhere I touched he yelped.

His buddies didn't seem altogether convinced by the performance. They stood around and tried to persuade him to fight.

'Don't you want to avenge yourself on the running dogs of imperialism?' says ever-eager Everestus. 'Do you want to miss a chance to help liberate the masses?'

'I would want my chance — but my back....'

'Come on, comrade — forget your back,' chips in Norest. 'This is your first chance to prove you are a man and kill the enemy.'

I wasn't so sure a promise of enemy to kill would improve things, so I repeated Biani's story that we were just going to break into a shop and there wouldn't be any action.

But no one seemed to notice. Comrades Everestus and Norest went right on persuading their buddy to fight and he kept on moaning about his back.

Watching the whole kerfuffle I felt tired. The two of them, they were so hot for action, so itchy to fight, and they had no idea what they were letting themselves in for. It was just like me and Headlights and the others back in my security force days in Binga all those years ago. Ya, for a moment there the whole pattern seemed clear: if these characters survived our raid without disgracing themselves, they'd swagger back as heroes who knew everything and, if they made it through the next contact and the next and the next, they'd start scheming they were now real hardcore ouens, ouens who knew what the story was. And then as they were knocked around by the war, by all the intricacies of the struggle, fighting would become just a job to them, a difficult, dicey, exhausting job, and finally all's they would care about would be getting from one day to the next. Maybe Comrade Lucky was smarter than the rest; he seemed to sense what he was getting into.

'If he's sick he must anchor here,' I said finally. 'The rest of us better get moving.'

We had to trap for maybe two hours to reach the shop, which was about 50 yards from the auxiliaries' camp, right next to this beerhall. We took up positions, anchored until the beerhall had closed and everyone had staggered off home and then moved in. Round both the shop and the beerhall was a fence, barbed wire and quite high. The guard was at the back of the building, behind a shed and, as we prowled around, we could check his shadow on the beerhall wall; he was perching next to a brazier, warming his hands.

'Old man, old man,' Biani called. The guy just sat there, trying to pretend he couldn't hear. 'Come over here, old man. We know you are there.'

'Who is it?' he asked, wrapping his blanket about him and picking up his kierie as he shuffled over to us. 'Who is it?'

'Don't you know us?'

'No.'

'We are the boys. Open the gate.'

'I haven't got a key.'

'Well, climb over and come here.'

'I'd fall.'

'Do you want to live?'

The old man nodded.

'Well, climb over then.' Koshkosh cocked his AK.

The guy climbed over.

'Where are the keys?' Biani asked.

'The barman has got the keys,' the bloke said, 'and he lives over there.' He pointed off into the night.

'How far?'

'Five, 10 minutes.'

So the guard went off with two comrades to fetch the keys. The rest of us waited in the shadows.

The moment they returned, we opened the store. There was no money in the cash register — the owner had taken it home with him, but even so, we made quite a haul: coffee, kapenta, blue soap, toothpaste, tea, flour, 'energy' (Koshkosh's word for sugar), corned beef, blankets, every last scrap of tobacco in the place, mealiemeal, cream biscuits, razor blades, matches, chocolate — it was like Christmas.

As we're stuffing all the goodies into bags, someone notices Comrade Norest isn't around. We drop everything and spread out through the yard to look for him. Was he lost? Had he deserted? Had he been ambushed by the auxiliaries? His gat was found lying next to the gate but there was no sign of our hero. Whatever, it was too risky to stick around. We grabbed our bags and gapped it, leaving Koshkosh to pour the paraffin and set the place alight.

The flames roared up and the auxiliaries opened fire, but by then we were nearly a kilometre away. We cached our haul, rendezvoused with Koshkosh and then headed straight to the camp. If the enemy had captured Norest they'd persuade him to talk, no problem, and first thing they'd want to know would be the location of the camp.

We rock up hot and panting and ready to run, and eeeh, first thing we check is our missing hero, Norest, sitting on a stone, half a slab of chocolate in one hand and a packet of biscuits in the other, whilst our patient, Comrade Lucky, who couldn't sit up just an hour before, is squatting in awe beside him listening to this gory story about how all the rest of us in the unit — every last man — had just been wiped out by a force of Smith's tanks.

Ou Biani, he's so mal, he claps both of them a couple hot ones, grabs hold of Norest and shakes him, and between gasps the bloke wheezes out his story: he'd seen shadows, these big black shadows, reaching out for him. He'd thought they were the enemy and he'd dropped his gat and run.

'Scared of shadows and calls himself a fighter,' scoffs Koshkosh. 'Why didn't you stay at home and get a job cleaning lavatories for the mabhunu?'

Biani claps the bloke to the ground and kicks him a shot in the gut. 'Why didn't you tell your comrades about this danger thing of yours — eh? Why?' — kick — 'what kind of fighter runs away and leaves his comrades to die in an ambush!' — kick — 'you're a deserter — that's all you are,' — kick — 'and you know what happens to deserters?'

Judging from the way he's snivelling and snotting there he certainly did. It was something you were told on your first day of training, and just about every day thereafter: deserters got shot.

'Well — have you got anything to say for yourself then?' Biani takes out his Tokarev, points it right between Norest's eyes.

Norest goes down on his knees, begging and pleading, crying no, don't shoot me, I won't do it again.'

'Okay, okay, that's enough,' says Biani finally. 'Seeing it was your first contact, seeing we are short of cadres — we won't kill you. But next time,' — Biani gives him another dose of the boot to underline his point — 'next time you'd better stick with us — because if you run, you are going to die — even if I have to chase you all the way back to Zambia myself.' The snivelling began to quieten a little. 'And, Comrade Lucky, you with the back pains — you are going to carry the RPG everywhere we go for the next month.'

Comrade Message was sent off to Katusha with Biani's report on the attack, and he returned with a note ordering us to continue harassing the auxiliaries.

Two-three nights later our connection at this kraal sent a lightie to tell us that four auxiliaries had commandeered one of the headman's huts for the night. We trapped over to check out the scene, and once we'd spoken to the mense and found out all the details we withdrew to discuss tactics. Norest reckoned blow down the door and charge in with gats blazing, but Biani wasn't convinced. 'What if one of them manages to get hold of his gun?' he says. 'We can't risk casualties.'

It was then that Vuso volunteered: he said he could creep quietly over to the hut, so quietly that the guard — if he was still awake — wouldn't notice him, and gooi the grenade inside.

Okay, quite fine, Biani told him, and you could see him thinking well, if it's a trap, we'll only lose an untrained lightie. He gave Vuso one of his grenades, wished him luck and ordered the rest of us to take cover.

Ou Vuso, he handled the business like he's buying five cents sweets at the shop down the road. He took the grenade and ambled off through the dark straight to the hut, and tossed the thing in through the door — gwaaa-a-a-a--aaah.

Next day we heard two of Muzorewa's mense had been blown to smithereens. The third lost his arm, but the fourth somehow wasn't scratched — though he was plastered with bits of his buddies and, according to the locals, was gibbering like a monkey the next morning when the auxiliaries came and buried their comrades and took him away.

'I have killed men,' Vuso boasted afterwards, 'I am a man. But these comrades from training — the one runs like a woman, the other one is sick like a woman. So they should then do the women's work, the cooking and cleaning. They are good for nothing else.'

Comrades Everestus, Norest and Lucky took exception to this. 'All you did was throw a grenade,' Norest told him. 'That's easy. Anyone can do it. Now shooting. . . .'

'I'd like to see you try,' Vuso jeered. 'I can see you walking to that hut: you would've shat your heart out halfway there.'

Norest tried to grab Vuso and beat some respect into him but the lightie ducked away before he even got close. The bloke went to Biani to complain. 'Green fruit always causes stomach aches if it is eaten before its time,' he told Biani, suggesting that he send Vuso back to his mother and find a more obedient boy to guide us.

Biani, however wasn't impressed with their arguments. Vuso in fact had a point, he reckoned, and he decided that from then on Vuso and Norest and Lucky would all do the same work, and Vuso would be trained to use a gat. 'Now we will really be able to see who is a man,' he told them all. 'Now you must prove it to me.' After that the new fighters quickly began to improve.

In the days after the attack the auxiliaries avoided huts when they had to sleep away from their camp, and hid out in the koppies — not that it always helped them much. Just four nights later herdboys guided us up this koppie where they'd spotted a stick pitching camp. We climbed this goat path which seemed to zigzag from clump of thorns to clump of thorns, pulling ourselves up cliffs which would've made your average dassie think twice. When we're all in position, maybe 10 metres from where the auxiliaries were snoring, we lobbed a couple grenades into their position and ironed them out as they ran.

One fellow ducked away but he broke a leg as he tried to run down a cliff in the dark, and he screamed so long and so loud that we found him without too much trouble.

He kept asking us if we were going to shoot him, and he spilt out everything he knew: how many gats they had, the state of their morale, a list of their connections, the news that at least one RAR unit would be reinforcing them just before elections. He told us how he didn't like Muzorewa and wanted to cross to Nkomo. After we'd cross-questioned him for about an hour, Biani said in English: 'That's it. We can finish him now.'

'Maybe we can recruit him,' Everestus suggested. 'If we sent him back to Zambia for training.'

'With that leg?' says Biani, and nodded to Vuso to cut the bloke's throat.

Then Manyara gave us a list of all the sellouts who'd been working for the auxiliaries. There were 10 on the list, and we got to five before the others fled. Afterwards Manyara told us morale among the auxiliaries was now so low a unit had mutinied when ordered to go on overnight patrol.

This meant that the whole northern area of our zone was pretty much freed from security force, and in the next report to Katusha, ou Biani described it as 'liberated territory'.

Comrade Message arrived back with this note from Comrade Katusha informing us that we must rendezvous with him at his HQ to prepare for a joint attack.

Katusha also requested half the stuff we swiped in our shop raid, half of our monthly contribution from Manyara and half of anything else we might happen to lay our hands on.

Well, quite fine, the struggle needs supplies, so we loaded ourselves up with our booty and off we trap. Two nights later we rock up at the HQ kraal.

Waay out in the bush you could already hear the music blaring from this gramophone, and when we sneaked in closer we could check all these blokes — some in uniform — drinking and eating. For a moment there we schemed it was a trap: that kind of jollification went on at some security force camps, not guerilla HQs. Hell, we hadn't even spotted any guards.

Ou Biani, he's not happy with this lot, not happy at all, and he sends ou Koshkosh in to check out the scene. Five minutes pass, 10 minutes, 15, before the fellow comes staggering back, a pot of beer in the one hand and a skyf in the other. 'It's okay,' he shouts to us from the edge of the kraal. 'It's okay. It's just a party. You can come on in.'

Feeling rather stupid we follow them into the kraal. There must've been about 20 guerillas there already, and more turned up during the night. There was beer — eeh there was a lake of beer — and meat and sadza too — enough for everyone.

'You comrades have been fighting hard,' Comrade Katusha says when we hand over the booty. 'Enjoy the party.'

'Is this safe?' asks Biani. 'All this noise. Your guards didn't challenge us when we came in.'

Well, Comrade Katusha, he schemes this is a big joke. 'This is liberated territory here,' he announces. 'HEY COMRADES — CAN YOU ALL HEAR ME? YOU ARE NOW IN LIBERATED TERRITORY!'

We all laugh of course, he's the area commander, but we aren't going to believe it just yet.

He goes on to explain that the security forces never set foot in the area cos they knew they'd be ambushed. 'There is only one road here,' he tells us. 'We will let them come in, but when they try to go they find trees across the road and mines and ambushes. After what happened to their last patrol six months ago, they've left us completely alone.'

He went off with Biani to a commander's conference. The rest of us ouens ate ourselves thick, and started seriously on the beer. Another two units rocked up, and a couple guys who were supposed to be guarding the place. I ended up perching next to this comrade, one Freedom who I knew vaguely from some of the scummier shabs back in Burg. He was a bloke who could pass himself as goffel or houtie, whichever was most convenient, and back in the old days us goffels were always prepared to have him along — so long as he was buying the booze.

Now he was a houtie, no doubt about that, and we chatted away in Shona about the bad old days, what'd happened to who, the struggle. 'But at least we're out here in the bush,' he chuned me. 'Eeh, but there in Zambia things are hard. Here at least you can lay your hands on beer and women and put a few dollars in your pocket.'

Me, I was quite shocked. That wasn't exactly fighting by the regulations. 'Ya, we've had one or two problems with that kind of thing,' I told him, 'but our commander, he doesn't let you get away with it.'

'Hell, this Katusha, he's got three girlfriends. He's quite a bloke,' this Freedom went on. 'He wears this big bag of emeralds round his neck, and he's always telling the people to collect them — give, give,

give because we need to finance our guns. He tells us we'll need to eat when the struggle is over.'

'But don't the people object?'

'What can they do? Katusha's happy so long as he gets his share and, hell, if you've got a gun out here in the bush, you can do what you like. Who can stop you?'

While we were talking, someone turned off the gramophone, and the night sounds flooded back like bush over an abandoned farm. Down at the river the frogs kra-aa-aaked, and off in the bush, mongooses and bushbabies yelped and squeaked. Or maybe — it certainly sounded spooky enough — there were ngozi out there, evil spirits prowling around in the darkness just beyond the firelight. Waaay off, a hyena howled — maybe witches.... Ya, the dark suddenly felt closer, and the massive see-sawing shadows thrown by the blokes feeding the fire in the centre of the ring of huts seemed to be those faceless figures which stood over me pointing their gats in my nightmares....

Then the drumming began, so low you could feel the drums beating in you, beating right in your heart, and the high twanging of the marimbas, the harmonies knotting and twisting together like thin bright wires wound around a strip of oxhide, tangling together with the night noises, catching them up into the rhythm.

The cadres stood, yawning and stretching, from their beer pots as the music began worrying at their feet, and women from the kraal sidled over to the drums, swayed together. A shave, a baboon spirit, grabbed hold of one of the cadres, and sent him prancing around on all fours. Some bloke makes as if to throw a stone at him, and he races up this tree just like a baboon — I never would've believed a man could move like that — and sits at the top and barks waurggh-waurghh, waugh-waugh.

Me and the Ndebeles, we've never seen anything like this lot before. 'Mad in the head,' says ou Koshkosh, tapping his skull as we're watching the performance.

'No, no, it's not quite like that,' Biani tells us, a little embarrassed. 'It's nothing serious; it's just the spirits.' He explained well, they often turned up at a big celebration. 'There'll probably be about half-a-dozen of them babooning around eventually — but by tomorrow they'll all be fine again.'

The women had made their own dance by then, and in the firelight you could check their breasts joggling around, the large dark discs of their nipples. Eeeeh man, I chune you, I went so hard I could hardly walk.

The drum was pulling the cadres into the dance too: they pulled off their boots, dropped their gats.

As Biani and Koshkosh stripped down I stood there uncertain, feeling my feet beginning to tap with the rhythm but worrying that there'd be some kind of repeat of that snuff scene.

'Give it a go,' Biani said as he hid his gat under these bushes. I shook my head. After all those years jiving at the Saturday night scenes, I felt my dancing was another kind of animal altogether.

'Come on, come on,' he tells me. 'You can't dance any worse than the Ndebeles.' Hell, by then the dancing spirits had already grabbed hold of me anyway, and no ways could I just sit on the sidelines and keep still. So I followed ou Biani out into the music imitating all his leaping and stampings until I realised no one was bothering about me anyway so I just let the music take over, and went where it took me.

Up in the trees the bloke taken by the baboon spirits screeched and jabbered. The rest of us danced, edging opposite the women, stamping together in a loose, ragged line. Then the music swirled, whirled up and flung us, spinning and shouting and ya, for a moment there, what with everyone so caught up in the dance, the drums seemed to drum us back, back hundreds of years, before whitey'd come with his colonisation, before the Arabs raided the coast for slaves, and it was as if we'd been drummed back across the centuries, back to our Shona ancestors, back to the peace and warmth of their original world.

After all that beer, I needed to piss, so I slip off into the shadows, and there I got talking to this mammoth mamma, who was also taking a quick break — actually, to tell the truth she got talking to me. After two minutes' politeness, she grabs my arm and drags me off to her hut — not that I needed much dragging — and we got right down to business. Though her tits were so large that they about smothered you, though all the rolls of her fat were greasy with sweat, though she stank like a four-day-dead fish, inside she was hot and live and the pair of us pomped away merrily until morning.

The next morning — well, let's pass over that. The next evening we were all still shaky with the babbelas when Comrade Katusha assembled us out in the bush. 'How are you feeling?' he asks us, 'how are you feeling after your contacts with the beer and the women last night?' Much laughter.

Then Katusha gets down to business and informs us ya, we're going to hit one of these convoys on the main Kariba road. Comrades to the north and the south of us have been harassing traffic, and now the big shots have ordered us to join the campaign to cut the town off from the rest of the country.

So off we trapped, and two nights later we reached the site and took up our positions in the koppies above the road, Comrades Norest and Lucky right in the middle in case they got scared and tried to run off. We weren't going to let them disgrace our unit. 'We will only fire for five minutes before we withdraw,' Biani informed them. 'If you try to withdraw before then — you will die — with my bullets in your back.'

We anchored there between the rocks and the aloes until about nine that morning, when this long convoy, about 40-50 cars and trucks, rolls into the killing grounds. Whooo, we open up, I chune you, we hit them with a blast of fire: five RPGs, a mortar, a LMG, and the rest of us blasting away with our AKs.

A rocket smacks into this army truck — bwaaaa — and it bursts into flame. A car suddenly slews across the road, its rear blown off. The Rhodesians dive from their trucks and cars, take cover and open up, and the cannon on this armoured car swings round and round blindly firing off into the bush on both sides of the road. A couple cars at the rear gooi a quick U-ee and race back towards Sinoia. This cannon shot crashes into the rocks a couple 100 metres off, puffing up this huge wad of dust.

The cadres with heavy weapons stopped firing, withdrew. Rounds zinged against metal and windscreens cracked and whitened as those of us with AKs rattled away. The return fire was closer now, ricocheting off rocks just a couple metres above us, and Lucky, he dropped his gat and knelt down whimpering. Norest didn't flinch. He lay there and kept on firing. There in this ditch I spotted these Rhodesians as they popped up to fire off a quick burst, and then ducked down again. I started raking the line of the ditch with fire in the hope that one of them would stand up to it, but they kept down, and one of them crawls up the ditch aways and fires off a burst and drops back before I can get at him.

Biani checked his watch, gave the order to withdraw. We slipped back through the rocks as the rounds spatter against them, down round the koppie to the valley behind. We put foot, I chune you, we put foot, as the firing dies away behind us, shitscared that the jets and the choppers would be swooping down on us any second now.

But nothing came after us and, that night, when we rendezvoused with the other units, we heard none of them had been pursued either, — and even better — we hadn't suffered a single casualty in the ambush.

That night on the Rhodesian news they announced there had been a cross-border raid on training camps in Mozambique and 'hundreds' of terrorists had been killed. Then they mentioned that a convoy en route to Kariba had been ambushed, Corporal Ronald Brookes had been killed, and four Africans, an army truck and a car destroyed, and several other vehicles damaged.... Ya, the second phase of the struggle was already underway.

Back in our area we found that the election campaign was hotting up. A platoon of RAR arrived to reinforce the auxiliaries, and they acted like they owned the place. Sticks from both armies roamed the area showing off their heavy weapons like mortars and MAGs, and forcing the mense to listen to their propaganda.

They didn't make themselves many friends, but they made themselves felt. At every kraal we visited, they'd left the stink of their sellout propaganda and we had to spend all our time tearing their lies apart.

As the mense'd never been given the opportunity of voting before, they spent a span of time explaining the whole procedure: since this was a 'free and fair' election each person had to vote once. And, to make sure nobody went voting more than once, everybody would have their hand checked before they voted. They would have to stick it under a special light and if the light said they were all right, then they would have to dip their hand in this colourless liquid which looked like water but left an invisible mark. Then you would enter the polling booth and there — if you liked Muzorewa you should put a large cross next to his symbol — and if you didn't like Muzorewa, well then, you put a small cross next to his symbol.

The mense didn't need us to make them see through the Muzorewa lies, and that talk of magic water made everybody suspicious from the start. We didn't disappoint them: if they so much as touched the stuff we chuned them, they'd become sterile. That water was Smith's last-ditch plot to exterminate all the blacks so's the whites could have Zimbabwe for themselves.

One morning, early-early, as we left this village where we'd been spreading the good word, Vuso, our scout, motions us — take cover. I'm flattening myself against the earth when eeh, I check a security force unit tramping along this path just below us as if they're the only people in the world.

Vuso cocks his gat, creeps forward. Biani signals to him to stay. He liked a contact to be planned down to the last detail; he hadn't ever been one for taking chances.

But Vuso ignores Biani. He'd been waiting, waiting for his chance to hit the auxiliaries head-on, and he's not going to forget it just cos Biani doesn't think it's safe. He jumps out onto the shelf of rock about 20 feet above the path along which the unit is tramping and, standing right out there in the open, without even a leaf for cover, he opens up. The bloke he's still new with the gat, and the thing lashes about like a decapitated snake. The enemy dives for cover — Biani's cursing — they return fire fast and furious — and eeh, it's FNs not AKs. Vuso has single-handedly ambushed this whole RAR platoon and eeh, I chune you, those blokes were one hell of a lot more jacked up than any auxiliaries. They hold their position, keep their fire hammering back at us, close and accurate, and every second I'm expecting Vuso to topple back dead.

'Retreat!' yells Biani. 'Retreat!' It's every man for himself. Me, I jump up and hare off, zig-zagging through the brush, and I chune you I put foot, put foot, and didn't stop until I reached our rendezvous point. There I anchored, anchored, panting and hoping like hell that the RAR hadn't captured one of us cadres and knocked our position out of him.

Everestus was the next to show. He wasn't quite sure whether to praise Vuso for his bravery or to damn him for disobedience. 'After all, we did get at least two,' he kept saying. 'I did see them fall.'

But, as we anchored there, anchored there, and still no other cadres came, the pair of us both fell quiet. Then in hobbles Biani half-carrying Koshkosh. Ou Koshkosh'd been hit in the gut — luckily the bullet had just torn the flesh on his left side. If it'd been just about a quarter inch closer, it probly would've ripped open his guts and his intestines would've spilled out, and the only thing we could've done for him then would've been to put a bullet into his head.

His wound was paining like hell, and the bloke he was about in tears. I stuck on a field dressing, gave him a shot of morphine, and leaving Everestus to organise the others, me and Biani helped him to a hideout where he could rest in safety.

When we got there I cleaned the wound which'd pretty much stopped bleeding by then, crushed a couple penicillin tablets and sprinkled the powder over it, smeared on some Vaseline, and gave the bloke something to make him sleep.

'Goddam Vuso,' swore Biani when ou Koshkosh finally began snoring. 'Comrade Koshkosh is one of our best cadres — I'd like to snap the little bastard's neck.'

'It was something though,' I put in. 'Standing up like that — I could never have done it.'

'Remember back in our Zipa days when you stood up and blasted that truck?'

'There wasn't much choice. It was either prove I'm a freedom fighter or a knife in the back. Now you —'

'Ya, I also used to stick my neck out,' ou Biani admitted. 'At first I was like Vuso, not worried about death or tomorrow or anything. I just wanted to liberate Africa.' Ou Koshkosh groaned as he shifted onto his side. 'Aaaie but look at us now: keeping our heads down, sticking to the shadows.'

'You get older,' I said, 'and more cautious. We're probly better fighters for it.'

'Ya, we didn't know about all the corruption back then. We didn't know about commanders who collected emeralds or logistics men whose wives buy cars. We didn't know about all the intricacies. Smith was the only enemy.'

'We've helped ourselves a little too.'

'A pair of boots and some beans — nothing. These blokes are grabbing everything they can get their hands on.' Ou Biani man, he was as hot as your gunbarrel in a contact. 'They're like hyenas, they swallow everything —'

'The struggle...' I began.

'If we hadn't fought for the struggle we would have wives, good jobs now. But we are like hippies — we have nothing.'

'The party will look after us.'

Biani, he checked me out a bit skew there. He always schemed I was a shade green.

The other blokes rock up with long faces: there's no Lucky, no Vuso.

'Why couldn't the goddam kid just obey orders?' mutters Biani.

'He has no discipline,' put in Norest, who'd never been any friend to Vuso. 'If you think you're an elephant you don't see the thorns in your path.'

'He could still turn up,' reckons Everestus. 'No one saw him fall. And the security forces aren't going to finish off a comrade like him so easily.'

When it was dark, we went to Chombo's kraal and asked him to look after Koshkosh for us: the elections were too close for us to nurse him. Chombo knew a cave deep in the gwashas where we could hide him, and volunteered one of his daughters, this 18-year-old who was hot with herbs. Knowing Koshkosh it wasn't actually the smartest thing we could have done, but at the time we were so pleased to find someone to look after him that we didn't think too much about it. Me and Biani, we carried Koshkosh to the cave, and settled him down on a bed of blankets. I gave Chombo's daughter bandages and penicillin and instructions, and when he was asleep we headed back to the others.

As we were trapping along there Biani told me that I was now deputy until Koshkosh recovered.

'Me!' I said. I was pleased, of course, that Biani schemed I was the most reliable and trustworthy comrade around, even though there wasn't much competition in that unit of ours, but I wasn't sure I could manage. 'The comrades won't listen to me,' I told him.

'Why?'

Well, I didn't want to say cos I was just a goffel, but that's how I felt and Biani knew it.

'You will have to make them listen then,' he said. 'You are the deputy.' The other blokes didn't say a thing when Biani announced I was now deputy. They had never been told to distrust me, and so they hadn't seen me as a coloured but just as one of the main mannes. If there was a disaster I would at least be able to lead the survivors back to Comrade Katusha.

Two days later, as we're preparing to doss, who rocks into our camp but ou Vuso himself.

Vuso had quite a story to tell. He'd been chased and he'd run till he'd become too tired to keep moving. He hid his gat under some leaves and crawled into an antbear hole where he fell asleep. As he slept, he was discovered by a pair of enemy soldiers. They pulled him out, slapped him around and kicked him, certain he was a 'terrorist' scout. Not true, Vuso chuned them. His old queen was very poor, she only had three goats and they had strayed so he was looking for them and he was too scared to go back till he'd found them.

'And why are your clothes so torn and dirty?' they asked.

His mother didn't have money for soap or new clothes, he explained, and when they asked where his father was, he told them how his old man had been killed by the 'terrorists' right at the beginning of the war.

Well, they weren't altogether happy with his story so they took him back to their camp and locked him up in a bunker. Next day a honky officer interrogated him and, when he asked to be let go so's he could find his goats, the bloke decided he was being cheeky and kicked him around before sending him off, handcuffed, with two soldiers who'd been instructed to take him to his village to check out his story. Well, that mother's village of his was a long way off and the day was hot. Before they were halfway there, the two escorts were yawning. 'Ag, he's just a child — he can't be involved,' the one said. 'Let's tell the dog to disappear and tell the officer he's just a bad little boy.' Well, the other bloke also felt like the day off, so they gave Vuso a kick, let him go and strolled to the next village where, so we later heard, they bought a pot of beer. Ou Vuso, he went to collect his gat and track us down. Ya, that officer was right: he was cheeky that one, and also very lucky, very lucky indeed. By the time he found us we had given him up for dead, and Biani was so pleased to see the lightie that he didn't punish him. Instead he took Vuso off to one side and told him what had happened, and informed him that if he was ever so undisciplined again he would be shot, if not by the enemy, then certainly by us, his comrades.

We never found out what happened to Comrade Lucky, though we kept looking for him for as long as we stayed in the area. Maybe he was injured and died out in the bush, maybe he deserted and headed back to his home.

Things were getting pretty hot. On three successive nights we revved up the auxiliaries' camp, twice together with this unit operating to the east of us, destroying a truck, ironing out two auxiliaries and an RAR corporal, and injuring half-a-dozen of their blokes — all with no loss to ourselves. They sent out patrol after patrol to try track us down, and from the mense in the kraals we heard all of us comrades now had a price of 3 000 bucks on our head and they were offering 5 000 for Biani.

Then Chombo informed us that the guards for the polling station — this white RDR platoon — were due to rock up in a week, just two days before voting began. Biani reckoned well, we'd better squash these lice before they get a chance to invade our blanket so he sent Comrade Message off to collect a mine from HQ.

Three days later Comrade Message staggers back, loaded down with weaponry and all the latest news: the Zipra unit to the south of us had been ambushed and two of their cadres had been ironed out. And, on top of everything else, a fire force unit had been stationed about 30 kays to the south of us for the duration of the election. Things were hotting up.

Two days before voting began the RDR convoy trundles into our zone. Up front was this weird vehicle, spidery and low, a mine detector of some kind. The thing detected our mine all right but we opened fire anyway, revving up the lead truck, smashing its wind-screens and puncturing its takkies. Smith's men hit back at us with everything they had: MAGS, a mortar — the works. Eeeh, we gapped it out of there but fast, I chune you — just as well cos within minutes the choppers were overhead looking for us.

We managed to disappear into this thick bush down by the river. After that Biani decided no more daylight attacks — they were just too risky.

We figured out okay, it's night attacks then. Come the dark we rendezvoused with the unit to the east of us, and crept towards the enemies' positions. About 200 yards out one of their blokes walked right into a booby-trap — bwhhaaa — Smith's men opened up with machine guns and us ouens squeezed ourselves against the earth as the rounds shredded the bush overhead. The bloke screamed and screamed, couldn't stop screaming. Their medic crawled over to him, and when the firing stopped, I went over too. Eeh, he was a mess: his whole right leg had gone all the way to his hip, and his left foot also. The blood was flooding out of him like beer from a broken bottle. It was hopeless.

After that ou Biani wasn't exactly keen on night attacks either. We just perched there in the bush and watched through our binoculars as the security force, moving in platoons so heavily armed that we didn't dare risk attacking them, marched whole villages off to vote. There was nothing we could do. We couldn't even order the mense not to co-operate as Smith's men would've just thrashed them until they changed their minds. Comrade Everestus did tell the mense to ask the soldiers if they really thought this election of theirs would end the war, but I don't scheme anyone was dumb enough to try.

'Smith must've mobilised every last one of his men,' I remember saying as we lay in the shade of this thicket one afternoon and watched as an RAR platoon collected all the mense in this kraal together and 'escorted' them off to the voting booth.

'It's a pity Zipra didn't mobilise a few more of its own,' Biani reckoned. 'If we had a couple of those cadres who are sitting there in the camp waiting for the conventional war....'

'It's a pity we don't fight,' put in Vuso. 'Better we try something instead of sitting and talking.'

'We can die but we can't stop the elections,' Biani told him, 'and a guerilla never fights when he knows he must lose.'

But even Biani found it difficult not to attack. None of us could come up with a good plan, so he sent Comrade Message off to Katusha to find out what the other units were up to. He returned with this note telling us not to try anything stupid: six comrades in an area to the north of us had been wiped out when one of the units tried to ambush a heavily-armed convoy.

From what we could gather from the radio, the situation was much the same throughout the country. Smith had organised such a show of strength that the comrades had to keep well behind cover. In Harare the radio reported mammoth crowds queueing outside polling stations, and all round the country farmers trucked loads of labourers to the polls and employers gave their workers the day off so that they could vote.

There was nothing for us comrades to do but argue about the size and significance of Smith's victory.

Ya, when the results were announced none of us were too surprised to hear the Rhodesian story that 64 percent of the people voted.

The radio said people were dancing in the streets of Burg, and certainly the imperialists had something to celebrate. Smith argued, of course, that the results proved that the majority of the blacks supported his Zimbabwe-Rhodesia, and many of the overseas observers, for instance members of the British Conservative Party and Freedom House, some American outfit, said as far as they were concerned the elections had been as free and as fair as possible under the circumstances. O, they admitted there had been a little intimidation here and there, but the way they saw it the majority of the people had voted voluntarily.

Us cadres, I chune you, felt like crawling into a hole and sleeping for a week. We had failed. The imperialists had the results they wanted, and they would use them as an excuse to prop up their puppet regime with guns and money. Ya, it looked as if we would be fighting for a very long time indeed.

We went off to collect Koshkosh. He was healthy; his wound had healed, but he didn't seem altogether happy to see us. I figured he just wanted a little more time for R&R. Then we stopped at Chombo's kraal to thank the people for looking after our comrade, and eeh the old bloke let us have it. What kind of army were we, he asked, were we really in the country to help the people? This comrade of ours had seduced his daughter, the one who was supposed to be nursing him, and another girl from the village. Now they were both pregnant, and what were we going to do about it? Biani managed to calm him down by giving him a 100 dollars and promising him more later, but when he returned to us, eeh he was so hot he was overheating.

'You are not allowed to have girlfriends,' he shouts at Koshkosh. 'It's against regulations. You are lucky that Chombo is a loyal Zapu man and didn't sell you out.'

'Comrade Katusha, he has girlfriends,' ou Koshkosh tries to argue. 'Why can't we have some fun?'

Which only enraged Biani more. 'Do you want us all to die because you can't keep your prick out of some whore's cunt? Do you want us all to die so you can have some fun?'

Koshkosh, he didn't even try to answer. Biani raves on and on. 'We can't trust you to be deputy,' Biani finishes. 'You think you're such a big shot that you can't even bother to think that you could've killed all our comrades. You are no more our deputy. Muzukuru is deputy.'

Koshkosh's face didn't change. He stared at nothing in particular. Me I chune you, I couldn't work out how I felt. I was pleased, of course, that Biani schemed I was doing a reasonable job, but there was also ou Koshkosh. How did he feel? I didn't want enemies.

Ya, after all the fighting, all the arguing and alles, us ouens needed a break. Biani came up with a plan to raid this bottle store in a village in the European farming area bordering our zone.

Comrade Everestus objected: hitting a bottle store was against Zipra regulations — and the regulations were strict on the subject cos a couple units had poured so much booze down their throats that they'd passed out and had been captured.

'No one bothers with the regulations anyway,' scoffed Biani. 'The big shots tell you one thing and then they do whatever they want.'

'After all our fighting we need to relax,' explained Koshkosh, 'and no one can find out about what we do here. . . .'

Comrade Everestus looked around, saw how the blokes were checking him out with a naked eye there, and was convinced.

Come the next night we headed over to the bottle store. We cut our way through the fence, and woke up the watchman. Though we beat him till he blubbered he stuck to his story that the boss had the keys. Finally, someone jammed a rag into his mouth and tied him up while the rest of us tried to prise the door open with a bayonet. No go. There was nothing for it but a grenade.

Us cadres retreat behind this ridge and Biani lobs the thing at the door: baahhhaahhhhhhhaaaammmmm — the door buckled and bent and out from under it oozes foam and glass and beer. We shoved the door out of the way and pushed our way inside. The stink of alcohol about knocked us off our feet. Splinters of glass crunched beneath our boots — the blast had blown all the bottles off the shelves. We pushed through to the back of the store where cartons of brandy and beer and Rhodesian wine were stacked on the floor and packed ourselves three kitbags full.

Once we'd taken what we wanted Biani lobbed in another grenade to finish the place off. FNs opened up there by the village. We ducked

into the bush, and headed for the koppies. Come morning the enemy
would be after us with trackers and choppers, expecting to find us
passed out along the path. We put foot, put foot, Vuso scouting the
way, Biani right behind him, and all the rest of us strung out behind
quietly lubricating ourselves with the occasional dop. After about
half-an-hour, Comrade Norest began to develop something of a
stagger, and next thing he suddenly halted right there in the middle of
the path, drained a brandy bottle, burped, patted his stomach, and
gooid the thing off into the bush where it smashed against a rock.

Biani swung around, sized up the scene in a second. Aaaie, and
then he laid into us: what did we think we were doing! We were going
to get ourselves killed. He rearranged the line, ordering me and
Everestus to take the booze and walk just ahead of him. 'If you are
going to act like kids, I'll treat you like kids,' he informed us. After
that lot, I chune you, we were all very well-behaved. We put foot, put
foot and by the time the birds began to call we were maybe 15 kays
from the bottle store.

As the sun rose we ducked into this mupungara thicket, seated
ourselves in a circle, opened a bottle of brandy and some beer and got
down to business.

After the first couple of sluks we all became quite philosophical.

Everestus remarked comfortingly that, sooner or later, elections or
no elections, the country would be ours.

'I hope there's still something left for us then,' cracks ou Koshkosh.
'But what whitey doesn't take with him, the big fish will probably
swallow.'

He takes another sluk of beer and brandishes the bottle. 'This can
be the only reward any of us will ever see.' Much laughter.

'But the party will take care of us,' says the earnest Everestus. 'I
heard Nkomo speak.'

'But the party has taken care of us already,' schemes ou Koshkosh
grinning. 'We've been taught a trade — how to use a gun — and as
long as we keep hold of our tools, we can never starve.' More
laughter.

Comrade Norest didn't think it was so funny though. 'It's not to
laugh at,' he says. 'The war can go on for years and when it's over we
can be old men. How will we eat? How will we buy wives? Our

brothers working in the cities are getting good jobs because we are fighting the mabhunu.' He had a point, a good point. These were things a lot of the ouens worried about.

'Ya,' reckoned ou Biani, 'after all the fighting we've done the struggle owes us something. Enough money to get started again, maybe buy a taxi or a few cows.'

Everestus suggested that the regulations didn't really make allowances for this sort of thing.

'At least we'll be stealing from Smith's men,' Biani informed him. 'There're plenty comrades these days who take from the struggle.'

'But still. . .' Everestus began to object.

'The struggle owes it to us,' Biani informed him. 'We are the ones who fight and risk our lives.'

'A couple cows and a car each?' schemes Koshkosh. 'You planning to rob a bank or what?'

Banks, well, there weren't any banks for miles, but there was a mine, a copper mine, just a couple of kays down the drag in territory which Zipra had not yet infiltrated. As we downed our dop we talked about that mine, and in the dust, we made a model with a few sticks and stones and tried to work out how we could rob it.

We finally passed out just before midday and it was only late that evening that, sick and groaning, we began to revive. Everestus, he sat there, his head between his knees, and puked and puked but nothing came up. Ou Koshkosh, he was crawling around checking all the bottles for a sluk to take the bite out of his babbelas. Norest was all smeared with puke: there was puke crusted on his clothes and on his boots, even puke in his hair. Me, my mouth was dry as a mummy's tit, and my head felt as if it'd been crushed under a pyramid. I swallowed the contents of my water bottle and closed my eyes and lay back and waited to die. Ou Vuso, he was still snoring away like a chainsaw.

'Come on, come on — time to get moving,' says Biani as he surveys the rest of us wrecks.'This place stinks of stale booze — Smith's men can find this place just by following their noses.'

'Leave me here to die,' groans ou Koshkosh. 'My comrades will have a better chance without me.'

Biani, he got the message. Besides, he was still pretty shaky himself. 'Okay,' he says, 'okay. You've got one hour — just one hour more — to recover.'

Chapter 22

*T*he mine was on the edge of a plain in the shadow of a ridge of koppies, riddled with caves and thick with mukonde, succulents with massive heads of grey-green branches. From our hideout we watched the mine with our binoculars: fences, that was the first thing you noticed, fences inside fences. The whole complex was surrounded by a six-foot fence with a barbed wire overhang, and the security office, the administration block and the white compound were all surrounded by a security fence, while the two compounds for blacks, one for those who now had their families at the mine and the other for those who were alone, were ringed with a barbed wire fence. Dogs and guards patrolled all the fences at least once a day, and at the gate next to the administration block there was this mammoth guard house. That mine was well-fortified, I chune you, and as I checked the place out I realised eeh, this mission wasn't going to be easy.

We needed more intelligence than we were ever going to get through binoculars so Biani decided to recce this kraal where the workers bought their stop and kachase. 'If I'm not back by 1 am,' he told us, 'rendezvous with me at the fence,' — he pointed out this spot next to a thornbush — 'at 3.00 if I'm not there — well then you might as well go back to Katusha.'

He was back by 11.00 that night. He'd gotten talking to a couple of blokes there by the shab, and after a couple drinks he told them he was looking for work, any kind of work.

The blokes — three of them — tried to talk him out of it, telling him how tough the graft was, how your bones ached after each shift and how the food was so bad you farted all the time.

Biani chuned them that he was desperate: his family was starving, he had to get money from somewhere, and so on and so forth until the blokes reckon okay, okay and told him how to go about looking for graft. The personnel officer liked his workers neat and tidy and yes-baasing and no-baasing every second word. Then the government said you had to have a situpa, and there was this nganga just up the way who could fix you a first-class charm which practically ensured you got the job — and for only 10 bucks.

When the three of them decided it was time to head back, they invited Biani along, telling him he could sleep on the floor and talk to the personnel officer first thing in the morning. Quite fine, except he didn't get any further than the entrance: the guards on duty wouldn't allow him in, not even for a bottle of kachase.

Well, there wasn't much he could do about it short of opening fire so ou Biani said he'd sleep back at the shab, and come back to find out about the job in the morning.

Back at our hideout he filled us in on what he'd learnt: they were paid on Friday — just two days off.

'So I'll go along tomorrow, and try to get inside,' he said. 'I can look around at least, and maybe I can find out a bit more too.'

So next morning first thing, ou Biani's there at the gate demanding to see the personnel officer, who turned out to be this old honky with a face as hairy as a dry mango pip.

'Good morning, my baas,' ou Biani says as he's shown into the office. Well that put a smile on the baas's dial.

Biani presents the bloke with this reference which I'd written to the effect that John Mawema was a good reliable hardworking boy who understood his orders, could understand a little English and had been employed on Sunset Farm for 10 years until terrorism had put a stop to farming operations.

Which Biani expanded by saying that his baas's farm had been burnt down by terrorists, and his baas went bankrupt and had to leave the farm.

'My heart is sore — even now,' ou Biani ends off, thumping his chest.

'These terrorists,' says the bloke, very sympathetic. 'They destroy everything including the lives of their own people.'

And with that he launches into such a long list of benefits available at the mine — free film show once a week, a soccer team, three meals a day, shifts which are never longer than 10 hours — that ou Biani is scheming that he's got the job all wrapped up in gift paper.

But the personnel officer finished the interview by telling ou Biani sorry, hey, we've got nothing for you now, John, I wish I had something to offer you, it's not often we get an applicant of your calibre. Biani must've looked a shade disappointed, cos the bloke then handed him a dollar, and told him to pray for the future of the country. Everything would finally come right, he said.

Biani wasn't too happy as he walked out. If he'd got the job he would've had an excuse to take a look around and ask all kinds of idiotic questions. If he left the mine now, he'd have to hang around in the shab for days, trying to cross-question the workers without them noticing it, and hoping hard that the mine security didn't start sniffing after him.

So, instead of heading down to the main entrance like he's supposed to, ou Biani slips into the bunch of miners who are limping back from the sick bay. Ya, all that day he sat in the sun in the compound and listened to the workers squabble and tell stories, nodding every once in a while but hardly saying a word. He looked as if he'd been part of the scenery for the past 10 years.

Within an hour he'd found out how many guards there were, where they were stationed, when everyone was paid — and, most important, where the cash was kept.

Ou Biani hung around until late in the afternoon when his three friends came off duty. No luck, he told them, there was no job for him, he had no more money and he wanted to rest a day or two before beginning the long trek back to his family.

'You get permission to stay here?' one of the three asked him, and Biani chuned him hey, what's this permission? He didn't know about any permission, he'd just come straight from the white man.

The three of them they were shaking their heads there. One of them explained that, at the end of the day, the guards on the gate would check through the lists of all those who'd come and gone. 'When they find that you haven't left, they'll come searching for you. They'll think you're a thief, and beat you up and hand you over to the police.'

Biani, he didn't have to act to look worried.

'Aah — it's no big problem,' one of the blokes chipped in. 'We'll hide you in our room. Then they'll never find you.'

A detachment of guards rocked up while Biani and his buddies were talking. They ordered the workers to show them their work cards and asked if they had seen a stranger about. Some said yes, some said no, and while everyone was trying to sort this lot out, Biani and Co. disappeared into their room. They hid him in a chest underneath a bunk, and he lay there dead quiet while a pair of guards poked around behind the door and in the bedding.

'The bastard must've buggered off long ago,' one of them complained.

'Those blokes at the gate — they think they're there to sleep,' the other one agreed. And with that they tramped off to the next room.

When the searchers had gone ou Biani brings out this bottle of kachase. The senior bloke, he goes to his trunk, unlocks it and brings out this lekker big radio which he switches to a Zambian station. There's a news bulletin, something to do with Muzorewa's manoeuvrings in the Zimbabwe-Rhodesia Parliament. After they've all had a sip or two he asks, well, what about Muzorewa, what do they think? And, first they're chuning him, well, you know, give him time, nothing has changed so far, but. And after a few more sips they're scheming, no, there'll never be any peace while our boys are out in the bush, and a few more sips later they're saying Muzorewa is Smith's black dog, and they're all praying for the victory of the struggle.

It was then that Biani told them that he was one of the boys from the bush, and his unit needed their help to continue with the struggle.

'Wait till tomorrow,' the oldest bloke says, very generous, then we'll all help you from our pay packets.

Biani explained that the comrades out in the bush were hungry, very hungry, there was no food in the kraals, and they needed money, plenty money to see them through to the rains. The only way to get this money, Biani said, was by robbing the mine.

Two of the blokes were keen to co-operate. Whether it was kachase or revolutionary spirit or what I don't know but they were inspired enough to join up with Biani there and then.

The third bloke, the generous one, wasn't so sure. 'Ya, ya — quite fine,' he kept saying. 'But I've got my children, my family. You can't take all my money.'

'We won't be taking your money,' Biani tried to explain. 'The mine still must pay you — you'll get your money Monday or Tuesday.'

But the bloke wouldn't believe him. Maybe he was a bit drunk. He just kept on repeating that he had a family to worry about, as well as the struggle.

Biani tried arguing, but the bloke he had taken up his position, and no amount of sense and logic was going to flush him out of it. 'I'll make a donation,' he kept repeating, 'but you can't take all my money.'

Finally Biani, who was also a little drunk, lost his temper, clapped the bloke across the ear, and told him to shut up.

The old man, he leapt up clutching the side of his head. 'I'm going to report you,' he screeches. 'I'm going to report you.'

The neighbours pounded on the walls and yelled at them to stop squabbling.

Ou Biani, he figured, well this was it. After how many years fighting he was now going to die like a rat in a trap, caught behind the fence of a mine compound. He took out his Tokarev. 'Any more shouting,' he told the old boy, 'and this will speak to you.'

The fellow staggered to the door, leant against it. 'If you shoot me,' he said, 'I'll die — but you'll die also. The guards'll be here in no time.'

This he seemed to think was a big joke, and he laughed and laughed so much that he slid down the door, and ended up sitting on the mat.

Biani grabbed the bloke before he could move or protest.

'Ya, it was a messy business,' he told us cadres later. 'I held him by the throat, held onto him — he was falling all over the room — and by the time I had him still, he was dead. We were worried someone would come in — there'd been a lot of noise — so we wrapped the body in a blanket and shoved it under a bed.'

Biani brought out the kachase again, allowed the other two workers a couple sluks to steady their nerves and then a couple more as well and, once they'd passed out, he grabbed the dead man's radio and sneaked from the compound, wriggling underneath the gate, over to our rendezvous point on the outer fence.

As we perched there in the dark he threw the radio over to us, and outlined his plan: the next day, Friday, an armoured truck would deliver the weekly wages at about 9 am, and a corps of clerks would immediately begin counting out the pay packets. We would attack round about 3.00, when the clerks were still counting — any earlier and the enemy would have too much time to chase us before dusk fell, any later and we could get tangled up with the first workers coming off shift.

First of all, said Biani, two of us would create a diversion by firing at the railhead, which was on the opposite side of the mine to the administration block, while the rest of us would then begin to cut our way through the wire and head to the paymaster's office where we would rendezvous with him and his new recruits.

I must say I wasn't completely convinced. 'How are you going to duck his guards until the afternoon?' I said. There were so many things that could go wrong that I didn't like to think about it. 'Let's forget the mine — there must be something else easier.'

But Biani, he just laughed. 'The deputy doesn't have to worry,' he told me, 'only the commander.'

I don't scheme many of us got much sleep that night. Ou Biani, he lay awake with the body tucked in beneath him, not daring to sleep in case one of the new recruits suddenly woke up with a change of heart. The rest of us ouens, we huddled wrapped up in our blankets shivering and scratching, scratching and shivering, as we waited for the night to end.

Your head kept on ticking, wouldn't stop, and suddenly you find yourself thinking that eeh, this plan of Biani's, it's suicidal. What if someone spots us crawling through the fence? What if they don't fall for our trick? We'd be caught like rats in a trap. Things go wrong: that's a natural law as sure as anything they tried to teach us at school — but this time our lives were at risk. Biani was one of the smartest strategists I'd come across in the years I'd been fighting, and his rule had always been pretty simple: don't take risks. Now he was breaking his own rule, and not just breaking it but smashing it. I was worried, I chune you, very worried, and being deputy I figured I had to say something.

But you don't damage morale, so I kept my thoughts to myself. Not only that, I also reminded everyone once again just how much coin we could collect and how useful it would be when the struggle was finally over.

When the first birds began to call I sent comrades Koshkosh and Norest off to the far side of the mine to prepare their positions.

The rest of us lay low, keeping well behind cover, as the day inched by. To keep ourselves entertained, we tried to come up with the slowest things we could think of: slow as a tortoise with arthritis, slow as a truck with no wheels, slow as water running uphill, slow as cooking food when you are hungry, slow as a beggar with no legs, slow as Smith's coming to his senses, slow as a speech by our beloved comrade Everestus, slow as Comrade Koshkosh on the march, slow as the last hours before a fight. Slow.

The game petered out and we all went quiet and I had this feeling that we'd left out something, that there'd been some mistake somewhere in the planning. The raid was pretty risky anyway, and one small fuck-up could wreck it completely. I reminded Vuso to be very careful, to follow instructions exactly and not to go wild with his gat again. 'We have a strategy,' I warned him, 'it is a difficult strategy, and so we must stick to it else comrades will die.' Step by step I began to sift through Biani's plan yet again.

Finally, at 3.00 on the dot, we heard the pop-popping of the AKs on the far side of the mine: at our distance they sounded like squibs at Guy Fawkes. Koshkosh and Norest were staging their diversion. Someone answered back with a G-3 and, judging from the shouting and the revving of cars, every last bloke with a gat was rushing off for his chance to be a hero.

With Everestus covering, me and Vuso we crept cautiously through the waist-high grass, yellowing now at the end of summer, to the outer fence. We snipped our way through and went on to the security fence, which we cut through too. Leaving Vuso positioned on this rocky rise to give cover, I pushed through into the garden of the administration block.

I ducked down beside this hedge of hibiscus — no one around. Keeping well under cover I followed it round the side of the administration building, down towards the road where I met up with Biani and his two recruits, all three of them wearing the bright orange plastic helmets and blue overalls of the mine. We didn't bother with how-are-you's, I chune you: Biani immediately ordered the two recruits to join Comrade Everestus in the rear.

The pair of us sneaked along the hibiscus hedge until we were opposite the back door of the building. All clear. In the distance the gats still banged away. Bent over like a quail Biani dashed past the dustbins to the door. Still no one. I shot over to join him.

The door opened at a push, and in we slipped, gats cocked, fingers on the trigger. No one in the passage. But someone had been around just a few moments before: steam was still rising from this teapot on a tea tray someone had left balanced on an ash bucket. A scrubbing brush lay beside a bucket in a pool of soapy water. The building felt spooky, deserted. I could feel the hairs on the back of my neck begin to stand: perhaps this was all a trap?

No one in the passage — into the office — a counter with a grille, and beyond it a long white room with a dozen desks covered with papers and files. On the wall was a calendar with a colour photo of some honky chick with only a beach ball between her and indecency. It was so still that for a moment we thought they had all gone off to fight. But there they were, kneeling against the wall, peering through the blinds, trying to figure out what all the commotion was about. They were all so keen to see what was happening that they hadn't noticed us come in.

Then one of the clerks, he turns and checks us there, gats at the ready, and grunts with surprise.

'Don't move,' Biani says, 'on the floor — on your stomachs — hands at the back of your necks.'

The mense all hit the floor like they'd seen a lot of movies. 'That's fine, just fine,' Biani tells them. 'Keep it like that, you'll be fine!' With me covering, he goes over and quickly searches them all. No gats, no knives. He prods one of the clerks with his gat. 'Where's the cash?' he demands, 'where's the wages?'

'Next door,' the bloke croaks. You can hardly hear him, his throat's so dry. The guns seem to be crackling louder.

'Who is next door?' Biani asks the bloke.

'No one — just the money — in a safe.'

'The keys — get me the keys.'

'Mister Jones. . .' and for the first time I notice this fat honky lying there among the others.

'Get them.'

The clerk stands up, very cautious, goes over to the honky and pulls the keys out of his trouser pocket.

'Okay,' says Biani, 'the cash — quick.' I stand guard in the office. The gats are still pop-popping off in the distance, and down by the gate the guards yell at each other. There's something moving about in the office next door. I grip my gat tight. I back over to the blinds, try to peer through, but I can't see a thing. If they got the back door covered we would be caught like fish in a net.

'One move,' I warn the clerks, 'one move — and the lot of you — you'll all be blown away.'

I check out my watch, and though I'm staring at it, staring at it, the hands won't move. Biani, why doesn't he hurry up? Why was he taking all damn day? In the other room I can hear rustlings and scrapings; maybe the guards have grabbed hold of him and are waiting in the next room, waiting for me to get impatient, for me to come out, to check what's happening. I wipe the sweat from my forehead and tell myself that I'm an idiot, a mudfish, a cockroach, calm down, cool down.

Outside the guards are still shooting and Biani still hasn't come.

One of the honkies moves, or seems to move, his hand sneaking toward his jacket, and me — it's like everything whirls together for a second, so quickly that I don't have time to think and before I know what's what the gun's jumping live in my hands and there's blood sprayed all over the wall and blood over everyone and this spreading brown stain in one bloke's trousers and three blotchy red bodies among the six blokes lying on the floor.

Biani was in the door.

'He went for his gat,' I said. 'He went for his gat.' I went through the bloke's pocket to show him. There wasn't any gat.

Biani, he grimaced. 'We'd better get moving,' he said. 'They'll know what we're up to now.'

I backed out of the room, my gat still trained on the clerks flattened against the floor.

Biani hands me a bag, a thick cloth bag, and I hare out the door after him as he zigzags to the security fence.

Vuso jumps up from his hideout behind these rocks. '**How was it?**

How was it? What you got?' he shouts just as three, four guards charge round the side of the building, spot us, and open up. The rounds zzing over our heads as we hit the deck and every time we try to wriggle off towards the hole, another swarm of rounds hisses inches above our heads.

'Vuso,' Biani yells, 'for God's sake open up!'

And he does, finally, sending his rounds whizzing off to orbit the sun and the moon. The guards are screaming for reinforcements, and a couple rounds splash in the dust inches in front of us — far too close for comfort.

'Lower — lower. Watch what you're doing!' That seemed to shake some sense into him. His next burst zips in just above our ears. The guards were forced to duck down, take cover.

Vuso jettisons his mag, sticks on another, opens up again, a short sharp burst. At the front of the administration building there's shouting as more of the mine mense head towards us. It's now or never: on elbows and knees we snake round the rocks through the fence as the rounds rattle about us.

Ou Vuso, he's so carried away with all this battling that when the time comes to withdraw after us, he stands up, fires a last burst at the guards and, as he turns to run — not even bothering to duck — he's suddenly lifted and spun as the rounds catch him and smash him down against the stones.

We ducked through the outer fence, rendezvoused with Everestus, and the two recruits, and raced off into the bush. We were only about a kay out when we heard the choppers. Quick-quick we ducked into this thicket of thorns, and lay there as the guards crashed through the bush looking for us, and the choppers patrolled up and down, up and down. We slipped from position to position, always moving towards the koppies and, when we'd reached this stretch of thick bush at the foothills, we faded fast.

Ya, once we'd reached the koppies we were safe. What with all the kloofs and crags and caves they would've needed an army to flush us out. We trapped on to our hideout, and waited out the day. I couldn't sleep. I sat in the sun and played patience, laid out the cards one by one, and wished that, like my mother, I could see the future in those bits of cardboard. Why did I have to make such a fuck-up? There was I scheming I was such a big shot, so proud of being deputy commander — and I panicked like a fresh-from-home. Now Vuso was dead and three clerks also — and all because I didn't think straight.

When Biani awoke, I apologised to him and launched into a list of all my sins.

'This is war,' he said. 'These things happen.'

As the moon rose we sat around in a circle, and Biani slit open the two cloth bags and emptied out all the hundreds of brown pay envelopes into this huge heap. We sat perched there for hours, sorting the cash in two- five- and 10-dollar notes which we paper clipped off into tens. The papers and the envelopes were stuffed back into the bags so we wouldn't leave any trace, and we buried them, with the coins, at the base of a thorn tree.

'Eeeeh, but I've never seen so much money before in my life,' ou Koshkosh says, eyeing the neat stacks of notes, and for once he wasn't joking.

'There must be enough just in this bundle to buy a car,' reckons Norest, weighing a wad of tens in his hands.

'I wonder how long we would've had to work to earn that,' one of the workers says. 'You've got years of work — of your life — in your hand there.'

'Money is blood,' breathes the other worker. Eeeh, the pair of them just couldn't take their eyes off all that cash.

Biani dishes out all the wads of notes: one clip of 10 each, one extra for him being the commander, and any remainder to one side for unit expenses. By the time he'd finished we all had more than a 1 000 dollars in front of us.

'We should do this more often,' cracks Koshkosh. 'Then we'd all become rich like the commissars say.'

But just then we weren't quite sure what to do with all that cash. Koshkosh suggested we should take off a couple of hours and hide the stuff. I was too tired — all's I did was walk off round the side of the koppie, and when I came to these three thorn trees bunched together on a rocky outcrop, I shifted the biggest boulder I could move, and shoved my share, wrapped in a piece of plastic I'd cut off my groundsheet, underneath it, and pushed it back into place. For all I know the stuff is still there.

Chapter 23

*W*e rock up back in our operational area and what do we find but one Comrade Message buzzing hysterically around the kraals like a blue-arsed fly that's smelt a large shit but can't find it.

It's nothing serious, we chune him, we just decided to take a week off — a holiday.

Then he wanted to know who the two new comrades were, where Comrade Vuso was, where we'd been, why we hadn't informed him. When the bloke quietened down Biani told him we'd been on a raid, hinting that our haul was only a couple hundred dollars.

Then Comrade Commissar Everestus sounded off about our great victory, proclaiming to the world that we'd got our hands on nearly 8 000 bucks. Ya, the idiot was so forthcoming that you'd scheme he was talking about the score at a soccer match.

'Comrade Message was interested. 'Eeh, that's a lot of money,' he says, very chatty, 'how did you get it?'

'We robbed a mine,' Everestus told him. We all knew the bloke was green, but eeh, this was more than green, this was weird. Hell, it was obvious to all of us that Message would tell Katusha, and if he got to hear of our raid he'd want a big share of the loot.

'Where is this mine?' Comrade Message wanted to know.

Biani broke in before Everestus could answer. 'I'll put it in my report to Comrade Katusha,' he said, checking that Message character out with such a naked eye that the bloke shut up. But it was too late, Everestus had spoken, and we all knew there was going to be trouble over this little lot — and soon.

We were right. A week later Comrade Message rocked up with a letter signed by Regional Commander Comrade Katusha demanding — in the name of the struggle — half the money we had taken.

'Half our money,' says one of our mine comrades in horror. 'This Katusha is as greedy as whitey.'

'Ask your baas what struggle is this that he needs our money for,' ou Koshkosh says, checking out Comrade Message with a naked eye there. 'Is it the people's struggle for liberation — or his struggle for cash?'

'No no no no no,' cries ou Message. 'Me, I'm my own man. Commander Katusha is nobody's baas.' And to make damn sure we understood, he shook his head so hard it looked as if it would come off.

'Well, go tell nobody's baas to go rob his own mines then,' puts in Norest.

'How are we going to buy our taxis now?' cries a mine comrade.

'If Katusha wanted 10 percent, that'd be okay, there would still be enough for us all to eat,' puts in Koshkosh.

'We won that money with our blood,' Everestus presses. 'Katusha can't just eat it. Vuso's spirit would never rest.'

'It's all for the struggle...' Message starts to say.

'Come on, man — we've been comrades long enough not to have to puke out that kind of nonsense for each other.'

Finally we decided well, then we'll write this Regional Commander

Katusha a note telling him that as we'd been risking our lives and had disrupted production at the mine, us comrades felt we had already made our contribution to the struggle as far as the raid was concerned.

'However,' Biani wrote, 'we will gladly donate 10 percent of the money we liberated because we are all greatly dedicated comrades.' We expected a bit of bickering about the percentage and reckoned that 20 would be a reasonable final figure.

Comrade Message left for HQ, and we settled down to the business of trying to throttle the auxiliaries' camp. Then one fine morning these herdboys come running to us with this report that strangers had been spotted on a koppie at dusk. Who was this lot? Selous Scouts sent to eliminate us? But then the auxiliaries were still ambling round the area — and, as we knew, Sku'Zapo only moved into an area after all Smith's other troops had been shipped out. An advance party of Zanla guerillas who'd been sent to win the hearts and minds of the locals? But then we would've heard about them from our connections in the kraals.

Next day the strangers were spotted again, this time wandering along a path. Eeh, I chune you us ouens were puzzled. Were they bandits, guerillas who'd gapped it from their parties and were now making their own way through the bush? But then surely, they would've robbed someone?

Then Comrade Message arrived with a story that he'd brought us some ammunition but it had been too much to carry and he'd had to cache it along the way. Well, this sounds a little suspicious so we follow him cautiously.

As we're going up the side of this hill, someone yells, 'Drop your guns — we're Zipra' and the mystery was solved: HQ was after us.

Well, we all dropped to the dirt quick enough, but we kept a tight grip on our gats.

'If you are Zipra why are you asking us to drop our guns?' Biani challenged. 'You sound like Selous Scouts.'

'Drop your guns,' Katusha repeated. He was somewhere up in the ridge above us. 'I want to speak with you.'

'This is not how comrades talk,' Biani says. 'Talk to us properly — like comrades — and we can listen.'

'Comrades don't break party rules; comrades don't rob.'

'Comrades don't deal in emeralds and ivory either.'

'You're a bunch of crooks, bandits — how can you talk about party rules?' Even there hidden by the grass as we were, you could sense Katusha's temper boiling up inside him. 'Drop your guns and stand up!'

'How can you lot talk about party rules?' Biani asks, adding that he didn't see any need for any kind of surrender.

Then one of their idiots opens up with his AK, I guess he just wanted to give us a fright, his fire was way over our heads, but eeh, I chune you we all answered back low and accurate. The whole bunch of them returned fire and the rounds snick-snacked off these rocks in front of us. They weren't playing around either.

This was just too much for one of the miners: he drops his gat, bolts — but before he's gone five yards they'd caught him with a burst which about chewed his body in two, and this thin spray of blood drizzled down around us. One of our blokes grabs a grenade and lobs it into their position — bwaaaaa-aaa-aa and then, for a shocked second, silence. 'Don't shoot!' Comrade Message was yelling, 'don't shoot!' and then suddenly we spot eight of their blokes all withdrawing down the right flank of the hill.

When we climbed up there we found that luck — of a kind — had been on our side: our grenade had bounced off a rock, and had rolled down into the HQ unit's position before exploding. One comrade had been decapitated — his head was wedged between these rocks, just the neck showing. Katusha's hand was gone: and the blood was spurting out in jerks. He just stood there, looking round sort of blankly.

Comrade Message dropped his gat and wrung his hands. 'Don't shoot,' he moaned. 'Don't shoot.'

Ou Biani, he was staring hard at the mess as if, if he stared at it long enough, and hard enough, it would all disappear. 'Patch him up,' he told me, nodding to Katusha, so I sat down and tied a tourniquet round his wrist, and gave him some water.

Then we withdrew, and went down to this kraal nearby and told the mense to go up to the koppies and help, there were comrades in trouble.

On we trapped. We put foot, I chune you, we put foot. At sunset Biani, called 'rush,' and we sat around in a circle and tried to sort out what was what.

'It's not our fault,' says Biani. 'Katusha, he eats like a hyena.'

'They started the firing.'

'We would've given him 20 percent, 30 even, if he'd been reasonable.'

'We are men; not even Zipra commanders can treat us like that.'

'He was asking for it.'

'He had it coming for a long time.'

'We should go back to Zambia and tell them what he's been up to,' Comrade Everestus tried to tell us. 'When we explain to the big shots they'll see that it was all a mistake.'

The rest of us, however, didn't have the same confidence in their sympathy and understanding.

But irrespective of the blame and responsibility and alles, one thing was for sure: Zipra was finished for us and there was no way back. We couldn't figure out what to do next. The struggle was still raging, no one knew when it was going to end. Katusha would be sending his fighters after us, and all we had cached was maybe 30 AK mags.

Us ouens, we were all so shaken that we even considered — and seriously considered, mind you — crossing to Muzorewa. Hell, we had to do something. But as desperate as we were, this Muzorewa medicine was too bitter, and none of us could bring ourselves to swallow it.

We discussed crossing to Zanla also, but the ouens weren't keen on that either. Norest and Comrade Mine were scared for their lives, while Koshkosh wanted to know if they would hand us back to Zipra and Biani wasn't exactly enthusiastic about returning anyway.

All that night we talked and talked, but come the dawn, we hadn't managed to agree on what to do.

Finally someone remembered the white farming area to the south of us. Zanla had forced about half the farmers off the land, and — so we'd heard — the remainder were fairly approachable, willing to keep the fighters in smokes and sadza just so long as they were left alone. It seemed to be the kind of place where we could safely hide out for a couple days while we worked out what to do next.

The next evening, at dusk, we began our trek southwards. For three nights we marched, cautious as chameleons, eating only raw roots and veld fruit, careful to leave no trace of our passing.

On the third night we found ourselves at the first of the white farms: skirting the workers' houses we saw the blackness of broken panes, doors standing open, and when we came closer we could make out, in the moonlight, the bullet holes in the walls. The wind shook the msasas like unquiet spirits and I felt the shivers sliding up and down my spine. We pushed our way in through the broken gate. The charred frame of a sofa had been thrown against the first house; weeds were pushing up between the springs. A heap of half-burnt cloth rotted in the doorway.

'People have been killed here,' whispered ou Everestus. 'I can hear the spirits crying.'

Round the back, in the gardens, we scratched among the weeds but all's we found was this one pumpkin, large and white, and a few handfuls of cabbage and spinach leaves. Better than roots anyway.

The farmhouse had also been gutted by fire. Holes had been blown in sections of the security fence and the fields surrounding it, acres and acres of unharvested maize and tobacco, were choked with weeds. Ya, as we trapped through the area in search of a hideout, we came across quite a few destroyed farms. The Rhodesians were suffering all right and, if this was the kind of damage throughout the country, you couldn't imagine them lasting much longer.

We eventually found a hideout, this stone pump house way up in the koppies which'd been abandoned and forgotten years back. We settled in, feeling, you know, that now's the time for a little peace and quiet, but eeh, I chune you from the moment we shoved open that door we never stopped arguing.

Everestus was still keen on returning to Zambia, Biani argued we might as well stay independent until we were all sure what we wanted to do. Norest and Koshkosh and Comrade Mine figured independence was quite fine but they wanted to get hold of some more coin, cos they figured we'd all need more than a few thousand come liberation.

'Just a couple simple robberies,' — that was Norest's favourite line — 'and then we'll all be fixed up.' Ya, with the promise of money Norest became as hot for action as ou Vuso had ever been.

'If we try anything we'll alert Zanla and the security forces — and we haven't got the rounds to fight them,' Biani told the bloke in his this-has-gone-far-enough voice.

But with his fortune to be made Norest didn't give up so easily. 'We managed to disappear last time,' he reminded us.

'We knew an area where we could hide out.'

'Well — couldn't we find a target a few kays from here?'

Suddenly ou Everestus pitched in: 'The spirits wouldn't like any robbery,' he told us.

'They must have been with us at the mine,' Norest scoffed.

'Because we were only taking our share. Taking more would be greed.'

We argued and argued for hours about that, I chune you, but no one could be convinced to change his mind and for days after that the argument kept breaking out again.

In between times we quietly visited the local squatters, who'd sneaked in from the overcrowded TTLs to the abandoned farmland, and the farm labourers on the few functioning farms. From what the mense told us there'd been a span of fighting a year or two back, but no one really bothered with the area now. The occasional security force patrol passed through and sometimes groups of Zanla cadres, but that was all. There wasn't much left to fight for.

Once we'd spoken to the mense, we'd loose Everestus on them, mostly to prove that we were really freedom fighters, and not Selous Scouts or bandits. By then we knew for sure that the bloke wasn't quite right in the head. He'd start talking of the spirits with a kind of weird certainty, as if they were his buddies, but when he spoke about anything else he seemed so out of touch you couldn't help scheming hey, this one's got a couple dozen screws loose somewhere.

But when he spoke to the people he was another something altogether. Some even schemed a spirit came to him. Whatever, you could actually see him change as he began: with every word he seemed to grow bigger, and his voice became stronger and clearer — I reckon he must've sounded like one of those old Bible prophets.

Everestus had only one subject, the new Zimbabwe, which he reckoned would be blessed right from the beginning: 'We are fighting the war our ancestors fought,' I remember him saying, 'and they will look after us. Rain will fall in the correct season, there will be no more droughts, and all across the land the mealies will stand 10 feet tall. . . .'

He spoke of huge herds of oxen, fat strong beasts which could pull ploughs with ease, and cows dripping milk from mammoth udders. He spoke of food, plenty of it, and meat, as much as you could eat, and beer brewed according to the old ways and a return to the traditions of the ancestors. He spoke of a return of all the lands the whites seized, the destruction of all their works, and the rebuilding of the city of Zimbabwe.

The mense, they could listen to him for hours, and after he'd spoken they always gave us food, and beer too, even though they had very little: it was winter by then, you check, and the authorities had burnt many of the squatters' fields and confiscated most of their cows and goats to make damn sure that they had only the bare minimum — or less — to eat, and couldn't feed any extras.

Then we saw soldiers patrolling the area, and so we withdrew to a block of undeveloped government land. There were some white farms about 10 kays away, and through them we found a way to fill our stomachs.

We sent a lightie off to one of the last farms with a note for his boss informing him that unless we were given a sack of mealiemeal, we would burn down his farm and kill his family and his cattle. The bloke got the message all right: as evidence of his goodwill he sent the kid back with a note agreeing to our demands, as well as two labourers carrying a sack of the stuff. To make sure it hadn't been poisoned, we took some to the labourers' wives and forced them to cook it and eat it. They survived well enough, so we had them cook this huge potful for us too. Eeeh, I chune you we grazed that night, we stuffed ourselves with sadza, just sadza, and after all the bush food we'd been eating it tasted as good as a roast leg of lamb.

But our fondness for sadza didn't last: the next day we had sadza for breakfast, lunch and supper, during the next two weeks about all we grazed was sadza.

Comrade Mine spent his spare time hunting for rats and hares and tortoises, but it was cold and there wasn't much around.

Then, one evening, while we're all perching there chewing over the skin and bones of our ration of rat, our stomachs all growling for more, more, more, Comrade Mine rebels.

'We've all got maybe a 1 000 dollars in our pockets — but there's nothing we can buy with it,' the bloke complains. 'Two hundred dollars — that's enough to eat for a year in the city — you could even buy steak with it, chicken — but out here what can we do? Hey — comrades — now who will sell me a chicken — just one chicken — for 1 000 dollars? Who can do it? I can't go to the kraals to buy — the masses have nothing. I can't go to the stores — it's too dangerous. So what must I do? Can I even make a porridge out of this money? — but no, it's just paper. I should've stayed there on the mine: there was always relish with your sadza.'

I began to explain but he didn't listen and ranted on and on. '... freedom fighters — from the bush — they don't need meat — they can eat the burnt hides of rats like herdboys in a famine — they eat their sadza plain — but where can an ordinary man get his chicken?"

'Eh, this is just nonsense,' I told him. 'Only a honky can buy where he likes. We're fighting a war, don't forget.'

'Well,' said the bloke, 'you're about the same as white. Why don't you go buy the stuff for us then?'

Eeeh, I chune you I wanted to clap that bloke: I hadn't had to worry about my colour for so long I'd pretty much forgotten it. But on the other hand a visit to a store meant salt, sugar, smokes! Just the thought was enough to get us all excited.

'Why don't we just hold the place up?' I said, trying to take the colour out of the idea. 'Why waste our coin?'

With which Norest and Co. all loudly agreed. 'Why not make a few bucks while we're about it?' he said. 'Even if — say — we all just get 10 dollars — it can help.'

But of course Biani wouldn't hear of it: we couldn't afford the risk, he said, we didn't want to advertise our presence, and we didn't have rounds to waste.

Norest pointed out that the security force would hear of our presence from its spies among the locals anyway, that there was as much risk in buying as in robbing, and there was no reason why, if we planned this properly, there necessarily had to be shooting. We argued and argued for a couple of hours but we didn't get very far. Finally Biani announced that he absolutely refused to have anything to do with a hold-up and that as far as he was concerned, that was that.

Anyway next afternoon we set out for the store, me marching up front trying to pretend like I'm the number one big boss, and all the blokes strung out in a line behind me.

We hid our gats in this koppie along the way, except for Biani's Tokarev pistol, that is, which I took along just in case, and then cut down to the road, and trapped along to the store. Me, I was shitting myself I chune you: what would happen if a truckload of Rhodesian soldiers came trundling along the drag? Hell, us blokes'd run, we wouldn't be able to control ourselves, and they'd shoot us down like vermin, and eeh, from the way the rest of the ouens went quiet you knew they were worried too. I was beginning to think this whole business was a very bad idea all round.

The shop was just your average bush store, a cement box with a faded aspirin ad over the door, and this large verandah on which half-a-dozen locals sat propping up the pillars.

It was quiet, there was hardly anyone around, and suddenly all I could think was ambush, this is an ambush. Then one of the blokes on the verandah asks us hey, you know, what is this thing? Why are you coming to the store on a Sunday?

Me, I wanted to laugh. Sunday — hell, Sundays happened in another world. When was the last time I'd worried about stores being closed on Sunday?

The bloke lights a smoke and eeh, I caught such a whiff of nicotine that I went weak at the knees. No ways were we leaving without tobacco. So I chune this bloke a long sob story about my truck breaking down, how this farmer just down the drag was now fixing it up for me. Cos of the breakdown we hadn't been able to get to the store earlier and now, unless I could buy some graze, all my workers were going to go hungry.

But the bloke was serious about Sunday. 'Sunday's a day of rest,' he tells us. 'We're not allowed to be open on Sunday. Rules are rules and that's that.' He took another hit of his cigarette.

That did it. I pulled the Tokarev out of my pocket and pointed it at him. 'Okay,' I told him, playing the heavy whitey, 'that's enough shit from you, houtie. Open up now — or else.' The comrades, they looked on, mouths open.

Man, that gat must've looked like business, cos that bloke he dropped his smoke and began hopping around like a frog in a frying pan, all yes baas, no baas, anything I can do for you baas. He unlocked the store for us, and scurried up and down behind the counter into the stockroom while I began to order. 'I want cigarettes — what've you got?'

Then Norest breaks in and informs the storeman that this is a hold-up. 'We are the boys,' he says. 'We need supplies.' Us ouens, eh we're dumbstruck. No one had ever contradicted Biani's orders like that before.

Ou Biani, he's so flat he about blew a couple fuses. 'This one he is mad,' he tells the storeman, and grabs Norest's arm and twists it behind his back until he's bleating with pain.

But the storeman, he figures out what's happening. 'I am for the struggle,' he assures us in a whisper. 'Take what you need. I'll say robbers —'

But you could be sure that, one way or another it would come out that the boys had been on another shopping spree. There wasn't much point in pretending.

'Fine,' Biani said after a moment. He picked out everything that we wanted: cartons of smokes, all that they had in stock, a box of packets of loose tobacco, a 10 kilogram sack of sugar, two bags of salt, corned beef, condensed milk, biscuits, chocolate, canned sausages, dried fish, tea and coffee.

'You should've come Friday,' the storeman kept saying. 'We had more stock then.'

'Now we'll be living in style,' cracked Koshkosh, slipping into his version of fancy English. 'Do you want coffee or tea in the morning?' But no one laughed. There was murder in the air.

Now that we were robbing the place, we figured we might as well take some new clothes cos the old ones were full of holes and lice. We stripped off then and there, and each chose two new outfits which we put on one on top of the other — what with all the boxes of food we weren't going to have too many free hands — and we stuffed our pockets with socks. Socks kept your feet lekker warm in winter but, as we didn't get much chance to wash them, they didn't last more than a couple of weeks at the most.

The till was next on the list. It was empty. 'You should've come Friday,' the storekeeper repeated. 'There was lots of money in the till then.'

As we left he asked us to tie him up 'otherwise the police can think I was helping you. Hit me too: they will trust me better if I am hurt'. Biani clobbered him until he screamed.

Once we'd safely cached most of the supplies the fun started: Biani announced that we would now be trying Comrade Norest for disobeying orders at a crucial moment, and thereby disrupting the unit's strategy.

Norest didn't take these accusations lying down. 'You were our commanding officer when we were Zipra,' he informs Biani. 'Then you could do these things. But who says you are our commander now?'

Ou Biani, he's just too shocked to say a thing.

'In fact,' Comrade Norest goes on, 'we must have elections here. We want a democracy — every decision must be taken by a vote. For too long you have been a dictator over us.'

'Bandits like you talking democracy?' Biani scoffs. 'You don't even know what democracy is.'

'One man, one vote,' says Norest. 'That's our democracy. Except for Everestus because he's mad.'

Ya, comrades Koshkosh and Mine were all for Norest, you could see that, and no one on this earth could say what Everestus would do.

'This sounds like a coup,' says Biani going over to Norest. 'This sounds like you are trying to coup me!' One thing you could say for Norest: he was certainly brave.

'A democratic vote.'

'Dogs shit your democracy.' And, with that, he grabs the bloke and cracks him one across the head and knocks him flat. 'That's for your democracy,' he says and kicks him one in the face — 'that's for disobedience to your commander, that's to remind you what we are fighting for.'

By the time Biani had finished there was blood everywhere and ou Norest's nose was as flat as a cat that's been run over by a steamroller, his eyes were jammed shut and he was spitting up bits of tooth. He crawled into a corner and lay there while we smoked and ate, not saying a word. Round about midnight we fell asleep.

When I woke up the next morning I saw that comrades Koshkosh, Norest, and Mine had gone, taking their gats, their money and some of the supplies.

I shook Biani awake. He didn't seem particularly surprised or upset when I told him we were now only three. 'It's a pity about Koshkosh,' he said. 'He's been fighting for quite a time now; you'd think he'd have more sense.'

As we didn't know where they had gone — to join the auxiliaries? to rob for themselves? — we had to disappear too. We were far too vulnerable to take any chances.

We never did come across any of them again, and we never heard what happened to them.

Chapter 24

We kept moving after that, we kept moving, tramping through the area at night, hiding out during most of the day. Everestus spoke at the kraals, and the people fed us, and we ate, knowing that they had very little. Weeks, months passed. There were more talks about talks, but we didn't pay much attention — it felt as if the war would go on forever.

I remember standing under these trees in the bright winter sun one morning, seeing the trees all bare and bare red soil beneath them and it was like, eh, I don't know — it was like that's all we were: like the trees we were hard and skraal and bare, we'd been stripped down to only what we needed to take us from one day to the next — everything else had been lost or abandoned somewhere in the bush. All the recces, all the running, all the thousands of kraals, all the speeches, all the days when I couldn't sleep and sat under a thorn tree playing patience, all the skirmishes and beatings, the deaths, all the stop we'd smoked — the whole lot seemed to fuse for a moment in my mind, and it was as if we were trapped into doing the same thing over and over and over and over again, and everything else that I'd ever seen or thought or done felt as if it'd faded into stories I'd heard about other people.

My dreams were so bad I didn't want to sleep. There was this one dream, an old dream which I'd been having from way back, before the Lusaka raids even, but only once or twice a year. This dream started coming every time I dozed off, and there was no stopping it. For a while there I tried to duck sleeping — cos I knew what would happen — and I'd sit up all day playing patience rather than close my eyes.

Putting it into words, saying it out loud, the dream doesn't sound so bad. It's just this: I'm half asleep, huddled in this shallow trench — sort of like a grave — and there's this huge shadowy figure standing over me, gat raised and just beginning to shout. And when you wake it's just the instant before the bullets begin to hit and you can feel your body burning at the spots where they'll strike.

Ya, that moment before you're properly awake, that moment when you are awake enough to believe it, but not awake enough to tell yourself it's a dream and you're an idiot, that moment — that burst of terror — left me cold and shaking every time. Me, I just couldn't get used to it, couldn't ever be quick enough to catch it.

I must have been going off a bit in those days, I chune you. Sometimes, as we walked, I'd doze on my feet, sort of putting myself mentally in neutral, still going on, still doing whatever had to be done. Then I'd check — there in front of me — this splash of blood, and suddenly I'd know for a moment that we'd all been wiped out and that we were a company of spirits tramping on through the bush, still not knowing that we were dead.

Then I'd look again and the blood would be only moonlight, moonlight reflected off a glossy leaf or maybe a shiny rock.

Then it was October and the hot season. The heatwaves rose off the bush and the mopane flies buzzed endlessly around your eyes. Our hideout was so hot that we shifted to a nearby thicket.

I stopped speaking, I didn't want to do anything. I felt as if I could sleep for months. We were in such a hopeless, such a pointless mess, and none of us could see any way out.

I was sick of everything. I was even sick of the struggle. It was supposed to liberate us and make us men but it had killed and maimed us, and sucked us dry like a mammoth tick, draining us of years of our lives, our friendships, our loves, our beliefs, our basic decencies — the things in fact we were supposed to be fighting for — and even our pasts. And now when we were empty, pure soldiers, we were condemned to wander about the earth like ngozi, hopeless and homeless.

I was sick of the comrades too: I was sick of Biani, a traitor and a tyrant and a thief who'd managed to con us all these years with his sounding phrases, I was sick of Everestus who swallowed his own propaganda like a dog swallows its puke, I was sick of myself for being such a weak fool as to land up in the middle of this muck. I was sick of everything.

I couldn't have said very much for about a week before Biani got hold of me. 'You've been odd,' he told me, 'go speak to an nganga. There's one at the kraal down the road.'

I just looked at him. 'Go talk,' Biani said, 'I've arranged it all. Some of these blokes are all right.'

I went. I was used to listening to Biani I suppose. The nganga was sitting alone outside his hut. When I came up, we smoked a reef, drank some kachase, and got talking. I told him about killings and fighting, Lusaka and Vuso and Lovemore, but I didn't mention Katusha or anything like that. If my loyalty was being tested, I made damn sure I passed.

We smoked another reef, and then this bloke got down to business. He fetched this calabash half full of water from his hut, and stared into it.

'You should sacrifice a goat to your ancestors and tell them why you are fighting,' he says. Me, I couldn't stop myself laughing: the only grandfather I knew about — and he's supposed to be the relation who looks after you — was the drunken Irishman, Adrian Edward Kiernan. How would his spirit and the spirit of his ancestors feel if I sacrificed a goat to them? My hand was halfway to my pocket — Biani told me to give the bloke 10 bucks when he finished.

'Wait,' he told me, 'wait. Your ancestors are fighting, black against white. As long as they fight you can never be easy, but you are also your own man. You must pay your respects, but look for your own way.'

'Ancestors,' I scoffed, 'they made me a coloured and gave me trouble.'

'You are alive,' the bloke said. 'Many have died. You have your arms and legs. You are not mad.'

Talking to the nganga did help, I scheme. It was either him or the rain, the first rains of the season, the gukurahundi, the rains which wash away the accumulated rubbish of the dry season. I was sitting in a patch of shade trying to play patience and ignore the haze of mopane flies buzzing around my eyes when there was a crack of thunder and this bank of cloud began trailing these grey snaggles of rain. The clouds looked like an old comb at first — one tooth here, a bunch of five or six here — and then, as the wind changed and it came closer, a great, grey wave.

Biani and Everestus sprinted up the koppie to this cave, but me, I just sat there, letting the first spots of rain thump against me, watching the drops disappear into the dry earth as if they'd never fallen. Then — down it came — a deluge, and in seconds I was drenched. I remember watching this rock across from me: the rain beat against it for minutes, but it was so hot that the water steamed off and it remained dry. The rain beat down harder, a few damp spots appeared, they spread, spread slowly, and when the rain slackened off for a moment, the spots lightened and shrank. Thunder banged again and the rain fell so hard that I couldn't see more than a yard in front of me. I couldn't even see the rock any longer. That's when I jumped up and ran to the cave.

After the rain the whole world felt cooler, cleaner. Even us cadres were calmer and easier. Ya, the only thing that wasn't improved by the rain was the radio. One night, the roof of the cave began to drip and the radio happened to be underneath it. We woke up to mud, and a radio so dead that not even a couple almost new batteries and my fiddling could get it working again.

After a month or so of rain our clothes were mouldy and rotten and it was time for a change. Well, a bus was usually a lekker soft target so

Biani decides, okay, we'll hit a bus.

So one afternoon we go down to this stop and he hails the driver like an ordinary passenger, and when the thing stops, me and Everestus rise up out of the grass, AKs at the ready. The driver, he takes one look at this lot and orders the passengers off. Ya, the bloke was so practised you couldn't help wondering how many times he'd been held up before. We lined the passengers up facing the side of the bus and Everestus gave them a few quick words about the struggle, while Biani went through their belongings and I hopped aboard to make sure that no one had forgotten anything like a bottle of brandy or a chicken beneath his seat. As I'm kicking through the empty bottles and old papers and stuff in the aisle and under the seats, this sheet of newspaper grabs my eye. I turned it over with my boot — it was still greasy from whatever it had been wrapping — and — there I check, in large black letters, 'SETTLEMENT'.

Me, I picked the thing up and there beneath the headline it's 'Agreement was reached at Lancaster House yesterday...'.

I took another look. I was seeing straight. I checked out the date — the 16th, Dec 16th 1979 and, jisis — it had to be two, three days old. So I stick my head out of a window and wave the paper around.

'Settlement,' I yelled, 'this paper says the struggle is over. There was an arrangement at the conference.'

'There's peace,' this bloke with his hands in the air pipes up. 'For two days now there's been peace. And there's a ceasefire too. You can't do this.'

Biani prods him in the gut with his gat and the protest stops. 'Read the article,' he shouts to me.

While the passengers stood with their hands up against the side of the bus, and Biani and Everestus watched with their gats, I stuck my head through the window and read them the story: the government of Zimbabwe-Rhodesia and the Patriotic Front of Zapu and Zanu had reached an agreement at the Lancaster House talks. A ceasefire was now in effect, the government of Reverend Abel Muzorewa would resign, Lord Soames would take over the country on behalf of Britain, a one-man one-vote election would be held within two months but the whites would still retain 20 out of the 100 seats in the house. All sanctions would be removed and international recognition was guaranteed. All comrades were to gather in 15 assembly points by

January 4.

'So we've won,' says Biani, in a kind of wonderment, as if he'd never quite believed it could happen. 'The people have won.'

So we withdrew with our clothes and our booty and, when we reached this hideout in the koppies, downed a couple celebratory tots from the brandy we'd socialised and, scraping off the crumbs of fried whatever, read the story again and again to check that it was all in fact above board.

'Looks all right,' reckons Biani finally, 'except this assembly camp business could be dangerous — what if Smith decides to bomb them?'

And ya, for a moment, the settlement seemed to stink of Smith's treachery. But, no, it was impossible: there it was in black and white — the British were coming, Commonwealth troops would supervise one-man one-vote elections which the Patriotic Front couldn't fail to win. Ya, we'd beaten whitey, whitey the inventor of guns and tanks and aeroplanes, whitey who painted the map in his own colours. They would never again be able to tell us that they were superior because at the bottom of their hearts they would never be able to believe it themselves. All that kind of nonsense would pass now, if for no other reason than that we would now be the bosses.

The struggle was victorious, we had liberated ourselves, forward with the struggle! We downed a couple more dops. Biani was quiet. Me, I didn't feel triumphant or even particularly joyful. There was just this enormous sense of relief; it was all over now, all the lunacy of the Smith regime was finally ending. Everestus jabbered on about children and wives and mothers and socialism, and whether Zapu or Zanu would win the election, though me and Biani weren't really listening. I closed my eyes and wondered about going home, I tried to remember Naomi's face, the purplish pinch in her bottom lip, the mole on her shoulder. Who was she with now? And the lightie, how old would she be now? Nine, nearly 10 — and I hadn't seen her for almost seven years! If we passed in the street we wouldn't recognise each other. And then my father with his campaign medals and the Rhodesian uniform that he was so proud of. Well, I wasn't exactly the kind of soldier son he had in mind. But there was ou Toofy, Comrade Revolution — he would surely be released from prison. Where would we go from here?

Chapter 25

Well, whatever the Rhodesians had in mind, one thing was for sure: it wouldn't be safe for us to rock up at an assembly point. Worse, we realised we couldn't stay in our hideout either cos the parties would be moving in to claim the area. Burg seemed our best bet — there at least we could disappear off into the crowd.

Then there was Comrade Everestus. We couldn't take him along with us cos sooner or later he'd open his mouth too wide. Biani reckoned well, he's so far gone that not even Katusha could blame him for anything, we might as well send him back to collect his fighter's benefits, if there were any.

So we told the bloke we were sending him on an important mission, and gave him this note to Katusha asking if we could meet to discuss our differences.

Everestus was ecstatic. 'We must finish these problems now,' he told us. 'Everything must be right in the new Zimbabwe.' He marched off smiling.

As soon as he was out of sight we cached our AKs and started for the nearest sizeable town, Miami. It took us three days to walk there, and when we rocked up we stuffed ourselved with bread and butter, boiled sweets and chips and polony.

The next morning we boarded a bus for Burg. It was a hell of a journey, hot and cramped and noisy. The bus was jampacked with mense heading to the city to search for relatives who'd disappeared. Even so there was such a spirit of happiness that it felt like Christmas, and people were smiling and singing. The struggle was victorious, the people had won!

Karoi, Sinoia. As the bus chugged along it struck me hell, I hadn't travelled this particular stretch of road since — when was it? — nine?— 10? — years ago when I was a member of the security force, and we were all being taken off into the bush for the first time. Those blokes — ou Soaps, Lootie Beauty, Clouds — where were they now? Through the window you could check this range of koppies, smoothed and softened by distance. Up in front a lightie howled; mirages shimmered on the hot tar. Already it was difficult to imagine myself ducking down the rocks, AK hot in my hand, and the rounds rattling overhead.

Then we round a corner and there was the city, all so familiar, as if nothing had changed, as if the entire war had been some kind of private hallucination. When I got off the bus I'd walk over to the second-hand furniture store that Naomi managed, and there she'd be perched behind the counter paging through a magazine, all very bored and itching to go home. I'd go to the cafe next door and buy two cups of coffee, and I'd pull up a chair, and sit there skinnering with her — crazy customers, brainless boss — until it was five o'clock and we could lock up and go home.

The terminus was packed solid. People were streaming in from all over the country. We pushed our way through the crush — so many people, I'd forgotten there were so many people — out into the streets where this human stream caught us, and we were rolled up towards town. A shoe repair store, radios, a dress shop. Nothing seemed to have changed. The cafe. And then my heart thumping in spite of myself, the second-hand furniture store. This fat white old queen sat behind the counter.

A truckload of Smith's men trundled round the corner, then another, then another. Seeing all those Rhodesian uniforms, me I caught such a spook that I about dived into the nearest shop. Ou Biani, he schemed it was a great joke. 'Hey, hey, hey,' he chunes me, 'hasn't anyone told you that there's peace now?'

Certainly those troops looked fat and happy enough for peace — in fact they were all so neat and clean in their camouflage uniforms that you'd never have schemed that they'd just lost a war. The whites too, they still behaved as if they owned the place, every second adult seemed to have a gat slung over his shoulder, and most of them wore T-shirts showing thick-lipped incompetent terrs being destroyed by lions, old ladies (white), mines that they had planted themselves, rhinos, crocs and choppers.

In fact this fading and torn news poster announcing that the PF generals were about to arrive in the city was about the only visible sign of defeat.

It'd been a long dry ride and we were thirsty, so we nip into the bar at the first hotel we came to, quite a fancy place. The bar was cool and dark, and no one, not the barman nor the four-five honkies perched at the bar seemed to notice our existence. Biani whistled, and as the waiter, a goffel, came over we were half-expecting him to tell us 'we don't serve blacks'.

But he just apologised for being so long, and, as if to prove his sincerity, he rushed back with our beers within about 30 seconds.

'To the struggle,' said Biani loudly. No one seemed to notice and we began to relax.

'One day we must have our tea and crumpets at a fancy hotel,' I said. 'Remember while we waited for that farmer. Comrade Koshkosh —' Silence. Neither of us particularly wanted to discuss Comrade Koshkosh just then.

'But this beer is lekker,' I put in, trying to keep the conversation going. 'Hell, when was the last time we had a proper, cold. . . .'

'Donk? Hey Ed, Ed,' someone was calling.

'It must've been back when we hit that bottle store. . . .'

'Ed — hey, Ed.' The bloke was shouting in our direction. He was looking at me. O hell, of course, Ed, Ed Kiernan. 'Ed — it's me — Soaps.' And ya, there he was, as fat and baggy as ever. Seven years of war didn't seem to have touched him at all.

'Well — come over. Siddown. Comrade Soaps — Comrade Biani.'
They nodded dubiously at each other.

'Man — long time no see, hey Eddie. Where you been hiding out?
Weren't you captured or something?'

'True,' I told him, 'I'm with Zipra now.' It was the simplest cover.

'I did think of crossing,' the bloke told us, and then gave us this
long spiel about how he'd sabotaged operations by pretending to get
lost and leading his stick away from the terrs' position.

'If it hadn't been for my wife and the lighties I'd've crossed over.'
And so on and so on. If I hadn't been captured I'd've probly been
standing there chuning the same kind of shit myself.

More beers. Ya, the way he told it, he was practically as good as a
'terr' himself, loudly protesting against the unequal pay of coloured
soldiers and the second-rate gats they were issued. Ya, he was still the
same Soaps all right, terrified of trouble. Now that us 'terrs' were
about to take over, you could see he was scheming he'd better get
onside but fast.

Then he started denouncing the racism of Smith and the
Rhodesians, and with all the beer he'd drunk he became very angry,
and he pounded on the table and shouted so loud that everyone could
hear us, and a couple whiteys checked us out with a naked eye.

Another round, and then another. Finally he came to the point:
what would happen to him, could he join the party — or was it too
late?

Ya, you could check that he wanted us to tell him, no, no, you
haven't been so bad after all, hell you were practically one of us. He
looked pretty disappointed when we told him to check with the party
HQ.

'Ed,' says Biani after Soaps had finally left. 'Ed — I could never
believe you were called that. Ed what?'

'Ed Kiernan, it's an Irish name. Pleased to meet you.' We shook
hands, very grave.

'And who might you be?' I enquired.

'Albert Chawaramibira.'

'Hell,' I said, 'you sound like someone else.'

We headed over to the black side of town, ate a double curry at a
takeaway, and downed another couple beers at this hotel before

jolling downstairs to check out the cherries at this disco.

We were very keen to get talking to the ladies, but though we had plenty of cash to flash, they just weren't interested. Me, I was still trying to figure this one out when I had to go off to the gents. On the way out I saw myself in the mirror — hell, I looked like a lunatic, my eyes had that crazy cooked look you get from rooking yourself sick every night for years, and I was so thin my skin seemed to have been painted onto my skull. My clothes would've been retired by a respectable tramp. I was fine for out in the bush but eeh, I chune you I was in need of a major overhaul before I was fit to face the city streets.

I rush down to tell Biani the bad news, and arrive just as he claps this bloke one shot — gwaa — knocking him spinning across the room. The bloke's buddies, half-a-dozen of them, close in. Biani pulls his Tokarev, threatens to blow them all into antshit if .... Someone lurches forward — pushed, I scheme — BAAAAMM — Biani fires. Everyone shrieks and stampedes for the entrance, a waiter drops a trayload of beers. Me, I shove forward and grab Biani's arm, and together we duck out back, through the kitchens, scaling the rear wall just as the cops, with sirens blazing pull up at the front.

'The struggle is over,' I chune him as we're lying panting beside this pile of rubble in a nearby builder's yard.

'Bastard had a knife.'

'But this isn't the bush. We can't go round firing gats....'

But when I looked to Biani to defend himself, I saw eeh, the bloke had passed right out. Well, hell, I couldn't exactly drag him off to a hotel and the place looked safe enough, so I dossed out too.

Next morning at six we were still snoring away when the night-watchman came shuffling around. The bloke wasn't exactly charmed to see us. 'Get out,' he yells, whacking Biani across the back with his kierie. 'We don't want any rubbish sleeping here.'

Biani wasn't charmed either: he jumps up, grabs the kierie from the bloke's hand and cracks him one across the skull.

The bloke, he lets out a yelp like a kicked mongrel, and stood there clutching at his head while the pair of us exit over the wall. This Portuguese cafe is open, and there we grazed a lekker big breakfast of stew and sadza and tea while we discussed what to do next. I wanted to see my father and Biani was keen to track down his cousin so we arranged to split up for the morning and to rendezvous at this bar we both knew at about 1.00 that afternoon.

It'd been nearly seven years since I last checked my father's cabin. The place looked as run down as ever: the green paint flaked from the walls leaving big orange patches, and a few roses survived amongst the weeds that had invaded the flowerbeds. The latest maid opened the door: she was dark and pretty and maybe 16 years old. My father sat at the dining room table working through a pile of papers.

'What are you here for?' he said without looking up. 'Trying to blow the place up?' I think he meant it as a joke but it came out all bitter.

'Just a recce,' I said, not wanting to have to go into all the intricacies.

'Why'd you join the terrs then?' he asked, finally looking up at me, and eeh, there beneath all the fat of his face you could check the terror of the trapped child.

I didn't want to make things worse for him. 'I would've been shot if I didn't,' I defended. And I chune you I felt sick then: there was I backing out of a fight — just like him. Hell, it was my struggle too, and he'd just better get used to the idea. 'I wanted to fight for our liberation,' I said. 'And I did.'

'What would your grandfather have thought?' he asks, as if now he's got me cornered.

'What about my grandmother?'

'What did these houties ever do for you?'

'Freed me from being whitey's arscreeper — that's what.'

'Those junglebunnies — they still haven't come out the trees!'

'They — we — beat you. You surrendered.' It wasn't the right thing to say.

'I've got news for you,' my father shouts, his voice suddenly rising to a high squeak, 'I've got news for you, Mr Terrorist. We didn't surrender — we just signed the Lancaster House agreement. We'll hold this election that the Brits want — and we'll win. And then, if Mr Mugger-bugger and old Fatso won't stop fighting the West will come in and clean them up in a week.'

'You could be in for a surprise,' I told him, struggling to keep my temper.

'Man — we could clean you up in an afternoon right now — just all you lot line up that side and all us lot line up this side, and we'd wipe you off the face of the earth in no time.'

'That's why we fought like we did — you had supplies and casavacs and fire force behind you — you had medicine and ammunition and choppers and jets. It's easy to fight when you've got all that.'

'Last election Muzorewa got 64 percent of the vote. This time round he'll get 80. We wouldn't have signed unless we were sure.'

'Are you as blind as whitey? Last time the masses were forced to vote.'

'No one was forced — we won fair and square — and we'll win again.'

'Just wait and see.'

'And even if you intimidate enough voters — we'll never let you take over.'

'We'll carry on fighting, we'll fight till we liberate our country.'

My father was quiet for a moment. 'My son — my only son with these communists — these barbarians!' The way he said it, so sad and slow, you'd have schemed I'd just died.

But by then, I chune you, I was flat. 'Your people are worse than us — you are the goddam barbarians. You should've seen what I've seen — how can you support these white devils?'

'If there's ever black rule, we'll have another Congo here. Look north — see what's happening to Africa.'

'Look at South Africa,' I told him. 'Why don't you go live there — if they will allow you in.'

Then, suddenly, no one had anything more to say. 'Ag hell,' says my father finally, sinking back into his chair, 'we can fight all week, and we'll get nowhere. We're just a bunch of goffels anyhow.'

'Zimbabweans,' I corrected, and then waved the flag of truce. 'How's the family?'

Well, Vera had three children now, lovely youngsters, very light. The oldest, Sandra would be starting school soon — 'though God knows what they learn in schools now.'

'Hell — what was so great about the old schools? The Rhodesians never managed to learn enough commonsense to know what was coming.'

'We're not finished just yet, you'll see.'

'You'll see.'

There was silence, and then my father began to tell me about Gladys: she had a boy, just the other day in fact, but that bastard Robson still wouldn't marry her, though at least he was paying support — 'maybe you should get your friends to do something about that one.'

'And the others?'

'Well, Mary and Rodney were struggling a bit up in Zambia, but then the whole damn country was struggling — what else could you expect from houties? Adrian was still locked up, but those idiots were sure to let him loose any day now.'

It was nearly time to go. I stood, muttered something about an appointment, made for the door. 'And my girl?' I tried to sound as casual as I could.

'She's fine — doing very well at school I hear.'

'And Naomi?'

'You should've seen the state she was in when you were captured — she was all for rushing off to Zambia — and then you turned terr and the government wanted to take the house — she had hard times, I'm telling you, hard times.'

'Come on — tell me.'

'She's remarried now, with three children. I saw them just the other day. They seem happy enough.'

'And the bloke?'

'Joe Josephs — from Gwelo. A goffel.'

I shook my head. I didn't know him. 'Got to go now,' I said and walked quickly to the gate.

'Come back,' he called after me. 'Come back and keep your gob shut and after the elections you'll be okay.'

'Burn your uniform now,' I shouted to him. 'Then maybe you'll live.'

By the time I rock up at the shab ou Biani was already there, and judging from the collection of bottles around him he'd been there for quite a while.

'Are you trying to refloat the ark or what?' I chuned him as I sat down. And out it all came: the cousin who'd been too scared to cross had stuck to his job and, over the years, had done pretty well for himself: he was now a personnel officer, and he had a car, a house, a truck, a hi-fi set, three lighties, a wife and a girlfriend — as well as a wardrobe full of flash suits.

Biani, he took one mammoth swig of beer. 'It's not right,' he said. 'We've fought the whites, and cos the whites were out fighting us he got promoted. It's not justice.'

Well, we had a couple more beers and then went off to Harare where we organised ourselves this room in a shack for 20 dollars a month. Once it was all sorted out, there was nothing we wanted to do particularly, so off we went to the nearest shab, someone's lounge, where about 30 mense were all crammed in with the radio blaring, and everyone sounding off about the elections. We bought ourselves a beer, and settled into a corner. It was a Zanu shab all right; there was a large picture of Robert Mugabe on the walls, and this drunk was announcing to everyone who bothered to listen that Zanu didn't need any help from anyone and, come the elections, they'd win big without any coalition with Nkomo and his Madzwitis.

After a couple of minutes the bloke staggered over to us, leans over the table, and demands to know who we support.

'Zanu,' reckons Biani, and the bloke spots the gat in Biani's jacket, and his eyes go big and wide. 'Ssssh — we are the boys — on a secret mission.'

But next thing the bloke is jumping up and down, up and down, flapping his arms about and screaming 'cock-a-doodle-doo, cock-a-doodle-doo — the boys — the boys' — and everyone yells 'jongwe', and crowds around, touching us and cheering. The old queen who runs the place presents us with a dozen beers, blokes are calling for more beer, more beer for the boys. 'Pamberi ne Chimurenga!' the drunk shouts. 'In our struggle for liberation we have overcome the forces of colonialism, racism, imperialism, tribalism....'

'Jongwe, jongwe.'

'We have smashed the security force,' the drunk roars joyfully. 'We have smashed that racist Smith and his black dogs, we have smashed him like an ant.'

'I wonder what fighting he did,' Biani mutters to me, very dry.

'We chased Smith's men out of the bush, and sent them scurrying like mice before us. We crushed them like mealies beneath a grindstone.'

Some bloke pushes me a beer and ya, you can check he was trying, he's trying very hard, to be friendly. He could hardly speak, he was so happy about the struggle. 'And you too — even a coloured was a comrade — you fought for us, risked your life for us,' he announces, 'you weren't like us blacks — you didn't have to do it. You are almost white,' and so on, and so on.

Me, I just couldn't stomach it. Hell, I hadn't fought as a favour, I'd fought for my life. Yet even now, even after I'd been fighting all these years, mense assumed I'd been a fighter only cos I'd been captured or cos I was a nice guy. Mumbling something I staggered outside and, leaning against the wall with one hand, I pissed pretty patterns into the dust.

That was the problem with being coloured, I realised. You couldn't call yourself just a Zimbabwean, cos people would also see a coloured and there was nothing you could do about it until this whole race business has been finally forgotten.

There was nothing else for it but to backtrack and down a couple more beers. Ya, we did nothing but drink all that day, we didn't know what else to do. We chased the chickies and drank and drank and within a week we were down to our last couple cents.

I remember that morning all right: eeh, I chune you, my head felt like a rhino had trod on it, and all's I could do was lie back and try to pretend that I didn't exist.

'We can't keep this up for too much longer,' I moaned.

'We can't,' ou Biani agreed. 'We got just enough cash for two more beers.'

Me, I just wanted to switch my mind off when I heard that. How could we raise some cash? All's we could come up with was a hold-up, and neither of us were too keen on the idea.

Dodging past the shab just round the corner where we already owed a couple dollars, we staggered off to find a place where boys fresh back from the bush were still a novelty.

We found this place which we reckoned was worth a try, and went in and bought ourselves a beer each.

As we're sipping quietly there, waiting to recover from the babbelas before we begin loudly reminiscing about some vital operation, one of Biani's buddies from way back, this bloke Shorty, a little fat bloke with a sneaky look, perched himself next to us, and we got talking. Once the bloke heard we were fighters, suddenly eeh, he's very interested, buying us this bottle of kachase and cross-questioning us about our exploits, and when he heard Biani was a commander, he even bought us a pack of cigarettes each.

Then somehow we ended up talking about coin, and how broke we were. Shorty, much to our surprise, beams bright as daylight and informs us he reckons he can help.

'What do you want to rob?' reckons Biani, cautious.

'No, no there's no robbery,' squeaks this Shorty character.

'Nothing like that. Look,' — and the bloke whips out his Zanu (Sithole) card, and trots out this long spiel about Comrade Sithole being the favourite leader of the majority of the freedom fighters.

'Come off it,' says Biani. 'You don't really believe this nonsense.'

'No, no, no, you don't understand,' Shorty says. 'Sithole pays.'

He took us off to Sithole's HQ to sign up. We were led into this big room where a dozen big shots were sitting round this table looking rather worried. They were having some kind of meeting about their election prospects.

Shorty introduced Biani as this Zipra area commander from up Miami way and me as his lieutenant. We shook hands, everyone all comrade, comrade, comrade, and very pleased to see us.

Then Shorty told them this long story explaining that we were only in those offices cos of his excellent connections among the comrades. 'I know there have been these rumours about me,' he tells them, 'but I haven't been round here because I've been at one of the assembly points speaking to the boys.'

Many, many Zipra comrades were not happy with Nkomo cos all he was interested in was his own fat stomach, and when they heard Sithole would allow them to join his party they were overjoyed. He recommended hiring all available Zipra comrades to spread the message, arguing that if there was a big enough push, practically the whole of Zipra could swing to Sithole.

Those big shots, man they swallowed every word of his like a cold beer on a hot day. With comrades like Shorty on their side, they figured maybe all this stuff about Sithole having the support of the freedom fighters was true after all.

After we'd repeated Shorty's story for the benefit of the big shots, Shorty pointed out that, to continue our good work, we needed money, a great deal of money. We had to sneak back to the assembly point, and fetch the rest of our men.

One of the main mannes reckons well, we're a little short of cash right now, why don't you fetch the rest of the unit and we'll pay you back?

Shorty informs him that the rest of the fighters weren't with us cos we didn't have enough cash to bring them all along. He then reminded us all that the elections were just around the corner, time was very short. Either they must act now or forget trying to win Zipra.

The big shot at the head of the table nodded. 'We need these comrades,' he declared. 'They can turn the elections for us.' And, with that, he ordered all the blokes at the table to make us a contribution. In spite of him telling them that they would all be paid back soon-soon, those main mannes weren't at all keen to part with their money.

They said 'Sorry, we haven't got much with us,' so he made each one of them stand up and empty his pockets, and he takes all the notes and throws them into the centre of the table.

'This will be a big boost for Sithole,' says Shorty, very happy with the way the pile of notes is growing and growing. 'Now I think he can win.'

We gave him 200 dollars, half our takings. What with liquor and ladies and new clothes, we blew our share in just three days. When we'd recovered, Shorty arranged for us to be recruited by Muzorewa's ANC. They had plenty of money, much of it from South Africa which wanted him in power again, and Shorty managed to talk them out of 800 dollars. Me and Biani ran through our 400 in a week.

When we recovered we agreed okay, okay, this was now too much. We'd been doing nothing but drink for nearly a month and enough was enough. It was now time to get ourselves organised.

First we had to check whether Zipra was seriously after us. We'd heard via Shorty that Comrade Hendrix was in town — he'd seen him drinking at this hotel where all the Zipra big shots hung out — so we decided to go over and say howzit and see what the story was.

We finally cornered him alone in the bar. He was drinking a beer and eating a plate of grilled biltong. You could see he was one of the big fish now. He looked well-fed, even fat, and he was wearing a suit.

He didn't look too pleased to see us. In fact he looked terrified.

'Calm down,' Biani told him. 'You are looking well.'

'I am all right,' he said, very nervous. 'What do you want with me?' He must have thought we were out to blackmail or assassinate him or something.

'We want to know what our position with Zipra is,' Biani said. 'Are they after us?'

Hendrix relaxed, downed a slug of beer, and leaned back against the counter. 'Why ask me?'

'You were my friend.'

'Can't we fix it?' I broke in. 'We've got coin.'

'Selling out like that? You think you can fix it like a broken gun?' Hendrix laughed as if this was all a good joke.

'Selling out?' Biani cut in. 'That's lies. Never.'

Comrade Hendrix shook his head, and began listing all these crimes that we're supposed to have committed: selling out the area HQ to the enemy bombers, the murder of 13 comrades, the attempted murder of a commanding officer, mutiny. 'There were some other charges,' he said with this you-can't-fool-me smile, 'but I don't remember them all.'

'It's all lies,' cried Biani, 'just lies.'

'No one can have enough cash to buy their way out of this one,' said Hendrix.

'It's all a mistake,' I put in and tried to explain that there had to have been some confusion somewhere.

Hendrix shook his head, and told us, look, no no, he was sure, there was no doubt at all. He'd looked into the whole business cos we'd been his buddies. First we'd mutinied, and then we'd gone banditing, then we'd ambushed Comrade Katusha when he'd tried to talk to us, murdering one of our comrades and shooting off our commander's hand. Finally, in an effort to destroy all evidence of our treachery, we told the enemy where the HQ was, and they blew it apart with their bombers, killing nine comrades and many of the masses too. There had been about 20 wounded, and guns and ammunition destroyed.

'You'd better disappear,' Hendrix told Biani. 'After this election they'll be coming for you.'

'What about me?' I was shitting myself, I chune you.

'They're only talking Biani,' he told me, 'you just keep out of the way.'

''A sellout,' ou Biani was muttering to himself. 'These comrades can think that I am a sellout.' We went to a shab and downed a couple of beers, and tried to work out what we were going to do next.

'Let's just head into the bush and hole up somewhere for a year or two,' I suggested. 'By the time we come back everyone will have forgotten all about us.'

'No one can forget this kind of sellout,' he said. 'Zimbabwe is such a small country that sooner or later we'll run across someone who knows us.'

'Then we can just move and hide out somewhere else.'

But Biani couldn't be convinced. 'I don't want to keep looking behind me for the rest of my life,' he said.

'Okay then,' I chune him, 'if Zimbabwe's too small, there's still Botswana, Zambia. With our cash from the mine we'd be able to buy ourselves papers and just disappear in some small town in Zambia, some place right on the Zairean border — or even in Zaire — no one would ever find us there.'

But Biani pulled every suggestion to pieces. He didn't want to do anything. He just sat there in his chair as if he wanted to sleep for a 1 000 years, and argued that wherever we went, there would always be the chance that the comrades would find us and finish us. The revolution would hunt the sellouts until they were all destroyed. And how were we going to get across the Zambezi anyway? These days you needed passports, and Kaunda would be so sick of Zimbabweans, he'd soon chase every last one of them from his country. Ya, with ou Biani you couldn't get anywhere.

I suggested writing the true story and sending it to Nkomo. I suggested heading to Mozambique or Zaire and hopping a ship to South America. I even suggested joining another liberation movement somewhere else in the world — everything I could think of.

But ou Biani wouldn't do anything. It was as if the steel in his soul had snapped. All's he wanted to do was lie back and drink.

The next few days we just hung around our room. I kept arguing with Biani, trying to persuade him to do something, but he just shook his head whenever I started up, like a cow bothered by a pesky fly.

'If they want me,' he said, 'they can find me here. I am not going to run from these corruptions for the rest of my life.'

'But what are you going to do? You can't just sit here?'

'If they want to finish me, then I'll finish some of them too.' And then he'd take his Tokarev out of his shirt.

Sometimes he'd rave on about how corrupt all the comrades were: here was Comrade Hendrix coming back a hero, and we all knew he'd made himself a fortune from the stores, there was his cousin who'd been too gutless to fight who now had a good job that the fighters' blood bought him. Katusha, how he'd stolen from the people — and

he was a hero too. 'I wish one of them would walk in here,' he'd say
taking out that Tokarev of his. 'I'd just like to watch them die.'

I'd try to talk sense to him, remind him that every fruit had its pips
and peels, and that we were still alive, that was the main thing, and we
would come up with a strategy sooner or later, but by then Biani
wasn't bothering to listen to me at all.

It was two days later, I think, that I went off to bum a couple of bucks
from my father. When I got back, Biani wasn't there, so I check down
at the shab, and there he is, sitting hunched up in front of this picture
of Mugabe, with half-a-dozen empties in front of him. Somehow he'd
also managed to lay his hands on a lump of cash.

We bought a bottle of kachase and went into the back yard to
drink. 'Where'd you get the coin?' I asked him, but he just grunted.

So we sat in the sun, passing the bottle between us, hardly saying a
word.

'I should have been killed during the struggle,' he tells me finally. 'I
should've died of malaria while I was carrying supplies for Zanla, I
should've been wiped out that time we lost Comrade Nyoni and that
kid.'

Another swig of the bottle. We were both pretty drunk by then.

'So,' I said, 'what's so wrong about being alive? We'll all be dead
soon enough anyway.'

'If I was dead I would be a hero — you know the song 'When the
names of the heroes of Zimbabwe are called, my name will be called
also'.'

This was pretty strange talk from ou Biani, but then he had
swallowed quite a quantity of alcohol.

'So, you're a live hero,' I chune him. 'What's wrong with that?
Scared of missing out on a posthumous medal or something?'

And then the bloke began to moan, a kind of low moan that you'd
expect from a wailing spirit. It was so nakedly unhappy that you
didn't know which way to look. It wasn't like Biani at all.

'Hey, hey, hey,' I chune him. 'Man, we're freedom fighters. We can
come up with something. We can improvise.'

But he just sat there slumped into himself, and moaning.

Then he told me that he'd crossed over to the South Africans.

At first I schemed it was just another one of Shorty's schemes. 'I
hope they paid you well,' I told him. 'Even for taking cash from those

people you need some compensation.'

But Biani shook his head. 'I can't stay here,' he said, not looking up.

He was dead serious. Me, I felt sick. The booze was burning a hole in my gut. I tried to cross-question him, but all he could or would tell was that he was going to cross into South Africa during the next few days.

'So — why? — hell —'

'It's like you told me,' he tried to explain. 'The first thing is — survive. These corruptions are killing the struggle and now they want to kill me.'

I wasn't so sure Biani could survive this. 'South Africa could kill you,' I told him, and babbled on about all the other ideas I'd come up with during the last couple days — joining another freedom struggle, disappearing into Zaire, hiding out in the country — but he wasn't listening. He had made up his mind and, even as I spoke to him I knew from the look on his face that he wasn't hearing me.

'There's nowhere to go,' he said.

I grabbed hold of the bottle and took a slug, burning gut or no burning gut and said everything all over again.

Biani burped. His eyes were pretty glazed. 'I can't stay,' he repeated.

'Well, then — but I'm not coming with you.' My words jumped out before I heard them.

'I didn't ask you to.' Then I realised how it sounded, like a betrayal, like a failure of my faith in him. He wasn't that kind of bloke. He would never have let me go with him anyway.

We spoke about the arrangements, sticking to practical things: how he could keep in touch with me, how I could get in contact with Rudiya and the child — I was just to tell them 'secret mission' and nothing more. And we kept on drinking and drinking until I passed out.

For years I'd stuck to Biani like a tick to a tortoise, and when I woke up the next morning and saw that I was alone I felt not quite properly there. I couldn't bear to stick around, I just wanted to get moving. I dressed, grabbed my stuff and sneaked out into the street — I didn't want to have to speak to the owner, didn't want to have to explain — and drifted through the townships, past the women selling roast mealies and matimbes, a barber with a customer on a rickety chair in the middle of a vacant lot, lighties wheeling wire cars around a dusty front yard, a uniformed lightie racing from school, an old man pedalling stiffly along on a bicycle, a group of youngsters wearing Zanu (PF) T-shirts, standing at a corner. No one noticed me, a goffel tramp staggering along by myself. I must've walked for hours, I didn't know where I was going, and I felt like throwing myself under a train. All around me the people swarmed about: an old woman carrying a basket full of vegetables home from the market, a drunk sitting on a rock with his head in his hands. These people had never had enough of anything — housing, education, decent food, a say in their own lives, but ya, with all our fighting, we'd begun to change all that. All at once I felt this glow inside me, and I felt like shouting to everyone — 'hey — comrade, comrade, comrade'. In spite of everything we'd won; in spite of everything we would win through.